आ नो भद्राः क्रतवो यन्तु विश्वतः ।

ā no bhadrāḥ kratavo yantu viśvataḥ

Let noble thoughts come to us from every side

- Ṛg Veda I - 89-i

BHAVAN'S BOOK UNIVERSITY

D1096939

KRISHNAVATARA
VOLUME III
THE FIVE BROTHERS
by
K. M. MUNSHI

BHAVAN'S BOOK UNIVERSITY

KRISHNAVATARA

VOLUME III

THE FIVE BROTHERS

K. M. MUNSHI

2019

BHARATIYA VIDYA BHAVAN
Kulapati K. M. Munshi Marg
Mumbai - 400007

First Edition	:	*1965*
Second Edition	:	*1972*
Third Edition	:	*1979*
Fourth Edition	:	*1983*
Fifth Edition	:	*1990*
Sixth Edition	:	*2006*
Seventh Edition	:	*2009*
Eighth Edition	:	*2014*
Nineth Edition	:	*2019*

Price : ₹ 540/-

Typesetting by Samir Parekh,
at Creative Page Setters,

PRINTED IN INDIA

By Nilesh Parekh, Paras Prints, at Gala 32, Singh Indu. Estate-3,
1st floor, Ram Mandir Road, Goregaon, Mumbai - 400104 and
Published by P. V. Sankarankutty, Joint Director,
Bharatiya Vidya Bhavan, K.M. Munshi Marg, Mumbai - 400007.
E-mail : bhavan@bhavans.info - Website : http://www.bhavans.info

KULAPATI'S PREFACE

The Bharatiya Vidya Bhavan—that Institute of Indian Culture in Bombay—needed a Book University, a series of books which, if read, would serve the purpose of providing higher education. Particular emphasis, however, was to be put on such literature as revealed the deeper impulsions of India. As a first step, it was decided to bring out in English 100 books, 50 of which were to be taken in hand, almost at once.

It is our intention to publish the books we select, not only in English, but also in the following Indian languages: Hindi, Bengali, Gujarati, Marathi, Tamil, Telugu, Kannada and Malayalam.

This scheme, involving the publication of 900 volumes, requires ample funds and an all-India organisation. The Bhavan is exerting its utmost to supply them.

The objectives for which the Bhavan stands are the reintegration of Indian culture in the light of modern knowledge and to suit our present-day needs and the resuscitation of its fundamental values in their pristine vigour.

Let me make our goal more explicit:

We seek the dignity of man, which necessarily implies the creation of social conditions which would allow him freedom to evolve along the lines of his own temperament and capacities; we seek the harmony of individual efforts and social relations, not in any makeshift way, but within the frame-work of the Moral Order; we seek the creative art of life, by the alchemy of which human limitations are progressively transmuted, so that man may become the instrument of God, and is able to see Him in all and all in Him.

The world, we feel, is too much with us. Nothing would uplift or inspire us so much as the beauty and aspiration which such books can teach.

In this *series*, therefore, the literature of India, ancient and modern, will be published in a form easily accessible to all. Books in other literatures of the world, if they illustrate the principles we stand for, will also be included.

This common pool of literature, it is hoped, will enable the reader, eastern or western, to understand and appreciate currents of world thought, as also the movements of the mind in India, which though they flow through different linguistic channels, have a common urge and aspiration.

Fittingly, the Book University's first venture is the *Mahabharata*, summarised by one of the greatest living Indians, C. Rajagopalachari; the second work is on a section of it, the *Gita* by H.V.Divatia, an eminent jurist and student of philosophy. Centuries ago, it was proclaimed of the *Mahabharata*: "What is not in it, is nowhere." After twenty-five centuries, we can use the same words about it. He who knows it not, knows not the heights and depths of the soul; he misses the trials and tragedy and the beauty and grandeur of life.

The *Mahabharata* is not a mere epic: it is a romance, telling the tale of heroic men and women and of some who were divine; it is a whole literature in itself, containing a code of life, a philosophy of social and ethical relations, and speculative thought on human problems that is hard to rival: but, above all, it has for its core the *Gita,* which is, as the world is beginning to find out, the noblest of scriptures and the grandest of sagas in which the climax is reached in the wondrous Apocalypse in the Eleventh Canto.

Through such books alone the harmonies underlying true culture, I am convinced, will one day reconcile the disorders of modern life.

I thank all those who have helped to make this new branch of the Bhavan's activity successful.

New Delhi
1, Queen Victoria Road,
October 3, 1951

INTRODUCTION

Who has not heard of Sri Krishna who delivered the message of the *Bhagavad Gita* and whom the *Bhagavat* calls 'God Himself'?

From the earliest days that my memories can go back to, Sri Krishna has been, in a sense, dominating my imagination. In my childhood, I heard his adventures with breathless amazement. Since then I have read of him, sung of him, admired him, worshipped him in a hundred temples and every year on his birthday at home. And day after day, for years and years, his message has been the strength of my life.

Unfortunately, his fascinating personality, which could be glimpsed in what may be called the original *Mahabharata*, has been overlaid with legends, myths, miracles and adorations.

Wise and valorous, he was loving and loved, far-seeing and yet living for the moment, gifted with sage-like detachment and yet intensely human; the diplomat, the sage and the man of action with a personality as luminous as that of a divinity.

The urge, therefore, came upon me, time and again, to embark upon a reconstruction of his life and adventures by weaving a romance around him.

It was an almost impossible venture, but like hundreds of authors in all parts of India for centuries, I could not help offering him whatever little of imagination and creative power I possessed, feeble though they were.

I have called the whole work *Krishnavatara, The Descent of the Lord.*

The First Part, which ends with the death of Kamsa, has been named "The Magic Flute", for it deals with his boyhood associated with the flute, which hypnotized men, animals and birds alike, sung with such loving tenderness by innumerable poets.

I have named the Second Part, which ends with Rukmini Haran, *The Wrath of an Emperor,* as the central theme is the successful defiance by Sri Krishna of Jarasandha, the Emperor of Magadha.

The Third Part is entiled *The Five Brothers* and ends with Draupadi's *Swayamvara.*

The Fourth Part is entitled *The Book of Bhima* and the Fifth Part is entitled *The Book of Satyabhaama.* The Sixth Part, which is now being serially published in the Bhavan's Journal, is entitled *The Book of Vyaasa, the Master.*

I hope to carry forward the series till the episode when, on the battle-field of Kurukshetra, Krishna reveals himself as the Eternal Guardian of the Cosmic Law—*Saashvata Dharma Gopta*—to Arjuna, if it is His will that I should do so.

I have followed the techniques since 1922 to reconstruct the episodes connected with Chyavana and Sukanya in *Purandara Parajaya* (a play), Agastya and Lopamudra, Vasishta and Vishwamitra, Parashurama and Sahasrarjuna in *Vishvaratha* (a romance), *Deve Didheli* (a play), *Vishwamitra Rishi* (a play), *Lomaharshini* (a romance) and *Bhagavan Parashurama* (a romance), and now Sri Krishna and the heroes and heroines of *Mahabharata* in these volumes of *Krishnavatara*.

Time and again, I have made it clear that none of these works is an English rendering of any old Purana.

In reconstructing Sri Krishna's life and adventures, I had, like many of my predecessors, to reconstruct the episodes inherited from the past, so as to bring out his character, attitude and outlook with the personality-sustained technique of modern romance. I had also to give flesh and blood to various obscure characters in the *Mahabharata*.

In the course of this adventure, I had often to depart from the legend and myth, for such reconstruction by a modern author must necessarily involve the exercise of whatever little imagination he has. I trust He will forgive me for the liberty I am taking, but must write of Him as I see Him in my imagination.

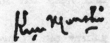

Bharatiya Vidya Bhavan,
Chowpatty Road, Bombay-7
August 15, 1967.

CONTENTS

CHARACTERS IN THIS STORY:

SRI KRISHNA:
BALARAMA—his elder brother;
VASUDEVA—his father, Chief of the Shoora tribe of
    Yadavas;
DEVAKI—his mother;
DEVABHAGA—his uncle;
UDDHAVA—his intimate friend and the third son of
    Devabhaga;
YUYUDHANA SATYAKI—his friend, a Yadava Chief, son
    of Satyaka;
KRITAVARMA—his friend; a Yadava *atirathi*;
CHEKITANA—his friend; a Yadava Chief, ruler of
    Pushkara;
GURU SANDIPANI—his teacher, with his *ashram* at
    Ujjain;
ACHARYA SHVETAKETU—his friend and Sandipani's
    principal disciple;
RUKMINI, SHAIBYA —his wives;
GADA—a Yadava Chief;
SATRAJIT —a Yadava leader;
SATYABHAMA —his daughter.

*   *   *

BHISHMA:
KING SHANTANU—his father, Emperor of Hastinapura,
    of the Kuru tribe;
SATYAVATI—his step-mother, the Dowager Empress of
    Hastinapura;
CHITRANGADA, VICHITRAVEERYA—his step-brothers,
    Satyavati's sons;

AMBIKAA, AMBAALIKAA—Vichitraveerya's wives;
   daughters of the King of Kashi;

*   *   *

PANDU—Son of Ambaalikaa, widow of Vichitraveerya,
   begotten by Vyasa, and King of Hastinapura;
KUNTI—his wife;
MADRI—his second wife;
YUDHISHTHIRA, BHIMA, ARJUNA—his sons by Kunti
NAKULA, SAHADEVA—his sons by Madri;
The Five Brothers

*   *   *

DHRITARASHTRA—blind son of Ambikaa, widow of
   Vichitraveerya, begotten by Vyasa, and father of
   the Kauravas;
GANDHARI—his wife;
SHAKUNI—his wife's brother;
DURYODHANA—Dhritarashtra's eldest son;
DUHSHASANA—his younger brother;
BHANUMATI—his wife;
KARNA, PRINCE OF ANGA—his friend;
PUROCHANA—his agent

*   *   *

KRISHNA DWAIPAYANA VYASA—the Best of Munis, son
   of sage Parashara by Satyavati and great-grandson
   of the Vedic Rishi Vasishtha;
JAIMINI, PAILA—his chief disciples;
DHAUMYA—his disciple, the preceptor of the Five
   Brothers;
VIDURA—Principal Minister of the Kurus in
   Hastinapura;
KUNIKA—a Minister of Hastinapura.

*   *   *

YAJNASENA DRUPADA—King of Panchala;
KRISHNAA DRAUPADI—his daughter;
DHRISHTADYUMNA, SATYAJIT—his sons;
SHIKHANDIN—his daughter who was transformed into
    a boy

* * *

ARYAKA—King of the Nagas, and father of Krishna's
    grandmother;
KARKOTAKA—his grandson;
RAVIKA—Karkotaka's wife;
MANIMAN—Karkotaka's son;
KAPILA, PINGALA—Karkotaka's daughters;
SIGURI—a Naga Chief.

* * *

HIDIMBA—a Rakshasa Chief;
HIDIMBAA—his sister, Bhima's wife;
GHATOTKACHA—Hidimbaa's son;
NIKUMBHA—a Rakshasa boy.

* * *

JARASANDHA—Emperor of Magadha;
SAHADEVA—his son;
MEGHASANDHI—his grandson.

* * *

DRONACHARYA—a pupil of Parashurama and teacher of
    the Pandavas and the Kauravas in the art of war;
KRIPAADEVI—his wife;
ASWATTHAMA—his son, a friend of Duryodhana;
KRIPACHARYA—Teacher of military science, brother of
    Kripaadevi;
STHOONAKARNA—a Yaksha, a master of the magic art
    of healing.

PROLOGUE

THE YADAVAS

In the days of the ancient fathers of our race, the Aryas, a vigorous people, spread over India, intermarrying with the Nagas, fighting with them or among themselves, and founding or destroying kingdoms.

The Arya *rishis*, dedicated to learning and self-discipline, lived in their hermitages, communing with the gods and spreading the Arya way of life based on *Satya, Yajna* and *Tapas*—Truth, Sacrifice and Purity—which they called Dharma.

Long before kingdoms were established in the fertile plains of North India by adventurous Arya kings, the Yadavas had pushed their way across the river Ganga, The confederated tribes of the Shooras, the Andhakas and the Vrishnis were the most powerful of them.

These confederated tribes cleared the forests in the valley of the Yamuna and established settlements which collectively came to be called Shoorasena after Shoora, the most powerful of their chiefs. Later they conquered Mathura, which in their hands grew in power, prosperity and influence.

The irrepressible Yadavas of Mathura had an inveterate horror of restraint. They would not have a king. Their affairs were carried on by a council of chiefs. However, Ugrasena, the chief of the Andhaka clan, came to be called 'king' by courtesy.

Andhaka Ugrasena's son, Kamsa, grew up, reckless, wild and ambitious. He distinguished himself by his valour and married Asti and Prapti, the daughters of Emperor Jarasandha of Magadha, who cherished the mighty ambition of subduing all the kings of the earth by guile and force. Kamsa became a trusted lieutenant, captured power in Mathura and used it tyrannically.

Shoora, the powerful chief of the Shoora tribe, married Marishaa, the daughter of the Naga chief, Aryaka, and begot sons, among whom were Vasudeva and Devabhaga and daughters, among whom were Prithaa and Shrutashravaa.

Prithaa, the eldest, was given in adoption to King Kuntibhoja and came to be known as Kunti. Marricd to King Pandu of the Kurus of Hastinapura, she became the mother of the Five Brothers known as Pandavas, three of them, Yudhishthira, Bhima and Arjuna, being born to her, and the other two, Nakula and Sahadeva, the sons of her co-wife, Madri, being adopted.

Shrutashravaa, the other daughter of Shoora, was married to King Damaghosha of Chedi and begot a son by name Shishupala, who, headstrong and ambitious, also wanted to win the favour of Jarasandha, the Emperor of Magadha.

Vasudeva, Shoora's eldest son, married Devaki, the daughter of Devaka, the brother of King Ugrasena.

To falsify the prophecy the the eighth son of his cousin Devaki would kill him, Kamsa put Vasudeva and Devaki in prison and killed their first six sons as they were born.

The seventh child, extracted from the womb long before his time, was secreted away and grew up as Samkarshana Balarama.

The eighth son, Krishna, who according to the prophecy was going to be the redeemer of the Yadavas, was taken away to Gokul at midnight as soon as he was born, and was brought up by Nanda, the chief of the cowherds of Gokul.

Devabhaga, the younger brother of Vasudeva, begot Uddhava, who, when an infant, was sent to Gokul to be brought up as Krishna's companion.

Balarama, Krishna and Uddhava grew up, strong, handsome and venturesome. Krishna, the most loving and lovable of them, became the favourite of the cowherd community and the darling of the milkmaids of Vrindavan, to which Nanda. had migrated.

When Krishna was sixteen, he was brought to Mathura, where he killed his maternal uncle, the wicked Kamsa.

Krishna, Balarama and Uddhava went to complete their education and training in arms in the school of Guru Sandipani. While living with Sandipani, Krishna rescued his son Punardatta from kidnappers by a miraculous exploit.

When Jarasandha heard that his son-in-law had been killed by Krishna, he marched on Mathura to avenge his death. Unable to face the siege of the town by such a powerful foe, the Yadavas allowed Krishna and Balarama to steal away from it at night. The brothers travelled across the Sahyadri to Gomantaka and lived among the Garuda tribes.

Jarasandha pursued Krishna and Balarama to Gomantaka but he and his friends were put to flight by the intrepid young men.

With their fame resounding through Aryavarta, Krishna and Balarama returned in triumph to Mathura, where the Yadavas, under their leadership, became strong and disciplined.

In order to destroy the Yadavas of Mathura, Jarasandha decided to strengthen his alliance with King Bhishmaka of Vidarbha and King Damaghosha of Chedi. He arranged that Bhishmaka's daughter Rukmini should be married to Shishupala, son of King Damaghosha of Chedi, while his own grand-daughter was to be married to Rukmi, the son of Bhishmaka.

To carry out this arrangement, a *swayamvara* was staged at Kundinapura, the capital of Vidarbha. In fact, it was a fraudulent imitation of the ancient ways of the Aryas, for no choice was to be left to Rukmini, but to marry Shishupala. Krishna, with several Yadava chiefs and their allies, went to Kundinapura uninvited and induced Bhishmaka to give up the false *swayamvara*.

Krishna's fame grew and his fabulous exploits gave him the halo of a demi-god.

Jarasandha, however, was unforgiving. He decided to destroy the Yadavas of Mathura. He, therefore, made up his mind not to take any Arya king into his confidence and entered into a pact with Kala Yavana, the savage king of the region beyond the river Sindhu. According to the pact, the Yavana was to march on Mathura from the west and himself from the east, destroy the Yadavas and burn Mathura to the ground.

To save the Yadavas from the fate which awaited them if they were trapped by these overwhelming forces, Krishna led them across swamps and deserts to far-away Saurashtra. There they settled in the kingdom of Kukudmin, whose daughter Revati was married to Balarama. Their capital, Dwaraka, soon became a flourishing port.

Kala Yavana could not reach Mathura. He became the victim of the anger of an old sage who went by the name of Muchukunda and whom he tried to kill.

Jarasandha, when he reached Mathura, saw to his desperation that the Yadavas had escaped him. He spent his fury in burning Mathura to the ground.

To force a dynastic alliance between himself and the kings of Chedi and Vidarbha, he issued orders that the *swayamvara* of Rukmini should be held at Kundinapura, where she should be married to Shishupala.

Krishna suddenly appeared at Kundinapura, carried away Rukmini to Dwaraka, the capital of Saurashtra, and married her.

THE KURUS

In the Arya world, the largest and most powerful clans were the Bharatas and the Panchalas.

In the old days, the Bharatas had established suzerainty over all the kings of Aryavarta. Their king, Bharata, was by tradition acclaimed the greatest of the *Chakravartins.* Hastin, who founded Hastinapura on the banks of the Ganga, belonged to the line of Bharata, the Emperor.

In later times, the Bharatas also came to be called the Kurus and held sway over a large dominion and suzerainty over many kings.

The lands occupied by the Kurus and their rivals

the Panchalas formed the heart of Aryavarta, distinguished for its learning and valour. The most eminent of the Arya *rishis* had their hermitages there and its kings upheld the ancient ways of Dharma.

Shantanu, a descendant of Hastin, was a great king. He begot a son, Gangeya, who grew in strength, valour and righteousness.

When he was well advanced in years, King Shantanu fell in love with a fisher girl, who later came to be known as Satyavati. However, her father would not agree to her being married to the king unless her son, if she had one, could succeed to the throne. To make his father happy, Gangeya took a vow to remain unmarried and not to claim the throne. The vow was a very stern one and so Gangeya came to be called Bhishma, the terrible.

By Satyavati, Shantanu begot two sons, Chitrangada and Vichitraveerya. The elder one died in battle. Bhishma installed Vichitraveerya on the throne of Hastinapura and carried away the King of Kashi's daughters, two of whom were married to the boy king.

Vichitraveerya, while still a boy, died issueless. Bhishma would not marry, nor accept the throne. The royal line of the Kurus was threatened with extinction.

On the advice of Bhishma, Satyavati, the Dowager Empress, called on Krishna Dwaipayana Vyasa, her son by Sage Parashara, to beget sons on the widows of Vichitraveerya according to the ancient custom.

Krishna Dwaipayana Vyasa had been brought up by his father in the highest tradition of the Vedic *rishis,* of which his great-grandfather, Vasishtha, was one of the founders.

By his learning and austerities, Vyasa had acquired the highest position among the *rishis* of Aryavarta. He had also redacted the divine Vedas, which the Gods had communicated to the ancient sages of immortal memory, of whom his forefather was one of the most eminent.

To perpetuate the line of the Kurus, the Sage accepted his mother's mandate. By Ambikaa, he begot Dhritarashtra, who was blind from birth. By Ambaalikaa, he begot Pandu, who was afflicted by disease from his very birth. By a maid-servant who offered herself in devotion, he begot Vidura.

Bhishma brought up the three boys with care and wisdom. Dhritarashtra being blind could not succeed to the throne, and the younger son Pandu ruled over the Kuru empire well and wisely, earning immense popularity. Vidura, the maid's son, grew up to become a wise and saintly minister.

The blind Dhritarashtra was married to Gandhari and by her begot Duryodhana, Duhshasana and several other sons.

Pandu was married to Kunti, the sister of Vasudeva, the father of Krishna, and also to Madri, a princess of Madra. Afflicted by a curse which denied him the pleasures of life, the King retired to the Himalayas with his wives. By the will of their husband and the blessing of different gods, they begot five sons, Yudhishthira, Bhima, Arjuna and the twins, Nakula and Sahadeva.

On king Pandu's death, Madri, his younger queen, followed her husband on the funeral pyre, entrusting her two sons to the care of the elder co-wife, Kunti. The sages brought Kunti and the Five Brothers to

Hastinapura, where, by the advice of Veda Vyasa, Bhishma accepted them as the sons and heirs of Pandu.

The Five Brothers grew up, handsome, strong and honourable and became the favourites of all, though this displeased Duryodhana, Duhshasana and other cousins of theirs.

Dronacharya, a pupil of Parashurama, the great master of the art of war, was employed by Bhishma to give training to the princes. During their training, the Five Brothers excelled their cousins in learning as well as skill in arms.

When their training was over, they helped their guru Dronacharya to win for himself the northern part of the territories of Panchala, ruled by King Yajnasena, otherwise known as Drupada.

All the Five Brothers became very popular with the Kurus. The eldest of them, Yudhishthira, came to be regarded as Dharmaraja—righteousness incarnate. Bhishma, therefore, installed him as the *yuvaraja* or the Crown Prince of Hastinapura, for, besides being fully fitted to be so, his father Pandu was the last king to sit on the throne of the Kurus.

After Yudhishthira was installed as *yuvaraja*, Bhima, the second of the Five Brothers, went to Mathura to complete his training in mace combat under Balarama, who was the recognized master of that art.

That was just before the Yadavas, afraid of being exterminated by the Emperor Jarasandha of Magadha, went away to Saurashtra, led by Krishna.

KRISHNAVATARA

VOLUME III

THE FIVE BROTHERS

1
KING DRUPADA'S RESOLVE

*T*he Panchalas occupied lands to the south of the river Ganga. After the Kurus, they were the most powerful of the Arya races and Kampilya was their capital.

Their king, Yajnasena Drupada, was an austere and unforgiving man, who had for years brooded over a humiliation. To avenge it, had become the sole purpose of his life.

In his young days when he was studying in the *ashram* of his Guru, he had an intimate friend, Drona, the son of a learned Brahman called Bharadwaja. With the airy unreasonableness of early youth, the friends took a pledge that each would share the other's fortune in life. After completing their studies, they separated, Drupada to become the king of the flourishing kingdom of the Panchalas.

When Drupada became a king, Drona went to him and insisted on the pledge being redeemed. The young king rejected Drona's demand to share the royal opulence and repulsed his former friend.

Drona took the insult to heart. He neither forgot nor forgave it. In order to avenge it, he underwent intensive training under the great Parashurama and acquired mastery in arms.

Later, he was lucky enough to link his fortunes to those of the Kurus, when he was appointed to train in arms the Kuru princes, the sons of Dhritarashtra and his brother Pandu.

When his pupils completed their training and became formidable warriors, Drona demanded a reward of them: they must avenge the insult Drupada had offered him years before.

In obedience to their tutor's commands, Arjuna, the third of the Five Brothers, an archer *par excellence*, organised a sudden attack on Panchala and captured Drupada. When the King was brought before Dronacharya, the Brahman warrior had his revenge. He extracted an apology from the King for the insult and as ransom demanded a part of the Panchala kingdom north of the river Ganga.

Drupada had to accept the terms imposed by Drona. However, smarting under the humiliation, he could never forgive Drona nor his pupil Arjuna. His whole life was poisoned by this bitter memory and all he lived for was to avenge it.

Drupada also transmitted this dominant passion of his own life to his two sons, Dhrishtadyumna and Satyajit, and to his daughter Krishnaa, from their very childhood. To fulfil their father's vow became the mission of their lives too.

The boys grew up into fine young warriors and began to prepare for the day when they could fulfil their father's pledge. Dominated by this same passion, Draupadi—the dark-skinned, stately, wondrously beautiful maiden—resolved to marry the most redoubtable warrior in Aryavarta, so that she could help in fulfilling the aim of her father's life. This aim became more difficult to attain as the years passed.

Dronacharya, his son Aswatthama and his brother-in-law Kripacharya, were in high favour with the Kurus, who, led by the powerful Bhishma, grew from strength to strength. Their hold over the Kurus increased as Drona's pupils became formidable warriors, notably Bhima and Arjuna, the sons of Pandu, Duryodhana, the eldest son of Dhritarashtra, and Karna, a charioteer's son, who had nevertheless been made the ruler of Anga by Duryodhana.

Drupada's growing frustration was converted into panic when his kingdom was menaced in the east by the Emperor Jarasandha of Magadha. That ambitious monarch, whose ominous power had cast its shadow over the Arya kings for more than a quarter of a century, had started encroaching on the territories of his easterly neighbour, the King of Kashi. Drupada was afraid that once Kashi came under the hegemony of Jarasandha, Panchala would have hostile powers on both its fronts.

He was growing old, Drupada felt. His sons, in spite of their best efforts, had not acquired either the ability or the skill of expert warriors. His hope of securing for Draupadi, now past twenty, a husband, who could carry on his ambition, had not been realized as yet. His pledge stood as far removed from fulfilment as when it was taken.

In the meantime, Yudhishthira, the oldest of the Five Brothers was appointed Crown Prince of

Hastinapura, and Arjuna, his enemy, was fast gaining the reputation of being the greatest warrior in Aryavarta.

Frustration made Drupada furious, and his determination grew more and more grim.

About this time, Guru Sandipani, one of the disciples of Parashurama in the art of war, came to the court of Drupada. Himself one of the great teachers of the martial art, the Guru conducted the most reputed school in Aryavarta which initiated promising young men into the Vedas and the Shastras as well as skill in arms and strategy in war.

His pupils were drawn from many of the royal houses of Aryavarta and some of the leading *ashrams,* for the Brahmans and the Kshatriyas received the same education till they chose their own special life of learning or war. Few kings or *rishis* ever thought that education of their aspiring sons and disciples would be complete without giving them some training in the Sandipani School.

Guru Sandipani trained his pupils as he travelled on foot all over the lands ruled by the Arya kings. They spent the rainy season in Avanti where Sandipani had his *ashram,* a month or two in Prabhasakshetra on the sea of Saurashtra and a few weeks at Kurukshetra in the *ashram* of the Best of Munis, Veda Vyasa, where Brahmans sought to acquire the highest learning. In between these stages, Sandipani visited the court of different kings or the *ashrams* of notable *rishis,* giving their young inmates the benefit of his training.

Sandipani always made it a point to stay for at least two weeks in a year at Kampilya, the capital of Panchala, as he had great regard for its king.

In spite of his unbending mind and the passion which dominated his life, Drupada was a king who ruled over Panchala in the best tradition of Dharma. Drupada held the Guru in great respect. In his company, he sometimes forgot the bitterness which had taken possession of him. And during Sandipani's stay, the Panchala warriors had the opportunity to learn the latest knowledge that could be acquired about skill in arms.

Sandipani, therefore, was the only person who knew everything about arms and also everything about kings and cadets in Aryavarta. So when he visited Kampilya this time, King Drupada unburdened his heart of the frustration and bitterness which filled it. And as the King spoke of wanting to wed Draupadi to an invincible warrior, his lean face was set in grimness and his hawk-like eyes flashed in ill-concealed hatred.

After hearing the King patiently, Guru Sandipani said: 'Noble lord of Panchala, I understand your feelings. But among all the young warriors, I know, Arjuna, the Pandava, is by far the most irresistible. He has brought archery to perfection. The Gods appear to have blessed him with miraculous skill.'

Then Sandipani mentioned several young princes of repute but Drupada rejected them outright. 'Find out for me a real warrior, one who can overcome all the pupils of Drona', said Drupada almost fiercely, for he was at the end of his patience.

Sandipani smiled indulgently at the King's impatience and spoke in sympathetic tones. 'The only other young warrior who can to some extent match the skill of Arjuna is Karna. But he is a charioteer's son, a loyal pupil of Drona and a dependant of Duryodhana, the son of Dhritarashtra. Any alliance with him is out of the question!'

Drupada was silent for a little while, gazing almost absently, and when he spoke, there was almost a ring of finality in his voice. 'I must find a suitable warrior to match the pupils of Drona. My pledge will not remain unfulfilled. And Krishnaa will keep her vow; she will marry the warrior who destroys Drona'.

Sandipani looked anxiously at the flaming hatred which burnt in Drupada's eyes. He almost felt that if Drupada's vow remained unfulfilled for long, he would do something terrible. 'Noble King, you have done her great harm in bringing her up in the way you have done', said Sandipani in a soothing voice. 'It will embitter her whole life'.

'No. She is the finest daughter a father could have. She often says that, had she not been a woman, she would have outstripped Drona's pupils and avenged the insult,' replied Drupada, a smile dissolving the sternness which overcast his face.

Sandipani tried to soften Drupada's grimness by smiling in his turn, persuasively. 'It is very difficult to think of a master bowman, for in these days so few practise the use of a bow and arrow that, when a man knows how to shoot with them, he can perform miracles. I know many excellent young warriors, but most of them are skilled in the sword, the mace or the battle-axe. Few of them have mastered archery to perfection'.

'I agree. In these days, the battle goes to the master bowman. He can aim from a safe distance and, given a sure aim and powerful arrows, he is invincible', said Drupada.

'That is why Arjuna has emerged as an irrestible warrior', replied the Guru. 'You must have heard that he can shoot at a target even in the dark'.

Drupada frowned, thought for a while and said: 'You are considered a great teacher of archery. I have already heard of some of your pupils who are experts in bowmanship'.

'The Princes Vinda and Anuvinda of Avanti are expert archers,' said Sandipani.

Drupada shook his head. 'Neither of them can ever come up to the best pupils of Drona. But there is one pupil of yours whose bow has been blessed by the Gods. He has the reputation for taking a deadly aim from a running chariot while he is handling four horses—a feat which even Arjuna cannot perform'.

Sandipani laughed at the earnestness with which Drupada said this. 'I know whom you mean. You mean Krishna Vaasudeva, don't you? He is the only pupil of mine who has out-stripped even his Guru in the use of arms. He can match the best archer in Aryavarta. But it is no use counting on him.'

'Why not?' asked Drupada, speaking with appealing insistence. 'I have heard so much about Vaasudeva. He routed Jarasandha, killed the Karavirapura Vaasudeva, destroyed the savage Kala Yavana. He led the Yadavas through the desert to the shores of the distant sea. Recently he is said to have inflicted a defeat on Shalva. And he has come to be recognized as the finest chariot warrior.'

'You need not tell me all that,' said Sandipani, glowing with pride. 'In Vaasudeva's hands, a bow is a formidable weapon of war. As you know, shooting an arrow from a running chariot is a very difficult art: speed, poise, swiftness and agility, all have to be timed to the movements of the rushing horses. All these have come to Krishna by the favour of the Gods.'

'It is said that he can not only shoot a deadly arrow, but can speed his *Chakra* at an opposing warrior from a running chariot, even when the enemy is rushing forward in his chariot,' added Drupada, who for the moment allowed his enthusiasm to overcome his grimness.

'That is true,' said Sandipani.

'What more do I want then?' said Drupada. 'Get him to wed my Krishnaa, I beg of you. He is your pupil and will listen to you.'

'I know Krishna,' said Sandipani. 'He will not wed a young woman unless she wins him, and it is very difficult to win him. I know what Rukmini and Shaibya had to go through to become his brides.'

'My Krishnaa is a wonderful maiden. She would

stand up to all the tests', said Drupada with pride.

'I know your daughter well, noble King. She would make a noble and heroic wife to the finest Kshatriya in Aryavarta', said Sandipani.

'She would be a fitting wife for Krishna, I assure you', remarked Drupada.

'Krishna is not likely to accept your proposal. If he does he will have to pledge himself to fight his cousins, the Five Brothers whom he loves greatly,' said Sandipani.

'Gurudeva, I am sure he would listen to you', said Drupada 'And if Krishna accepts my daughter, I will give him all that he wants, even a part of my kingdom, and see that the Yadavas are rehabilitated in Mathura.'

'Will your daughter be willing to win Krishna Vaasudeva?' asked Sandipani. 'Krishna may not accept a bride who wants him, not for what he is, but for what she wants him to be.'

'Draupadi has heard the story of his exploits. She admires him very much. But she is a proud girl,' said Drupada with a smile. She inherits her father's spirit and may not stoop to conquer'.

'It may be that she will forget her pride when she meets him who knows? His being a master charioteer is the smallest part of him,' added Sandipani.

'What is he like, by nature?' asked Drupada.

'He is not merely a warrior. In three years, since the Yadavas settled in Saurashtra, his leadership has given them not only freedom from fear, but strength and riches. Their horses and cattle have multiplied.

Their ships fare forth from the port of Dwarka on to the high seas and bring back immense wealth from unknown shores,' said Sandipani.

'Now I can understand why the Yadavas worship him as if he was god', said Drupada.

'He releases mysterious streams of faith and has become the source of inspiration to the Yadavas; they are no longer what they were—turbulent and irrepressible. The trials they have endured and the leadership of Krishna have given them a wonderful sense of discipline. That is why the Yadavas can subdue the surrounding principalities and, as a crowning achievement, inflict a crushing defeat on Shalva, the ally of their arch-enemy Jarasandha,' said Sandipani, and carried away by admiration he added with a smile: 'Besides, Krishna is a very dangerous person to meet, I tell you. To meet him is to love him. To love him is to surrender oneself to him. Though he is my pupil, if god could be a man, he would be Krishna.'

'Then, I beg of you, Gurudeva, help me', said Drupada folding his hands. 'I will do everything that I can to win him for my daughter. He would fulfil the pledge for me. That would also bring about an alliance between the Panchalas and the Yadavas'.

'Noble King, when I go to Prabhasa Tirtha next, I will tell him what you have offered. But I have yet to see a man who can make a decision for Krishna', said Sandipani, and the Guru's face glowed with pride.

2

SANDIPANI ARRIVES

Guru Sandipani and his pupils were arriving at Prabhasa Tirtha from Bhrigu Tirtha by sea by about mid-day.

Krishna, the son of Vasudeva, the chief of the Shoora Yadavas, rose earlier than usual from his bed. When he received the respectful greetings of his spouses, Rukmini, the Vidarbha Princess of flaming beauty, and Shaibya, the dark Princess of Karavirapura, whose smile was a song of beauty, he said with mock solemnity: 'Today Gurudeva is coming and is going to decide whether you are keeping your husband happy or not'.

Rukmini put out her tongue impudently. 'We are going to complain that our husband is keeping every one happy but ourselves'.

'Try. Who will believe you, looking at your face? No one will, will he, Shaibya?' asked Krishna and departed.

He proceeded to the beach with his elder brother Balarama and his friend Yuyudhana, the son of Satyaka, generally called Satyaki.

Balarama was a giant in size and strength. By nature he was good-natured, frank and hearty, though when engaged in a mace combat he could smash skulls, with amazing skill. He loved Krishna above everything else, and being free from personal vanity, took greater pride in the achievements of his younger brother than in his own,

Satyaki was a fiery young man, lithe and sinewy, skilled in arms and an athlete, and an expert chariot warrior too. He followed Krishna like his shadow and keenly shared any adventure he embarked upon with steadfast loyalty.

As was their daily routine, Krishna, Balarama and Satyaki joined the Yadavas on the beach, where most of the young and able-bodied ones gathered every morning to acquire greater skill in weapons and keep themselves in fighting trim.

These exercises were in the nature of daily training for collective action and had stood the Yadavas in good stead in their swift rise to power. They had come to look upon physical endurance and bodily vigour as the essential requirements in life.

As Krishna met the young Yadavas gathered on the beach he accosted some by a word, some by a smile, still others by nod or gesture of friendliness. In response he was greeted with spontaneous shouts of "Jaya Shri Krishna", for out of devotion they had come to add the honorific word "Shri" to his name.

A retainer was waiting with his mace named *Kaumodaki* and his bow, *Sharnga,* which he alone could wield. Today, however, he did not enter the mace combat nor shoot an arrow as was his wont. He rested content merely to cheer others who excelled in the performance.

The exercise over, Krishna and Balarama, with the Yadavas, went for a swim in the sea. After swimming, they stood in the water and performed their morning worship of the rising sun. Then they offered their daily worship at the shrine of Somanatha, the God of gods.

It was a cold, crisp winter morning. Gargacharya, the venerable preceptor of the Yadavas and Krishna, accompanied by Balarama and Satyaki, went to the jetty to receive Sandipani and his pupils. Many Yadavas of note and other people had also collected on the beach to give the Guru a hearty welcome.

When the pupils, led by the principal disciples of Sandipani, stepped ashore from the boats, the venerable Gargacharya received them with his blessing. The disciples and the pupils also paid their respects to Krishna and Balarama, whom they held in great admiration as former pupils of the school, who had miraculous achievements to their credit.

With a staff in his hand and dressed in the skin of an antelope, Sandipani, tall, gaunt and sinewy, stepped out of the last boat, his greying hair blowing about his face in the sea breeze, and enveloped Krishna in an affectionate embrace.

Sandipani looked at his favourite pupil with frank admiration. A strenuous life, led with great intensity, had scarcely left any marks on him. The brow was as smooth as a young woman's; the eyes sparkled with joy; the laughter was spontaneous. The grace of his body gave little evidence of the muscular power which could, when required, keep the four stormy horses of a running chariot under control and speed the whirling *chakra* to sever the head of an enemy.

The Guru observed with great satisfaction that his pupil wore his eminence without a trace of vanity. Not a word or gesture escaped him which could indicate that he had performed exploits which were heard with awe-inspired interest in courts and village squares alike.

A fresh garland of *champaka* flowers was swinging cheerfully from his neck. His peacock feather waved gaily on his diadem as he laughed. The yellow *pitambar* which he wore was folded impeccably.

Sandipani's heart overflowed with joy. It was the greatest feat of his strenuous life, thought Sandipani, to have fathered such a spiritual son.

Krishna stepped aside and Sandipani hastened to embrace Balarama. The heavy-bodied giant encircled the wiry Guru in his massive arms and left the old teacher breathless.

'And where is Uddhava?' asked Sandipani.

'Krishna has sent him to Hastinapura,' laughed Balarama, 'as if Dwaraka was not good enough for him.'

During these years, Krishna, while looking after the interests of the Yadavas, had never failed to follow the happenings in the outside world. Even in the prosperity which had come to the Yadavas, he had never forgotten that the fate of Dharma was ultimately bound up with the fortunes of Aryavarta.

Krishna had also never ceased to cherish the memory of the happy days he had spent with Arjuna and Bhima when, one after the other, they had visited Mathura, and he had followed their career in the distant north with great interest.

Vinda and Anuvinda, the twin Princes of Avanti, had been his loyal friends from the time they had all been pupils at Sandipani's school. Avanti was developing into a great centre to which men from all parts of Aryavarta were attracted, and the Princes, whenever they could, kept Krishna informed of the developments in different parts of the country.

The Brahmans too kept the common consciousness flowing throughout the Arya world. They visited one country after another, going on pilgrimage, attending sacrificial sessions, visiting schools of learning, reciting the exploits of ancient kings, imparting the teachings of the sages, and seeking the patronage of kings or warriors or the rich members of the community.

In their peregrinations, the Brahmans never missed visiting the holy shrine of Somanatha at Prabhasa, and when there, invariably received generous hospitality and lavish gifts from the Yadavas, and in return, gave an account of whatever they had learned in the countries they had been visiting.

All who came to Dwaraka were as much fascinated with Krishna's graciousness and wisdom as they were awed by the superb way in which he had built up the power of the Yadavas. When they left Dwaraka, they carried with them the tales of his exploits to retail them wherever they went.

It was Guru Sandipani's school which steadily

maintained a flow of communication between the different parts of the country. The Guru himself, on account of the confidence which was placed in him by the kings and the *rishis*, was an authority on the policies of both of these.

Krishna, therefore, knew what was happening in the outside world.

After Rukmini's proposed *swayamvara* had been turned by Krishna into a fiasco, Jarasandha had returned home to Rajagriha, the capital of Magadha, frustrated and furious. During these three years he had made no attempt to invade any of the kingdoms ruled by the Arya kings, though reports had it that he was waiting for an opportunity to overwhelm the King of Kashi.

However, as Krishna knew, the final victory of Dharma largely depended upon the attitude of the Kurus of Hastinapura, and of the Panchalas of Kampilya—the two most populous of the Arya races.

The fertile lands which the Kurus and the Panchalas occupied along the banks of the Ganga formed the heart of Aryavarta. It included Kurukshetra and Brahmarshidesh, where the most revered of the sages had their *ashrams* and where the standard of Kshatriya conduct was set by the venerable Gangeya. Generally called Grandfather Bhishma, this pillar of the Kuru power, single-minded in the pursuit of Dharma, was as strict in personal and public life as he was terrible in war.

Krishna felt the situation in Hastinapura

heartening. The blind King Dhritarashtra had had the wisdom to appoint Yudhishthira, the eldest son of his deceased brother Pandu, and Krishna's cousin as the *yuvaraja*. Within a short time, with Grandfather Bhishma's blessings, he had gained the love of his people. and a reputation for being a just and benevolent ruler.

Krishna was also delighted to hear that Arjuna, the third of Pandu's sons and the friend whom he cherished, had given stability to the empire of the Kurus by his victories in the wars. His fame as a warrior of miraculous power had spread everywhere and his exploits were sung in every royal hall.

However, the situation was not free from uncertainty. When Yudhishthira was installed as the *yuvaraja*, Duryodhana, the eldest son of Dhritarashtra, came to Saurashtra on the pretext of perfecting the art of mace combat under Balarama, its recognised master.

Duryodhana after his arrival wormed himself into the affections of Balarama and became his favourite pupil. He was also at pains to make friends with Krishna, who was the last person to repulse a proffered friendship.

Spiteful and malicious by temperament, this Kuru prince, as Krishna could see, had lashed himself into a jealous rage at Yudhishthira being appointed the *yuvaraja,* and had really come to Dwarka to ascertain whether the Yadavas would befriend him if there was a clash between him and the Five Brothers. Krishna had been, therefore, glad that with him away for about a year all intrigues would be hushed in Hastinapura and the Five Brothers would happily be left free to strengthen their hold on the Kurus.

Krishna knew that Yudhishthira was pledged to Dharma; that the Five Brothers were devoted to each other; that they were held in high regard by their venerable Grandfather Bhishma, and in great affection by the Best of Munis, Veda Vyasa, foremost among the seers.

With Yudhishthira as the *yuvaraja* and later the Emperor of Hastinapura, and Arjuna too, the irresistible warrior, by his side, Krishna felt confident that Dharma would come to be respected, and violence and wickedness subdued. That was the only hope of the Arya way of life flourishing and reclaiming those people who were alien to it.

When, after a year's stay with him, Duryodhana left for Hastinapura, Krishna could see that things would now be not too easy for the Five Brothers. The time, therefore, had come for him to go north, give strength to his cousins, the Five Brothers, and forge an alliance which would stand as a bulwark for Dharma.

The long-awaited opportunity to go north had presented itself two months before when be had received a pressing invitation from Yudhishthira to come to Hastinapura. In response, Uddhava, his beloved friend and cousin, had been sent in advance to announce that he, Krishna, was coming.

■

THE TEACHER AND THE PUPIL

*S*ince his Guru desired to see him, Krishna went to Gargacharya's *ashram,* after the midday meal.

Sandipani was seated on a deer skin under the shade of a banyan tree, surrounded by some pupils. When Krishna joined him, the other disciples left them to themselves, sensing a special purpose in this visit.

Sandipani soon came to the subject which was uppermost in his mind. His voice was earnest and his deep-set eyes grave. He said: 'Krishna, my son, I am glad to see you so well and so happy. What are your plans, now that the Yadavas are thriving? Are you content with what you have done so far?'

'Gurudeva, because of your blessing, the gods have been very kind to me,' said Krishna with equal seriousness, for between the two of them there was a close bond of understanding. 'The Yadavas are now free from the fear of Jarasandha. They are strong and united, and also prosperous—perhaps more prosperous than is good for them,' he added with a smile. 'Some of us are prone to lapse into riotous living.'

'Remember you were not born to make the Yadavas rich,' said Sandipani. 'Riches and Dharma do not go together.'

'I don't know what I was born for. Many people seem to know more about it than I do,' remarked Krishna with a mischievous twinkle in his eyes. 'You must discover what I should do next.'

'I wish I was fit to do so, my son,' said Sandipani with an apologetic smile, for he often wondered whether it was not his pupil who kept him on his mettle all the time. 'However, is it not time, Krishna, to think of all men, not of the Yadavas only? You alone can achieve the impossible and establish Dharma among men,' he added.

'I must rest content to face whatever task confronts me for the moment, without going specially out of my way to seek new ones,' said Krishna thoughtfully.

'Well, the task has come to you in the shape of your Guru,' said Sandipani with a smile. 'He brings you a message from King Drupada of Panchala. He wants a favour from you. After telling you all about it, I can, if you like, speak about it to King Ugrasena and your noble father.'

'King Drupada is sending me a message?' said Krishna, his eyes wide with surprise.

'Krishna, he offers you his daughter Draupadi, in marriage,' said Sandipani slowly, watching the reactions of his pupil. 'She is beautiful, gifted and highly intelligent. In return for your accepting her, he also offers to give you a part of his kingdom and to help the Yadavas rebuild Mathura which is now a wilderness.'

Krishna started smiling, his eyes shining merrily. 'I wish every task you asked me to perform were so tempting, Gurudeva. It seems I am a very desirable son-in-law. But how have I merited this favour from so great a king? Everyone, except myself, seems to have forgotten that the kings would not sit with me, a *gopal,* at the *swayamvara* of Bhishmaka's daughter.'

The teacher was also infected by Krishna's merriment and laughed heartily before he said: 'Drupada, does not merely confer a favour on you; he also asks for one.'

'In what way could I possibly be of service to the noble lord of Panchala?' asked Krishna.

'In a very real way,' replied Sandipani. 'Drupada, as you must have heard, has suffered brutal humiliation at the hands of Dronacharya, that great master of war, the military leader of the Kurus. He made the King part with some lands north of the Ganga. Since then, the King has only one aim to live for—to avenge the humiliation. And he wants you to help him do so.'

Krishna laughed aloud. 'And Draupadi will be my fee for destroying Dronacharya!'

Sandipani raised a warning finger. 'Don't think this a foolish jest, Krishna. I know Draupadi. Don't be unjust to her. She is noble; she is devoted to her father; she will marry none but the most redoubtable hero in Aryavarta, so that his pledge may be fulfilled. Few daughters live for their fathers as she does.'

'But why me? There are many redoubtable heroes in Aryavarta who will do what her father wants them to,' said Krishna, again laughing merrily.

'She thinks you are the best of them or perhaps the

only one she would choose,' said Sandipani. 'And she is the finest woman in existence.'

Krishna, holding up his hand with his thumb and finger joined together, as teachers often do when explaining something, summarised the offer with a smile. 'Drupada's favour then comes to this: I am to marry a very determined woman. I then fight Dronacharya, and if necessary all his pupils, the Kuru Princes, to avenge her father's defeat. I leave my position as a humble Yadava to become a tributary of Panchala. Incidentally I induce the Yadavas to leave this beautiful land and rebuild a wilderness. It is a very tempting offer indeed!'

There was no irony in what Krishna said. He was only analysing the situation with an unerring clarity. Sandipani looked on admiringly; this pupil of his had the sanity of outlook which he wished many other kings and warriors possessed.

'I knew, Krishna, that you would not be tempted by the offer. I frankly told Drupada so, but as he was very insistent, I had to promise him to convey his message to you,' said Sandipani as he smiled appreciatively. 'I also told him that you are a very difficult person to deal with. You will not allow anyone to make up your mind for you.'

'What a poor opinion my Guru has of me!' said Krishna, and both the teacher and the pupil laughed, each eyeing the other with affection.

'I wish I had more disciples I had such a high opinion of as I have of you, Krishna,' said Sandipani. 'What reply shall I convey to King Drupada?'

'Gurudeva, take him my humble greetings and tell

him that I am beholden to such a noble king, for the preference he has shown for me.' said Krishna. 'But the Yadavas are too well settled in Dwaraka to think of returning to Mathura. Tell him also that I feel unequal to the task which he wishes to call me to.'

'You can't brush this affair aside lightly. Have you realised what we are in for, if you refuse the offer,' asked Sandipani, his face becoming grave.

'No,' replied Krishna.

'Hate consumes Drupada. At times I have felt that it may drive him to any madness. He may offer Draupadi. to Jarasandha and precipitate a war with the Kurus. Then even the Gods cannot save the Aryas,' said Sandipani.

Krishna thought for a while. 'That disaster must be averted,' he said, anxiety creeping into his voice.

'I shudder to think where Drupada's bitterness will lead him,' said Sandipani.

'And Dronacharya is no less determined?' said Krishna.

'Perhaps,' said Sandipani.

'Gurudeva, we shall have to think over this matter,' said Krishna.

The teacher and the pupil exchanged meaningful glances.

They understood each other's unspoken thoughts.

'Please convey my homage to Drupada and tell him that when I come to Hastinapura where I am invited by my cousin Yudhishthira, I will visit Kampilya to pay my respects to him,' said Krishna.

'You are going to Hastinapura!' exclaimed Sandipani

in surprise. 'You need not go there now. Yudhishthira is no longer the *yuvaraja*'.

'What!' exclaimed Krishna, taken aback.

'Shvetaketu was there in Hastinapura when the Five Brothers were banished by King Dhritarashtra. He will be able to tell you more about it. He has just arrived from Bhrigu Tirtha.' Sandipani clapped his hands and called his principal disciple.

Shvetaketu came to where they were sitting and folded his hands before the Guru. Krishna got up and the two friends held each other in a happy embrace.

Shvetaketu was the pride of Sandipani's school. He was learned in the Vedas; he was a first-rate teacher of the martial art. His honest face was framed in a short, dark beard and dark matted locks.

Sandipani said: 'Shvetaketu, tell Krishna all about the banishment of the Five Brothers from Hastinapura'.

'Yes' said Shvetaketu, taking his seat in front of Sandipani. 'When I went to Hastinapura to collect the three cadets who were to join our school, I met Uddhava, who was preparing to accompany the Five Brothers to Varanavata. It seems that King Dhritarashtra, egged on by Duryodhana—whom, Krishna, you know very well—asked Yudhishthira to give up his office as Crown Prince and to proceed to Varanavata with his brothers and mother. When the people heard of this misfortune they were stricken with grief; many Kurus raised protests; women wailed publicly. And when the Five Brothers left Hastinapura, a large crowd followed them for about a *yojana* with tears in their eyes'.

Krishna was thoughtful for a while. 'Shvetaketu, I

do not understand this. Yudhishthira was appointed Crown Prince by the advice of the venerable Bhishma who is the real power in Hastinapura. How could he allow such a thing to happen?'

'I did not stay in Hastinapura long enough to find out the details. But some people whom I met said that no sooner had Dhritarashtra conveyed his wishes than Yudhishthira cheerfully expressed his willingness to leave Hastinapura. His brothers were against it, but ultimately they submitted to him', said Shvetaketu. Krishna, oppressed by his thoughts, remained silent.

'It is no use your going to Hastinapura now', said Sandipani. 'It would be better for you to go to Kampilya after I have communicated your reply to King Drupada through Shvetaketu. The Five Brothers were highly respected by the Kurus, but now, with Duryodhana as Crown Prince, things will change—and change for the worse. It is not worth your while to go there'.

Krishna looked up. The boyish smile had disappeared from his face. The eyes which had twinkled merrily so far, grew unfathomably deep. 'Gurudeva', said Krishna slowly and deliberately 'we were talking about my appointed task. It has come to me now. I must do it. I will go to Hastinapura'.

'Go to Hastinapura now? Duryodhana will not offer you a welcome', said Sandipani.

'I am not going in order to secure a welcome. With Yudhishthira, Bhima and Arjuna in Hastinapura, Dharma was soaring skywards. Now it is eclipsed. That is why I should go there', said Krishna.

The atmosphere suddenly became tense. 'I can leave

Dwaraka in two days' time,' continued Krishna. 'Satyaki will be ready with sixty chariot warriors and the necessary retinue. And I will go by the short-cut through the deserts',

'But why so hurriedly?' asked Sandipani.

'I feel that something is going to happen to the Five Brothers', replied Krishna. 'I must reach Hastinapura before that.' Krishna's mind was made up; his eyes were now compelling. The majestic calm of a god had settled on his brow. 'And Gurudeva, don't convey to King Drupada the message that I gave you just now. Send Shvetaketu with me and he will go to Kampilya and deliver another message from me',

'What message do you want to send?' asked Sandipani.

'Shvetaketu, my message to King Drupada is this', said Krishna decisively. "I am obliged to His Majesty King Drupada, for offering me the hand of Draupadi. If the noble lord of Panchala permits me, I shall come to Kampilya from Hastinapura and discuss the offer personally with him before I place it before my revered lord, Ugrasena, and my Father". Shvetaketu, get ready'.

Sandipani was struck at the transformation which had come over his pupil. The gay youth had become almost a god of destiny.

'Krishna, my son, you are the best judge of the situation', said Sandipani. 'I will not ask you for your reasons for coming to this decision. If that is the Dharma which lights your path, follow it. My blessing, my son, is always with you.

■

DRONACHARYA'S DECISION

*T*he *Yuddha shala*—military academy—of Hastinapura, situated on the bank of the Ganga, enclosed a very large area. Warriors were trained there, also arms were fabricated, horses bred, elephants trained and war chariots manufactured.

In the *Yuddha shala* there was a large mansion. In it there lived Dronacharya, the teacher of the Kuru Princes and the great leader who directed all the military preparations which upheld the Kuru power.

In front of the mansion, under an ancient peepal tree, he sat in deep thought, though he only appeared to be gazing intently at the wavelets which lapped against the bank of the river. He was seated on a sort of throne placed on a small platform and now and again threw parched gram to the fish and tortoises swimming in the shallow waters. Here he always sat, making plans, talking to pupils or giving orders to subordinates. Feeding fish was the only distraction he permitted himself at the time.

As a Brahman of high rank, Dronacharya wore his locks matted and had no jewels or ornaments on his body. Unlike other Brahmans, however, he was dressed in silk. The throne on which he sat was covered with a tiger skin—a tribute to his great guru

Parashurama, who was always clad in one. A gold-encrusted bow and arrow adopted by him as the insignia of his office, rested against his knee, also reminiscent of the manner in which his master always kept his famed battle-axe with him when seated.

His beard and locks were dark, thick and well trimmed. His pointed nose, firm set lips and small but brilliant eyes testified to the fire which burned within his small but sturdy frame.

His forehead was deeply furrowed, for his affairs had come to a crisis. Just when his ambitions were on the point of being fulfilled, he was faced with a reverse.

Dronacharya was the son of Bharadwaja, a very learned Brahman who, pledged to austere poverty, had taken the traditional vow of not keeping more food in his house than was needed to provide his family for three days. From his childhood, therefore, he had smarted under the privations which his father's self-imposed vow entailed.

When Drona went to the house of his guru to pursue his studies, he had to accept self-imposed poverty—the privilege of a *brahmachari*, a celibate student. He had to maintain himself by collecting his daily food from generous neighbours, sleep on a deer skin, collect fuel and perform other domestic tasks.

Other Brahman fellow-students who stayed in the guru's house, took pride in living this way, not Drona. He hated poverty, self-imposed though it was. He saw no sense in self-imposed nonpossession and envied some of his fellow-students who came from princely families and who found ways to live in comfort.

Drona was as proud as he was ambitious. He was

sure that he had it in him to outstrip all his fellow-students in whatever he undertook—now or at any time. But invariably his poverty shook his self-confidence. He had an insistent urge to command, to control, to bend men to his will. He scorned the Brahmanical discipline which gave up worldly gain in the pursuit of high learning and austere self-discipline—*vidya* and *tapas.*

With a view to overcoming the helplessness which his poverty imposed upon him, he ingratiated himself with a fellow-student. Yajnasena Drupada, the Prince of Panchala, a generous young man, who had no hesitation in sharing his comforts with him.

However, Drona was not content to be the Prince's friend, he wanted to be his master. With that object in view, he won the confidence and affection of the Prince, whom he came to dominate by his superior intelligence and resourcefulness. Led step by step, Drupada, in effusive friendliness, pledged eternal friendship to the young Brahman.

The Prince was impressionable to a fault. His friendship for Drona soon turned into worshipful devotion. In a fit of childish generosity skilfully engineered, he took a solemn vow with the sacred waters of Ganga in his hands that when he ascended the throne of Panchala he would share his royal authority with his friend.

Some years went by. On the death of his father, young Drupada succeeded to the kingship of Panchala. Drona was happy. His dream had come true. So when he finished his studies, he went to his royal friend and claimed a share of his power; the time, he urged, had come to fulfil the Prince's vow.

The young King had even forgotten the vow that he had taken in a moment of boyish enthusiasm. During the short time that he had been on the throne, he had also been awakened to new values and responsibilities as the king of one of the most powerful kingdoms of the Arya world. But he still held his friend in affection. He welcomed him with lavish presents and even offered to provide an *ashram* for him or confer an office suited to his learning.

For years, young Drona had nursed the hope that the young Prince would keep his promise when he became king and accept his domination as in their student days. He was, therefore, affronted. He had not come to Kampilya to assume the role of a guru or a minister; he wanted a share of the royal power and was determined to have it.

Drona, therefore, insisted on the pledge being fulfilled. Drupada, now wise in the ways of the world, ridiculed the idea of his fulfilling a silly pledge taken in his teens. He simply could not share his royal power. He held it in conjunction with the chiefs of Panchala and with the ministers who had served his father all their lives. He could not, he pointed out, do such an absurd thing as to share his royal authority with a friend, however beloved he was.

Drona was furious. He charged Drupada •with breaking his pledge. In reply, Drupada was polite but firm; he could not fulfil a promise given in ignorance of his responsibilities.

Exasperated, Drona, in the presence of the assembled court, hurled insults at the young King and threatened him with dire penalties. The position became impossible and the King was forced to turn this irate, erstwhile friend of his out of Kampilya.

Drona was not prepared to accept defeat. He decided to acquire the necessary force to coerce Drupada into performing his promise.

He was a hard realist, with a cool, calculating brain. Mere learning, he saw, was not enough to satisfy his ambition. He must, therefore, follow in the footsteps of Parashurama, and, through mastery in arms, acquire a power greater than that of the kings.

Undaunted by hardships, he travelled to the *ashram* of Parashurama at Shoorparaka, walking through forests, sleeping under the open sky, often going without food. The old Master, pleased with the intelligence of this aspiring young man and his zest to be trained in arms, accepted him as his pupil.

A few years passed by. Drona mastered all that the old Master and his *ashram* had to teach about the fabrication and use of arms and about the making and winning of wars. Even his guru, the ancient master of the art of war, who had trained generations of pupils, was amazed at the unbending will with which the brilliant young man completed his training.

Drona became a matchless teacher in the art of war. He saw, as few had seen before him, that the era of the battle-axe and the mace, the sword and the trident, had gone, never to return. The bow and arrow were the only weapons of the future. He therefore acquired complete mastery of the flying missile—the arrow which, when he willed, could serve him with the readiness of an intelligent slave.

Before leaving the *ashram,* Drona married Kripaadevi,

the daughter of the teacher in whose house he was residing. Accompanied by her and her brother Kripacharya, also an expert in training young men in arms, he returned to Aryavarta to carve out a career for himself, which would ultimately enable him to avenge Draupada's insult.

With rare self-assurance, the young teacher presented himself to no less a person than Grandfather Bhishma at Hastinapura. Bhishma, himself a pupil of Parashurama, immediately saw the worth of such a competent expert in military affairs and engaged him, and also his brother-in-law, to initiate the Kuru princes into the art of war.

Once appointed as the head of the *yuddha shala* of the Kurus, Dronacharya bent all his energies to imparting to his pupils the art which he knew so well.

However, that was not enough for his bursting energy, nor was it the aim he had set himself. He rebuilt the Kuru machine of war, reorganized the corps of swordsmen, archers, experts in mace combat, masters of elephants and chariot warriors. He also became an adviser on the affairs of the State to Bhishma, to whom his penetrating intelligence was useful.

His students, the Kuru princes and other cadets, proved worthy of their master. Of them, Bhima and Duryodhana excelled in the art of mace combat; Arjuna, and also Karna, the charioteer's son, became master bowmen. His own son, Aswatthama, also became a formidable warrior.

His pupils not only fulfilled his hopes, but helped

him to secure the primary aim of his life. Through the
miraculous bowmanship of his pupil, Arjuna, he also got
King Drupada to fulfil his promise.

In a sudden and unexpected attack, Drupada was
captured by Arjuna and laid at his feet. The helpless
King of Panchala had to offer an abject apology for
breaking his vow, and, by way of ransom, part with a
slice of his kingdom to the north of the river Ganga. The
fair city of Ahicchatra in this territory now became
Dronacharya's to rule.

Drona's ambition waxed higher. He was not content
with being the master of Ahicchatra. He had no illusions
about kings and held kingship in contempt. He scorned
the pomp and ceremony which glorified them into little
divinities. His aim now was to be the real master of the
Kuru empire, so that the fortunes of many kings might
depend on him.

The situation in Hastinapura was to Drona's liking,
and he knew how to alter as he wished whatever did not
please him. Grandfather Bhishma, in spite of the
supreme power he enjoyed, was getting old. King
Dhritarashtra lacked both character and vigour. His
pupils, the Kuru princes, were divided among themselves; The sons of Dhritarashtra were jealous and
distrustful of the sons of Pandu. This hostility provided
him with the necessary opportunity to manipulate
things as he liked.

The Five Brothers—the Pandavas—all able in their
own way, were his supporters. Of them, Arjuna was the
most devoted. Duryodhana and his brothers—the sons
of Dhritarashtra—though loyal to him in a sense, were

intrinsically unreliable, but he had seen to it that his fiery son, Aswatthama, should be Duryodhana's close associate.

Drona knew that only the Five Brothers could extend the Kuru empire to the ends of the earth. Yudhishthira, righteous and noble, would make a very good emperor, Bhima and Arjuna were formidable warriors. Nakula knew the art of breeding and training horses for war, as no one else did. Sahadeva was learned, wise and farsighted. And he fondly hoped that in view of their ungrudging loyalty to him, he would be the master of the situation when they came to power.

So, when the time came, Drona heartily approved of Grandfather Bhishma's suggestion that Yudhishthira should be appointed the *yuvaraja,* the Crown Prince. He was the wisest of all the Kuru princes and loved by all, and, as the eldest son of the late King Pandu, he was justly entitled to succeed to the throne.

No sooner had Yudhishthira become the Crown Prince, than he, in his very conscientious way, took upon himself all the responsibilities of the office. He commanded the full confidence of Bhishma in the affairs of State and acquired the respect of all the ministers, particularly of Vidura, the wisest of them.

When Yudhishthira was appointed *yuvaraja,* Drona felt that he had now become all-powerful, more powerful than Bhishma himself.

However, he was annoyed at Yudhishthira's attitude. As a *yuvaraja,* he was no longer the docile pupil which he had been in the *yuddha shala.* He was a monarch, with the self-confidence of one who knew his business and with an honesty of purpose which could not be deflected by personal loyalties. No doubt, when he had military affairs to discuss, he took his teacher into confidence.

Hard as he tried, Dronacharya could not dominate Yudhishthira. At all times, the young Prince was fair, just, correct and cordial, but firm in his determination to fulfil his royal duties conscientiously. Intrigues did not affect him. He sought advice from many, but accepted guidance from no one except Grandfather Bhishma, and he governed the empire to the satisfaction of all concerned.

Then the blow fell. Without even mentioning the matter to him, Yudhishthira sent an invitation to Krishna Vaasudeva of Dwaraka to visit Hastinapura. He also heard that Drupada, his enemy, had offered his daughter to Krishna.

All the fabric of power which he had built up was threatened. For some years, he had received reports about the formidable exploits of Krishna, but so far it had caused him no worry, for the Yadava hero was too far away to be of any significance. But now he was coming. His cousin, Uddhava, was actually arriving in Hastinapura within a week to announce his arrival.

The crisis had to be met, and met with cold-blooded decisiveness. Yudhishthira could not be permitted to ally himself with Krishna. In no event was it to be thought of, if Krishna was to wed Drupada's daughter.

Drona carefully considered all the possible moves on the chess-board. He had to checkmate this new move of Yudhishthira's. Yudhishthira, in matters of State, was not pliable. Bhima and Arjuna could not be parted from Yudhishthira. Bhishma was not likely to refuse an alliance between the Kurus and the Yadavas.

The game which he had been playing all through his life had suddenly changed shape. It demanded drastic moves. The Five Brothers must not rule in Hastinapura if he was to have his way.

The only course left was to inflame the rivalry between the Five Brothers and Duryodhana and his brothers. He himself had no confidence in Duryodhana's character or ability; but his son Aswatthama, he knew, provided Duryodhana with fire and energy. So far it had been his influence over Duryodhana exercised through his son which had prevented Duryodhana and his friends from taking violent steps to displace Yudhishthira.

It was the most decisive moment of his own life. He had to make the final bid for assuming complete power over the Kurus, which was only possible with Duryodhana as the *yuvaraja*. True, he was unstable, insolent, badly advised, but he would be an easier instrument in his hands than the righteous Yudhishthira.

Drona clapped his hands and ordered the servitor, who came in response to his call, with folded hands, to send for his son, Aswatthama. The teacher went on feeding the fish and the tortoises.

Aswatthama soon came and prostrated himself before his father. Unlike his father, he was a tall and well-built man with large eyes and apparently an impatient temper.

'I want to talk to you, my son,' said Dronacharya, his face showing a winning smile, which he could assume whenever it suited his purpose.

'As my venerable father pleases,' said Aswatthama.

'You were displeased with me the other day when I

told you that the salvation of the Kurus was in the hands of the Five Brothers. You told me that I was unjust to Duryodhana and his brothers.'

Aswatthama's eyes were full of annoyance, but he lowered them out of respect. 'I was sorry to have said so, but, venerable father, if I do not tell you what we feel, to whom should we say it?' These words, though humble in their meaning, were not spoken in humility; they suggested suppressed displeasure.

Dronacharya smiled affectionately. 'Son, I have thought over what you said. There is some truth in it. I have not been fair to all my pupils equally, as I should have been.'

Aswatthama looked up in surprise. This was almost the first time that he had found his father confessing that he was wrong. He did not know what was coming next and waited.

'Have you told Duryodhana what I said to you?' asked Dronacharya.

'Yes, venerable father,' replid Aswatthama.

'You are now free to tell Duryodhana that I do not propose to take sides in his quarrel with the Five Brothers,' said Dronacharya with a show of fairness.

'Oh, Father, I am so pleased!' exclaimed Aswatthama happily. 'May I have your permission to go and convey to Duryodhana what you have now said? Now we can see our way.'

'Yes, my son, you have my blessing.'

As Aswatthama hastily left his father, Dronacharya threw a handful of gram to the fish and the tortoises, and smiled to himself. It was a smile of supreme satisfaction, for he felt that his mind retained the same crystal clarity which had characterised him throughout life. He could cut any knot with uncanny precision without being affected by sentiment. Yes, he had done it more than once in the past.

A Nishada boy, Ekalavya by name, once, had fallen at his feet begging to be trained in archery. He had refused him. His mastery in bowmanship was not to be distributed freely to all pupils who might or might not be useful to him. He was going to concentrate on the Kuru princes—among them, above all, on Arjuna, the left-handed bowman of immense promise.

Now, the picture of Ekalavya rose before the teacher's mind. The boy had a blind devotion to him, and would not take a refusal. He had gone to his forest home, constructed an image of himself and, in his name, practised archery and gained perfection.

When he learnt about it, Drona at first had felt very proud. Students could learn archery not only under his direct guidance, but even under his distant inspiration!

But the moment he saw the supreme bowmanship of Ekalavya, he sensed the danger which lay in a Nishada boy raising a generation of Nishadas to practise advance archery, of which he was the master. That could not be allowed to happen; it would come in the way of his personal ambition. Ekalavya would some day overcome Arjuna and all his other pupils, and his project of building power with the aid of the Kuru princes would come to naught.

The foolish, trusting Nishada boy, true to tradition, wanted to give Drona the present due to his guru on completion of his studies. At that moment, Drona saw the way to avert the danger. He asked the boy to give him the thumb of his right hand as a present!

It was a terrible thing he had asked for; it would make the poor boy utterly useless as an archer. But Drona could not allow anyone to stand in his way. Ekalavya's skill must be made entirely ineffective.

The Nishada boy fell at his feet, and begged of him to spare his thumb without which he could not speed an arrow. But he, Drona, was not to be shaken in his calculated decision.

He now remembered the words that he had then spoken: 'My boy, either you give me the present of your thumb or you can have your skill as a free gift.'

'No, no,' the boy answered, tears rolling down his cheeks. 'You have been to me the master not only of my skill, but of my body and soul. I have lived all these years in the hope of pleasing you. I shall not fail.'

With a broken heart, the brave boy took the blade of his arrow, cut off his thumb and presented it to him.

For a moment his heart, he recollected, had moved. He had been inclined to countermand the order. But no! He could not permit a pupil of his to thwart his ambition. He accepted the bleeding thumb as a present, blessed the boy and came away. And he was not sorry for it.

Today he had a similar crisis to deal with. But now he had not merely to ask for the thumb of his pupil. He had to remove five of his favourite pupils—and among them, his dearest—to clear his path.

After all he was Drona and no one should stand in his way.

5

THE UNCLE'S COMMANDS

The mansion of the Five Brothers in Hastinapura stood near the palace of King Dhritarashtra. Persons wanting to meet one or other of them on affairs of State, waited on the verandah in front. Archers with bows and arrows stood guard at its gates.

In one of the long corridors of their mansion overlooking the wide expanse of the river Ganga, Uddhava sat talking to Arjuna, the third of the Five Brothers, who was sharpening the blades of the arrows of the giant bow at his side. The corridor was full of all sorts of arms—maces, swords, battle-axes, tridents, spears and bows of various size and strength with a variety of arrows. This was the arsenal of Bhima and Arjuna.

In that age when battles were fought and won by the prowess and skill of individual warriors, every warrior worth the name had to fabricate his arms to suit his strength and skill.

Arjuna was not merely a master bowman, but could make his own weapons and give them an edge and potency peculiarly his own. The gods had given him the skill to make his arrows more deadly than any on earth and he had the eye and the skill to speed them as he liked.

Uddhava and Arjuna were both of medium height. Their bodies showed long and continuous training in wrestling and in arms.

Uddhava had regular and attractive features, which, however, bore the stamp of an austere mind. His general behaviour too showed a habit of conscious self-restraint. His eyes also bespoke a seriousness not commonly found in a man of his years.

His cousin, Arjuna—Mother Kunti being the sister of Uddhava's father, Devabhaga—was different. He was well shaped and graceful in every limb. His face, fairer than uddhava's, was strikingly handsome. His eyes were intelligent, his brow noble. His voice was well modulated and his smile sensuous. There was also an air of temperamental fastidiousness about the dress and ornaments he wore.

When Uddhava had arrived in the morning, Bhima and Arjuna had received him at the city gates. When he was brought home, all the Five Brothers and their Mother, Kunti, had given him an affectionate welcome and made enquiries about his family. Uddhava had informed them of the purpose of his visit to Hastinapura. He had come to announce that Krishna was arriving within a few weeks in response to Yudhishthira's invitation.

Yudhishthira had left for the royal palace to join the *parishad,* the assembly of experts, with whose assistance he transacted the affairs of State and dispensed justice to the citizens. Sahadeva, the youngest of the Five

Brothers, had gone with him; he had already come to be recognised as an authority on the ancient laws of the Aryas and worked as a member of the *parishad* when it advised Yudhishthira.

Bhima and Nakula had also left to attend to their work and Mother Kunti had gone to the kitchen to get the meal prepared for them.

When Uddhava enquired about the affairs of Hastinapura, Arjuna told him all that was happening to them.

'Uddhava now you see how unhappy we are though our Eldest[1] is *the yuvaraja,*' said Arjuna with a genial smile which made light of the import of his words.

'But, by all accounts. the Eldest is loved by Grandfather Bhishma and also by the chiefs and the people,' said Uddhava.

'Yes,' replied Arjuna with a touch of sarcasm, taking up a fresh blade to sharpen. 'Our Eldest rules over the Kurus. but his commands are defied by our cousins and their friends. People love us and shower blessings on us; and every day our cousins plan to destroy us.'

Uddhava could not help comparing Arjuna's smile with that of his friend Krishna; yet he discovered a difference. This smile was fascinating and evoked friendliness; the other was enchanting and won hearts.

'It is very strange of Duryodhana to behave so,' said Uddhava. 'You have brought fresh renown to the house of the Kurus—the Eldest by his righteous ways, Madhyama[2] and you by your valour. Anyone else would have been proud of you,'

—— and Nakula by the wonderful horses he has trained and Sahadeva by his uncanny wisdom,' interrupted Arjuna with an affectionate twinkle in his eyes as if Uddhava had done an injustice to his younger brothers whom he loved so well. Then he laughed. 'But that is our misfortune.'

Arjuna paused for a while. Then, weighing his words, he proceeded: 'Our cousins hate us for what we are. Duryodhana thinks that brother Yudhishthira has usurped his place as Crown Prince; he could never forgive his father for being born blind,' added Arjuna with a wink and smile. 'That cost him a throne.'

'But your father was the last king of the Kurus and a good one too,' said Uddhava. 'And according to our ancient canons, the Eldest has right to succeed to the kingship.'

'That is true,' said Arjuna, giving a proud smile at the mention of his father. 'That is why Grandfather Bhishma decided that the Eldest should be the Crown Prince. But our cousins will not accept that decision.'

'But obviously you are qualified to rule,' said Uddhava.

'That is the trouble,' said Arjuna with a smile. 'Our cousins hate us because we excel them in skill in arms, win victories and bring wealth to Hastinapura and our Eldest commands the love of the people. They would particularly like to murder Bhima, for he makes them look foolish every time they try to humiliate us.'

'I can't blame them either,' said Uddhava with his usual sense of fairness. 'You are all so good, so brave and so lovable. I am myself jealous of you.'

'Brother Uddhava, I wish we had not been born into a royal family,' said Arjuna. 'Then we would have come with you to Dwaraka and lived happily with Krishna and Balarama.'

'Oh, we would welcome you heartily if you ever came to us,' said Uddhava, for a moment allowing a little warmth to creep into his even voice. 'Krishna loves you so much. He has never forgotten the happy days he spent with you.'

Arjuna smiled a little apologetically. 'Nor has Bhima ever forgotten the attention which Krishna and Balarama showered on him when he was in Mathura. And I often dream of the days when Krishna and myself as boys lay side by side talking sometimes till the morning star rose.'

'Oh, Bhima was so good. We all loved him so,' said Uddhava, carried away for a moment by the memory of Bhima's visit in the happy days at Mathura. 'And he was so fond of all of us.'

Arjuna was thoughtful for a minute. 'We would have left Hastinapura in disgust long ago. But if we did so, it would break the Grandfather's heart.'

'Why? If he can't keep your cousins in check, he should give you a separate principality to rule. That would be the best way to end this torture,' said Uddhava.

'Uddhava, Grandfather has borne a heavy burden throughout life,' replied Arjuna with fairness. 'When young, he gave a pledge to his father, the Emperor Shantanu of glorious memory, to see that the royal house of the Kurus was maintained in greatness, upholding the rule of Dharma. To fulfil that mission, he has sacrificed everything. Now that our cousins are proving so irrepressible, he thinks we alone can help him to carry out his mission.' Then Arjuna's face became solemn as he added: 'And that is what Bhagavan Veda Vyasa thinks, too. When he last came, he told us: "My boys, you must not swerve from your appointed task. The future of Dharma is bound up with you".'

'Then why don't they do something about Duryodhana and his brothers?' Uddhava asked.

Arjuna looked up, and, with a laugh that rang out pleasantly, asked: 'What can the righteous do to the unrighteous? They will meet their own doom in their own time. At present they have rallied a few chiefs to their side.' And Arjuna looked cautiously at the door to see that no one was within earshot and added in a voice which showed how distressed he was: 'And Guru Dronacharya has, we hear, withdrawn his support from us.'

Both of them looked up as the echoes of a heavy tread were heard coming towards them.

'Arjuna, I have arranged everything.' came the loud cheery voice of Bhima, the second of the Five Brothers, as he came in. Taller than Arjuna by a cubit, sturdy beyond the measure of men, with his muscular neck standing out like a pillar from his massive shoulders, he was the very image of irresistible strength. His face bore a broad smile and his deep, resonant voice had a rare heartiness as he addressed Uddhava.

Arjuna put aside the blade that he was sharpening, and asked: 'What have you arranged, Madhyama?'

Bhima sat down on a seat which lay in front of the others. 'Duryodhana and Shakuni, his uncle, his mother's brother, have planned a sinister action. Aswatthama has thrown himself into the fray with vehement energy. One of these nights they want to kill us,' Bhima said gaily, as if he was talking about some sport,

'How have you come to know of this?' said Uddhava.

'Sahadeva learned of the plot and told me. Perhaps uncle Vidura told him about it. So I decided to beat them at their own game,' he said with a boyish laugh, and added: 'We are now ready. Arjuna, prepare your arrows on which you waste so much of your time. I have already put guards around the house. When they attack as, we will finish them off. Won't we. Arjuna?'

Bhima rubbed his hands in glee and added: 'I would like to smash the head of Duryodhana and break the neck of that charioteer's son, Karna.' He breathed a stentorian sigh of satisfaction as if he had already disposed of their enemies.

'Now, Madhyama, don't be so wicked. Nothing is going to happen to us,' said Arjuna, winking at Uddhava to impress upon him that such outbursts were not uncommon with Bhima.

Bhima looked up proudly. 'I was born to destroy the wicked,' he said with complete self-confidence. Then he flung an indulgent smile at Arjuna. 'I am not a weakling like you, nor a saint like Yudhishthira. If they fight, I fight, and if I fight, I win'.

'But is there no way to stop this family feud? If you

try to kill each other, you will shake the foundations of the power of the Kurus,' said Uddhava. 'It might destroy the whole of Aryavarta.'

'Aryavarta requires to be shaken to its foundations', replied Bhima indifferently. Then he added with an air of finality: 'You cannot stand for ever in fear of wiles and violence, and you cannot compromise with untruth. So, Arjuna, you had better sharpen your arrows this time in real earnest; it is going to be a fight to the finish.'

They did not notice that Mother Kunti, who had come in to call them to their meal, had heard Bhima's last words.

'Bhima, don't always talk of fighting; it frightens me,' said Prithaa, the adopted daughter of King Kuntibhoja, generally called Kunti. She was a small, well-preserved woman, now nearing fifty, and bore herself with great dignity. Her face was pale and her eyes sad. Her smile, however, had the supreme quality of attracting affection, and, to her sons, grown into splendid manhood, she always spoke with the accents of an indulgent mother talking to small children—as if they were still her babes who had scarcely learnt to walk.

Bhima laughed aloud. 'We are Kshatriyas,' said he, slapping his chest. 'Fighting is our primary duty.'

'In defence of Dharma only, Bhima, and not for the love of it,' Kunti quietly corrected him.

'It is my Dharma to protect all of us at all costs, and, if Duryodhana is unrighteous, it is my duty to fight him,' said Bhima.

'Uddhava, have you men like this among you, who are always longing to fight one another?' asked Kunti with an indulgent smile, as she turned towards Uddhava.

'Aunt, we also used to have men who fought each other. But now thanks to Krishna we are learning to fight against our enemies,' said Uddhava.

'How I wish Krishna were here!' burst out Bhima with enthusiasm. 'He would help us fight our enemies.'

'I have heard so much about Govinda that I want to meet him,' said Kunti, with a reminiscent look upon her face. 'He must have grown so since I saw him last. Do they still call him Govinda?'

'Oh, he is Govinda to us Yadavas, though I find it hard to call him, by any name but Krishna. I called him so when I learnt to speak, long before they called him Govinda,' said Uddhava.

'We have been waiting for him all these days,' said Arjuna with a smile. 'Uddhava tells us that he will still take about three weeks before he arrives.'

'I wish he had brought Rukmini with him. I have never seen her.' said Kunti. 'I hope she makes him a fitting wife.'

'Krishna often says that a Gopala is not a fit husband for the Princess of Vidarbha, and that makes her very angry.'

'I also sent word for Krishna to bring her with him.' interrupted Bhima, laughing. 'She must come and fall at my feet. I am Krishna's elder brother. I would also like to see whether she is worth all the trouble which Krishna took to carry her away. If I had been in his place, I would have borne her on my shoulders.'

'And what is Shaibya like?' asked Kunti with a smile. 'Does Rukmini quarrel with Shaibya?'

'Shaibya is a wonderful woman,' said Uddhava, suddenly becoming serious. 'It was she who helped Rukmini to secure Krishna in marriage.'

'Oh, here is Nakula,' said Bhima.

Nakula, the fourth brother, a slim, sprightly and well-mannered youth with a vivacious look, came in. In sharp contrast to Bhima and Arjuna, he looked every inch a dandy. He folded his hands before Mother Kunti, his brothers and Uddhava. 'Madhyama, I have made all the arrangements as you suggested,' he told his elder brother.

'For what?' Kunti inquired anxiously.

'I have already told you, Mother, that, if Duryodhana fights us, we are going to finish him off this time,' said Bhima in his cheerful voice, and assumed a mock ferocious look to frighten his mother.

'Oh, Bhima, please don't talk like this. He is your cousin,' pleaded Kunti.

'And my greatest enemy—thirsting for my blood,' remarked Bhima.

'No, no, you are exaggerating, Bhima,' said Kunti. 'And if he is your enemy, you must win him by your love.'

'The wicked can't be won by love,' retorted Bhima.

They lapsed into silence as they heard footsteps coming towards them, and turned, to receive Yudhishthira, who looked like a larger Arjuna, of heavier build and with less grace in his limbs. His eyes and beard gave him a very elderly appearance. Gentleness was obviously the key to his nature.

Vidura also came in with him. A darkish skin, a stocky build, a pleasant face, a short nose, large eyes beaming benevolence, a smile of humility and a flowing beard went to make up the externals of the most respected and trusted minister of Hastinapura.

He was the illegitimate son of a palace maid, but no one thought of him as such. Every one knew that Best of Munis, Veda Vyasa, according to ancient custom, begot Dhritarashtra. the blind, and Pandu, on the two childless queens of King Vichitraveerya, Ambikaa and Ambaalikaa.

Ambikaa, when asked to bear another son the same way, was unwilling to go to the Sage, and sent her maid instead. Vidura was born to the maid as a result of this union.

In his boyhood, Vidura had dedicated himself to the pursuit of learning and mastered all the ancient laws of polity and royal conduct, and in view of his innate wisdom and saintly outlook, his views on men and things were sought even by so august a person as Grandfather Bhishma.

Vidura was gentle, just and generous. His charity knew no limits. He lived liked a hermit, spending all his ministerial emoluments to help the poor and the needy. He was always anxious to offer solace to the unhappy, and every orphan found a father in him.

To the Five Brothers, he was not a minister, but a well beloved uncle, and they gave him all the respect due to one. For a moment, Vidura's face was clouded with sorrow.

'Bhima, why have you posted archers around our mansion?' asked Yudhishthira.

'To protect us', said Bhima. 'Duryodhana is plotting to kill us'.

Yudhishthira quietly commanded: 'Bhima, withdraw the archers. We do not need them'.

'Why?' asked Arjuna. He sensed a note of unusual earnestness in Yudhishthira's voice.

'We leave Hastinapura the day after tomorrow', said Yudhishthira.

'Why?' shouted Bhima, as the others looked at Yudhishthira literally stunned.

'Those are the commands of our uncle, King Dhritarashtra', said Yudhishthira.

'And go where? Into a forest?'

'No, to Varanavata'.

'I won't obey them', shouted Bhima impetuously. 'I am not going to be banished.'

Yudhishthira looked with gentle sorrow at his tempestuous brother. 'Bhima, I have accepted the commands'.

6

BANISHMENT

It had happened in this way. When Yudhishthira was dispensing justice in the *parishad*, Vidura came to summon him to the presence of King Dhritarashtra. In obedience to this call, Yudhishthira with slow steps proceeded to the royal palace.

As they were going up the steps, Vidura whispered: 'My son, something terrible is going to happen. Don't let you courage fail you'.

'Uncle, I have no courage, but faith in the God of gods. Whatever He wills is sure to be for the good', said Yudhishthira with a trusting smile.

'Do you know that Duryodhana has hatched a plot to kill the five of you and all your friends?' asked Vidura in a low voice.

'Sahadeva told me about it,' said Yudhishthira quietly. 'Bhima is taking the necessary precautions. But I don't believe in them. We can only be killed when our time comes—not a moment before'.

'May the Great God protect you, my boy. If you are in danger, you can always rely upon me to do my best to save you', said Vidura.

'You are always so good, Uncle', said Yudhishthira gratefully, smiling trustfully at Vidura. 'I don't know what we would have done but for you.'

They stepped into the room in which King Dhritarashtra was seated on a throne of gold. Grandfather Bhishma was similarly seated by his side. Evidently they had been in consultation for a long time, for the King looked helplessly woe-begone, while Grandfather looked stern.

The King was about fifty, but his hair, grown prematurely grey, gave him the look of a much older man. Fair and well-built though he was, he sat on the throne with his mouth sagging and his shoulders hunched. His sightless gaze was fixed on the door as his uncanny powers of hearing identified the coming tread of his nephew.

Granfather Bhishma, his face framed in a white beard and mane, looked the image of ancient strength, the strength of a solitary and snow-capped mountain peak which had withstood the storms and shocks of many ages and yet remained unshaken. His body, in spite of the weight of years, was unbent. His giant frame still spoke of vigour undimmed by age. Though his eyes flashed sometimes with a rare fire, his face was lined with care.

Grandfather had been the pillar of Kuru power for three generations; in fact, since he gave up his right to the kingship of the Kurus and pledged himself to celibacy, to enable his father Shantanu to marry the fisher-girl Satyavati.

'Is that you, Yudhishthira?' asked King Dhritarashtra, trying to introduce an element of affectionate welcome into his voice.

Grandfather, as Bhishma had come to be universally called, undaunted by repeated set-backs, had brought up the five sons of Pandu and the numerous sons of Dhritarashtra as if they were his own sons, had them educated and trained under Dronacharya, the best of teachers and appointed the most worthy of them, Yudhishthira, to be Crown Prince.

During all these sixty years and more, he had been inflexible in his resolve to uphold Dharma. Due to his leadership, many of the misfortunes which befell the Kurus' royal house had passed by without damaging the stability of the most powerful kingdom of Aryavarta.

Now a new calamity was developing, which he had steeled himself to face grimly.

'Yes, lord. I am here to await your commands', said Yudhishthira, as he prostrated himself, first before Grandfather, who touched him on the head, and then, before Dhritarashtra.

'Who is that with you?' asked the blind King Dhritarashtra. 'Is it Vidura? And there is also another. Is it Sahadeva?' The blind King blessed him with his extended hand.

'My sons, may you live a hundred years', greeted Bhishma, but his voice was sad and his eyes overclouded, as he looked affectionately at Yudhishthira.

'When I sent for you, Yudhishthira, you were just going home from the *parishad*. It is also time for your morning meal', said Dhritarashtra apologetically, trying to make his voice as kind as he could. 'But, unfortunately, what I wanted you for could not brook delay'.

'I am always at your command, noble lord,' said Yudhishthira. 'What are your orders?'

'Take your seats, boys,' said the King. 'Vidura, have you taken your seat?' he asked Vidura 'My son'—for, Yudhishthira, 'you are dearer to me than my own sons— a grave crisis has arisen in our affairs. My son, Duryodhana, and his friends are filled with jealousy and hate.'

'Why are they so unhappy? What offence have I given them?' asked Yudhishthira with humility. 'Please, noble lord, let me know.'

'It is not your nature to give any offence, my son. Arjuna is courtesy itself. And Nakula and Sahadeva are very gentle, polite and considerate,' the King said with a clumsy effort at being fair.

Yudhishthira saw the difficulty which Dhritarashtra found in expressing himself frankly, and helped him out of it. 'Noble lord, sometimes Bhima does give offence,' he said in an apologetic tone. 'But you know that, though he is outspoken by nature, he bears no malice. Whenever he sees that the other man is hurt, he is always ready to make amends.'

Grandfather continued to pass his hand over his beard, listening intently to what was being said, but remaining silent himself.

'I know that, Yudhishthira,' said the blind King and,

in a voice of simulated despair, added: 'This time, however, things are beyond repair. The situation has become serious. You know how badly my sons are advised by their friends—that charioteer's son Karna and Aswatthama, the firebrand son of Dronacharya. They are trying to bring things to a head,' he added as if every word was extracted from an unwilling heart.

'What do they want, noble lord?' asked Yudhishthira. with a glance at Grandfather who continued to look on in unmoving sternness.

The King moved his head from side to side, as if unable to bear the burden of his anguish. 'My son. I hesitate to tell you the truth. However, I must take you into my confidence; you are such a wise man. You Five Brothers, they think, are becoming too great for their liking—also too popular. They have heard rumours about you, too,' added the King and paused.

'That is not true,' said Yudhishthira sadly but frankly, trying to rescue the King from embarrassment. 'They started the rumours themselves. They say we have decided to remove you from your august position and deprive them of their heritage.'

King Dhritarashtra nodded in assent. 'Yes, that is the rumour.'

Yudhishthira, deeply hurt, spoke in a sad voice. 'Noble lord, do you believe this rumour? Grandfather knows that we are incapable of entertaining any such sinister design.'

King Dhritarashtra silently turned to Grandfather.

'You have been a father to us, Uncle. Tell me the truth, I beseech you. Do you believe in the truth of this rumour?' asked Yudhishthira.

Grandfather's brilliant eyes were fixed on the King with concentrated fury, and even the sightless monarch felt it.

'I know, I know', said the King in a pleading voice. 'I have full faith in you—in all you Five Brothers. None of you could ever dream of such a design. You give me all the honour due to your father, I know'.

The King paused for a moment to conquer his nervousness. He turned his sightless eyes towards Grandfather, his sagging mouth slightly trembling. Evidently he was afraid that Bhishma would intervene in the conversation, but the old man was grimly silent, his gaze unflickering. 'You know, my boy,' added the King with a forced laugh, 'there is no remedy which can allay suspicion.'

'Not even truth?' asked Yudhishthira.

'One who suspects can never see the truth', said the King. 'And even if he sees it, he cannot act up to it'.

'Noble lord, I do not know why we are suspected of such a heinous plot. Ask Grandfather; he will assure you that we bear no ill-will to Duryodhana and his brothers. The other day I offered him that we should share the responsibility of my office. He rejected the offer', said Yudhishthira sorrowfully.

'He is very headstrong, you know', said Dhritarashtra. 'Once he takes a dislike, he takes it for ever. What can I do?'

'What ought we to do, noble lord? Show us the way and we shall obey', said Yudhishthira.

'No, no. I don't want to be unfair to the sons of my beloved brother Pandu', said the King, again turning his blind eyes towards Grandfather in mute appeal for approval. 'But if this situation worsens, Hastinapura may be spilt into warring camps.'

'I know that my efforts to remove Duryodhana's distrust have not succeeded', said Yudhishthira.

The King was now growing more nervous, for he felt Grandfather's silence more effectively disconcerting than any words he might have spoken. 'It is no longer a question of distrust', he said hurriedly. 'They are planning action, my son. I tried to dissuade them from it, but they would not listen. They are bent on a fratricidal war.'

'I am not ignorant of what they want to do, noble lord. They are planning to kill us—and that too very shortly,' said Yudhishthira.

Yudhishthira looked at Grandfather, whose eyes were now full of concentrated rage, but who still would not speak. His speechless anger was instinctively felt by the blind King who hurriedly exclaimed: 'God of all gods, no, no, no; they would not do that.'

'I want your orders, noble lord', said Yudhishthira, with the calmness of a man who was just discussing a matter of routine, 'Let me have your decision. Is it my noble lord's wish that we should defend ourselves, or should we submit without offering any defence?'

'Of course, defend yourselves', said Grandfather's

deep voice firm and decisive. 'The sons of my Pandu shall not be killed in cold blood. I am clear as to that'.

The incisive words made the others feel as if lightning had fallen in their midst. No one spoke for some time. Grandfather resumed passing his hand rhythmically over his beard.

The King turned his blind eyes appealingly towards Grandfather, paused a little and changed the conversation. 'My son, my son, let us not talk about conflicts. Don't you agree, Yudhishthira?' he asked.

'We will do everything to avoid a conflict, noble lord. I would not fight my cousins even to keep my throne', said Yudhishthira in his straightforward way, guessing what the King was leading up to.

Grandfather looked at him with sympathy.

'There, there, there,' said Dhritarashtra, putting as much appreciation as he could into his voice. 'There speaks the son of my beloved brother. He was very noble, and so are you, my son.'

Yudhishthira did not look at Grandfather for help, nor did he hesitate for a moment to come to a decision. He was ready for any sacrifice. 'Noble lord, I said it once and I say it again: Whatever your commands, they shall be obeyed. Do you want me to give up the office of Crown Prince? Grandfather gave it to me with your consent; I did not covet it; it is yours to take it back. Install Duryodhana tomorrow as Crown Prince and let him be happy.'

The King gave a long sigh as if he was most unhappy at what Yudhishthira had said. "That may not be the end of the affair, Yudhishthira,' the King said hurriedly. 'The people love you very much—you and your brothers. They worship you as if you were Dharma incarnate. If Duryodhana displaces you in that fashion, they will rise against him.'

'Noble lord, pray be frank with me. Let me know what you want us to do. Our first concern is to preserve the greatness of the royal house of the Emperor Bharata', said Yudhishthira.

'That is it,' said the King as he struck the arm of his throne vigorously. 'But Duryodhana will not let you live in peace in Hastinapura. That is my difficulty.'

Yudhishthira laughed a little audibly, as if to assure the blind King that he was all too willing to help him out of the difficulty. 'Noble lord, do you want us to leave Hastinapura? Shall we go into a forest? I am ready.'

'No, no. I don't want you to do that,' said Dhritarashtra, turning a little nervously towards Grandfather. 'I want you to go to Varanavata for a few months. A festival is being held there in honour of the God of all gods. Oh, it is a great occasion and thousands of people will go to the rejoicings. All of you Five Brothers have been working too hard.' Then the King added hurriedly : 'Once you go away for some months, their suspicions will be allayed. Then you can come back to Hastinapura.'

'Uncle, I now know what you wish us to do. Your wishes are my commands,' said Yudhishthira promptly without a trace of regret. I will proceed to Varanavata the day after tomorrow,' said Yudhishthira.

The King felt relieved. 'A new palace has already been constructed for you. You can enjoy yourself fully there. But will Bhima and Arjuna agree to go? They might create difficulties', he added with a touch of anxiety.

'They will not like going; they will protest; but I assure you, all of us will obey your commands, noble lord,' said Yudhishthira.

'My son, you are so noble,' said Dhritarashtra, with relief. 'You are just like your father, my large-hearted and beloved brother. You have saved the Kurus from a great calamity.'

'Noble lord, give us your blessing.' Yudhishthira, impatient to leave the King's presence, touched the King's feet. Then he prostrated himself before Grandfather, who, stern as ever, bent low, lifted him from the ground and embraced him.

'Yudhishthira,' said Grandfather, 'you are Dharma itself, my son. May the God of gods protect you and your brothers. May your path be blessed.'

As Bhishma breathed in the scent of Yudhishthira's hair a tear trickled down his ancient cheeks.

In that tear lay exasperation, helplessness and sympathy, which brought a choking sense of gratitude to Yudhishthira.

∎

7

THE BLOW

*Y*uyudhana, the son of Satyaka, was in charge of the party which travelled with Krishna to Hastinapura.

Satyaki, as he was generally called after his father's name, was an *atirathi*, an expert chariot warrior of the highest rank, and commanded a contingent of Yadava chariot warriors. Each chariot warrior had a trained assistant and a charioteer to ride with him. Each chariot had, besides the horses harnessed to it, a relay of two horses and two riders to protect the rear in a battle. Each horse had a groom. The retainers, when on duty, travelled in bullock carts, which also carried provisions, tents and other equipment.

The party camped at Pushkara Tirtha which was ruled over by the Yadava chief Chekitana. A miniature town sprang up round the open space. In the midst of it Krishna's chariot stood flying his eagle banner. They had travelled by the very route along which three years back the Yadavas had been forced to flee on their way to Saurashtra.

Now it was a well-defined caravan route. As it passed through the deserts, shelter and water were provided at several halts. Villages had sprung up at several places on the way. Convoys had been stationed by neighbouring chiefs at short distances throughout to provide safety to the caravans.

Shalva, in whose territory lay a part of the route, was now at peace with the Yadavas, the might of his camel chariots broken. Though restive at the Yadava hegemony, Shalva had, as a friend, played the host to Krishna at several places.

Krishna had already sent advance riders to Hastinapura to summon Uddhava to Pushkara Tirtha, and one evening, Uddhava, in obedience to the summons, arrived. Wan and tired after a long and breathless journey, he flung himself into the arms of Krishna who was waiting to receive him.

The horses of Uddhava's chariot were foaming at the mouth. His retinue, unable to keep pace with their impatient chief, was more than a day's journey behind.

Satyaki and Acharya Shvetaketu, the principal disciple of Guru Sandipani, were surprised at the speed and haste of Uddhava's arrival. Sensing some impending disaster, they stepped aside, forgoing the usual salutations.

'Brother, Krishna, a calamity has overtaken us,' Uddhava managed to say in broken accents. 'The Five Brothers are dead.'

'What!' exclaimed Krishna in astonishment, and disengaged himself from his friend's embrace. With some effort, he regained his composure and said, 'Wait till you regain your breath.'

Uddhava, quite exhausted, flung himself down in the shade of a tree. Krishna sat by his side, his arms around him. Shvetaketu took his place near them, while Satyaki went to fetch water for Uddhava to drink.

'Now tell me what has happened.' said Krishna.

'The Five Brothers are dead!' repeated Uddhava. 'Burnt to death in a palace fire at Varanavata. Mother Kunti too is dead.'

It cost Krishna a strong effort to regain his composure. 'Take your own time, Uddhava, and let me know all that happened, from the beginning.'

Satyaki brought water, which Uddhava drank. His breath restored, he sat up and placed a hand helplessly on Krishna's shoulder. 'When I went to Hastinapura, Krishna, I was met by Bhima and Arjuna at the city gates. They took me to their mansion where I paid my repects to my Aunt, Kunti. She enquired about all of you. Yudhishthira and the twins were also there. Unexpectedly, Vidura—you have heard of the saintly minister—came to call Yudhishthira. The King had summoned him.'

'How were the Five Brothers—happy?' asked Krishna.

'They were worried over a plot reported to have been hatched by Duryodhana with the assistance of his uncle Shakuni, Karna, the charioteer's son, and Aswatthama, the son of that great warrior, Dronacharya.'

'Yes, I have heard about them too,' said Krishna. 'What was the plot?'

'The plot was to kill the Five Brothers. And Bhima

was making preparations for counter-action,' resumed Uddhava. 'It seems Grandfather Bhishma, after holding a long consultation with King Dhritarashtra, summoned Yudhishthira, so as to find a way out.'

'What did the King tell Yudhishthira when he met him?' asked Krishna,

'The King told him that Duryodhana and his friends has decided upon drastic action and that the Kurus were threatened with a fratricidal war,' said Uddhava.

'Duryodhana, they say, is capable of anything,' said Shvetaketu.

'The only way to prevent a catastrophe, the King said, was for Yudhishthira to give up his office,' said Uddhava.

'Did he agree to do so?' asked Krishna.

'Yes, without any hesitation,' replied Uddhava. 'But the King was not satisfied. The Five Brothers were held in high regard by the people; and, if they had lived in Hastinapura, Duryodhana would never have been able to act as Crown Prince. Yudhishthira would still have continued to be the darling of the people.'

'And so......?'

'So Yudhishthira was asked by Dhritarashtra to go for a few months to Varanavata where a festival was being held. He agreed', said Uddhava.

'What did Bhishma say to this suggestion?' asked Krishna. 'I thought he was fond of the Five Brothers.'

'Yudhishthira told us how at the interview Grandfather sat stern and silent. He only intervened to say that the Five Brothers should defend themselves if they were attacked,' replied Uddhava.

'Did Bhima and Arjuna agree to the suggestion?' asked Krishna.

'Not at first,' replied. Uddhava. Bhima was very angry. Arjuna protested. The twins disliked the idea. But Yudhishthira had given his word, and their mother Kunti insisted that it should be honoured. So ultimately all of them agreed. They are a wonderful family. Each one is a part of the rest'.

'Their strength lies in that—and their glory too,' declared Krishna. 'Please go on with your account'.

'Immediately it became known to the people of Hastinapura that the Five Brothers were going to visit the festival, they were troubled. No one believed that the Five Brothers would voluntarily leave their post of duty. And two days later, when they left Hastinapura, a large crowd, oppressed by grief, saw them off,' said Uddhava.

'What did you do?' asked Krishna.

'I accompanied them to Varanavata and lived with them for a few days. Wherever the Five Brothers went, people honoured them with shouts of victory. But the air was fraught with portents of an impending calamity. The new palace, which had been temporarily constructed for them, was lightly made, plastered with some strange substance. Purochana, the *mlechha* officer, who looked after them, was more of a spy than a servant, and he saw to it that the palace was guarded day and night', said Uddhava.

'If they suspected foul play, why did they not go back to Hastinapura?' asked Satyaki.

'They could not return to Hastinapura', said Uddhava. 'Yudhishthira had given his word. And apart from that, if they had returned to Hastinapura uninvited, they would have been killed in cold blood. Duryodhana, now that he had become Crown Prince, was not going to take any chances.'

'I learnt of the banishment of the Five Brothers from Shvetaketu', said Krishna, 'He was in Hastinapura when the Five Brothers left. When did you learn of the death of the Five Brothers?'

'I was at Utkochaka, when the news came that the palace had caught fire and the Five Brothers and their mother Kunti had been burnt alive. I immediately returned to Varanavata to ascertain things for myself. The palace was completely gutted. As I suspected, it was made of an inflammable material. Purochana, the officer, was also burnt to death. Later, the bodies of the Five Brothers and their mother Kunti were cremated,' said Uddhava, in great sadness.

Krishna sat lost in thought.

'Did they not suspect that the palace was made of inflammable material? They could have found a way to get away in time,' said Shvetaketu.

'They were preparing for the emergency. Vidura had also been suspicious of a plot and had sent an expert to construct an underground passage through which they could leave in case of emergency. But the expert could carry on his work only when Purochana was not present. I do not know whether the underground passage was completed, but the Five Brothers had no chance to escape,' said Uddhava.

'This is a terrible blow', said Krishna slowly. 'Destiny has played a trick, a wicked trick. Our cousins, whom we loved and upon whom we counted, are dead. Aunt Kunti, that gem of a woman, is dead too, though I am glad she died with them, for they were the very breath of her life'.

'What shall we do now?' asked Shvetaketu.

'We must go back to Dwaraka. What else?' replied Uddhava. 'I do not want Vaasudeva to go to Hastinapura where Duryodhana rules as Crown Prince. Even Grandfather seems to have lost his hold over the Kurus'.

'Uddhava, think again. Can we go back to Dwaraka?' Krishna asked slowly, as if speaking to himself. 'All our plans have gone wrong. When I learnt that the Five Brothers were banished, I decided to go to Hastinapura to meet the venerable Bhishma and to find a solution. I had other plans too. Now they are dead,' said Krishna. The others respected his anguish and sat there quietly.

'And they had not even the solace of having you, Uddhava, with them till the last,' added Krishna sadly, as he looked at Uddhava with tender eyes.

Suddenly a pang of conscience shot through Uddhava's heart. He was with the Five Brothers when they were in danger but left them to shift for themselves. Not that he could have been of much help to them, but it was wrong, he felt, to have left them at Varanavata.

Krishna looked affectionately at Uddhava as if reading his thoughts.

'Krishna, Krishna, I think I was a fool to have left them in those circumstances,' said Uddhava.

'I wish you had stayed with them, Uddhava. Now it is no use regretting the past,' said Krishna, and then lapsed into a mood of self-communion. 'With the Five Brothers gone, the Kurus will be in the power of Duryodhana. And worse. With his uncle Shakuni in power, the venerable Bhishma will no longer maintain control. The Kurus will drift away from Dharma,' he added.

'What can we do?' asked Uddhava.

'What ought to be done', replied Krishna.

Krishna sat silently for a little while. Then, as if he had seen the light in a flash, he looked up, and his face bore that look of majestic calmness which made him so irresistible when he took a decision.

'I now see what we have to do. I must pay a condolence visit to Hastinapura and meet the venerable Bhishma. There I will fathom the mystery which surrounds the death of the Five Brothers,' said Krishna, and asked, 'which way did you come?'

'I received your message at Utkochaka. I was given an escort through the territory of the venerable Aryaka, the noble Naga king and our maternal great-grandfather, and crossed the Yamuna near Mathura,' replied Uddhava.

'Is Mathura inhabited again?' asked Krishna.

'It broke my heart to see that Mathura was a wilderness. Our mansions and palaces are in ashes and ruins. A few hundred poor Yadava families have come back to their homes and are cultivating some patches of land. And quite a settlement of Nagas and Nishadas has sprung up there,' said Uddhava.

'Some day, Uddhava, we shall have to restore Mathura to its ancient glory, but the time is yet to come,' said Krishna.

'Need I go to King Drupada?' asked Shvetaketu.

'Of course, you must. My visit to him has become all the more imperative,' said Krishna. 'Take the road which brought Uddhava here. On behalf of Uddhava and myself, pay our humble respects to the venerable Aryaka—he must be more than a hundred years old now. Convey to him that I will do my best to come on my way back and offer my prostrations at his feet'.

8

DURYODHANA IS AFRAID

A yojana away from Hastinapura, the capital of the Kurus, three men, evidently of high rank, sat on the banks of the Ganga, engrossed in serious talk. They had just returned from hunting, for their bows and arrows lay by their side. They ate and drank while they talked.

At some distance stood two chariots, their horses unharnessed and grazing. The charioteers squatted on the ground near them, awaiting the return of their masters. Two deers lay at their dying gasp in a bullock-cart near the chariots, blood oozing from their wounds.

The eldest of the three was elderly, short, fat and pleasant looking. He wore a well-trimmed beard, had small, round eyes, puffed cheeks, and a satisfied smile on his lips. He was reclining on the ground, facing the two younger men, and was sipping his drink leisurely. He was Shakuni, the younger brother of Queen Gandhari. He was a well-known figure in Hastinapura, and perhaps the most hated.

Duryodhana, the eldest son of King Dhritarashtra and Gandhari, and the newly appointed Crown Prince of Hastinapura, was handsome and tall. His sturdy frame and bulging muscles testified to his skill in wrestling and mastery in mace-wielding. His large and intelligent eyes flashed intensely whenever he spoke with emphasis. As befitting his princely state, he wore costly ornaments on his wrists, arms and neck. His bejewelled diadem lay by his side.

The third was Karna, the charioteer's son, whom Duryodhana had raised to a princely station. He was very handsome, well-built and lithe. His face bore the stamp of courage and honesty; his sparkling eyes bespoke rare intelligence. The ornaments and the diadem he wore indicated a lesser rank than Duryodhana's.

'I don't like this cowherd coming to us at this time.' said Duryodhana, looking at his uncle for corroboration. 'I know him well. He is likely to prove dangerous.'

Shakuni gave a broad smile, shifted his position on the ground and leisurely took a sip from the cup. 'I don't like him at all, at this time or at any other,' he said. 'But I don't agree with your calling him a cowherd. If you don't like a man, Duryodhana, the best thing is to load him with compliments'.

'What can Krishna do to us?' asked Karna, sitting up from his reclining posture.

'You don't know him, Karna,' said Duryodhana. 'There is nothing that he does not know and nothing that he cannot accomplish. That is what the Yadavas believe. They are all puppets in his hands. He is not likely to forgive us for sending his cousins into banishment'.

'He might also try to find out how they died', said Shakuni with a mischievous twinkle in his eyes.

'They are dead and have been cremated with the proper ceremonies,' said Karna. 'That is the end of them'.

'I know Krishna. He is a smiling rogue, if ever there was one,' said Duryodhana.

Shakuni looked indulgently at his nephew. 'Krishna has extraordinary achievements to his credit. Some even say that he is a god', he said with a view to teasing him.

'That is nonsense,' said Duryodhana, his eyes flashing angrily. 'He can fight. He can intrigue. He can eat, drink and make love. He can gossip with old women and play with children. Who says he is a god? But, god or no god, why should he come all the way from his distant land? I don't believe that he comes merely to pay a condolence visit'.

'My dear nephew, there you are, getting nervous again', said Shakuni with a laugh, patting Duryodhana's knee with a fat hand. 'When you don't believe a thing, always say that you believe it. Supposing we take Krishna to be a god, what can a god do? He cannot bring the Pandavas back to life, can he? And remember, gods are only pleased with those devotees who flatter them most'

'The misfortune is that Grandfather thinks very highly of him,' said Duryodhana. 'Last night, he was telling Father about Krishna's exploits. He said that Krishna was the only man who would bring some measure of Dharma into this wicked world. What can you do with a foolish old man like that?'

'Where does Grandfather get all these reports from? asked Karna.

'Vidura must be retailing all this gossip to Grandfather', replied Duryodhana.

Shakuni winked at his nephew and said with a smile: 'A saint is always a nuisance. You can't get rid of him and you can't trust him'.

'But I should prefer to see for myself what Krishna is like,' remarked Karna.

'Father intends to receive him as if he were a king', said Duryodhana. 'Why should we give him so much importance?'

'My boy, nothing is lost by giving a man a ceremonial welcome. It fools him and keeps stupid people happy. But I can guess why Krishna is coming here with so many Yadava warriors', said Shakuni.

'Why?' asked Karna, and then answered his own question. 'With his Yadavas he had to flee before Jarasandha and seek an asylum at Dwaraka. Now he feels that he is strong enough to push his way among the kings of Aryavarta'.

'Karna, I wish you would think a little coolly', said Shakuni. 'He need make no effort to take his place among the kings. People say that he defeated Jarasandha at Gomantaka; that he halted the swayamvara of Rukmini at Kundinapura; that he eluded Jarasandha and carried his people safely to Dwaraka; that he carried away the Princess of Vidarbha single-handed before the very eyes of the assembled princes. He has recently inflicted a severe defeat on Shalva, the king of Saubha. He is already held in high esteem by our kings.'

'That makes his coming here all the more mysterious,' said Karna.

'There is a wicked purpose behind his visit,' said Duryodhana.

'Boys, you will never know how to deal with affairs of State,' said Shakuni. 'You always form hasty opinions. Krishna is a powerful person; that is clear. He is held in high regard by Grandfather Bhishma and even your father. We have, therefore, to see how he behaves, before making our plans.'

'Uncle, what shall we do when he comes tomorrow?' asked Duryodhana.

'I will tell you what you should do, Duryodhana. Flatter him. sing his praises, try to be obliging, worm yourself into his confidence. When you were at Dwaraka, you made a mistake. You should have made friends with Krishna and not with Balarama,' said Shakuni. 'And, Karna, I would advise you not to meet him. You are too forthright. If he is the clever man that we all think he is. we should be cleverer, Duryodhana.'

'What have I done that I should be forced to play the hypocrite all the time?' asked Duryodhana, his face red with indignation. 'I was born to be the king of the Kurus. Why is everyone conspiring to keep me out of power, even now when Yudhishthira is dead? Why does everyone think that Yudhishthira had a better right to the throne than I?'

'He was the son of a god', remarked Shakuni sarcastically.

'Was my uncle a god?' asked Duryodhana with a sneer.

'He was highly respected by Grandfather and loved by the people,' replied Shakuni in a mocking vein.

A hard ferocious look came over Duryodhana's face. 'Yes, I know. I am better any day than he ever was, and yet everyone, even you, Uncle, looked upon him as my superior. I am an expert warrior, invincible in mace combat and wrestling. Yet, even my guru, Dronacharya, accepted Bhima and Arjuna as my betters'.

'Ask your Grandfather Bhishma,' said Shakuni. 'It is he who decides in Hastinapura who is good and who is not'.

Duryodhana worked himself up into a rage. His handsome face became ugly and cruel. 'Yudhishthira was worshipped by the people; I am considered a nuisance by my Father,—even by you. I am disliked by all, except by my mother. Why am I not given a chance to become a great king some day and be a *Chakravartin?*'

'Duryodhana, don't be impatient. If I can help you, you will be a *Chakravartin* some day', said Shakuni, trying to pacify him.

'I know you are my only support, Uncle, but why

has the God of all the gods denied me the fair and easy way to what is my due?' asked Duryodhana.

'You can't say that now! Your rivals are out of the way', said Karna.

Duryodhana, for the moment obsessed with only one idea, continued to speak in bitterness. 'Now this Vaasudeva is coming. He will talk sweetly, and the gullible old man will smile at him. And Uncle Vidura, the pious fraud, will prostrate himself before him and unburden himself of whatever is in his mind. Then this cowherd, if he discovers that the Pandavas were tricked into going to Varanavata to their death, will shout for all the world to hear that it was *adharma!* And the people will echo that it was *adharma,* and everyone will say that it was the work of the wicked Duryodhana. Why is it that nobody talks about Krishna killing his uncle Kamsa?'

'My dear boy, if you want to follow in his footsteps, start by killing me too. I am your uncle,' said Shakuni with a grin.

'Don't make fun of me, Uncle. I am going to be the king of Hastinapura—but, O gods, when? My Father is old, but he may live for many years yet. Grandfather should have been in the Land of the Manes years and years ago. So should that venerable Veda Vyasa, who is always old and never looks older. I am getting old, while the grandfathers are growing younger every day!' said Duryodhana bitterly.

'If you get so excited, you will go to the God of Death before you are old', said Shakuni.

'I don't care what happens to me,' said Duryodhana, his face a fierce mask. 'I will wipe out everyone who stands in my way, before I die. I am sick of being told that it is my Dharma to sit quiet and let everyone walk over me.'

'My boy, don't think of the future; Think of what is before you just now', said Shakuni, placing an affectionate hand on his nephew, and added: 'Krishna must be sent away without becoming wiser. After he goes, we will think out all the rest.'

'I wish I could throttle the cowherd,' said Duryodhana.

'Uncle Shakuni. I know you will not accept my advice', said Karna without mincing his words, 'but I give it to you for what it is worth. Let us talk frankly to Vaasudeva. Ask his advice now that Duryodhana is Crown Prince, as to how we can ally ourselves with the Yadavas.'

'—And be swallowed up by Krishna instantly!' completed Duryodhana. 'We should soon be his vassals'.

'Duryodhana, listen to me,' said Shakuni. 'Do not let him discover that anything is wrong. And remember the advice which I have always given you: Speech is given to man to hide his thoughts, never to express them.'

A frown crossed Duryodhana's brow as he got up impatiently and ended the discussion.

█

9

GRANDFATHER BHISHMA

*A*ccording to the usage of the Aryas, whenever a queen died. a mission of condolence was dispatched by her parent's family. The visit of Krishna to Hastinapura at the head of such a mision, coming as it did from Vasudeva, the brother of Kunti, was therefore a ceremonial event of importance.

As was the custom, Krishna and his party were received with due ceremony at some little distance from the city gates of Hastinapura by Duryodhana and his brother Duhshasana, accompanied by important men associated with the court of Hastinapura.

Krishna, Uddhava and Satyaki, as well as the other Yadavas, changing their usual clothes, ornaments and weapons, dressed themselves in simple white *dhotis* and scarves. The receiving party, similarly dressed, conducted them, first, to the banks of the Ganga where they offered obsequies to the soul of the departed.

Then the mourners, the guests as well as the hosts, walked to the royal palace along the main street crowded by onlookers anxious to have the *darshan* of the famous guest.

Krishna's heart was weighed down with sorrow not only at the death of Aunt Kunti and the Five Brothers, but at the genuine grief of the people who appeared to have cherished a deep affection for the Five Brothers. Also, for the first time in his life, he saw no light. The opportunity that he was seeking for, to fulfil the mission of his life in partnership with his cousins, was gone for ever.

Krishna who had more than a suspicion that his cousins had been tricked to their deaths by Duryodhana, watched him carefully. The Kuru prince was evidently play-acting when appearing to be overwhelmed with grief. It was so out of character.

He watched Shakuni too—Duryodhana's reported adviser of evil fame. He wore a desolate look. His eyes were swollen; tears welled forth from them now and again. He carried his grief to the extent of even suppressing an occasional sob. He was overdoing his part, concluded Krishna.

He also immediately spotted Karna. There was no mistaking him. The noble brow, the flashing eyes, the dignified bearing and the frank smile, all indicated the man of courage that he was reputed to be.

His father, Vasudeva, had told him about Karna's true lineage: it was a terrible family secret which no one, except three or four persons, were privileged to share.

Krishna could not help wondering at the strange vagaries of fortunes. Karna, a charioteer's son, was the henchman of Duryodhana. The Five Brothers, whom Aunt Kunti had brought up with care in spite of the hardships she had had to go through were dead, and with them had gone the hopes of Dharma becoming triumphant among the Kurus!

The palace grounds of Hastinapura covered a very large area, with small mansions studded all over it, each with a garden behind. Krishna, Uddhava and Satyaki were given a separate mansion a little away from the central one which was occupied by the dowager empress Satyavati, the grandmother of Dhritarashtra, 'the most venerable Mother' as she was called.

Duryodhana, with effusive cordiality, placed himself at the service of Krishna, Uddhava and Satyaki who were the guests of Grandfather Bhishma. He was all too anxious to please. Behind Duryodhana's cordiality, however, Krishna could sense the real man, evidently oppressed by fear, anxious to create a good impression.

His watchful glances showed his evident distrust of Krishna. What reasons could he have for distrusting him? Were the Five Brothers burnt to death under his instructions? Was he capable of such a dastardly deed? Would Duryodhana, now that he had attained his ambition, be able to begin a new life of righteousness, Krishna wondered. Could he be converted to such a life? Not till he was separated from Shakuni, with his false smile and obsequious manners.

Krishna paid a ceremonial visit to King Dhritarashtra in the adjoining palace where he lived. Prematurely hunched, he sat on a throne, his month sagging, his blind eyes fixed on the door. He was dressed appropriately in mourning clothes. On one side stood Duryodhana; on the other, a young man named Sanjaya, who on occasions of State served the blind King as his eyes and ears. Two men armed with maces stood unmoving like statues on the two sides of the room.

The Minister, Kunika, led Krishna to a throne placed in front of Dhritarashtra, who before taking his seat, exchanged appropriate salutations. Uddhava and Satyaki, who had accompanied Krishna, after offering similar salutations, stood on each side of him.

The blind King was full of suppressed excitement and afraid of his own words lest they might express too much. Duryodhana sat next to his father, and, whenever his father said something he disapproved of, he corrected it. There was no doubt, Krishna felt, that King stood in awe of his son.

Throughout the interview, the King was all too anxious to convince Krishna that he had held the Five Brothers in great affection. They had been like his own sons. He had brought them up with a parent's care He had appointed Yudhishthira Crown Prince and looked forward to his succeeding to the throne—a wonderful man, so straightforward, so affectionate, so loyal! Had he lived, some day he would have added to the glory of the Bharatas.

He was sorry, said the old King, that he had given his consent to the Five Brothers going to Varanavata. But who could resist fate? What happened was predestined to happen. Fate leaves no choice to man.

False, false, false to the core, Krishna thought.

Then Krishna was received by Grandfather Bhishma. The old warrior was seated on a gold-encrusted seat, Vidura standing by his side. A similar seat was placed in front for Krishna.

Krishna was charmed with the gracious courtesy of Grandfather, who gave an intimate touch to the interview by not receiving him seated on the throne in the middle of the room. Krishna immediately sensed the significance of this and responded similarly by leaving Uddhava and Satyaki outside the room.

Grandfather sat, erect and unwrinkled, the very image of ancient strength, a relic of the days so often sung of in story and song, when Parashurama dominated life and Veda Vyasa had not yet been born.

Before Krishna could prostrate himself, the old man had risen from his seat, taken a step forward and flung his arms around him. 'Vaasudeva, I am delighted to see you. I have been hearing so much about you.'

The old man placed his hands on Krishna's shoulders and turned his face towards the light. 'Vaasudeva, let me look at you carefully in the light. You look like a boy. What is the secret of your youth?'

Krishna laughed with charming modesty. 'The blessing of the Great God and of elders like you'.

'These are your friends? Uddhava and Satyaki, are they? Call them in,' said the old man.

Vidura led Uddhava and Satyaki to the old man, who, after they had fallen at his feet and received his blessing, retired.

The old man then turned to the guest and smiled, which he rarely did, and his eyes looked Krishna up and down appreciatively. 'Now sit down. I am glad that I have seen you with my own eyes. I thought you were a tall, battle-scarred warrior always fighting tirelessly.'

'Are you disappointed in me, venerable Grandfather?' asked Krishna as he fell under the spell of the old man's unexpected geniality.

'No, I am happy to meet you, After what I have known in my life, it is a solace to see someone who has faith in the glory of our ancestors and aspires to walk in their footsteps', said Grandfather, his habitual sternness all but gone.

'Venerable sir, I understand your grief.' said Krishna, folding his hands. 'You hoped that Yudhishthira would revive the glory of the Kurus. Now he is dead.'

Grandfather leaned back on his seat eying the young man, whose wise and tender eyes were fixed on him as if he understood what was passing in his ancient mind.

Grandfather drew a long sigh. 'I had great hopes of him, Vaasudeva. He was the very image of my Pandu— so truthful, so just, so considerate, so good to the people'. Then he paused. 'I never expected that I would lose him'. The old man's eyes were moist with tears.

'Venerable Grandfather, I fully realise what you feel. You have always been the very image of strength—never giving way to fate. And I am sure the God of all gods will give you strength even in this calamity', said Krishna.

The sympathetic voice, the kindly eyes and the understanding half-smile, so characteristic of Krishna, were working their magic. Bhishma found the stranger, not a young chief distrustful of him, not a warrior known for his exploits, but a man who genuinely loved and honoured him. His self-confidence, which had been shaken by the events of the last few weeks, was restored, and the aloofness in which he had kept himself wrapped fell from him.

'Vaasudeva, the Great God has been trying me all these years,' said Bhishma. His voice was sad. 'For seventy years and more, I have borne the weight of the Kurus on my shoulders. Every time relief was near, fate intervened and laid a greater burden on me'.

'You are like the Himalayas—always strong, always unbowed. You have given us smaller men an example for all time, of what a man with a sense of Dharma can do,' said Krishna.

'I do not know whether I will be able to bear the burden now. The Five Brothers are gone,' said Grandfather with a sigh.

'How did they come to be banished, with you here?' asked Krishna.

The question touched the tenderest spot in the

unhealed wound in Bhishma's heart. Against his will, in defiance of his instincts, he had had to surrender to the pressure of circumstances, and he had had never ceased to blame himself for his submission to the dictates of practical wisdom.

Bhishma felt a yearning to unburden himself before the young man, whose eyes were full of compassion and who appeared to appreciate the difficulties he was facing, with sympathy. 'Vaasudeva, they were not banished,' he said. 'They went of their own accord. Yudhishthira saw the difficult situation in which we were all placed, as he always did. Had he not voluntarily stepped down from the office and agreed to leave Hastinapura, there would have been conflict. Rivers of blood would have flowed, and...., the old man's voice sank into a whisper, 'they would have been killed all the same.'

'Could you not have prevented it?' asked Krishna.

'Vidura and I thought about that for a long time', said Grandfather, shaking his head and turning to Vidura for corroboration. 'Duryodhana and Shakuni had spread their net very wide. Karna, the formidable warrior, is their ally. So is Aswatthama, the son of the leader of our army, Dronacharya. Drona is devoted to his son, and so is his brother-in-law, Kripacharya. Surprisingly, in spite of his great affection for the Five Brothers, he would not—or could not—intervene. I could not have helped the Five Brothers if a bloody conflict had begun'.

Then the old man, in spite of the strength which was writ large on his face, said with a sad smile. 'A new generation has sprung up, Vaasudeva. I am no better than a dead ancestor—to be invoked when necessary, to be ignored when convenient.'

'You are all-powerful—if you decide to use your power', said Krishna. 'Did you think, Grandfather, that if the Five Brothers left Hastinapura, tension would relax?'

'Yes Vaasudeva', said Grandfather. 'I thought that, after a little while, we could set them up in some independent principality. But, alas, that was not to be.'

Krishna turned to Vidura, 'Vidura, are you sure that they were burnt alive?'

'That is what is said, noble Vaasudeva,' said Vidura, with folded hands.

'What do you say?' asked Krishna.

'Everything is in the hands of the Great God', said Vidura and added: 'Dead bodies were found. They were charred beyond recognition.'

'What will happen to the Kurus, Grandfather, with Duryodhana as Crown Prince and Shakuni as his adviser?' asked Krishna, 'I am asking you, for the future of Aryavarta is bound up with the fortunes of the Kurus. Will it be safe in their hands?' Then in a low voice, as if speaking to himself, he added: 'If once we compromise with *adharma*, we can never get away from it.

'Many years hence—and possibly far away from here—we shall have to pay a heavy price.'

Bhishma was surprised at the perspicacity of this young man. The words had a prophetic ring. He saw clearly the meaning of what was happening, which had so far come to him in fitful glimpses, and a slight shudder passed over him.

'The Great God, I am sure, will look after the Kurus, my son. I agree with you that a lie never deceives—but it takes a long time to find it out'. The old man was in no mood to answer Krishna's query, and changed the subject.

He added: 'I want to spend the rest of the days that the Great God may grant me, in keeping the empire of the Kurus together. That has been the mission of my life. I have lived all these years in the hope that it will be fulfilled.'

Grandfather lapsed into silence and for a moment continued to gaze at the ground. Apparently his mind was busy tracing the course of the cruel events of his life.

'I am sure the Great God will see that your mission is fulfilled,' murmured Krishna. He saw that Bhishma was reluctant to carry on the conversation, further, and asked: 'May I have your permission to withdraw, Grandfather?'

'Yes, Vaasudeva, you may go,' said Grandfather. 'After your stay with us is over, are you going back to Dwaraka?'

'No. I am invited by King Drupada to go to Kampilya,' said Krishna.

Grandfather's eyes were wary. 'He is our enemy. What do you go there for?'

'To find out whether the King of Panchala stands firm in Dharma, as is reported,' said Krishna frankly.

'Promise me, Krishna, that you will not seek an alliance with Drupada against the Kurus,' said Grandfather.

'I promise, Grandfather—unless Duryodhana takes to *adharma*,' said Krishna. And, as he stood with folded hands before Grandfather he added humbly: 'Today, Best of Kurus, I have been blessed. I feel as if I had worshipped at the shrine of a god'.

Then Krishna and his friends withdrew as Grandfather extended his hands in blessing.

10

A GOPI IN HASTINAPURA

$\mathcal{K}$rishna spent two days meeting people who came to pay him their respects and paying visits to shrines conducted by Duryodhana, who was evidently determined to make friends with him.

On account of the mourning, all ceremonial events, other than those connected with the obsequial rites of the departed, had been postponed. · When the mourning was over on the expiry of three months from the death of the Five Brothers, the court went back to its usual round of ceremonial and social events.

On the third day thereafter, Dhritarashtra invited Krishna, Uddhava and Satyaki to dinner with his family. On that occasion, Krishna paid his respects to Gandhari, Dhritarashtra's consort, who, since her husband was blind, had taken a vow on marriage to remain blindfolded all her life. She was a shrewd and powerful woman, who, as Krishna found, doted on her sons and encouraged them in their ambition.

Among the ladies of the royal family whom he met was Bhanumati, Duryodhana's newly-wedded wife. Krishna had heard reports of her beauty, but could never have imagined that a slightly-built young woman of seventeen could be so exquisite and at the same time so sensuous. Her eyes were dreamy, her cheeks rosy like the dawn, her curves moulded to perfection. She walked with a dancing grace.

Krishna had been told that she was the daughter of the King of Kashi and had brought the free ways of her homeland into the rather strict atmosphere of Hastinapura's court presided over by Grandfather Bhishma. She moved, laughed and talked to people in an uninhibited way. She was not so decorously correct as a princess might have been expected to be in the presence of elders and guests, but her forwardness was characterised by a childlike impulsiveness, so charming that one could never have thought of her as being immodest.

At a first glance, Krishna, the lover of beauty in all shapes and forms, was full of admiration for her. The looks which Bhanumati shot at him as she served him were now and again frankly worshipful.

When Krishna left after dinner was finished, she stood in front of the other princesses of the family and smiled familiarly at him as a sweet favourite child would, and to the horror of the other princesses, asked him: 'I hope you are comfortable here?'

Krishna's eyes danced merrily at this bold but anxious query, and he replied in a tender voice: 'When so much affection is shown to me by all of you, how can I be unhappy—and, with you to serve me, I have taken more food than I should have,' he added in a bantering tone, lapsing into the merry way in which he always talked to the young Yadava girls of his family.

He would have loved to say a few more things in the same vein, but he saw Grandfather, with severe eyes, waiting for him so that they could go back to the mansion where he had been housed.

Krishna returned to the mansion. During the day, though he was engaged in talking to several people, the rosy cheeks, the exquisite curves and limpid eyes of Bhanumati were before him.

The next evening Uddhava and Satyaki had not returned from Vidura's, where they had been invited for dinner, even after the lamps were lit. Krishna was preparing to retire for the night, when he heard the gay laughter of men and women approaching him. He put on his diadem and his necklace again, turned to the door, and saw Duryodhana, Duhshasana, Bhanumati and two other princesses coming towards him very gaily.

'Vaasudeva, we have come to invite you to the Gouri *Puja* (Worship of the Mother Goddess) which Devi is performing', said Duryodhana, who, like his companions, appeared to be under the influence of heady drink.

'Forgive me, Duryodhana, I am just retiring to rest,' replied Krishna.

'You cannot disappoint us,' said Bhanumati, her eyes dancing and her dimpled cheeks showing the most enchanting smile. 'We know all about you. You were the darling of the *gopis* of Vrindavan. Surely we are not worse than those cowherdesses!' She said it with such a childish insistence in her voice—as if she were seven and not seventeen—that Krishna found it difficult to disappoint her.

'Those days were different. I am no longer what I was in Vrindavan. Moreover I am not in a mood to join your gay company,' said Krishna.

'No, you must come,' said Bhanumati, stamping her feet in her sweet girlish way.'Oh, please come. We want you to be happy, now that the mourning is over.'

Krishna forgave her for the familiar way in which she talked, so out of tune with etiquette of the court.

Duryodhana and others added their insistence to Bhanumati's and Krishna accompanied them to the quarter of the royal grounds where Duryodhana's mansion stood. He left a message for Uddhava and Satyaki with a retainer that he had gone with Duryodhana to attend the Gouri *Puja* held by Princess Bhanumati and would be returning soon.

Krishna 'could easily see that in one of Duryodhana's crude attempts to make friends with him, he was displaying his wife's charms—the easy method of the dastardly husband. But he did not want to repel these attempts to win him.

Bhanumati, who had been married to Duryodhana only a few months before used to dress in the fashion of her own country, except when she was to see the elders. A gold-embroidered bodice encased her girlish breasts, and her skirt, tied below her navel, showed her dainty stomach to the best advantage. Unlike the fashion generally adopted by the princesses of the day, her neck, arms and wrists had only stringed buds of *Kunda* flowers for ornaments, and the braids of her hair were interwoven with them. Her waist-band was also made of thickly woven buds, and from it again was suspended a strap woven with buds which reached up to her ankle. She looked like a maiden made of flower buds rather than of flesh and blood and a cloud of sweet aromas surrounded her.

Bhanumati was charming beyond description. She often lisped like a little child and was always bubbling with laughter, very often without any provocation. The surprising part of her behaviour was that she talked to Krishna as if she had known him all her life.

On the way she monopolised the conversation, 'I know all about you; also how you dance with *gopis* on moon-lit nights. If you are here on some such nights, you must teach us what you taught the *gopis*,' said the irrepressible young Princess.

'How do you know all that? It is all gone and forgotten,' said Krishna.

'Oh, I know all about it,' said Bhanumati mischievously, pressing her hand on Krishna's arm, a gesture which would have been highly indecorous for a young lady of gentle birth. 'I am not such an ignorant person as you think me to be. After Mathura was burnt, a number of ballad singers from your city came to my father's court and entertained us with songs of your exploits, particularly how you played the *rasa* with the *gopis*. Oh, I even know some of the ballads by heart and often sing them. Ever since those days, I have wanted to meet you.' She said looking at Krishna with longing: 'That is why, I had no sooner heard that you were coming to Hastinapura, than I told Aryaputra[1] that I must meet you. I have so often dreamt that I was your *gopi*.' She said this with a charming sigh, an exquisite addition to her talk. And it was clear that she had taken more *madira* than was good for her.

'Duryodhana, if I had known that I was such a dangerous person, I would not have come to Hastinapura at all,' remarked Krishna.

'Oh, she has been a great trouble to me. Since she heard that you were coming here, she has been talking of nothing else but you. you must have been a very gay person in your boyhood, Vaasudeva, to be able to make girls at strange homes so mad about you,' said Duryodhana.

'Let me talk to Vaasudeva, Aryaputra. All these days you have been talking to him. I will never get another opportunity to speak to him again. Noble Vaasudeva, do you remember the *gopis* or have you forgotten them?' asked Bhanumati lifting her eyes, now full of passionate admiration.

'Princess, how can I forget them? They are part of my life,' replied Krishna.

'Then, if I am your *gopi*, will I also become a part of your life?' asked Bhanumati.

'You cannot be *gopi*, Bhanumati. You are the consort of the Crown Prince and some day will become the Empress of the Kurus,' said Krishna in a bantering tone.

'Don't evade answering my question,' said Bhanumati with impatience, pouting her pretty lips fresher than the buds she wore. 'I don't care whether I am an Empress or not. I want to live among flowers, songs and dances, as you did at Vrindavan, and all the time hear your flute which sent the *gopis* of Vrindavan fleeing from their homes to come to you.'

'Duryodhana, you had better take care,' said Krishna, lapsing into one of his charming smiles, which of late had been seen so rarely. 'She is talking of running away from you and coming to me.'

'She is a chatterbox. Don't listen to her, Vaasudeva, All through the day and half the night, she keeps talking of the most absurd things. I should not be surprised if some day she went mad,' said Duryodhana laughing.

'Am I mad? Just listen, Vaasudeva,' exclaimed Bhanumati in mock horror. 'It is he who is mad, all the time talking about becoming Crown Prince and destroying this man and that, and whispering all sorts of things in the ear of his uncle—may the Great God ever make him fatter and fatter—who does not know even how to smile from his heart.' Then she laughed, and all the others, except her husband, began to laugh.

'Be silent, Bhanumati,' said Duryodhana with a frown. He was also feeling the worse for drink, but knew what dangerous ground his wife was treading on. 'You do not understand affairs of the State and you must not talk about them.'

'I do not want to understand them, and I never like talking about them,' she said laughing. The way that her husband snubbed her made no difference to her cheerful mood. 'Vaasudeva, tell me that you will stay here till the next moon-lit night and play *rasa* with us.'

'Bhanumati, you are asking for the impossible. I cannot stay here till the next full-moon. I have left the flute you are thinking of in Vrindavan, and no flute that I have played since has had that magic. I have almost forgotten how to dance the *rasa*. And don't forget that we are not in Vrindavan.'

'I wish I were,' said Bhanumati in a voice almost choking with emotion, for, a little worse for drink, she had reached the mood of expressing her feelings in an exaggerated way.

'We wish for many things which we cannot get. But you are the Crown Princess of the Kurus. I dare say that there have to be rigid codes of behaviour, and Grandfather would never forgive me if I took liberties with them,' said Krishna.

'Yes, I know, It is Grandfather who always makes life difficult here, Oh Vaasudeva, I wish I had been born a *gopi*,' Bhanumati said as they reached Duryodhana's mansion.

11

GOURI PUJA

$\mathscr{D}$uryodhana and his companions led Krishna to his mansion which was at the far end of the palace grounds. They crossed over to a small secluded garden in the rear which was surrounded by a high hedge of flowering creepers.

This garden was reserved for Bhanumati, who almost daily performed the worship of Gouri there with songs and dances in the fashion of her native country. In the centre was installed a stone image of the Mother Goddess under a canopy of silver.

The garden was lit by torches tied to posts, which fitfully illumined the garden. In front of the Goddess burnt four lights on silver pedestals, fed by ghee. In the middle stood a huge jar filled with aromatic wine, with a number of silver and gold cups lying on the ground around it.

Krishna, with his sense of the beautiful, had taken a liking for Bhanumati, who chattered happily like a bird which has tasted the elixir of the *shimal* flowers in the month of Phalgun. From her sprightly talk, he learnt that she performed Gouri Puja every day with some of her women friends; she did so for the health and glory of her husband. Only sometimes the princes and princesses came to see the strange ritual.

'In Hastinapura they think that every one else is a barbarian. Do I look like one?' she asked Krishna, her little face tilted ravishingly.

'If you are a barbarian, we are worse,' replied Krishna.

'Aryaputra rarely comes to the *puja*,' she complained. 'I want him to come always. He never listens to me. Today he has come only because you have come. I am very angry with him,' she said laughingly. 'He has also brought his friends,' she added pouting her lips in unconcealed disgust at the type of friends that he had brought. 'And their wives have come too—for the first time to the *puja*—to welcome you, Vaasudeva. They are dying to have your *darshan*. They were terribly excited when I told them what the ballad singers have been singing about you in my father's court,' she said, and looked at Krishna with a show of anger. 'Why did you not bring your flute with you? Next time when you come to Hastinapura, you must bring it,' insisted Bhanumati.

'I will have to fetch it from Vrindavan', said Krishna smiling in response to the appealing requests of Bhanumati. His eyes for the moment had a distant gaze. Another loving childish figure—Radha's—stood before his mind. 'But it is so far, far away,' he said reminiscently.

'Aryaputra has ordered so much *madira*. Can you

drink it all?' asked Bhanumati, pointing to the jar which lay in front of the Goddess.

'It is enough to drown me, I confess' said Krishna.

Six or seven young chiefs in different stages of drunkenness stood there, laughing without restraint in a manner scarcely appropriate to the occasion. Krishna acknowledged their greetings with distant formality.

When Duryodhana and Bhanumati led Krishna to the shrine, two maidens of striking beauty were performing the ritual of *arti* by waving lights before the Goddess; four others were singing the hymn to the accompaniment of hand-claps. Two of them could easily be identified as having come from Kashi, Bhanumati's country, from the style of dress they wore. The others evidently belonged to high families of Hastinapura.

When the *arti* was finished, every one first touched the flame with the tips of their fingers and then touched their eyebrows with them. Krishna offered worship by placing flowers at the feet of the Goddess and recited the hymn.

Bhanumati, laughing all the while, distributed the cups to the persons present, who drank the wine copiously. Krishna, never tempted to depart from his well-regulated habits, took only a few sips from the cup which Bhanumati held to his lips. In any other young woman, this would have been unforgivable brashness, but Bhanumati did it with such childish glee that Krishna was inclined not only to forgive her, but to like her for it.

A few hand-drums were then brought forward by the young women, who began to sing in honour of the Goddess. As they started dancing in groups or in circles, beating time with their feet or whirling in pairs with extended arms held together, their swaying figures cast artistic patterns on the ground in the flickering light of the torches. The dances and songs continued for a long time with intervals in which the young ladies replenished their strength by sipping wine.

Of all the young women there, Bhanumati was by far the most striking. She sang in a melodious voice of great richness. As she danced, her small graceful body swayed with a perfect rhythm. Her gleeful laughter resounded at intervals over the songs and the drum beats. It showed how thoroughly she enjoyed the festivities, and her happiness proved infectious for every one including Krishna.

The young men stood on the two sides, keeping time by clapping their hands, and admiring the sensuous movements of the graceful bodies rather than the dance or the song. But they soon passed the limits of sobriety and their eyes were lit with a fire which had little to do with the religious or aesthetic significance of the festivity.

Krishna soon saw that the festivity was taking a different turn. The women stopped at short intervals to drink wine and also to force it on the young men, who reciprocated the compliment. Krishna did not like what he thought was an outlandish ceremony and detached himself from the crowd of young men. Only Bhanumati came now and again to press him to drink with such affectionate insistence that, not to make her unhappy, he sipped the wine a little.

Both men and women, Krishna could see from their eyes, were intoxicated not only by wine, but by passion. This surely could not be the *puja* which Bhanumati performed every day. It must have been specially staged by Duryodhana. Was it for his benefit?

The dancers, thoroughly exhausted, gave up dancing and now and then threw themselves on the ground or rolled on the grass laughing shamelessly. When they stood up they were unsteady on their feet and their eyes were rolling in drunken animality.

When the dance came to an end, four young women extinguished some of the torches. The scene was then dimly lighted only by the feeble, flickering green-lights which stood in front of the Goddess.

Krishna was getting disgusted at the form which the festivity was assuming. He had felt equally disgusted when his Yadavas indulged in such unrestrained drinking. He could put up with Balarama's habitual massive drinking because of his unbounded affection for his brother and because it only made the Big Brother expansive, never drunk. His disgust. however, was mixed with compassion for the foolish unfortunates who courted temporary insanity in a vain search for happiness.

The women, some of them lying exhausted on the ground, clapped their hands hysterically and shouted: 'Victory unto Mother Gouri!' The young men shouted in response.

All the women then began to shout in merry excitement; their vague, dark shadows were seen pursuing the young men: their giggles and laughter and words of endearment were heard as they sought one another—not necessarily their married partners. Soon they were all chasing each other or rolling on the ground in pairs.

The festivity was evidently coming to a climax and Krishna almost decided to withdraw, but he had no heart to leave Bhanumati unprotected. She must be saved, he felt, from herself, from the possible promiscuity which he thought was likely to follow once the remaining lights died out.

The lights went out. Most of the company lay on the ground, some murmuring half-formed words, some in each other's arms.

Krishna heard the guttural voice of Duryodhana as he lay on the ground, whispering to someone, who, from her voice, was clearly not Bhanumati. It was no longer a ritual; it was an orgy.

Suddenly a woman fell on Krishna. There was no mistaking it; it was Bhanumati. She threw her arms round his neck, trying to find his mouth to make him drink with unsteady hands. Her flower-laden body was quivering with passion. Krishna realized the terrible implications of the situation. Duryodhana had exploited his wife's unthinking childishness to trap Krishna into a situation which would bind Krishna to him forever as his boon companion!

In this home of the proud Kurus, the canons of Dharma were being flouted shamelessly. He had seen the Yadavas, during some of their festivities, behave just as badly. But this orgy was terrible and unforgivable in a Crown Prince of the Kurus. His heart went out to the solitary old Bhishma, who, by sheer strength of character, was trying to uphold the traditions of the ancient Kurus.

However, there was no time to think. The situation must be saved. He lifted Bhanumati in his hands— she was as light as a bundle of flowers. She clung to him, nesting her head against his chest whispering all the while: 'I am your *gopi*; I am your *gopi*.'

Krishna held Bhanumati in a close grip against his body, as if she was a very naughty child bent on mischief, or a wild animal. Even her endearments were stifled by the way he kept her pressed against his chest.

A vast compassion for this lovely, girlish beauty swept over Krishna. All her gifts were wasted in the arms of the self-willed, thoughtless Duryodhna. Keeping her body locked to his by the vigorous pressure of his arms, he stalked out of the garden.

Bhanumati was too intoxicated to know what was being done with her. Guiding himself slowly by the dim star-light Krishna made his way round Duryodhana's mansion and then slowly proceeded towards that of Dhritarashtra. Whatever happened, the reputation and

happiness of this poor girl, and with it the prestige
of the Kuru house, must be maintained, and her sense
of decency aroused.

On the way, Krishna stopped for a moment to
adjust Bhanumati's skirt which, in her struggle, had
curled up to above her hips. The flower buds had all
but dropped off. The bodice at one time or another had
fallen off, the knot which tied it having been loosened
during the vigorous dances. In the dim star-light, her
exquisite body shone as if she was made of pearls.
Krishna sighed; all this was to go to waste, with
Duryodhana as her husband.

Krishna introduced himself to the watchman who
stood at the gates of the King's mansion and explained
that Bhanumati had been taken ill at the Gouri *puja*
and it was most important, he said, that she should
be with her mother-in-law, Gandhari. The watchman
was shocked that at that time of night the distinguished
visitor should bring the Crown Princess dead drunk.
But he knew the vagaries of the Crown Prince and
was in the habit of making allowances for unexpected
situations in connection with his married life.

The watchman brought along an elderly maid-
servant. who after hearing the distinguished guest's
strange errand, went into the mansion and after some
time led the blindfolded Gandhari out of the enclosed
garden in which, with Dhritarashtra, she had been
sleeping.

'Vaasudeva, you! At this time!' she exclaimed,
utterly surprised.

Krishna waved the watchman and the maid-servant away and whispered: 'Yes, Mother. Forgive me. I have brought Bhanumati. She is in a terrible plight and must be saved.' He then explained to her all that had happened, and added: 'When I saw that the Gouri *puja* had been transformed into a bestial orgy, I thought it necessary above all to save the reputation of Bhanumati. If she was found in the morning lying drunk in the garden with men and women in compromising positions, you can imagine how Hastinapura—and perhaps the whole of Aryavarta—would have been shocked. The only way, I thought, was to save her at any cost. She is a harmless, little child'.

Bhanumati was now fast asleep, only whispering at intervals some words which were incomprehensible to others, but which Krishna understood. She was happily dreaming that she was a *gopi.*

Gandhari asked the maid-servant to lift Bhanumati and place her on her own bed by her side. It was a piece of good fortune for the Queen that she was blindfolded; otherwise she would have seen her daughter-in-law in a condition which she would never have forgotten.

'Vaasudeva, you have conferred a boon on the Kurus. I will never forget it, my son', said Gandhari. 'And, who knows, this may become a turning point in the poor girl's life.'

Krishna left the sorrowing mother-in-law to ponder over the future of her family. Bhanumati slept on, unconscious, lying in the same bed as her mother-in-law, only the words, 'I am a *gopi'*, escaping her lips now and again. Mother Gandhari loved her sons more than she cared to confess, but shuddered at the fate of the Kurus if these irregularities were to be a feature of their family life.

In the morning, Gandhari got the maid-servant to wash Bhanumati's face in cold water. Slowly consciousness returned to her. She opened her eyes and found herself in her mother-in-law's bed, with her mother-in-law sitting by her side. She looked at herself, clothed only in a torn skirt, and bitter tears fell from her eyes. 'Oh, Mother! What has happened to me?' she said and clung to Gandhari.

'My daughter,' said Gandhari in a sad voice, putting her hand on Bhanumati's head, 'don't fear. Everything is all right. Thank God, Krishna Vaasudeva brought you to me last night. If he had not done so, the whole royal line of Bharatas would have been disgraced for ever.'

Bhanumati broke down and clung to Gandhari helplessly, as the scenes of the previous night came to her mind. 'Mother, Mother, what could I do? Aryaputra, your son, wanted me to win Vaasudeva, and I did my best'.

'My child, I know you would not have done it of yourself. You are too immature. But remember one thing: the woman, who tries to win friends for her husband by shedding her sense of propriety, ends by making an enemy of him as well as of her own self. Thank God, in this case it was Vaasudeva. What would have happened if it had been another man?'

The dawn broke. The retainers who looked after Bhanumati's enclosed garden, when they came to prepare for the morning worship, followed by two priests with what was needed for the ceremony, saw a strange spectacle. Men and women, with scarcely any clothes on, were sleeping off their drunkenness on the ground in all manner of compromising positions. Among them they recognised the Crown Prince.

They were frightened. They did not know what to do. Not to perform the *puja* at the proper time would be a sacrilege. But with those men and women lying in front of the Goddess, this was difficult. Besides, they had not the courage to carry away the drunken people because they were of such high rank.

The priests hurriedly went to Vidura, the Minister, for whom everybody had great respect, and told him of what they had found in Bhanumati's garden. He came there with three or four men who were in his confidence. He was struck aghast at what he saw.

His first care was to remove Duryodhana from the garden to his own mansion. But it was difficult to do so. He was a strong, well-built man, still dreaming of his experiences of the previous night and very angry at being shaken prematurely out of his enjoyable torpor. The others were removed by Vidura to his own house in the palace ground, where, with some difficulty, he awoke them to the situation in which they had placed themselves.

Most of the young men and women in the garden were persons of high rank. Naturally, therefore, the scandal took the palace by storm and convulsed the whole of Hastinapura by its impact.

When Bhishma heard of it, his anger spread awe around him. He called the *parishad* and the principal courtiers, and issued his commands, at which every one trembled.

Duryodhana and Duhshasana were to go to Kurukshetra to perform penance for a month. The other young men had to go to Badrinath for a year's penance.

The two young relatives of Bhanumati, who had accompanied her to Hastinapura, had to return to their homes. All the other young women were to perform *chandrayana vrata* every month for twelve months under the supervision of the High-Priest of the Kurus.

Two of them, who were found in the arms of men other than their husbands, had an additional penalty to pay; if their husbands and fathers-in-law did not accept them even after purification, they were to enter the fire.

The garden of Bhanumati was uprooted. The plot of land on which it stood was purified by lustrations, and regular shrine of Gouri and Her lord, Shankara, the Great God, rose in its place.

Bhanumati, thinking of the fate which she had narrowly escaped, developed a high fever.

∎

12
THE DOWAGER EMPRESS

*I*t was the evening of the day before Krishna was leaving that Vidura came to invite him to an interview with the old Empress, the Most Venerable Mother. It was a rare honour, because she rarely saw any visitor who came to Hastinapura.

Born of a fisherman on the banks of the Yamuna, Matsyagandhi—as she was then called—had borne a son to no less a person than the great Sage Parashara, In a moment of weakness the sage had fallen under the spell of her dark eyes, her lithe form and her vivacious charm.

When the son—called Krishna, for he was dark, and Dwaipayana, because he was born on a *dwipa*, an island—had grown up, the father had carried him away to his *ashram* in Kurukshetra, where the learned *rishis* dwelt. Inheriting the mighty traditions of Vasishtha, one of the founders of the race, Krishna Dwaipayana became Veda Vyasa, respectfully termed the Best of Munis, or the Master, and revered by the whole of Aryavarta.

The Emperor Shantanu of the Kurus, once when he was out hunting, fell in love with Matsyagandhi. Then she was barely sixteen, and the river, the sun and the winds had given her health, freshness and a challenging freedom of behaviour, and the Emperor could not long withstand their onslaught.

The Emperor asked her father for her hand. The latter was a hard-headed fisherman and refused to give her in marriage unless he was assured that her son—and not the Crown Prince Gangeya—would succeed to the throne of the Kurus of Hastinapura on his death. Gangeya, to make his father happy, took the terrible vow of lifelong celibacy, renouncing his claim to the throne. Shantanu married the fisher girl, who thereafter came to be known as Satyavati.

The fisher girl emerged as a shrewd and vigorous Empress, upholding the best traditions of the imperial house of *Chakravarti* Bharata. But fate was unkind and put all her wisdom and courage to the test.

She bore two sons to Shantanu, Chitrangada and Vichitraveerya. Chitrangada died when a boy, fighting. Vichitraveerya was a weakling from birth. Bhishma, in order to maintain the continuity of his father's line, abducted Ambikaa and Ambaalikaa, two daughters of the King of Kashi, and had them married to Vichitraveerya.

Luck was against the Kurus. Vichitraveerya died childless. The Empress shouldered the responsibility in a brave manner. She begged of Bhishma to give up his vow, ascend the throne and marry. But Bhishma was firm; he would not give up his vow. She then invited her son, Veda Vyasa, to beget children on the childless widows of the deceased King.

Fate, however, pursued the royal line of the Kurus relentlessly. Ambikaa gave birth to blind Dhritarashtra and Ambaalikaa to Pandu who was diseased from birth. Not all the efforts of Satyavati had succeeded in giving to her deceased husband what she thought was his due—a line of vigorous kings.

According to ancient custom, Dhritarashtra, being born blind, could not succeed to the throne. Pandu succeeded him and ruled well and wisely, but in a few years, overcome by disease, retired to the Himalayas and died, leaving his widow Kunti, sister of Krishna's father, and five sons.

With Bhishma by her side, Satyavati again faced this calamity with courage. Pandu's sons, the Five Brothers, were accepted in the family as gifts from the gods. Dhritarashtra begot numerous sons, and the burden fell on the aging Empress to see that these princes were brought up with care and affection.

Now, when the princes had grown to manhood, and the Five Brothers had given great promise of redeeming the glory of the Kurus, calamity had again struck the royal house of the Kurus. The sons of Dhritarashtra developed a venomous hostility towards the Five Brothers, who, to escape a catastrophe, had to be banished to Varanavata. And as report had it, they met their death in the burning palace.

Satyavati was a very devout woman. She sat the whole day in *puja*, praying to the Great God that her husband's empire should continue intact in able and righteous hands. And though she rarely interfered in the affairs of the State, her watchful eye and wise guidance helped Bhishma and Vidura in making important decisions. She was not an old, dowager Empress; styled the Most Venerable Mother, she was treated by the Kurus as the presiding deity of Hastinapura.

When Krishna met her, she was on her usual seat in front of a small shrine of the Great God Shankara which had been installed for her in the room in which she spent most of her time. Even at seventy, she bore the traces of her early beauty. Her dark skin was fresh and soft, her small figure compact, her eyes undimmed in spite of age and grief. The crown of white hair over her dark face gave her the halo of a goddess.

Satyavati's smile was sweet as she pointed to a wooden seat in front of her. Krishna prostrated himself before her and then took the seat.

'Vidura, you can sit down too', she said to Vidura.

'Yes, Venerable Mother,' said Vidura and took his seat on the ground. His respect for this legendary figure was mixed with admiration.

'I understand, Vaasudeva, you are proceeding to Kampilya tomorrow morning,' Satyavati spoke slowly and her voice was sweet and sad. 'I am glad you came to Hastinapura, though I wish the occasion had been a joyful one. We are faced with a great calamity.'

'I looked forward to the Five Brothers re-establishing the glory of *Chakravarti* Bharata,' said Krishna.

'Yes, I thought so myself, but the Great God willed otherwise,' she said. 'Vaasudeva, when you go to Dwaraka, convey my blessing to Vasudeva and Devaki and to Balarama. Few parents are as lucky as yours, for they have Balarama and yourself as sons,' she added, not being able to keep a touch of tragic sadness out of her voice. Her progeny, she could never forget, had failed her.

'Venerable Mother, I shall convey your message to them, and I thank you for the gracious hospitality shown to me,' said Krishna

'Have you any children?' she asked.

'Yes, one son,' replied Krishna.

'By the Princess of Vidarbha?'

'Yes,' said Krishna.

'What is his name?'

'Pradyumna,' said Krishna.

'Give him my blessing when you see him next.'

'As the Venerable Mother commands,' said Krishna.

'We are extremely beholden to you, Vaasudeva,' she said, though with an air of dignity befitting an empress. 'Had you not saved Bhanumati, the Kurus would never have been able to face the world,'

Krishna smiled. 'Oh, even you have come to know of it?'

Satyavati smiled in reply. 'How can I give up looking after my family? I will never forget the debt of gratitude which we all owe to you'.

'Don't think of it, Venerable Mother. I saw that the situation could have terrible implications if allowed to develop. Forget all about it. And I beg of you, don't blame the poor child. She is as innocent as a small child and as impulsive. She has it in her to be a great woman some day, for her instincts are noble,' said Krishna.

'Do you think that it was the doing of Duryodhana?' she asked.

'I cannot say who engineered it. But her childish admiration for me as the cowherd of Vrindavan was worked upon by some clever person in order to lay a trap for me', said Krishna.

'A trap for you! What could be the motive?' she asked.

'Evidently to bind me to the Crown Prince by the ties of boon companionship', said Krishna.

'Do you think so?' asked Satyavati.

'Yes, I am sure,' said Krishna. 'She is incapable of wickedness. She has sent me a present as a sister. I have conveyed to her my pledge to be a brother to her.'

'Vaasudeva, I never thought that you were so good', said Satyavati warmly.

'How do you know that I am good?' asked Krishna with a sly laugh.'I am a very wicked person. I killed my uncle and ran away with Bhishmaka's daughter. You cannot be sure what I may do next,' he added, for he did not want her to receive the impresion that he pledged himself to an unconditional support to the policies of Hastinapura.

'My son, all these years it has been my lot to sit here and judge the real worth of people,' she remarked with a smile, 'I have had reports about you all time that you have been here. And I have come to agree with my son, Dwaipayana, about you'.

'What has the Best of Munis been saying about me?' asked Krishna.

Satyavati gave a winning smile, '—that you are born to re-establish Dharma.'

'All of you are so kind,' said Krishna with charming humility. 'I try to do what I can; the Great God favours me with some success.'

'Who knows what the Great God wants you to accomplish?' Then her face dissolved into a smile, maternal in its tenderness. 'Vaasudeva, shall I address you as Krishna? Remember that it is a dear name to me; my son Dwaipayana bears it too,' she said graciously. 'Will you answer me frankly, honestly, if I ask a favour of you?' she asked with pleading eyes as the uncertainty which had been oppressing her for days came back to her with poignant insistence.

'Have you any reason to doubt my frankness or honesty?' asked Krishna, moved by the manner in which the question was asked.

Satyavati smiled gratefully. 'Krishna, answer me frankly. Will you stand by me?'

'I stand by you!' exclaimed Krishna. 'You are the most powerful Empress in the world, and, with Bhishma by your side, you are irresistible.'

'But not against fate,' she said quietly, looking around to see whether any person, beyond the two, was within hearing distance.

'I am always at your service,' said Krishna.

Satyavati's face assumed a solemn look. She glanced at Vidura, lowered her voice to almost an inaudible whisper and said: 'Will you stand by the Five Brothers?'

'Stand by the Five Brothers!' exclaimed Krishna as a thrill of expectation went through his heart. 'Are they alive?' This was a strange mystery, after their funeral obsequies had been duly performed!

Satyavati again looked on all sides carefully to see if anyone, except the two sitting in front of her, was within hearing distance, and whispered: 'They escaped from the burning palace.'

'Escaped!' Krishna opened his eyes wide in disbelief. 'But their dead bodies were ceremonially cremated'.

She put her finger on her lips, 'sh....sh....
sh....sh....,' and added: 'They escaped from the burning
palace by a tunnel which Vidura's man had dug'.

'But what about dead bodies?' asked Krishna.

'They were not of Kunti and the Five Brothers,' said
Satyavati. 'If the dead bodies had not been found there,
Duryodhana and Shakuni would have discovered that
they were alive and had them pursued and killed.'

'Then where are they?' asked Krishna.

'Vidura kept a boat ready for them to cross the
Ganga, but after they left it, they disappeared into the
forest,' she said.

'Could they not be traced?' asked Krishna.

'That is our difficulty', she said. 'We cannot trust
anyone here to trace them. If we do so, someone or other
in Hastinapura is sure to discover that the Five Brothers
are alive. Then they will be hunted down. I want you to
find out where they are and whether they are safe. No
one will suspect you of trying to do so. It will be easy for
you to have a search made, for they are lost somewhere
in the forest where the Nagas live. Perhaps your
maternal grandfather, King Aryaka, might be helpful. We
cannot even take him into our confidence, Who knows,
Shakuni might bribe the Naga chiefs to kill them. If you
can find them, take them away to Dwaraka, without
anyone knowing it.'

Krishna looked up, his face glowing. 'Venerable
Mother, your commands shall be obeyed. The Five
Brothers shall be found.'

'May your path be victorious, my son,' said the old
Empress with a sigh of relief.

∎

13

THE BEST OF MUNIS

$\mathscr{K}$rishna and a few leading members of his party took boats to go to Kampilya, the capital of Panchala. The other Yadava chiefs were left behind to follow with chariots, horses and carts by the land route to Nagakoota, the headquarters of King Aryaka, the maternal grandfather of Vasudeva, whom Krishna wanted to visit on his way back to Dwaraka.

The Ganga was a very wide and rapid-flowing river, and the boats, as was the way with the river traffic of the day, skirted along its banks, rarely crossing to the other side.

From infancy, Krishna had worshipped the mighty Ganga as the Mother of Rivers, though at a distance. This was, however, the first occasion he had had to see the wonders of this living divinity: the ducks, in shoals, drifting leisurely on the water; the graceful swans floating by; the flying fish cheerfully jumping out of the water; the alligators, their snouts protruding above the surface, suddenly disappearing on their approach: the birds of various hues wheeling over them; the tree-tops on both banks nodding at each other across the blue sky.

On both banks there were huge virgin forests, sometimes impenetrable. Their continuity, however, was broken at places by foot-paths along which people from adjoining villages came to bathe or fetch water. And the Nagas, almost naked, continuously plied little canoes from one place to another.

On the way the Yadavas also came across large settlements built on open spaces recovered from the forests. These were the new frontiers of Aryavarta where adventurous Aryas had made their homes.

The residents at such settlements, as soon as they saw the procession of boats, came to the bank of the river to receive the guests, offered them garlands and fruits, and sometimes insisted on their resting a night with them or at least taking a meal.

On every such occasion, the settlers, on learning who the principal guest was, would wash Krishna's feet, worshipping him as a divinity; for the fame of his marvellous feat in vanquishing Jarasandha and later leading the Yadavas to Dwaraka had reached most of the Aryan settlements in the north.

At infrequent intervals the Yadavas came across the *ashram* of some *rishi,* easily identified by the smoke of the sacred fire trailing up to heaven, or by the chant of Vedic hymns breaking the silence of the forest with its moving rhythms. When they came across such an *ashram* Krishna and his party landed and paid their respects to presiding *rishi,* joined him in his daily worship of the sacred fire and accepted his hospitality.

The sadness, which had settled on Krishna before meeting the Empress Satyavati, was completely dissipated as he watched the swift-flowing waters of the Ganga. As he breathed in the beauty of the serene moon-lit nights on the river, he felt a new strength coming to him.

Only when they were by themselves, did he share with Uddhava his thoughts of rescuing the Five Brothers. They—the Five Brothers—must be traced, and that too without its being suspected even by their Yadava comrades—not even by Satyaki who was too outspoken by nature. Krishna himself was out of the question for the purpose of seeking them; he was too prominent—so was Uddhava, his friend and cousin.

Uddhava agreed that the search, if it was to succeed, must be carried on in complete secrecy. 'Why not take King Aryaka into our confidence?' he suggested. 'The Nagas know the forests inside out and will be able to trace the Five Brothers'.

'I don't know whether we can trust him', said Krishna, but added: 'But we have to take that risk'.

'I will go to Nagakoota to find out whether the old man can be trusted. That is the only way,' said Uddhava.

'But I want you at Kampilya,' said Krishna with a mischievous smile.

'Why me?' asked Uddhava with a meaningful smile, 'Satyaki would do as well.' He could always divine his friend's innermost thoughts without being told.

'You have guessed my purpose, you cunning fellow,' laughed Krishna. 'I want you to be the son-in-law of King Drupada'.

'Who would accept me in your place?' asked Uddhava, also breaking into a laugh. Krishna's laughter was infectious. 'Krishna, I am a very simple man. I have no ambition to wed at all—much less such a fiery princess as Draupadi is reputed to be. I cannot tame wild mares as you can.'

'Uddhava, how long will you surrender your individual life to me?' asked Krishna, pressing Uddhava to himself with an unusual outburst of emotion. 'You cannot always look after me. Sometimes I must look after you also.'

'Don't think of me. Besides, it is more important to think of the Five Brothers than of the Princess', said Uddhava.

'Uddhava—' interrupted Krishna, as a sudden thought struck him.

'What is it?' asked Uddhava.

'Suppose the Five Brothers are alive—.'

'And—?' enquired Uddhava.

'Drupada could give his daughter—'.

'To Arjuna,' said Uddhava.

'I am afraid it cannot happen', remarked Krishna with a sigh.

One day, as they were travelling on the river, they heard at a distance the solemn chants of Vedic hymns issuing from many throats in perfect tones and harmonies. The magic quality of the chant as it floated the air transformed the landscape into a scene of ethereal beauty. On enquiry they learnt that it was Utkochaka Tirtha, where Dhaumya Rishi had his *ashram.*

They soon came to where a group of trees surrounded a large landing place to which several boats had been moored. Evidently, some distinguished guests had come to visit the *ashram.*

Krishna and his party moored their boats by the side of the other ones. After landing, they proceeded towards the *ashram* where the hymns were being chanted, and found a large settlement surrounded by a cactus hedge. In an opening in the center, a fire was burning in a sacrificial pit, and a large company of anchorites of both sexes were offering oblations, accompanied by chants. About two hundred Nagas and Nishadas, with their chiefs in many feathered head-dresses and quaint costumes, were also sitting there. Some men carried spears in their hands or crude bamboo bows on their shoulders, and many women had babies in their arms. There were a number of ailing men and women among them.

When some disciples informed Dhaumya Rishi of the new arrival, he came out to welcome the guests, and his joy knew no bounds when he learnt who the principal guest was. In fact, Shvetaketu had already informed him that Krishna would be halting there on his way to Kampilya.

Dhaumya blessed Krishna and his companions, and led them to the sacrificial fire, before which a venerable figure sat, offering oblations.

'This Tirtha is always lucky. You have come, Vaasudeva, when the venerable Veda Vyasa himself is here', said Dhaumya.

Krishna felt excited as never before. The MASTER, as Veda Vyasa was generally called, the fountain-head of Dharma—of whom he had heard so much from sages, elders and priests—was before him. He prostrated himself before the Best of Munis when Dhaumya Rishi presented him.

For a moment the large eyes in the swarthy face widened in surprise, then grew soft with the light of recognition.

Krishna introduced himself. 'I, Krishna, the son of Vasudeva, the Best of Shooras, bow to thee, Master. This is Uddhava, son of my uncle Devabhaga. This is my friend, Yuyudhana, son of Satyaka.'

'Vaasudeva, I was waiting to meet you', said the Master in the clear, rich voice of a fond father . 'May you live for a hundred years—nay, a hundred and twenty'. The Muni patted Krishna's back and added: 'I met your father Vasudeva—oh, years ago—in fact, before you were born.'

'Mother Devaki told me the way you blessed us all', said Krishna, feeling overwhelmed by the brimming love which the smile expressed much more eloquently than any words.

'When I came to Mathura thereafter, you and Balarama had been to Gomantaka,' said the Master.

The Sage was dark-skinned and of heavy build,

clothed in the skin of an antelope. His most outstanding features which created a tremendous impression on whoever saw him were his massive brow, short broad nose and large luminous eyes which looked at the world with inexpressible kindness, all framed in white hair, matted on top, rising like a snow-capped mountain peak. The smile fascinated Krishna; it played upon his lips, inviting every one to share in an abiding love which knew no reservations and made no distinctions.

'Let us finish the *homa*', said the Sage.

Krishna and his companions sat down beside the Naga chiefs and joined in the chant.

When the *homa* was over, the Sage enquired of Krishna how his people were and what brought him to the land of the Ganga.

After Krishna had replied to these questions, Dhaumya called one of his disciples and gave him instructions to distribute milk to those who were ailing, maimed or struck by palsy. Each of them came limping, crawling or in pain, as his disability permitted, up to the Sage, who put a small leaf in each pot of milk, taken from an improvised bag which was suspended from the shoulder of his principal disciple, Jaimini.

The unfortunates, pot in hand, sat down in front of the sacred fire, their heads bowed. The rich voice of Veda Vyasa rose in a chant, invoking the twin Gods, the Aswins, who healed men.

There was a hush over the assembly. The chant rose and fell in well-toned cadences. The atmosphere was surcharged with a new vitality, as when the fresh, crisp breeze blows at dawn in spring.

The chant was over. The Sage then asked each ailing person to drink the milk, which he did. In the case of sick children, their mothers gave them the milk.

In a voice affectionate and yet irresistible, the Master said: 'Come, I will give you my blessing'.

Each one of the ailing came before him and bent his or her head in deep veneration, trying to pay homage in the best way he or she could, by folding hands, touching his feet, or, when that was not possible, by falling to the ground before him. Afflicted babies were held up by their mothers in front of him. And between the eyebrows of each, the Master applied the sacred ashes from the fire pit.

'Now go home,' he said in a cheerful way. 'The Aswins have cured you.'

The ailing people shouted in exultation as the malady fell away from some of them. The lame began to walk steadily: the blind began to wink their eyes, finding a glimmer of light: the palsied began to totter to their feet. And the many who remained uncured with helpless hands, begged the Master to come to their rescue, in piteous ways. The Sage extended his hands in blessing and said: 'Go home and pray to the Great God who destroys all sufferings.'

The others who saw the miracle shouted: 'Victory to the Master!'

After the confusion caused by the excitement of the

crowd subsided, the disciples served fruits, roots, barley cake and honey on banana leaves to everyone. Most of this food had been brought as presents by those who had come to see the Master; the rest was supplied by Dhaumya from his *ashram.* And as they ate it the Sage went round among them, serving them with whatever they wished and invariably making some friendly remarks.

The Sage, Krishna was informed, never sat down to his meal till all others who had come to him had been served their food first. When every one was served, the Master himself sat down between Krishna and Dhaumya eating the same food as was served to others.

When the meal was over, the Master chanted the words: 'Shantih, Shantih, Shantih' (Peace, Peace, Peace). It was a sign for the others to take their leave of him.

The Master stood up, after washing his hands, folded them and, with his usual parental smile, walked away, while many people rushed to touch his feet.

Krishna had heard many things about the Master, but for the first time he felt humbled, for he found one who was a friend of all and alien to none, and who gave to others, life, both spiritual and physical.

Soon Krishna, Uddhava and Satyaki were installed in a hut near the *rishi's.* After the meal Krishna was called to the hut in which the Master had been housed.

While Krishna sat before the Sage with folded hands, he could not help feeling the magic of his personality. He felt as if he was in the presence of a being from some other world, who knew, understood and loved all men.

The large eyes as they turned to Krishna were full of kindliness. The voice had a liquid note of deep affection. The manner was that of a man deeply interested in all' that one said and did.

'Why did you come to Hastinapura?' asked the Sage.

Krishna told the Sage of his decision to come to Hastinapura; of the shock that he had received when he heard of the death of the Five Brothers; of his talk with Dhritarashtra and Bhishma; and of his impression of Duryodhana and Shakuni.

In the benign presence of the Sage, Krishna, to his surprise, felt that keeping back anything would be a sin, but he was not sure whether he would he justified in sharing the secret which the Empress Satyavati had confided in him.

'I had hopes, venerable Master, to bring the Yadavas nearer to the Kurus. With Yudhishthira in Hastinapura allied to King Ugrasena in Dwaraka, we could have brought King Drupada to overcome his distrust of the Kurus. Then I hoped to bring the three peoples—the Kurus, the Panchalas and the Yadavas—together in a common effort to re-build our life,' said Krishna.

'How did you expect to do that, Vaasudeva?' asked the Sage with a smile of understanding.

'I hoped that the kings, once reconciled, would take to *rajadharma* and lead their people more easily to the way of Dharma,' said Krishna, and added sadly: 'But Yudhishthira is now gone, and my hopes have vanished.'

The Muni's face was wreathed with a broad smile, disclosing his bright flashing teeth. 'Remember, Vaasudeva, Dharma, never dies. You, who destroyed Kamsa and defeated Jarasandha, should be the last to forget that your first duty is to uproot *adharma* wherever it may be.'

'Venerable Master, you are the supreme teacher, and can enlighten me. How can *adharma* be uprooted when Jarasandha flourishes in Magadha, Duryodhana rules in Hastinapura and Drupada nurses bitterness in Kampilya? They live in hatred; they pursue violence. The only Dharma they recognize is satisfying their hatred,' said Krishna, explaining the problem which he found insoluble.

The Sage smiled indulgently. 'If I even thought of things like that, I should never have survived a day. Vaasudeva, when I was young, the Aryas had all but destroyed Aryavarta by internal feuds. The Vedas had been forgotten. The *ashrams* were a wilderness.'

'And you brought back Dharma. How?' asked Krishna.

'I had faith—faith that Dharma is timeless. It may be obscured for a moment, but it never—never—dies,' said the Sage with the confidence of one for whom the infallibility of Dharma was the firm foundation of life.

'But kings like Jarasandha and my uncle Kamsa would destroy it, if they could,' said Krishna.

'I never put my faith in kings. Hate and distrust, fear and jealousy, often guide them,' replied Veda Vyasa.

I put it in the *ashrams*. As I travel from *ashram* to *ashram*, I find most of them to be the homes of *vidya* and *tapas*—knowledge and self-discipline—where *rishis* live in austere poverty and rise above the lures of the flesh, fighting untruth in whatever form it appears.'

'Yes, Master, the *ashrams* owe their faith mainly to your inspiration,' said Krishna.

The Muni spoke reminiscently. 'At first I had to fight single-handed, but the Great God gave the faith to hundreds of *rishis*. These Brahmans, by leading their life in Dharma and enduring sufferings in defence of it, gave it a vitality which even kings had to respect. Look at Dhaumya, for instance. He came here years ago and established this *ashram*. By virtue of his *tapas*, he has brought about a change even in the ways of the Nagas. Aryaka and his people have taken to Arya ways. This was not done by the valour of kings; it was Dhaumya's *tapas* which brought about the change.'

'Is King Aryaka still well and active?' asked Krishna.

'He is very old now,' replied the Sage.

'Tell me, venerable Master, how can Duryodhana be won over to the ways of Dharma?' asked Krishna, as the Gouri Puja orgy came into his mind.

'The God of all gods will see to it in His own good time. We have no right to insist that He must give us what we want *when* we want it,' said the Muni with a smile.

'And now Yudhishthira is gone,' said Krishna.

The Muni smiled. 'Yudhishthira, they say, is dead,'

continued the Master with an inscrutable smile. 'I am sure he is alive, if not in body, at least in spirit.'

Krishna saw the opportunity to find out whether the Sage knew what Satyavati had told him. 'Do you think, venerable Sir, that the Five Brothers are alive?' he asked.

The Sage did not answer the question directly. 'If they are dead, at any rate you are here, Vaasudeva. It is for you to teach the kings the ways of Manu, Vaivasvata and Janaka. You are now going to King Drupada. Try to win him over to the ways of love. The bitterness between the Kurus and the Panchalas must be converted into friendliness. The Panchalas are a great people and devoted to Dharma.'

'Venerable Master, I doubt whether I can help in this matter, but I will try,' said Krishna.

'You are a Kshatriya, Vaasudeva. Act in truth and purity, honour those who live in Dharma and leave the rest to the Great God,' said the Sage.

'The venerable Bhishma said almost the same thing,' said Krishna.

'I wish he had stopped the intrigues of Duryodhana instead of driving the Five Brothers to their death to oblige him,' said the Sage. Then he smiled. 'Each man has to follow truth as he sees it. Bhishma thinks that his life is pledged to keeping the Kurus strong,'

'Yes, I found the venerable Bhishma torn by an inner conflict. The Five Brothers were dear to him, but the strength of the Kurus was dearer,' said Krishna.

'Vaasudeva, put all that is in you into the deed which confronts you and perform it with faith in the Great God,' said the Sage, as Dhaumya came in to take him to the Veda *shala*. 'That is what your life is for, and that is your empire which no king can filch.'

'Give me your blessing, Master,' said Krishna.

'My blessing is always with you. May you always win, Vaasudeva.'

After the evening worship and the meal of fruits and roots which the foresters had brought with them as an offering, they retired for the night. Throughout the night Krishna felt the presence of the Muni by his side.

In the morning, Krishna heard that, before dawn, the Muni and his disciples had left for the interior of the forest to meet the King of Nagas.

'Where is Uddhava?' asked Krishna.

'He has left with the venerable Master', said Satyaki. 'He wants to pay his respectes to King Aryaka, your father's maternal grandfather. He will join us when we reach Utkochaka on our way back.'

'Why did he leave so suddenly?' asked Krishna to find out whether Uddhava had taken Satyaki into his full confidence.

'Perhaps he wants to find out whether the Five Brothers are really dead,' replied Satyaki. 'After his talks with the venerable Veda Vyasa, Uddhava evidently thought that the Master himself was perhaps going on the same mission.'

Krishna smiled. Satyaki was clever.

14

KAMPILYA

$\mathscr{K}$rishna and his party resumed their journey by the river. At Ekachakra Tirtha, with only one stage of the journey to Kampilya left, he was received by Dhrishtadyumna, the *yuvaraja* of Panchala, and its Prime Minister, Acharya Udbodhana. Acharya Shvetaketu, Krishna's friend, who had preceded him to announce his arrival, was also there to receive him.

The guests and the hosts travelled in gaily decorated boats to the capital of Panchala. At intervals they halted at flourishing settlements on the banks of the river, where the residents gave the guests a hearty welcome with drums and fifes and lavish hospitality.

On the journey, Krishna was delighted to find that Dhrishtadyumna was a fine young prince who bore himself with dignity and reserve. He also learnt from him and others how happy and prosperous the Panchalas were under King Drupada's just and benevolent rule. On the way they also came across several *ashrams* of *rishis* whose blessings they received.

When they reached Kampilya, a large and prosperous city, King Drupada turned out to receive

Krishna at the head of the courtiers and a crowd of citizens. Tall, gaunt and bony, he was severe in his manner almost to a fault. However, he had put aside some of his gravity on this occasion in order to give a warm welcome to the guest whose arrival he had been looking forward to for a long time.

Krishna could not help feeling that everyone stood in awesome respect of the royal presence.

'Panchala is very lucky to welcome you here, noble Vaasudeva,' said Drupada in a resounding voice.

'The good fortune is all mine, seeing that I am meeting you, my noble lord,' replied Krishna, as he was locked in the King's embrace before he could touch his feet.

The King invited Krishna to ride with him on an artistically painted and caparisoned elephant. Dhrishtadyumna and his brother Satyajit sat with them, and the courtiers and the guests followed the elephant in chariots. The procession passed through the main street to the palace, the drums beating and the fifes playing a joyous welcome.

The King, Krishna found, spoke little, but whatever he said was charged with intense feeling. He appeared to be well informed about the affairs of the Yadavas; no doubt he had his own sources of information, besides his close contact with Guru Sandipani.

Krishna took to the princes, Dhrishtadyumna and Satyajit. Like their father, they spoke little, but in whatever they said, their outlook was straightforward and their admiration of Krishna genuine. Brought up and trained as soldiers, they scorned every kind of subterfuge.

When they arrived at the palace, Drupada, with evident reluctance, introduced to Krishna a third son of his, Shikhandin by name. He was a shrinking, undersized, but very good-looking boy, almost girlish in his behaviour. The frightened air with which he came forward to salute Krishna was intriguing; Drupada and his two other sons were looking on, apprehensive lest in some way the boy should disturb the cordiality of the occasion.

The ceremonial dinner at which, besides the guests, there were the leading chiefs of Panchala, was a grand event. The food was rich, the arrangements perfect. Music played softly at a distance. The women of the royal family, richly dressed and gorgeously decked out, served food. Among them was Krishnaa, Drupada's daughter.

Krishna was lost in admiration at the splendorous beauty of the Princess, who, fair, tall and graceful, moved in self-assured dignity. Her face reflected the native modesty of a well-born maiden, though her every movement and every gesture expressed a strong will.

In spite of the luxurious richness of the dinner the King as well as the Princes were abstemious in their habits; none of them drank, though every one else did. Shvetaketu whispered in Krishna's ear: 'The King and his sons have forsworn drink till the family vow is redeemed.'

Krishna spent that night thinking of Drupada, of his cultured people and of his apparently well-governed State, of the two Princes who were so upright, and the third who looked so frightened, and of the Princess who was so wondrous.

The next day, after the morning meal, the King invited Krishna to the mango grove behind the palace. Now that they were alone, Drupada knit his brows and for a moment gazed steadfastly at Krishna. Then he raised his greying head and looked Krishna in the face with a wry smile.

'Vaasudeva, I have invited you here to make a very strange offer,' the King said abruptly without any introduction.

Krishna folded his hands. 'I shall be beholden to you, noble Lord, if you tell me what is in your mind.'

Krishna could see the agony which the King was suffering in order to throw off his temperamental reserve and make the suggestion which was uppermost in his mind. But he was trained to exercise rigid self-control over himself, and in a stern voice said: 'Guru Sandipani must have told you about it. Will you take Krishnaa for a wife?' Then he quickly added: 'I feel humiliated at having to make this offer to you myself.'

Krishna himself felt hurt at seeing such a proud and noble person undergoing such distressing humiliation. He looked at him with sympathetic understanding. 'Noble lord, I realise your feelings. Your offer has already been conveyed to me by Guru

Sandipani.' Krishna stopped because he saw a look of disappointment on Drupada's face.

'You will not accept the offer?' the King asked bluntly.

'I do not reject the offer which is so generously made,' said Krishna, giving one of his enchanting smiles. 'Forgive me, noble lord, if I am frank about it. I do not feel equal to it and I hate to be put in a position in which I cannot fulfil the expectations of such a noble king as yourself.'

'Are you afraid of Drona?' asked the King, knitting his brows.

'No, lord, but I would not like to be a cause of war between the Kurus and the Panchalas,' replied Krishna frankly.

'Why?' asked the King abruptly, with suppressed impatience.

'Our Dharma can flourish only if both the Kurus and the Panchalas defend it. If they fight each other in a bitter war, where will we be?' asked Krishna.

'No one ever thought of these things when Drona and his pupils attacked me unprovoked, made me a prisoner, filched my land and drove out my people,' said Drupada bitterly.

'That was wrong,' said Krishna persuasively, trying to overcome the bitterness which was in the King's heart. 'Dronacharya should have forgiven the personal wrong if any was offered to him. Perhaps, being trained in arms, he had forgotten that a Brahman's first duty was to overcome anger. And I am sure Arjuna would

never have treated you, noble lord, in the way he did,
had he not been commanded by his guru.'

For a few moments Drupada looked steadfastly at
the ground. Then he knit his brows again and said in
a determined voice: 'There cannot be any peace between
the Kuru and the Panchalas so long as Drona and his
pupils rule over Hastinapura.' Then he turned to
Krishna and said brusquely: 'If you do not accept my
offer, I will have to seek alliance elsewhere.'

'Noble King, your offer is generous, more than
generous, munificent. But of what use can an alliance
with the Yadavas be to you? If you help us to re-settle
in Mathura, instead of our being helpful to you, we will
bring upon you the wrath of Emperor Jarasandha,' said
Krishna, smiling persuasively.

Drupada obstinately shook his head. 'We are fairly
strong. If Jarasandha invades Panchala, Bhishma, in
his own interest, might come to our rescue—Drona or
no Drona. But I do not want his help. I do not care it.
If you accept my offer, I can defy them both,' said
Drupada firmly.

'Would it not be better if we brought about an
understanding with Grandfather Bhishma, irrespective
of Jarasandha?' asked Krishna.

'You are mistaken, Vaasudeva, in thinking so. You
do not know how powerful Drona is in Hastinapura. He
will have no settlement with me. Nor will I have with
him,' said Drupada.

'If only the Five Brothers had been alive!' suggested
Krishna.

'It would have made no difference. The Five Brothers would never have become friendly to me. They were very loyal to Drona, and even if they had been inclined to be friendly with me, Drona would have seen to it that Duryodhana destroyed them,' said the King and added: 'I have heard that Bhishma had to banish them—nay, send them to their deaths—because Duryodhana had become irresistible on account of Drona's support.'

Krishna saw how shrewd the King was, in spite of his bitterness. He was right. The Five Brothers would never have been banished from Hastinapura if Drona had given them full support. Aswatthama was Duryodhana's friend; Drona could have insisted on his son withdrawing his support. He could have thrown his weight on the side of Yudhishthira. But he did not. The thing became clear to his mind.

'I have met Grandfather Bhishma,' replied Krishna. 'He agreed to send the Five Brothers to Varanavata to avoid a conflict with the Kurus.'

'Well, that only shows that you do not know Drona, that is all,' said Drupada bluntly.

'I confess it is a difficult situation,' said Krishna, appreciating the dilemma in which King Drupada found himself. 'Noble lord, anyway I cannot be of much use. I cannot live all the time on the banks of the Ganga and the Yamuna. The Yadavas will not leave Dwaraka. And I will not go to war with the Kurus. If I did so, it would be against my Dharma!'

'What is your Dharma?' Drupada asked bluntly.

'To help righteousness—particularly in Kings,' replied Krishna. 'For, an unrighteous king is the cause of chaos.'

Drupada flared up and his pent-up fury was let loose in a flow of words. 'Vaasudeva, I have never done an unrighteous action. I have stood for Dharma all my life. I have honoured Brahmans; I have protected the ancient ways; I have looked to the happiness of my people; I have seen to it that no one starves in my kingdom.' The King opened his heart to Krishna, and his thoughts were now seeking expression before his sympathetic listener. 'If you come to my help, we will be able to consolidate Aryavarta in the ways of our ancestors.'

'I still fail to see how the Panchalas would gain by an alliance with the Yadavas who are far away and could not render much help,' said Krishna.

'I want you to be with me, Vaasudeva. Then I can be strong enough to fight *adharma*. Drona supporting Duryodhana and his brothers in Hastinapura is a danger to Dharma. If you accept my offer, Panchala will be strong. Then Bhishma may see the wisdom of making a peaceful alliance with me by getting rid of Drona,' said Drupada.

'Is there no way to change Drona?' asked Krishna.

Drupada laughed bitterly. 'To change Drona! I have known him from the time we were boys. He is conceited, unforgiving, implacable. He would fire the whole world if it suited him.'

'Perhaps you are very harsh, noble King,' remarked

Krishna. 'Even the wickedest man has a small corner for a noble impulse in his heart.'

'It only shows that you have not met a man like Drona in your life. Shall I take it that you reject my offer?' asked the King.

Krishna shook his head. 'I have yet to see my way to accept your offer, noble King.'

King Drupada was sorry at having let himself go before a youngster, and pulled himself up. 'Well, if you do not accept my offer, I must think of other ways.'

'Certainly you can choose any husband you like for the Princess,' said Krishna.

'I may accept Jarasandha's offer,' said Drupada, watching Krishna's reaction keenly, for he knew that Jarasandha was his lifelong enemy.

'Jarasandha's offer!' exclaimed Krishna in surprise.

'Yes. He has sent an offer for the hand of Draupadi for his grandson, Meghasandhi. With him on my side, I can overrun the Kurus,' said Drupada.

'Noble lord, have you any idea what an alliance with Jarasandha means? You know the fate of Damaghosha of Chedi and Bhishmaka of Vidarbha. An alliance with Jarasandha spells death. He is living in *adharma*,' said Krishna.

'Do you think Duryodhana will be different, once Bhishma goes to the Land of Yama?' asked Drupada, as he showed his intention of terminating the interview. 'Anyway, I will keep to my vow, whatever happens,' he added decisively.

'Forgive me, noble lord, for asking: if Krishnaa accepts Jarasandha's grandson for a husband, will she be happy with him?' asked Krishna.

'Find out for yourself. I have no objection to your meeting her. She also thinks that my pledge can only be redeemed if you accept her,' said Drupada.

Krishna was visibly moved. 'Noble lord, I am overwhelmed by the confidence which all of you repose in me. I want to do everything to help you, but I must see that the way I take is right. But can you be so carried away by your bitterness, noble lord,—forgive me if I am frank—to sacrifice the happiness of your daughter and wed her to the cruel old Emperor's grandson?' asked Krishna.

'We have no loves and hates, Vaasudeva. We have only one aim in life, and that is to punish Drona for the wrong he has done me and my people. We all live for it. We are prepared to sacrifice every feeling to win that end,' said Drupada.

'But, noble lord, would you not be sacrificing the happiness of a noble young woman by making her live with Meghasandhi for all her life? I shudder at the very idea,' said Krishna.

'I understand my daughter very well. She is at one with me. She would immolate herself in the fire, if by that we could secure our end. And who knows how Meghasandhi will turn out as a husband? A good wife can change any husband,' said Drupada.

'Oh, noble lord, where will all this end?' asked Krishna with a sigh.

'It will end in the destruction of Drona,' said Drupada firmly. You have doubts whether Draupadi will willingly sacrifice herself for this end. Will you meet her? Perhaps then you can see your way. She is a brave young woman. I wish she was a son,' said Drupada with a sigh.

'Certainly, I will meet her, if those are your commands,' said Krishna.

'I will call Dhrishtadyumna. He will take you to her,' said Drupada.

As they rose to go, they heard the faint sound of retreating feet. Drupada listened, grew pale with irritation and bit his lips. Someone was eavesdropping! Then he led his guest into the palace where Dhrishtadyumna and the minister were waiting.

As he glanced back, Krishna could see the youngest prince, Shikhandin, hurriedly crossing the mango grove.

It was this Prince who had been eavesdropping—to the annoyance of the King! Evidently there was a mystery about this unwanted child.

Krishna was moved by the impact of Drupada's personality.

When he had started for Dwaraka, he had only wanted to establish contact with the great powers in the North, to be able to fulfil his Dharma in relation to the situation in the Arya world. Now, unexpectedly, he found himself in a maze of powerful hates and passions.

Krishna told Shvetaketu and Satyaki, when they were by themselves, of what had passed between him and King Drupada, and added: 'We are flung into a vortex of *adharma*.

'Why is it a vortex of *adharma?*' asked Satyaki, who loved to look on the bright side of things.

'Because it is sucking every one of us into a whirlpool of hate' explained Krishna. 'How one little act of hate affects everyone! A foolish young prince insults a foolish young Brahman. The young ascetic is filled with hate. He spends his life training his pupils so that the insult may be avenged. To achieve his end, he—untrue to the Brahmanical canons of conduct—humiliates a good and noble king. Mortified, the king resolves to destroy the powerful Brahman, makes hatred the passion of his life and brings up his children to live for it. The ascetic, now a great warrior, wields power in Hastinapura only to satisfy his passion nourished by hate. The King, here, wants to build up his power to crush him. The Panchalas and the Kurus are estranged; they may soon be drawn into a fratricidal war. Now we are in it.'

'Are you not drawing conclusions too rashly?' asked Shvetaketu. 'The Yadavas won't be drawn into it unless we want to be.'

'No, Shvetaketu. If I accept Drupada's offer, the Yadavas will be drawn into the whirlpool. If I do not, King Drupada will barter away his freedom to Jarasandha. Then the whirlpool will grow larger, more destructive, and we will be drawn into it all the same, whether we want to be or not,' said Krishna.

'Then let us go back and leave this whirlpool to its fate. We are happy at Dwaraka as we are,' said Satyaki.

'It is not so simple as that, Satyaki,' said Krishna thoughtfully. 'If we go back to Dwaraka and refuse to have anything to do with this world of hate, we may be saved for a time, but destruction is sure to come to Aryavarta. The edifice of Dharma, which our ancestors have built for the benefit of the world, will be doomed. Violence and hate will spread everywhere. Chaos will overwhelm us in the end.'

'How can it affect us if we remain aloof from the North altogether?' asked Satyaki.

'No, Satyaki, we cannot isolate hate. We can only live by trying to conquer it. Perhaps, in doing so, we may have to face extinction. We will have preferred death to running away from the mission which the Gods gave us. But then at any rate we will have left a mighty tradition of Dharma behind us. Then some day a new saviour will arise and carry on our work,' said Krishna.

'What do you suggest we should do?' asked Shvetaketu.

'I see no light at present. Perhaps I may see it after I meet the Princess,' said Krishna.

Satyaki, in his boyish way, laughed. 'We cannot find light from the Best of Munis—nor from King Drupada. Now we are seeking it from a young and beautiful woman. Lord, you have remained the same as you were in Vrindavan.'

Krishna laughed merrily too and said: 'Satyaki, light comes from the humblest of teacher if the pupil is in earnest. And it more often comes from a forthright woman than a wise man. I am going to Draupadi to find light.'

'Please, lord, do not take her as a consort. Her life is wrapped up in hate,' said Satyaki.

'Don't lose faith, Satyaki. If Draupadi remains wrapped up in hate after I meet her, it is I who will have failed. But I want to believe what you friends have been telling everybody—though it is just flattery, I know— "Wherever there is Krishna, there is Dharma— *Yato Krishnah Tato Dharmah—*",' said Krishna.

In the evening, Dhrishtadyumna, anxiety-ridden, came over with profuse apologies. That evening, the King would not be able to join the guests. He had been suddenly taken ill. Dhrishtadyumna also begged to be excused. An important embassy from King Hiranyavarma, the father-in-law of his youngest brother Shikhandin, had arrived for important consultations. The matter was very urgent. Would the noble guest excuse his absence too?

Krishna could see that the embassy had come on a disquieting mission, and he himself pleaded the need for a day's respite. However, he wondered what the matter could be. There was clearly a mystery which surrounded Shikhandin. But that was no concern of his.

15

THE LOYAL DAUGHTER

*O*n the morning of the next day, Dhrishtadyumna, who showed signs of having passed a sleepless night, came to invite Krishna to the mango grove to meet Draupadi.

Taking his scarf, Krishna put on his diadem and went to meet Krishnaa, the Princess of Panchala.

The Princess, with her brothers Dhrishtadyumna and Satyajit—again Shikhandin was absent, Krishna noted—took a seat opposite Krishna's, offering him a respectful salutation. She looked down modestly, gracefully bending her head decked with flowers.

'It is rather contrary to custom, noble Princess of Panchala, that I should meet you thus. But the noble King wanted me to do so,' said Krishna.

Draupadi looked up and fixed her large beautiful eyes on Krishna. Then, in a low, hesitant voice she said: 'I told my father to let me meet you, though it was forward for a well-born maiden to do so.' And she added with a bluntness, possibly inherited from her father, which, however, was entirely out of keeping with her modest behaviour: 'I wanted to ask you myself whether you would come to our help.'

Krishna was lost in admiration at the frankness of this young woman and smiled in his irresistible way. 'Noble Princess, your father and you are both so gracious that I cannot refuse you anything,' he said. 'But will you tell me why you choose me for the privilege of helping you?'

'We have been thinking of you for the last two years,' intervened Dhrishtadyumna, 'in fact, since you led the Yadavas to Saurashtra.'

'How can I help? The Yadavas are far away— perhaps not very strong. And I am not a king', said Krishna.

'You are more than a king. You are a god, so rumour says. Anyway, you are the one warrior among Aryas whom all respect,' said Draupadi with downcast eyes but in a voice of deep conviction.

Again Krishna admired the boldness with which so young and modest a woman faced the problem which confronted her father.

'Guru Sandipani has been telling us all about you, noble Vaasudeva,' interrupted Dhrishtayumna. 'Even Jarasandha, he said, is afraid of you,'

'Gurudev is always kind to me', said Krishna. 'But what noble Drupada demands of me is beyond me. I can't fight Drona, for I won't fight the Kurus.'

A cloud of disappointment crossed Draupadi's glowing face. Her lips were trembling. She looked at the ground intently for some moments and heaved a sigh. 'Then you won't come to our help?' she asked almost inaudibly.

Krishna was moved by the pathetic tone in which she spoke and the tears that were gathering in her beautiful eyes. 'I can and will help the noble lord,' said Krishna 'but not in the way you all want me to.' To destroy the deep faith which the whole royal family had come to have in him would, he felt, be cowardice, it would be a failure to face the tremendous task which his Dharma set him.

'They say that you live to vindicate Dharma,' said Draupadi slowly. 'We only want you to vindicate it, by helping us. Do you know how brutally we were treated by Drona?' she asked, looking at him with some renewed hope in her voice.

'I know a little, but not everything,' remarked Krishna.

'Then I will tell you,' said Draupadi, as she looked up bravely into his face. 'My father had been celebrating a festival at Ahichhatra. He had just come out of the shrine after worshipping the God of gods, surrounded by pious Brahmans. Drona and his pupils encircled the unarmed crowd in the very precincts of the temple, against the canons of Dharma. Arjuna took aim from a distant tree. With one arrow he brought my father's crown to the ground: with another he cut his right ear-ring into two; with a third, he wounded him in the leg. Before my Father could take up his bow he fell. The people who surrounded him fled out of fright. Then Bhima and Arjuna bound my Father—the noblest king in Aryavarta—and dragged him to Drona, as if he was a thief.' The Princess stopped speaking, her beautiful eyes flaming with indignation, her breast heaving.

Krishna waited in silence for her to continue.

'My Father would not have taken it to heart if Arjuna and he had fought each other as warriors should. But Drona did not have it in him to fight a battle. He wanted to take my Father by surprise, to humiliate him before his people, to force him to crawl before him. Ultimately, my Father was set free only after he had offered an apology for having broken his promise and had relinquished some of our lands. Even then Drona was not satisfied. He took possession of our lands, robbed our men of whatever they had, and drove them out, starving and helpless.'

Draupadi was not narrating an old story; she was recounting the drama of her father's humiliation as if she saw it in her imagination at the moment. And as she re-lived the events, her voice quivered with anger, her eyes were afire and her face glowed. Then she abruptly controlled herself and stopped for a while.

'You tell us, Vaasudeva, that you won't help us in the way my Father asks you to. But we all want it the way he wants it,' said Draupadi, looking up with pride as she defended her father.

Krishna could understand the feeling of the Princess, and smiled appreciatively.

After a little pause, Draupadi continued: 'Vaasudeva, you don't know my Father. He has always lived a righteous life. He has been a father to his people. He has never harboured malice against anyone.'

A look of deep affection came into Draupadi's eyes. 'But he cannot forget the bitter moments when Bhima and Arjuna tied him and led him to the feet of Drona. From that moment, he has been different, we have all been different. For months thereafter, my Father felt so terribly hurt that he would have, out of shame, flung himself into the Ganga. But we, his motherless children, whom he had brought up with more than a mother's care, promised him to avenge the insult.' She looked up with resolution: 'And we shall avenge it.'

Krishna saw the glowing cheeks, met the eyes of fire and heard the vibrant voice—they all told of a rare filial devotion. He almost felt as if he was in the presence of a divine being. 'Noble Princess, your devotion to your father is beautiful,' he said.

Draupadi looked up at Krishna to see whether he was being sarcastic, but was relieved to observe the generous impulse which had led him to express his admiration. 'My Father gave us life. We are ready to give it up for him,' she said.

'If I do not agree to help, have you decided to accept Jarasandha's offer?' asked Krishna.

'My Father has discussed that matter with us also,' replied Dhrishtadyumna. 'If you refuse help, we will accept Jarasandha's offer. If Draupadi is married to his grandson Meghasandhi, the allied armies will be led by my Father against the Kurus.'

'And Aryavarta will be in flames,' said Krishna with a smile.

'Aryavarta was reduced to ashes when so saintly a king as my Father was captured in *adharma* and made to fall at the feet of that proud Brahman,' said Draupadi bitterly.

'Where was Bhishma then, who calls himself the pillar of righteousness? Where was Dhritarashtra, the King of the Kurus, who claims descent from *Chakravarti* Bharata? They all gave a welcome to Drona at Hastinapura, as if he had conquered a mighty *chakravartin* in battle,' she added.

Krishna was lost in thought. He could not help being drawn to this noble-hearted maiden. 'Suppose I promise help—and fail?' he asked.

Draupadi's face suddenly broke into a smile. 'We know all about you, Vaasudeva. You will never fail.'

'Why do you feel so?' asked Krishna, smiling in return.

'Drona has two pupils whose bows are gifted with miraculous powers—Arjuna and Karna. Guru Sandipani has only one pupil, Vaasudeva, whose *Sharnga* is more destructive than the *Triyambaka* of Lord Shiva Himself,' said Draupadi.

'That is all an exaggeration. As I told you, the Guru is very fond of praising me', said Krishna.

'If you fail, we are prepared to accept failure,' said Draupadi with candour.

'Will you accept my help even if I don't accept the offer of your hand?' asked Krishna

'Don't you like me? Am I so unfit to be your wife?' asked Draupadi, throwing a mischievous glance at Krishna.

'You know I am a cowherd and not fit to be a princess's husband. And I hate the way princesses are bartered away to secure alliances. Marriage is not a matter of commerce', said Krishna. Then he added: 'Let us not talk of marriage. You will be free to choose whom you like, regardless of your Father's pledge. But this I promise; I shall stand by noble Drupada—and you—if you take me as your own.'

They all stopped talking. Drupada was walking towards them in great agitation, his face grimmer than ever.

'Dhrishtadyumna,' he said in a voice choking with anger. 'Shikhandin has disappeared!'

Dhrishtadyumna, Draupadi and Satyajit stood up in excitement, 'What?''

'Shikhandin is gone. No one knows where,' replied Drupada. 'I have had a search made in all possible places. He has left no trace.'

Drupada sat down on the platform built round a big tree, his hand to his forehead. 'I wish he was never born,' he muttered.

Krishna out of delicacy, quietly withdrew.

The beautiful picture of Drupada's family, united in affection, remained vividly in Krishna's mind: the father, stern and parental, feeling amazed; Draupadi, sitting at his feet, with her hands on his knee, looking into his eyes; Dhrishtadyumna, standing by his side protectively; Satyajit, looking at his father in distress—all united in affection and purpose.

Shikhandin, the frightened prince, Krishna thought, was the wayward child of this proud family and his sudden disappearance was both a shock and a relief, because he presented an insoluble problem to them.

Krishna's heart warmed towards Drupada and his children. In spite of their being steeped in hatred, there was a nobility about each one of them, which it would be difficult to find in all the members of a royal family.

Krishna thought of his conversation with Draupadi. Because of it, he had to take a decision to commit himself to a definite course of action.

The situation was difficult and complicated. At any time it might turn into a conflagration. Bitterness had entered the hearts of Drupada and his children. The ambitious and proud Drona was not likely to become friendly towards them.

Hatred equally dominated Duryodhana and his friends—hatred for the Five Brothers, hatred of all those who stood in the way of their self-willed course.

Duryodhana was certainly a problem. He was at Kurukshetra for the moment, but when he returned to Hastinapura after three or four months, he as Crown Prince of the Kurus, would be in a formidable position. Advised by Shakuni and supported by Dronacharya, he might even celebrate his assumption of office by a military adventure against the Panchalas.

Any conflict between the Kurus and the Panchalas, as things were at that time, would be to play into the hands of Jarasandha. He would immediately overrun Kashi and march into Panchala.

A crisis was developing. He could not, Krishna thought, run away from it. He must play his part, whatever it might cost. This possible conflict might be postponed, if not avoided, by creating a new situation. Of such a solution, Drupada alone could be the key.

Anyway he should be prevented from aligning himself with Jarasandha or any other ambitious prince. Possibly he could conquer his bitterness if he could develop such power as would make the humiliation inflicted on him by Dronacharya cease to be the real passion of his life any longer. Krishna's mind was made up.

The next day Drupada, his sternness a little subdued by the misfortune which had overtaken the family, asked Krishna what decision he had come to after he had met his daughter.

Krishna replied: 'Lord, I have met the noble Princess, your daughter. I have promised her that if you are willing, I am ready to help you as best as I can.'

'Vaasudeva, I was sure that after meeting her you would come to our help,' said Drupada, his face showing the pale semblance of a smile. 'She is a wonderful girl, this daughter of mine'.

'I will be frank with you, lord. I shall help you in every way to redeem your pledge. I shall stand by you so long as you consider me as you friend. But please, I beg of you, don't ask me to marry the Princess,' said Krishna.

'If you pledge yourself to stand by us, why don't you marry her? She is willing,' said Drupada.

'She is the greatest jewel among princesses. If she likes, she can marry the most redoubtable warrior in Aryavarta. But such a warrior must be ready to marry her,' said Krishna with an enigmatic smile.

'You do not choose her as your wife?' asked Drupada with a toss of his head. His pride was evidently hurt.

'Do not misunderstand me, lord,' said Krishna. 'I would not allow her to choose a husband because he is clever enough to kill warriors in battle. But she has made up her mind. She wants to marry the best warrior in Aryavarta. I will, therefore, help her to fulfil her pledge in the way she likes.'

Drupada felt that Krishna was equivocating, lapsed into his severe mood, knit his brow and asked: 'Then you refuse to help us?'

'No. I would be yours, no matter whom she marries,' replied Krishna.

'Even if she marries Jarasandha's grandson?' asked Drupada.

'You, noble lord, have the final decision about the choice of her husband', replied Krishna. 'If I were you, I would choose a husband for her regardless of your desire to avenge the insult and marry her to a noble prince who fully deserves her.'

These distinctions were beyond Drupada. 'What if she prefers to marry you?' he asked.

'Noble King, let us not forget what her heart is set on at the present moment. She has taken a pledge to marry a man who can vanquish Drona's pupils in war. She must have such a one as her husband and will be happy with no other,' said Krishna.

'That is true', said Drupada.

'Then may I suggest to you that you hold a swayamvara for her?' asked Krishna.

'Swayamvaras are getting out of fashion among us. Most of them are mere formalities now,' said Drupada.

'And there is no saying that such a *swayamvara*, will reveal the best warrior in Aryavarta.'

'Why not hold a true *swayamvara*, such as was held by our ancestors in the past?' said Krishna, lowering his voice. 'Let the noble King set up a real test and let the Princess marry the warrior who proves to be the best archer in Aryavarta.'

The idea of a *swayamvara* took Drupada by surprise. He took some time to realise its implication. 'But you are the best archer in Aryavarta,' he said.

'I am not sure. The race of master bowmen is not extinct amongst us,' said Krishna with a smile. 'But why even select me behind the backs of others? Invite as many princes as you can. Put them to a severe test and let the Princess choose as her husband the one who succeeds at it.'

With his chin on hand, Drupada tried to understand the implications of this proposal. Its possibilities were dawning on his mind.

Krishna continued: 'Most of the powerful kings and expert warriors, who are desirous of aligning themselves with you, will come to the *swayamvara*. In this way you will be the center of power on that occasion. You will acquire more allies. You will not alienate anyone, for you will have the credit of being fair to all. In the end you will emerge stronger, I assure you.' Then he laughed aloud and said: 'If you selected me now as your son-in-law to secure an alliance, many princes would be your enemies.'

Drupada thought for a while. 'But if no one is able to stand up to the test?' he asked.

'Then naturally, lord you and the noble princess can choose any of the princes gathered in the *swayamvara*,' said Krishna.

'And supposing she chooes you?' asked Drupada with a smile. His mind was diverted from the hatred of Drona as he thought of possibilities of holding a *swayamvara* and making friends.

'If I am not able to win the test, I will certainly not be fit to marry Draupadi, for she wants a redoubtable warrior as her husband,' said Krishna with a responsive smile, and added: 'Anyway the Yadavas would be on your side and I would keep my pledge.'

Drupada sat silent for a little while, thinking hard. Then he spoke slowly. 'Vaasudeva, the *swayamvara* that you suggest is sure to enhance my power'.

Then he looked at Krishna in a new light. His proffered friendship, without seeking anything in return, was a challenge to his own innate goodness and sense of honour. For a moment, he forgot the bitterness which was in his heart and was lost in genuine admiration for this young man. He said: 'Vaasudeva, give me one promise. You will remain my friend, whatever happens— even if Meghasandhi or Duryodhana or Shishupala wins the contest'.

'Yes, I promise,' replied Krishna. 'But I assure you that it will not be easy, for any of them.'

'Why do you say so?' asked Drupada.

'If you permit me, noble King, I will leave Acharya Shvetaketu to arrange the *swayamvara* for you. When Guru Sandipani comes here, he will decide upon the nature of the archery test,' said Krishna, and added: 'But no one must know till the last minute that the choice is to depend upon a test in archery.'

'You want them to remain under the impression that Krishnaa will be free to choose any one she likes? That would be deceit,' said Drupada.

'Why? Is not the bride in a *swayamvara* free to decide for herself even at the last moment what her husband's merit should be?' asked Krishna.

'Yes, she is,' replied Drupada.

'Well, the noble Princess can make up her mind before the assembled kings and declare how she will choose her husband,' said Krishna.

Drupada heaved a sigh. 'I do not know, Vaasudeva, why I have come to acquire such confidence in you in so few days or whether I am doing the right thing in accepting your advice. But somehow I am inclined to accept it, if you will stand by your promise that you will help me to redeem my pledge.'

'Noble lord, if the *swayamvara* goes well, as I think it will, you will have grown so powerful that you will have avenged your humiliation without striking a blow. You will win the best marksman among the Aryas as your son-in-law. His friends will then be your friends also. Those who are frustrated will have no reason to complain,' said Krishna.

'And the Yadavas will come too?' asked Drupada.

'Yes, all of us will come with Balarama at our head to stand by you. And Drona, in spite of the Kurus being here to help him, will no longer be worth a thought', said Krishna.

Drupada frowned, 'This is not redeeming my pledge,' he said, lapsing into his dour mood.

'Noble King, don't be impatient,' said Krishna. 'Your pledge is to avenge the humiliation inflicted upon you. What better way is there to redeem your pledge than gathering strength to reduce Drona to insignificance?'

Drupada was impressed at the tone in which the remark was made. The handsome, boyish face, strangely transformed, expressed power. The eyes bespoke a stern resolve. And he was convinced.

'Then are you sure that my vow will be redeemed?' asked Drupada.

'I am sure. I will remain pledged to see it fulfilled,' replied Krishna.

'Will you enter the lists in the *swayamvara?*' asked Drupada. His mind was still fixed on winning Krishna as a son-in-law.

'If I am so minded, not otherwise,' replied Krishna. 'But I assure you, whoever stands the test will be the best archer on earth.'

It was difficult for Drupada to fathom the working of the young Yadava's mind. Suddenly a vista of vast power opened up before him. He felt that, if his guest's plan come to be followed, he would be in a better position to redeem his pledge than if be continued wallowing in bitterness as at present. He looked gratefully at Krishna.

'Vaasudeva, I will hold the *swayamvara* as you

suggest. I am going to repose complete trust in you. I can lose nothing if your plan fails,' said Drupada.

Krishna smiled. 'If the plan fails, I will be the only man who will have lost everything.'

'Lost everything!' exclaimed Drupada.

'I will have lost you as a friend. I will have broken my promise to Draupadi. I will have humiliated the Yadavas in the eyes of the princes of the world,' said Krishna, and added as if speaking to himself: 'What is Krishna after all? He is what he is because he has never failed in his Dharma.'

With a rare onrush of emotion, Drupada put his two hands on Krishna's shoulders. 'Vaasudeva, I will leave everything to you. Give any instructions that you like to Udbodhana and Shvetaketu.'

'Will you accept one more piece of advice from me?' asked Krishna.

'What is it?' enquired Drupada.

'Announce tomorrow that you will be holding the *swayamvara* next year in the month of Chaitra,' said Krishna.

Drupada's face flushed with enthusiasm. 'Yes, I will,' he said, and smiled.

∎

16

UDDHAVA AMONG THE NAGAS

*U*ddhava was by temperament slow at making decisions, but when occasion demanded it, he could make one and follow it up by prompt action.

The moment Krishna told him that the Five Brothers were believed to have escaped death, Uddhava made up his mind to pay a visit to his father's maternal grandfather, King Aryaka, the Naga lord of the forests between the Ganga and the Yamuna, who alone could help in finding out the fate which had overtaken the Five Brothers after they had escaped from the burning palace at Varanavata.

When he met the Master in Dhaumya's *ashram,* he somehow felt that the Sage, who himself was proceeding to Nagakoota, the capital of Aryaka, could provide the key to the mystery. So, late at night, after Krishna had retired, he sought the Sage's permission to accompany him, which was readily granted.

The Sage's party, which Uddhava joined, consisting of ten disciples headed by Acharya Jaimini, besides a few Naga chiefs, travelled in boats, and reached Ekachakra Tirtha after three days.

Uddhava soon found that the presence of the Sage
had a powerful influence over the Aryas and the Nagas
as well as the Nishadas.

On the way, wherever the news of his arrival had
preceded him, the villagers gathered on the bank of the
river to welcome him. At times, on their pressing request
the Sage even stepped down from his boat and received
the homage and gifts of the hospitable villagers, most
of whom were Nagas.

Wherever they were invited to halt for the night, the
Sage presided over the *homa* which his disciples
performed. Led by Jaimini, whose rich voice sent waves
of inspiration surging forth, they chanted the Vedic
mantras and invoked the gods. Then, as in the *ashram*
of Dhaumya, the ailing and the maimed were either
cured or taught to pray to the Aswins, the twin gods of
cure, for their recovery. The Sage with his own hand
distributed food to those who had assembled, and gave
them his blessing. And as he came, he left, giving the
people a new life of hope.

From Ekachakra, the Sage, who was the guest of
the King there, and his party proceeded on foot through
the forest to Nagakoota, the Naga chiefs acting as his
guides. On the way also, crowds of Nagas came to touch
the feet of the Sage and received his blessing.

From his infancy, Uddhava had heard the name of
Veda Vyasa, the Best of Munis, spoken with reverence.
Now, for the first time, he saw with his own eyes the
magic of his presence and the depth of affectionate
reverence which he evoked. For years, the Sage had
been going up and down the Ganga and the Yamuna

visiting the *ashrams* as well as the settlements of both the Aryas and the Nagas, inspiring the *rishis* and their disciples to live a life of high ideals according to the strict Arya code, bringing the Nagas nearer the Aryas wherever he could; allaying their distress and stilling hostilities; conferring his blessing on all the people who came to him and curing the ailing and maimed; above all, giving all in distress a new zest for life which flowed from the love which he had for everyone who came to him.

After four days' journey on foot, they came to Nagakoota, the capital of King Aryaka. Large crowds of Nagas headed by King Aryaka and his grandson, Prince Karkotaka, had come to the outskirts to welcome the Sage.

The old King, now over a hundred years old, came in a litter. A body of skin and bones, thin hands, palsied legs, a shrunken face like a death mask, wide open yellowish eyes which watched every one, a brain still alert, a tongue which on occasions could lash out, and a terrific will—these formed the relics of what was once the great Naga King, whose word was law in the forests which lay between the valleys of the Ganga and Yamuna.

The King had survived his six wives and eleven sons and numerous grandchildren, and, though a living corpse, dominated the life of the Nagas, who looked upon him with a curious mixture of affection and awe. He was one-third a King and two-thirds a god, for he was believed to receive direct messages from Lord Pashupati, the guardian deity of the Nagas.

When the Sage introduced Uddhava to him as the grandson of his daughter Marishaa, the old King asked him to come to him, embraced him warmly and entrusted him to the care of his great-grandson Prince Maniman, son of Prince Karkotaka, his eldest grandson, who was the ruler.

Karkotaka and Maniman were both fine-looking warriors of the Naga race, one of about fifty and the other of about twenty-five. Their bodies were painted with red and white stripes. They wore feathered head-dresses, and each carried a shield and spear as a royal Naga should.

Uddhava had been to the Land of the Nagas beyond the seas when he had gone with Krishna to rescue Punardatta, the son of Guru Sandipani, but so far he had never been among the Nagas from whom his father's mother had come. He was, therefore, delighted to meet them.

On their way back to the settlement, Aryaka insisted on Uddhava walking by his litter, on both sides of which went the priests of Pashupati, with their shaven heads and their long staffs in their hands. On the way King Aryaka asked Uddhava whether he knew how his grandfather, Shoora, came to marry his daughter, Princess Marishaa. When Uddhava replied that he did not, the King told him the story with an old man's garrulity.

It was in the old, old days, said Aryaka, when the Yadava tribes of Vrishni, Shoora and Andhaka had been clearing the forests on the banks of the Yamuna to establish a home for themselves.

Shoora was a bold chief. Once he went hunting and in the forests was attacked by a pack of wolves. He would have been killed by the beasts but for the timely arrival of a party of Naga chiefs, who rescued him.

Shoora had received severe injuries and was unconscious. The Naga chiefs brought him to where he, Aryaka, was camping.

'I immediately saw that Shoora was a brave chief and took him into my own hut, and my family nursed him back to health, said Aryaka. 'Marishaa—she was my eldest daughter—attended on Shoora during his illness,' continued the King. 'She was a fine woman, bright, vivacious and bold. She had a serpentine grace. Marishaa decided to become the wife of Shoora, and, when Shoora recovered, he was also captivated as much by her attentions as by her charms.'

Aryaka paused for a while and continued: 'When the Yadava chiefs came to take Shoora away, he went with them, but left his heart with Marishaa. Once he had fully recovered, he returned to me and asked for Marishaa's hand in marriage. His Yadavas were angry at first; they were a very proud people. But Shoora was a brave man. He came with me to Nagakoota, married Marishaa and took her away to his people.'

The old King paused for breath and then added reminiscently: 'Oh, it was a great occasion, and the Nagas and the Yadavas held high festivities. And my Marishaa was a fine woman. She became the mother of many brave sons and beautiful daughters,' he added proudly.

'Did you ever go to Mathura?' asked Uddhava.

'Your grandfather was not settled in Mathura when he married Marishaa. Later I went to Shoora's home in Mathura only once. That was when his eldest son, your uncle Vasudeva, was born,' said the King.

These Nagas were simple, unsophisticated folk, who lived in brick houses or mud huts and, except for the barley and gram which grew effortlessly in their fields, on what the forest yielded—fruits and roots, and the fare which the birds and animals of the forest provided.

Men and women went bare-bodied except for a short piece of cloth wrapped round their lower limbs. At first Uddhava was shocked to see the women with their bosoms exposed, freely mixing with men—an unpardonable sin amongst the Aryas.

They were a happy-go-lucky people, not venomous as reports stated. Their cattle was meagre. They only cared for goats, sheep and donkeys which they had in abundance.

Uddhava also found the Nagas easy-going. Their priests did not hesitate to give a hearty welcome to Sage Veda Vyasa. They also worshipped their Great God, Pashupati, in their own way, with water and flowers and leaves, but had no objection to the Sage and his disciples worshipping alongside them in the characteristic Arya way of setting up the sacrificial fire.

When the Sage performed the daily *homa* in the open-air shrine of Pashupati with Vedic chants, the priests were happy to sit by his side and listen very reverently. Even their magic priests betrayed no jealousy when the Sage, cured the ailing and the maimed. And throughout, King Aryaka sat in a litter by his side, his uncommonly wide eyes fixed intently on him.

Possibly this was the secret of the Sage's magic, thought Uddhava. Wherever he went, he created in people an instantaneous desire to come to him, to have him in their midst and to worship him. So, whenever he came to Ekachakra, the King insisted on his visiting Nagakoota. In the company of the Sage, he always recaptured a part of his old vitality, and his large family somehow felt a little more united. His people also felt as if he was one of their elders. No one thought that his race and ways and worship were alien.

Day after day, a huge crowd came from long distances to have the Sage's *darshan*. Every day the *homa* was ritually performed. Milk pots were distributed; a sacred leaf was put into each of them. The ailing and the maimed drank the milk in hope and faith. There was a rush to get the Sage to apply sacred ashes to their foreheads. Then a miracle followed.

Some, who had lost the use of their eyes, saw. Others, whose legs, had been palsied, began to walk. Some, who used to fall rolling to the ground, had the demons driven out of them. A huge feast was then held at which the Sage served with his own hands. And as later he took his seat with Aryaka and Karkotaka a great shout of joy went up in the Sage's honour.

The report had gone round that Uddhava was the grandson of Princess Marishaa. So, to his extreme embarrassment, he found himself surrounded by Naga chiefs, dressed in war paint and feathered head-dresses, and carrying spears. The elders patted him on the back. Others gazed at him in warm admiration.

The younger chiefs were particularly fascinated with his diadem, his well-shaped, unpainted body, and the large bow which he carried—a strangely accoutered stranger and yet of their own blood.

The Naga women also gave him an effusive welcome as if he had been a long-lost prodigal son returned home after years. Some old women of the royal family looked him all over and even made him tilt his face back at an upward angle in order to discover whether it bore any traces of the characteristic features of the royal family.

Uddhava was tempted to run away when he found himself surrounded by forthright women, all wearing only a short cloth round their waists. He had never been besieged by so many women in his life before.

The young Naga women were shapely, slim and free in their movements. Though dark compared to the Arya women, their bodies shone like gold because of the constant application of turmeric powder. The young princesses—and they were legion—surrounded him, talking to him with easy familiarity. Their graceful, sinuous movements justified the name of Nagakanyas (snake maidens) given to them, thought Uddhava.

Uddhava took to his uncle, Prince Karkotaka, as if he had known him all his life. He was a sturdy man and had a frank and open countenance. His son, Prince Maniman, younger than Uddhava by a few years, wrapped in the pride of his tribal superiority, could never overcome his fascination for the long bow and arrow and the sword which Uddhava carried. For the first time in his life, he felt an urge to be something more than what he was. He was dying to learn everything which Uddhava could teach him about the art of war.

On the night of the full-moon, the Nagas held festivities in honour of Uddhava's home-coming. At the feast, Aryaka sat in his litter next to the Sage, who despite his reputation as the most revered being in Aryavarta, sat amidst the crowd, smiling broadly, for all the world like the fond grandfather of a large and devoted family.

After the feast, there was dancing till the early hours of the morning. Men and women joined in it freely, facing each other in groups; the men with multi-coloured war stripes on their bodies, with feathered head-dresses and armed with spears and shields; the women with jingling bracelets from wrist to elbow and anklets almost reaching up to the knee. Karkotaka and Maniman, by their affectionate insistence, even dragged Uddhava into the dancing, though he awkwardly stumbled at every step to the good-natured merriment of the group of princesses opposite.

Uddhava was surprised to learn that, in spite of their warlike propensities, the Naga warriors' finest weapons were only copper-head battle-axes and spears of different sizes, which they could throw from a great distance to kill an enemy or a wild beast or to fix a fish with great accuracy.

The Naga warriors prized personal bravery and scorned the use of their crude bows and arrows, considering it degrading for an expert to take an aim against an enemy at a safe distance. Many warriors prided themselves on killing bears and lions in hand-to-hand fights. That, they said, was the true test of a warrior.

Uddhava found it difficult to understand this attitude towards archery. He could not believe that expert bowmen such as Krishna or Arjuna or himself were lacking in courage. But the Nagas had their own standards. Possibly because of them, they were paying a heavy price in their skirmishes with the Aryas. No wonder, he thought, that his people with their might were driving the Nagas into the interior of the forests or leading them into their world as inferior beings.

The more he saw the difference between his own people and the people of his grandmother's father, the better he understood the significance of the Sage's life. This mighty descendant of Maharshi Vasishtha, the noblest of Arya sages, showed no trace of contempt. To him both Aryas and Nagas were his own people, and he could make each of them feel that he was one of them. It was no wonder that Bhishma, the terrible, the great Guru Sandipani and King Aryaka and his Naga chiefs—and even the lowly and the ailing—saw in him a friend who gave them such solace as no one else could. He no longer wondered at the new world that the Sage was trying to create—a nobler life than the one Brahma had created.

Uddhava was lodged with Prince Karkotaka, who, with his three wives and numerous children, lived in a group of huts. Prince Maniman, his wife—he had as yet only one—and his twin sisters, Kapila and Pinagala, looked after Uddhava with such effusive solicitude that, unaccustomed as he was to such ministrations, he felt embarrassed.

The next day, Uddhava was surprised at the change that had come over him. For many years he had schooled himself to behave like an ascetic. Now he found his self-restraint falling away from him. He felt different. So far as he could remember, he had never been so unrestrained in his behaviour since he had given up Shaibya and surrendered himself to Krishna. He even could not help feeling dissatisfied with himself for having studiously cultivated austerity. Uddhava felt obliged to sigh. He had missed something in life.

However, he was impatient to fulfil his mission. Three days later, he told the Sage the purpose for which he had accompanied him. The Sage replied with a laugh: 'Didn't I know it? I guessed your reasons when you asked my permission to come with me,' he said, and added: 'Karkotaka has already entrusted some of his chiefs with the mission of finding out whether anyone has seen the Five Brothers and Kunti in these forests.'

'We must find the Five Brothers, Master,' said Uddhava. 'It would be best if the Five Brothers and Kunti return to Dwaraka with us, when Krishna comes here on his way back'.

'I cannot stay here long', said the Sage. 'I will have to leave for Ahichhatra on the tenth day from now. You can stay here till you receive the news. Would you like me to leave a few disciples here to help you?'

'No, Master,' replied Uddhava. 'My Uncle Karkotaka will give me all the help I need.'

While they were talking, Karkotaka himself came and prostrated himself before the Sage. 'Master, we have some news,' said the Prince. 'Siguri Naga, one of our chiefs, who has been going round the villages, has sent word that one of the Nagas from our frontier village Lahuria, seems to have seen five Aryas some months ago. One of them, to use his words, was as big as an elephant and carried an old woman on his shoulders'.

'Brother Bhima and his mother, possibly,' said Uddhava.

'But where did they go?' asked the Sage.

'Siguri's message is: the Naga who saw them was so frightened at seeing the strangers that he ran away; he does not know where they went,' said Karkotaka. 'Siguri has gone to Lahuria to make further enquiries. We will get some news when he returns.'

17

UDDHAVA'S TRIALS

*P*ingala and Kapila, the twin sisters of Maniman, were slim and graceful, and of the same height. Both had heart-shaped faces. Both had delicious dimples in their cheeks. It was difficult at first sight to distinguish one from the other. They each wore a yellow cloth of exactly the same style. They even tied up their hair in identical ways, each with a lotus flower in it of just the same shade of colour. They smiled in the same way and very sweetly, and did it very often almost at the same time. They did not have the sophisticated coyness of the Arya maidens; they were just happy in their natural way to meet a member of the family and tried to make Uddhava pleased in the best way they could.

The twins, who were never tired of being near Uddhava whenever possible, were full of admiration for whatever he said and did, hanging on his words, and asking questions with wide-eyed curiosity. By sheer worshipful attention, they succeeded in drawing him out to talk about himself, and, whenever he did so, Krishna naturally figured very prominently in all he said.

They became deeply interested in the adventures of Krishna and Uddhava; how they had played with *gopis* at Vrindavan; how Krishna killed Kamsa, he, Uddhava, being ready to jump into the fray if his life was in danger; how they were educated by Guru Sandipani; how they went to Nagaloka across the seas to rescue their Guru's son; how Krishna went away to Gomantaka and routed the terrible king Jarasandha about whom the twins had never heard; how Balarama and he, Uddhava, conquered Dwaraka; how he helped Krishna rescue Princess Rukmini from Kundinapura and how wonderful Krishna's two wives were, on hearing which[1] the twins exchanged significant glances.

The twins had never heard such adventures before, nor had they met anyone who could perform them. They soon began to live in their imagination with Krishna and Uddhava, and talked of Krishna as a god—of course, always associated with Uddhava.

In all his dedicated life, Uddhava had never met with such avid and innocent listeners before, and so great was his delight in retailing his exploits that he was often carried away by an enthusiasm to which he had been a stranger so far. He thought that the twins were interesting children. They, however, thought that he would make a wonderful husband.

Uddhava was very happy. He liked the Nagas. He was moved by the warmth with which Aryaka and his family surrounded him. He thoroughly enjoyed initiating Prince Maniman into the Arya skills in arms and horsemanship. He revelled in the affectionate attention of Prince Karkotaka, his wife and the twin Princesses. And, now that the prospect of going in search of the Five Brothers and taking them to Dwaraka was before him, he was full of enthusiasm for the new adventure. He had never felt human relations so welcome as now.

That night he went to sleep in this cheerful mood and had pleasant dreams in which Krishna and Maniman were mingled and the large eyes of the twin Princesses twinkled like distant stars.

His dreams changed. He felt a tingling sensation which gave him an unfamiliar experience. A soft arm was touching his body. Gradually he awoke to a sense of reality. He was not dreaming. He was lying on his right side, and soft arms encircled him from the left!

Uddhava was horrified. A Nagakanya was by his side. Was it Pingala or Kapila? Oh, the Great God!

He was seized with trembling. He had never known the touch of woman—except that of his mother, sister and little Subhadra. Years ago, he had felt a mad infatuation for Shaibya, the Karavirapura Princess, and had dreamt of marrying her. But when he found that she loved Krishna, whom he adored above everything, his single-minded devotion to his beloved friend came to his rescue. He gave up and forced himself to look upon Shaibya as a divinity to be worshipped at a distance. Thus he succeeded in sublimating his passion, but in doing so he acquired a detached attitude towards all women. To him they all became goddesses, distant and to be worshipped. And his concentrated devotion to Krishna provided a fortress which Kamadeva, the God of Love, had not been able to penetrate so far.

Now he felt that he was on trial. He was away from Krishna. His heart had been softened by the welcome that Aryaka's family had given him. The attention which the twin Princesses had given him, and their frank and effusive admiration, had also helped to tear down the pedestal on which he had set woman as a goddess. And now one of them was turning the idol into living flesh.

It was a loathsome situation. The worshipful attitude that he had adopted with regard to all women was in danger. 'Krishna, Krishna, where are you? Why are you not here at this critical time?' he cried to himself helplessly. 'I am in the coils of a Nagakanya!'

For a moment he was inclined to think that this could not be a reality; it must be a dream; no princess of the royal house—and that too his grandmother's—could be so shameless. But no! It was not a dream; it was a reality. He clenched his teeth. He was determined not to yield.

The soft hands tried to turn his face towards their owner. But he would not move.

Time passed. The maiden's efforts grew less insistent. Evidently she had begun to feel frustrated. She burst into tears and sobbed tragically. His heart melted. For a fleeting moment he felt inclined to take her in his arms, but he prayed to the Great God for strength.

And He gave it.

The sobbing maiden went away, Uddhava was, however, not very happy, though he had vanquished Kamadeva. With some effort, he dozed off, but there were dreams.

Then it dawned on him—horror of all horrors!—that it was not a dream! It was now the other twin. 'Oh, Great God, is there going to be no end to my trials?' he muttered.

Again, he clenched his teeth; he stiffened his body; he exercised inexorable control over his limbs. He invoked the help of his revered ancestors.

The maiden burst into tears. She stood up in despair and left the hut, sobbing all the while.

Uddhava was half-inclined to call her back. But no! The strict code of the Aryas forbade intimacy with women other than one's wife. He would not be guilty of a sin.

'Oh, Great God!' he muttered, 'Why did I come here? In adhering to my solemn pledge when I renounced Shaibya and conforming to the great and glorious Arya code of life, I have unconsciously broken the hearts of these innocent maidens. Oh, Grandmother Marishaa, why did I not listen to you?'

Uddhava spent the rest of the night tossing in bed. He got up early, in a curious state of mind. He was unhappy that he had made the girls so miserable; he was however, happy that he could stand the test. He went to the river and had his bathe.

When Maniman met him, he saw in his eyes a sense of injury, and, in his behaviour towards him, an aloofness which he had never seen before. The brother appeared to know how he had treated his sisters, and was angry!

Then it dawned on Uddhava that the ways of the

Nagas might be different from those of the Aryas. Possibly Naga young women chose their mates in a manner which Aryas would consider sinful. He remembered how Asika fell in love with Krishna when they were in the Land of Yama.

Evidently, Pingala and Kapila had made advances to him with the consent of their brother—perhaps even with the approval of their parents, and any repudiation of such advances by him would be at the risk of inviting the hostility of their parents. Had he, Uddhava, defied the Naga code of conduct? Was he guilty of a breach of etiquette?

It was nearing the meal-time when Acharya Jaimini came to call Uddhava to the Sage. As he went with him to Aryaka's residence, he felt like a goat being led to the slaughter-house.

The Master sat beside Aryaka who was in his inseparable litter, and Karkotaka, his forehead puckered into an unpleasant frown, on the other side of him. Next to him again sat Karkotaka's wife, the fat Princess Ravika, one or two other elderly ladies, Maniman's wife, and—oh! horror!—the twin Princesses, with their red, indignant eyes brimming with tears turned towards him as if he had been guilty of murder.

Uddhava was in acute distress, not so much for fear of any consequences to himself, but at having inflicted so much unhappiness on the people who had given him such a warm place in their hearts. Particularly the sight of the heart-broken twin Princesses almost choked him.

Of all of them the Sage was the only one who was his usual grandfatherly self, smiling at him with understanding.

'Uddhava, sit down,' said the Sage, pointing to a seat in front of him, which he took, expecting a volley of bitter curses.

The Sage's smile, however, was encouraging; he looked as if he was enjoying the situation. 'Uddhava, you have deeply wronged the noble lord of the Nagas— in fact, the whole of your grandfather's family.'

'I! What have I done, Master?' asked Uddhava, trying to make his tone as innocent as he could. But he heard the sobs of one of the twin Princesses and his heart condemned him as a brute.

'You rejected the twin Princesses,' said the Sage, glancing at King Aryaka, whose shrunken head nodded approval.

'But—but—I never invited them,' said Uddhava, feeling like a boy found in the very act of stealing.

'You see! That is what I told you, noble Aryaka,' said the Sage turning to the King with a hearty laugh. 'He does not know the ancient ways of the Nagas.'

Sobs....................

'He has disgraced our whole family,' said Karkotaka. 'What will happen to my pooor girls?' he asked.

More sobs....................

Uddhava could not understand these complications. He had been brought up in the noblest traditions of his people. 'But, Master, what have I done?' he cried in real anguish. 'The twin Princesses are not married to me. It would have been a heinous sin if I had accepted them. And you, Master, would have never forgiven me.'

There were more heart-rending sobs and angry frowns, till the whole-hearted laughter of the Sage relaxed the tension.

'Now you see, noble Aryaka, it was exactly as I told you,' said the Sage. 'Your ways are different from the ways of the Aryas. What you consider a legitimate ritual of marriage would be a sin for Uddhava. The twin Princesses were right in their own way. Uddhava was right in his own way. Both acted with propriety,'

'But what will happen to my daughters?' asked Princess Ravika, the mother of the twins, indignantly, casting a venomous glance at Uddhava. 'Rejected by Uddhava, they will not have another chance of getting a husband. They will have to drown themselves in the Ganga.'

An indulgent smile spread over the broad face of the Sage. 'We must find a way out of this difficulty,' he said. 'Uddhava, why don't you marry the twins according to our rites? I am sure they will be willing. And take them away to Dwaraka as your grandfather Shoora carried away Marishaa.'

Uddhava shuddered, not only at the idea of breaking the pledge which he had taken when he renounced Shaibya, but at the prospect of appearing before the Yadavas with a couple of young Naga princesses as his wives.

'But, my Master, I have forsworn marriage,' said Uddhava almost pathetically. 'I have come to look upon all women as goddesses.'

The remark evoked a humorous twinkle in the Sage's eyes.

'Master, you are the greatest *tapaswin* alive. Forgive me if I am impudent. How can you ask me to forswear my pledge to remain unmarried?' asked Uddhava.

'I have tried to be a *tapawin;* that is why I know what is it to fight Kamadeva, the God of Love. You know that I have a son, Shuka. It is foolish to think that all can successfully conquer the God of Love. It is only given to a few, a very, very few. The rest can only make terms with him by rendering him what is his due through marriage. Then, he will be our ally, and make us strong and happy,' said the Sage.

Uddhava heard the Master in humility, but without conviction. The Nagas sat listening, impressed by the Sage's effort to persuade Uddhava, but evidently bewildered at the turn the talk was taking; they could not grasp its significance. That a young Prince should have to be persuaded to marry the Princesses of Aryaka's house passed their understanding.

Uddhava wanted time to think of some way of getting out of the difficulty.

'Master, to me your advice is a command, but I cannot decide now; he said. 'Krishna is coming here to pay his respects to the venerable Grandfather. I would like to consult him.'

'That would lead to much scandal,' said Prince Karkotaka. 'It would not do.'

'You are right, Karkotaka,' said the Sage. 'Ravika,' he addressed Karkotaka's wife, 'can you trust me?'

'Yes, Master', replied Ravika.

A shiver went down Uddhava's spine lest the Sage might say something which would commit him to marrying the twin Princesses.

'Master—' Uddhava began, but his sentence remained incomplete.

Suddenly there was a hue and cry and a sound of many rushing feet. Loud cries of 'Rakshasa, Rakshasa' were heard outside the precincts of the royal compound.

The women forgot their distress and huddled together in fright. Karkotaka, Maniman and an old uncle waiting outside sprang up, their spears and shields in their hands, and rushed out. Uddhava slung his quiver round himself, took his bow and followed.

A storm appeared to be brewing outside.

18

IN THE LAND OF THE DEMONS

A large crowd of Nagas, brandishing spears, had halted a little beyond the King's residence. Many were shouting. 'Kill Kill,' 'Rakshasa, Rakshasa,' and trying to rush at a boy suspended in a sort of cage of fibres hanging from a pole carried by four Nagas.

Siguri Naga, a young chief, was keeping the crowd at bay. The boy had fainted and was moaning piteously and muttering in a strange tongue. Prince Karkotaka stepped in front of the crowd and commanded silence. 'What is this?' he asked.

A Naga chief came before Karkotaka and said: 'Siguri Naga has brought a Rakshasa from the forest.'

The Nagas stood in terrible dread of the Rakshasas who lived in the inaccessible forests on the frontier of the land which they themselves occupied between the Ganga and Yamuna and on the banks of Charmanwtai. Weird stories of the grisly deeds done by these demons were the common theme of Naga folklore. Tangible support was lent to them by the occasional visit of a Rakshasa to some distant village. It was invariably confirmed by the disappearance of a straying person or by the remains of a human body all but devoured by sharp teeth in the night. On the frontier, it was therefore customary for the villagers to keep bonfires burning the whole night at the outskirts of their village to prevent the Rakshasas from coming.

However, no Rakshasa had ever strayed into Nagakoota, the capital of Aryaka. So when it was reported that Siguri Naga was bringing a live Rakshasa, all the Nagas—men, women and children—in the town turned out to see what they had never seen before, but the very name of which brought fear to everyone. Most of the men had come out with spears. The boys howled in anger, throwing stones at the little Rakshasa, and whenever a stone struck him he snarled and showed his pointed teeth.

As a Rakshasa was considered impure, Siguri Naga was only able to bring the boy Rakshasa to within a certain distance of the royal palace. Then, leaving him outside the court, he approached Prince Karkotaka, greeted him by prostrating himself and explained how he had come to bring a living Rakshasa into the royal presence.

Uddhava, however, was influenced by no such taboo. He saw the piteous spectacle, of the boy, moaning and whining by turns, his body lacerated, blood oozing out of his nose. Disregarding the horrified look of the Nagas, he stepped up to the cage and tried to give him a sympathetic touch with his hand.

'He is a Rakshasa,' shouted the Naga who was in charge, 'He will eat you', said one of them.

'Let him do so,' said Uddhava and undid the knot

which tied the boy to the cage, and lifted him in his arms.

It was a strange creature, more of a beast than a man. His head was steep and narrow. There were wooden chips, painted red, inserted in his lips, which made him look very ferocious. His teeth were filed as sharp as those of a wolf. His long nails, hard and black, were curved like a bear's. His shifty eyes were blood-shot and the cries which he uttered were more like those of a wounded animal.

Uddhava laid the boy on a verandah nearby, where he lay so to speak, on all fours, resting on his elbows. With some effort he was induced to drink some water, which he did, not by taking the pot in his hand, but bending low and lapping from it dog-fashion.

Siguri Naga was one of the ablest chiefs among the Nagas. Obeying the orders of King Aryaka, he had gone from village to village, gathering information about the possible direction which the Five Brothers and Kunti had taken on their way through the jungle. All that he could gather after great difficulty was that five Aryas, one of them very huge, and an old woman, had crossed over into Rakshasavarta, the dread Land of the Demons.

Tracing the route taken by the Five Brothers, Siguri Naga ultimately reached the frontier village Lahuria. Beyond it lay the almost inaccessible barrier of huge crags, boulders and hills which skirted the impenetrable forest in which the Rakshasas lived.

When Siguri Naga reached the village, he found that only the previous night it had been raided by the

Rakshasas despite the bonfires. An old man and a dog had disappeared. Following the foot tracks, he found that the raiding party consisted of five Rakshasas, one of them a boy. Their traces were ultimately lost in the narrow, stony trail over the craggy spurs.

With difficulty, Siguri induced some brave Nagas to accompany him to where the trail began, and proceeded along it for some distance, though with great trepidation.

Following the trail over the crags, they heard piteous whines as of a wounded animal. After a search, they found a Rakshasa boy lying in a hollow, with one of his legs broken. Evidently, in the dead of night, his companions, in too great a hurry to get away with their prize, had not discovered the boy's fall and not cared to come to his rescue when they did.

The Nagas wanted to kill him by throwing stones at him. But Siguri was bent on getting some information about the Five Brothers and stopped his companions from inflicting further injuries on the boy. He then crawled into the hollow and, placing the unconscious boy on his shoulders, came up with some difficulty.

Siguri's companions would not come near the Rakshasa boy. They shuddered at the protruding teeth, the murderous talons and the fierce-looking red protuberances from the mouth, which they soon found to be red-painted chips of wood inserted in his lips. Siguri, however, was firm. Clenching his teeth to stop himself from running away should the boy suddenly grow in size, as the Rakshasas were believed to do, he bound him hand and foot.

Securing him with great care, Siguri applied medicated mud to his wounds and tied up his broken leg with chips of bamboo. Then he gave some water to the boy, who drank it dog-fashion.

At first, every time the boy tried to bite him, he hit him. Then it dawned on the Naga chief that he did so because he was really hungry, for whenever he was denied a bite of his flesh, he began to cry like a hungry child.

Siguri got a rabbit and handed it to the boy, who clutched it avidly. In a moment, with long, sharp nails, he tore off its neck, skinned it a little and began to eat its flesh with relish. Soon a smile of happiness was on his curiously shaped lips.

The Nagas, after Siguri had tied him hand and foot, placed him in a cage of fibres and slung it on to a pole. But even then they glanced at the boy with trepidation now and again, lest any moment he might grow in size, break through the cage and devour them.

On the way Siguri had a difficult time carrying the young Rakshasa from one village to another. Whenever the villagers came to know that a live Rakshasa was being carried, they came out with their spears ready to kill him.

The boy Rakshasa was also intractable. He generally behaved as an animal would.

Siguri's labours, however, were not in vain. The boy instinctively felt that he was his protector and his ferocious attitude underwent a change whenever he patted him.

The Nagas, in their hundreds, surrounded the verandah on which Uddhava sat cleaning the wounds of the Rakshasa boy and treating him with the medicinal applications which every warrior in those days knew how to administer to a wounded person.

Karkotaka came and stood a little away from the verandah. King Aryaka had his litter carried there. The princesses followed. And the eyes of the twin Princesses, timidly peeping from behind their father and mother, almost came out of their sockets with fright on seeing Uddhava patting the little Rakshasa as if he was a ferocious dog.

The Master came to where the boy was lying, and patted his head. The boy tried to snap at the Sage's hand.

'Be quiet, my son. You will be all right,' said the Sage in a language which the boy seemed to understand.

At the Master's behest, Jaimini untied the bamboo chip with which Siguri had tied up his broken leg, treated it with some boiled leaves and tied it up again with expert skill. The Rakshasa boy, his fright overcome, looked at the Sage, and snuggled close to him like a pet dog seeking protection.

When his eyes fell on Uddhava, a curious look of recognition came into them. In response, Uddhava looked at him kindly and extended a hand to protect him. The boy's face took on an awkward, ugly smile and he uttered something in his language, part of which sounded like 'Bhima.'

'He says that you are king Bhima's brother,' said the Master with a broad smile.

Uddhava was taken aback at being so accosted. But the Sage understood the significance of what the boy was saying, and spoke to him in his language. 'You know Bhima?'

The boy nodded vigorously and repeated the word Bhima a little more distinctly, half closing his eyes in respect.

'My son, is Bhima huge and very tall, very bulging at the arms and thighs?' enquired the Sage.

The boy was delighted at this conversation, part of which he understood, and replied by making happy gestures to indicate how big Bhima was.

'Fair like me?' asked Uddhava and pointed at his own fair skin to indicate what he meant.

The boy nodded assent vigorously.

'Were there five Bhimas?' asked the Sage, taking the boy's hand and counting 1,2,3,4 and 5, on his fingers and his thumb.

The boy smiled and nodded assent again.

'I am Bhima's brother,' said Uddhava as he sat down by his side and began to pat him.

The Sage repeated: 'This is Bhima's brother.'

The boy nodded in the affirmative, though a little grudgingly.

'You want to go to Bhima?' asked Uddhava, indicating his meaning by gestures.

The boy smiled and nodded vigorously, but by way of comment, he raised his thumb and said 'Bhima' and indicated that he was very big. Then he showed the remaining four fingers and contemptuously referred to other 'Bhimas' who were small and insignificant.

The Master laughed at Yudhishthira, Arjuna, Nakula and Sahadeva being described in such a manner by the Rakshasa boy.

'Where is Bhima, the big man?' asked the Sage.

The boy smiled and pointed out in the southerly direction, saying in his language 'There, there.'

'Oh! They are there! In that direction!' commented the Sage.

'Master, let me take charge of the boy,' said Uddhava. 'I will look after him till he recovers.'

'Why?' asked the Sage. 'Jaimini will be able to look after him better.'

'But, venerable Master, the Great God has come to my help,' said Uddhava. His mind was working very fast and he saw that the only way out of the unfortunate situation he had walked into as regards the twin Princesses, was by risking death in Rakshasavarta.

'How?' asked Karkotaka.

'Uncle, the Five Brothers are alive,' replied Uddhava. 'So I will go to Rakshasavarta with this boy to bring them here. And when Krishna comes here, we shall take them to Dwaraka.'

Every one who heard Uddhava stared at him as if he had gone mad.

'You! Go to the land of the Rakshasas!' asked Karkotaka.

The fat Ravika could not restrain herself. 'How can you go? You will be eaten up. What will happen to my daughters then?'

'Yes, I will go, Aunt. I am here for that very purpose,' replied Uddhava firmly, as his heart sang merrily. He was going to Rakshasavarta to be eaten up.

The Sage saw through Uddhava's decision. He had decided either to rescue the Five Brothers and Kunti or die in the attempt and escape the twin Princesses.

'You can do so, my son,' said the Sage. 'Don't worry. Lord Pashupati will protect him. He has been sent here for this purpose.'

Ravika beat her forehead with the palms of her hand and the numerous bangles on her arms jingled dolefully. The twin Princesses fainted.

King Aryaka, who was listening to the conversation intently suddenly fixed his gaze on the Master, and in a shrill voice trembling with excitement, said: 'You are right, Master.'

Every one turned to look at the aged King, who appeared to be in a fit. They knew what it meant. Lord Pashupati was conveying his mandate through his lips.

The King tossed his head about as if in pain. His eyes rolled. The next moment he was quite steady. The eyes glowed with power, and a strangely forceful voice issued from his lips: 'He has the blood of Aryaka in him. He shall go and conquer and make the Nagas fearless.'

The eyes closed, a sigh issued from his lips, and the people stood awe-struck. Lord Pashupati had spoken.

Uddhav felt care-free as he bade good-bye to Siguri Naga on the outskirts of Lahuria, the last village on the boundary of Aryaka's kingdom. He had discovered the whereabouts of the Five Brothers. He was loyally carrying out the mission entrusted to him by Krishna. He had saved the twins from committing suicide; with him away, they would soon forget the unfortunate episode and, in a year or two, find suitable husbands for themselves.

Curiously enough, Nikumbha—Uddhava soon discovered the name of the little Rakshasa—came to show affection for him, because he was the brother of Bhima. In the twilight mind of the little Rakshasa, Bhima was a shining luminary of strength.

Uddhava could not help thinking of what would happen if he were to be eaten up. When Krishna came to Nagakoota, he would wait for him in vain. He would feel his loss as he had never felt the loss of anyone else before. The twins would go on crying for a few days before they forgot him; he hoped they would not do something silly out of grief, Uddhava thought with a smile. His father, Devabhaga, would be sorry to lose him, and his mother Kamsaa would shed copious tears, though not really sorry to have got rid of a son whom she disliked.

Yes, the Rakshasas would eat him up and that would be the end of Uddhava, he thought, and laughed.

Nikumbha was now his old sturdy self, except for a limp, and led the way towards the chain of barren crags which formed a barrier separating the land of the Demons from the rest of the world. The ground on which they journeyed was stony all the way; sometimes it was difficult even to see how the path ran; but Nikumbha knew every inch of the way, over which he climbed merrily with steady and sure steps.

Crossing the barrier of sharp rocks was a risky affair. Some of them were very steep; in places the imperceptible path wound over narrow ledges overhanging the valley. Nikumbha, however, skirted them with swift steps and laughed at Uddhava's efforts to maintain his balance, for at some places he had to make use of both his hands and feet to do so.

At midday the sun was fierce and the rocky ground became burning hot. Uddhava found it impossible to carry his arms. He dropped his sword. He even had to throw away most of the arrows from his quiver. He unslung his bow and used the shaft only, so as to keep steady.

By the afternoon, they had crossed the stony heights and began to descend to the densely wooded valley, beyond which the land of the Demons was situated.

By the time the sun set, they had entered the deep forest. Nikumbha was in high spirits; it was his native land, where hearty meals of small beasts were plentiful, and he left Uddhava to take a hasty repast by himself of what they had left. Then both lay down side by side under the shade of a tree.

It was midnight; the moon had risen high in the heavens. Suddenly Nikumbha sat up, began to sniff the air and listened intently as the wind whistled through the top branches of the trees.

Nikumbha awoke Uddhava by pulling at his hand and pointed a warning finger in a southerly direction. Uddhava rubbed his eyes. Yes, Nikumbha was right; he could hear a very faint sound of distant drums. 'What is it?' asked Uddhava, unable to understand why Nikumbha looked so frightened.

'Rakshasas,' he replied laconically in a whisper and tried to drag Uddhava on to an untrodden path. Uddhava unaccustomed to walking on thorny paths, refused to follow him.

A party with drums could be heard coming nearer. Their shouts of joy could also be heard.

'Rakshasas, Rakshasas,' Nikumbha said again in a furious whisper.

'Let us go back a little,' said Uddhava.

'You cannot. They will catch you,' said Nikumbha, as the sounds, which were coming still nearer, suddenly stopped and the shouts sounded as if the men were smothering them in their throats. For a moment there was silence in the forest, except for the whistling wind and the croaking of frogs.

'They have smelt you,' whispered Nikumbha. 'They will catch you.'

Soon a crackling sound was heard in a different direction coming nearer to them all the time. Nikumbha was right. The Rakshasas had smelt his presence and were approaching him in a semicircle.

Uddhava ground his teeth. The fateful moment had come. Automatically his hand went to his quiver. Nikumbha stopped him. 'They will eat you up,' he said in a whisper. 'Go up this tree,' he added, pointing to a very tall tree with sturdy branches.

The sound of cracking twigs trodden by cautious footsteps was approaching them. Even the breathing of men could be heard in the still night. It was terrible, this unknown, invisible death which was closing in upon him.

'Go up,' Nikumbha insisted. 'Don't come down whatever happens. They will eat you.'

The silence was broken by a strange, violent screech as if of a giant bird. Nikumbha would wait no longer. He went on all fours and glided into the undergrowth of the forest with the swiftness of a wild beast and disappeared into the tall grass which grew at some distance.

For a moment Uddhava felt that Nikumbha had decoyed him to his death. But the little Rakshasa had been so affectionate that it was difficult to believe that he could be so wicked. He, therefore, decided to accept his advice, and, strapping the shaft of his bow on to his back to give free movement to his hands, he began to climb the tree.

He was just in time. He had barely climbed to one of the upper branches, when he saw shadows creeping up to the tree, and halting under it. A terrible howl broke the silence of the forest. It was the howl, not of a beast but of ghouls. Uddhava shuddered with fright. Almost instinctively he was going to give up his hold on the branches to which he was slinging, when the sage advice of Nikumbha came to his mind: 'Don't come down whatever happens.' He clung on to a strong branch of the tree with all his strength.

It was a party of fourteen or fifteen Rakshasas carrying a couple of prisoners. In the clear moon-light, Uddhava could see that several of them had spears in their hands, while one or two carried axes.

The Rakshasas, standing under the tree, continued to howl frightfully; some of them even began to stage a frantic dance around the trunk. They were trying to frighten him into letting go of the branch to which he was clinging.

After a little while, however, the Rakshasas gave up trying to frighten him, and lay down for a rest. The ends of the fibre ropes with which the prisoners were bound were tied to the foot of one or other of the captors, so that the unfortunate men could not make any movement without waking their enemies.

Uddhava, determined not to be frightened to his death, clung to the branch of the tree for his very life. When he felt that most of the Rakshasas were asleep, he cautiously began to climb up to a higher branch. But the slightest noise awoke one or other of the Rakshasas, who howled at him in the most terrific manner.

When he had climbed to a higher branch, he could find only one way of not dropping off through inadvertence or fright. He untied the scarf which was wrapped round his waist and bound himself to another branch.

The morning star rose. One of the side branches broke under his pressure. Immediately the Rakhsasas woke up and again went round and round the tree howling all the time to frighten him into falling. When ultimately they found that he would not fall off in fright, two of them tried to climb up the tree. He took the first of four arrows which were still in his quiver and aimed it at one. The arrow hit the mark. The Rakshasa fell down with a piteous howl as blood spurted out of his wound. The other climber slipped down the tree.

The dawn began to break. There was whispering among the Rakshasas. They appeared to have given up their intention of frightening Uddhava; four of them sat down as watchmen under the tree and the rest led the prisoners on to an opening in the forest.

Now, in the light of the dawn, Uddhava could see the strange, fearsome creatures, with their sharp, pointed teeth protruding from their mouths, the scarlet chips inserted in their lips making them look blood-thirsty, the feathers inserted on both sides of their noses and even on their faces giving them a weird appearance. Their heads were covered with these long feathers and their faces were painted scarlet and white. Their nails were black and curved like Nikumbha's, only more pointed. They were all but naked and wore necklaces of bones. Their spears and axes were stone-tipped.

Some of the Rakshasas bound the prisoners to a tree and gave them food, which they were forced to take, though they were really too frightened to do so. Others collected firewood and lit a huge fire in the open space, placing stones on it and began to dance around it. When the stones grew red hot, they untied the prisoners with spears pointed threateningly at them, got them to sit down on the ground and tied branches of trees to them.

Then they shouted challenging war cries, dancing round the victims, who after a while were placed on the heated stones. The Rakshasas went about their business, heaping earth on them, though the piteous screams of the victims rent the sky.

The cries of the victims turned to moans, sank into low anguished whimpers and stopped altogether.

Fascinated, Uddhava continued to gaze at the ceremony which was being conducted around the fire. He felt neither hunger nor thirst and did not realise how the time passed. The Rakhsasas continued to dance around the fire in which the two victims were being roasted, yelling defiantly.

The sun began to decline in the sky. Uddhava gave up all hopes. He could not continue to sit on the top of the tree for ever; some time or other he would fall off and would be roasted in the fire.

When the bodies were cooked to satisfaction, they were taken out of the fire, still in a sitting posture. After having their faces painted with soot, they were carried to a stone shrine on one side of the open space and offered as a ceremonial sacrifice.

Two of the Rakshasas, who appeared to be either leaders or priests, conducted the ceremony.

After the offering was made, the Rakshasas again began to dance and shout to the accompaniment of drums, swinging their spears and axes with furious joy. The two priests got busy cutting up the bodies with sharpened sticks of bamboo, and, when the dance was over, distributed the pieces among the worshippers, who ate them with relish.

Shuddering, Uddhava looked at this grisly ceremony, almost unable to breathe.

It was long past midnight when the feast was over. Then, one by one, the Rakshasas dropped off to sleep; it was almost early morning before all of them were sound asleep, heavy with the festive meal.

∎

19

KING VRIKODARA

*T*he Rakshasas, weighted with the heavy fare that they had taken and tired with continuous dancing, slept, some snoring, some breathing with their mouths wide open, some rolling uncomfortably on the ground.

Uddhava, perched on one of the top branches of the tree and self-bound to another upright one, felt giddy. Hunger, thirst, the grisly sights he had seen, the stench of burning human flesh—all of which he had borne so far with stoical courage—had their cumulative effect. Despair seized him. His mind began to lose its grip. He felt like loosing his hold on the tree and dropping on to the ground out of a sheer lack of a will to live.

To keep up his failing resistance, he went on muttering:

He Krishna Govinda Hare Murare,
He Naatha Naaraayana Vasudeva.

But now he could not even repeat the favourite chant of Mother Devaki. He found the early morning breeze very refreshing, and began to doze. Only now and then he woke up with a start, for fear he should drop off the tree.

As he sat there half awake and half asleep, picture after picture flitted before his eyes. Krishna came with his flute, playing for Radha...........The angry Shaibya stood cursing him furiously............His mother Kamsaa, disgusted with him, turned away in scorn.........The twins also came now and again, looking at him with sweet smiles and loving tenderness. And every few moments he woke up with a start, adjusted his seat firmly on the branch and looked down upon the demons, all lying on the ground, sleeping soundly, round the tree on which he was seated.

Thoughts came to him fitfully. Some time or other he would drop down from the tree, be roasted alive and eaten by the demons.... Without him, Krishna was sure to feel lonely; there was no one else who could anticipate all his wishes... What would the poor twins do when they came to know that he was dead? Perhaps they would throw themselves into the Ganga all the same....

With the bright sunshine around him, he felt fresh for a while. He opened his mouth to breathe in the fresh morning air. He chewed a few green leaves from the tree: they only made him feel sick. He had now been on the tree for two nights and one day....

He was tired—tired beyond endurance.... He would have loved to die in a battle. He could then have sacrificed his life for some noble cause. But now the only prospect before him was to drop like a ripe fruit on the ground, be roasted alive and swallowed by the demons...

All his noble aspirations had come to an ignominious end .... Off and on he dozed off or lay in a faint of utter exhaustion.

....All hope of life had gone, he thought...

As his limbs begam to ache, he almost felt inclined to hasten the end by letting himself drop down from the tree of his own free will. The torture was too great to be borne any longer.

It was now midday. The fierce rays of the sun penetrated through the foliage. His mouth was parched. His tongue cleaved to his palate. He felt a burning sensation all over his body. He was dying for want of water.

He again prayed to Krishna—last prayer, a last goodbye, he thought it was:

He Krishna Govinda Hare Murare,
He Naatha Naaraayana Vasudeva.

'...My Krishna, my only satisfaction is that I brave death in order to carry out your mandate. Yes, your wish was always a command to me and I carried it out as I always have done throughout my life. Krishna, in my last moments, as throughout my life, I have been thinking of you and no one else. But how are you to know of it?....'

Uddhava fell asleep.

It was evening when he woke up. The demons were still sleeping soundly, except that one or two got up for a moment to drink at a stream flowing nearby and went to sleep again....

The forest bestirred itself. The birds were chirrupping. Soon there was silence throughout the whole landscape as the moon rose, shedding her liquid beauty over the top of the tree on which Uddhava was seated. Some of the demons woke up, went hither and thither, came back near the tree and again went to sleep.

Uddhava could not now sustain himself any longer. Hunger, thirst and exhaustion were all working on him. His limbs were stiff. His back ached. His head was splitting. The moment of his death was coming nearer.....

It was now impossible for him to sleep. He looked at the beautiful moonlight, with its silver gilding the top of the trees, weaving beautiful patterns on the ground and on the bodies of the sleeping demons....

It was strange, he thought, how he was going to his death. Possibly no Arya had ever met such a fate before.

He laughed at himself. Kacha was eaten by Sage Shukracharya, and, at the call of *Sanjivani,* he had come out of the Sage's stomach, hale and hearty. But no one would call him back after he was eaten up. He wished he knew the *Sanjivani mantra* of Shukracharya to tear open the stomach of the demons and come out alive. No such luck for him!

There was a film before Uddhava's eyes. He was not sure whether he was awake or asleep. He heard the voice of the twins: 'Uddhava has been eaten by the demons'.... No, that was not correct. He was still sitting on the tree... But there was no doubt that he was soon going to be eaten.

Suddenly, across the corridor of his half-conscious mind there rang out words: 'Uddhava shall not die while I am alive.' It was the beloved voice—the voice—of power. Uddhava shook himself awake. Had he heard the voice? Or was it a trick played by his senses?....

There was no mistaking the voice, or the tone, telling of an unshakable destiny, in which the words were uttered....

The dark blue face was before him. The eyes flashed a loving assurance. The head, with its curly hair and diadem crested with a peacock feather, was bent towards him in infinite tenderness....

For a moment his despair disappeared. Hope entered his heart....

He smiled as if Krishna was before him—a smile of affection, loyal devotion and surrender. 'Lord, I am yours. Even if I die, I will die carrying your mandate, with name on my lips.'

He was startled again.... The same voice, the same accents were borne on the breeze. 'Uddhava shall not die while I am alive'..... He smiled. His imagination was playing tricks upon him. He had heard the beloved voice once more. He was happy to die having heard it.

The demons began to wake up, to yawn and to twist their bodies into activity as the dawn broke.

Now they were all awake and active round the tree on which he sat, howling, grimacing, trying to frighten him into falling off. It was a matter of moments, thought

Uddhava, for he had not the same stamina as the day before. Any time he would fall off.

The Rakshasas danced and howled and shouted and screamed round the tree. Some of them brought dried twigs from the forest and heaped them around it. Evidently they were going to light a fire to bring him down.

The demons lit the fire. The smoke was choking Uddhava's nostrils as he sat there on top of the tree.

'Oh, Krishna, I am yours in life and death. Don't ever forget me,' he muttered out of sheer exhaustion. He decided to let go his hold and plunge into the fire.

Before his decision was completely made, above the jungle noises, suddenly, he sensed rather than heard a creeping and encircling movement as on the earlier occasion when the Rakshasas has been coming up to him. Evidently another party of Rakshasas was approaching. The Rakshasas who were sitting round the tree feeding the fire, pricked up their ears and looked at each other in fear, for they too had heard the sound.

Suddenly tom-toms were heard beating fiercely. Then came a sound like the terrible roar of an angry lion, reverberating through the forest glades. The Rakshasas who surrounded the tree on which he sat evidently knew what it meant and scampered away as fast as their legs could carry them.

From one end of the opening a mighty Rakshasa came forward, taller, sturdier and stouter than any person Uddhava had ever seen before. A long dark beard swept his chest; a mantle of feathers covered his body; a huge club, almost like an uprooted tree, rested on his shoulders.

Uddhava's heart missed a beat. He had just escaped one calamity to be plunged into another. Evidently this appeared to be the king of a more ferocious breed of Rakshasas than the one which he had been facing. There was, however, one difference. This Rakshasa, who had painted himself scarlet and white like the others, though more gorgeously, had no feathers on his nose and no chips in his lips, and he did not walk with the same animal-like gait as the others.

The Rakshasa chief stopped in the center of the opening and sent off a thunderous roar once again. In response, his followers—they were Rakshasas of just ordinary size and kind—came running out of the thickets.

The chief sniffed the air and looked on all sides, expecting to find someone. From a thicket by his side, a boy Rakshasa rushed forward on all fours; Uddhava recognized him; he was Nikumbha. The boy stood up, pulled the hand of the chief and pointed out Uddhava sitting in the tree. 'The wicked, ungrateful wretch!' muttered Uddhava.

The chief looked up. The giant frame, the sturdy shoulders, the pillar-like neck, were strangely familiar, Uddhava thought, though he had never seen the Rakshasa before.

Recognising Uddhava, the face of the chief broke into a broad smile—a smile with which Uddhava was all too familiar. He shouted, laughing: 'Uddhava come down. What are you doing there, you monkey?' The words were spoken in the sacred language of the gods, in the pure tones which Uddhava loved so well. His heart bounded with joy.

'Come down the tree. Don't go on sitting there like a monkey', repeated the deep hearty voice. 'If you can't climb down, jump I will catch you as you fall. Don't be a coward I am not going to eat you up.'

Uddhava tore away the scarf which bound him to the tree, and dropped down with the words: 'Oh, Krishna, you have kept your promise.'

Bhima received Uddhava in his hands, lifted him aloft and said with a laugh: 'King Vrikodara has come to save you, and you thank Krishna for it. You ungrateful wretch! That is just like my luck.'

Uddhava, overcome with emotion and exhaustion, fainted in the arms of his mighty cousin.

20

KING VRIKODARA WINS A WIFE

*W*hen Uddhava regained consciousness, he felt faint with hunger and thirst. He could not even stand; his legs were shaking. He allowed himself to be led by Bhima to a stream running nearby and impatiently bent down to slake his thirst.

In the meantime Nikumbha brought some fruits, which he ate. 'Now you lie down and go to sleep', ordered Bhima. 'In the meantime I will deal with these Rakshasas.'

When Uddhava woke up from the sleep, into which he immediately fell, he found Bhima busy hanging upside down some of the culprits who had eaten human flesh and who had been caught in the neighbouring thickets. Bhima was not content with merely hanging them; he stood before them as they threw out whatever they had eaten, enjoying their discomfiture with uproarious laughter.

When Uddhava went up to him, Bhima turned to him and said with a laugh: 'These fellows can never overcome the taste for our flesh. I am getting them to disgorge whatever they have eaten.'

Uddhava shuddered when he recalled the

nightmarish experiences which he had had the night before.

When punishment had been meted out to all those who were caught and sentinels were posted to watch them, Bhima led Uddhava into the interior of the forest. Nikumbha kept Uddhava company, holding his hand as he had done when they first entered the Land of the Demons.

Having regained his strength, Uddhava looked carefully at the strange transformation which had come over his cousin.

'Don't look at me as if you had never seen me before. You have always been a fool, Uddhava. If you wanted to come to me, why didn't you send word by Nikumbha? I would have come to receive you myself,' said Bhima.

'But how was I to know that you were the king of these maneaters?' asked Uddhava wryly. 'And you seem to like being it!'

'Of course I like it immensely,' said Bhima. 'It is better to be their king than to have to fight that wily Shakuni and his nephews in Hastinapura. Here you know where you are. You can fight; you kill; you can be killed. If you are alive you can live as you like.'

'But how did you come to be here? Where is Aunt Kunti? And where are the other Brothers?' asked Uddhava.

'Oh, they are all safe. I am going to take you to them, if they have not been already eaten up before we meet them,' said Bhima, chuckling to himself. 'It is all my doing.' He laughed as if it was a great joke, and added: 'I don't know why these things happen to me, of all the Five Brothers.'

'Krishna—in fact, all of us—have been troubled about you Brothers,' said Uddhava.

'Nothing can happen to us if I am there,' said Bhima with the bragging air of a naughty boy. 'Uncle Vidura told us that we would be safe only if we were thought in Hastinapura to be dead. So, after you left Varanavata, when a beggar woman and her five sons happened to come and stay with us, we found an opportunity. We set fire to the palace and escaped through the tunnel which, as you know, had been excavated by Unlce Vidura's mason. A boat propelled by machines was waiting for us—thanks again to our Uncle. We were soon across the river. We did not want to be recognized and so we passed by Ekachakra and took the way of the forest. Oh, it was great fun!'

'Why did you come to this wretched land?' asked Uddhava.

'Oh, that is another story. But don't call it a wretched land. It is my country; I am its king—King Vrikodara,' said Bhima, and slapped his chest. 'On our way we had to pass through some Naga villages. The villagers were so frightened of us that we thought they would go and report our presence to their chief, who would come and recognise us. You know, Uddhava, we are such a peculiar family that it is difficult to miss us—an old woman who can't walk, a giant who can roar and four others—a wise man, a dandy, a nincompoop and a star-gazer—none of whom can take care of themselves! So I led them deeper into the forest,' he added laughing at the funny description of his mother and brothers which he had given.

'It must have been terrible for Aunt Kunti to walk through the forest,' said Uddhava.

'Oh, I would not allow her to do so,' replied Bhima. 'The soles of her feet are as tender as lotus leaves. I carried her all the way, and sometimes had to carry the others too. They all think themselves very clever, but without me they would not be able to live for a moment. Whenever there is a difficulty, they, like helpless babes, look to me,' added Bhima, and laughed proudly.

'But how did you become the King of Rakshasas?' asked Uddhava.

'Oh, that was because I was fit to be their king,' said Bhima proudly. 'Oh, it was great! Even our ancestor, *Chakravarti* Bharata, would not have lived through this adventure. Listen: For two days we went deeper into the forest, sleeping under the trees and eating fruits. Then Hidimba came.'

'Who is Hidimba? asked Uddhava.

'Don't you know? He was the King of the Rakshasas. He was going through the forest with his men, when he smelt us. You know, they can smell men a *yojana* away,' said Bhima.

'Don't I know it?' said Uddhava.

'Then they began to creep near us in a semicircle on padded feet,' said Bhima.

'I know that way of theirs too, by bitter experience. It makes me shiver every time I think of it,' said Uddhava.

'We had no arms except the staffs we brothers carried. So I put the brothers behind me with mother in the centre, asking them to look after her. Then I stepped forward a few paces towards Hidimba. There he was, as fierce a Rakshasa as ever was, howling for all he was worth. He roared. I roared in reply. Mother fainted and poor Sahadeva had to work all his miracles in order to revive her. Hidimba and his men then howled at me. I replied with a bigger howl. Uddhava, you have never heard me roar; even the lions are frightened by it,' said Bhima looking at his cousin happily.

'I heard you do it this morning. It was frightening enough,' said Uddhava. 'I could have fainted myself. Then what happened to you?'

'They howled and howled; I roared and roared. They did not dare to approach me; they had never seen anyone like me before. Then Hidimba advanced with his stone-tipped spear pointed at me. As he hurled it at me, I jumped high, eluded it, and rushed at him with a thunderous roar. I did it so suddenly that the Rakshasas, who generally frighten people, were frightened themselves. They retreated a few paces,' said Bhima with a smile, his eyes glistening merrily.

'How could you be so terrifying?' asked Uddhava. 'Generally you are so kind.'

'Oh, Uddhava, you don't know your cousin! If you want to frighten people, leave it to me. When the Rakshasas fell back, I found an opportunity. A huge rock, which even ten people could not move, was lying on the ground in front of me. I lifted it with all my strength and hurled it at Hidimba. The rock did the trick. It crashed his skull, and with a fearful scream the Rakshasa fell to the ground. He was a very powerful Rakshasa—and tall too, though he only came up to my shoulders. But he had no chance against me. Thank your stars that you have a cousin like me.'

Bhima continued gleefully, patting Uddhava on the back. 'His followers began to run away in fright. I caught hold of one Rakshasa by the leg, swung him round and dashed him against a tree. They stood watching. Then a miracle happened. A sudden change came over the rest. They had considered Hidimba to be a demon of magic strength. When he was killed, they were stunned. They threw their spears. and hatchets to the ground and prostrated themselves before me,' said Bhima, laughing triumphantly.

'How was that?'

"These Rakshasas are very strange. They believe that their chief inherits the invincible strength of their great ancestor, Virochana. Once they find that he is not invincible, he no longer remains fit to be their king. I have heard that sometimes, when a chief is found to have lost his strength, he is roasted alive and eaten, so that his strength may enter those who eat him. So, when I proved stronger than their king, they were willing to offer their loyalty to me. To them I was a Rakshasa of greater invincibility,' said Bhima.

'What did you do with them?' asked Uddhava.

'I went to them, kicked a few, collected their spears and hatchets and distributed them to the Brothers. Then we tied them with fibres and ordered them to lead me to the place where Hidimba lived,' said Bhima.

'Did they obey you?' asked Uddhava.

'Only one Rakshasa tried to play a trick on me, I lifted him and flung him high up into the air. He came down with a crash and died,' Bhima chuckled. 'Thereafter no Rakshasa ventured to play any tricks. You know, Uddhava, how ferocious I can be when I want?' Bhima turned to Uddhava with mock ferocity. 'My Eldest was shocked at what he called my brutality and scolded me. If I had not been brutal, he would not have been alive; he forgot that—ha ha!' said Bhima, laughing uproariously.

'What happened to the dead Hidimba?' asked Uddhava, curious to know what obsequies he received.

'We took his dead body with us. He was carried by four Rakshasas,' replied Bhima.

'Did you go to the settlement of Hidimba?' asked Uddhava.

'Of course we did. Our procession arrived there with myself at the head, I roaring all the while. When we arrived at the settlement, the Rakshasas who were with us sent up piteous wails to announce the death of their king. The village turned out wailing in response—

the Rakshasas, their wives and their children—all with pointed teeth and lips pierced with red chips. Before them all came Hidimbaa, the sister of Hidimba, a stout Rakshasi, her whole body painted, her hair covered with fibres, wearing necklaces of bones. She was wailing as if her heart would break,' said Bhima.

'How did the Rakshasas receive you when they learnt of your exploit?' asked Uddhava.

'When they learnt that I had killed Hidimba, they fell at my feet. They believed that not only the spirit of the invincible Hidimba, but of the great Virochana himself, had passed into me,' said Bhima.

'So, that is how you became their king?' asked Uddhava.

'The funnier part of the story is still to come, my dear Uddhava. Hidimbaa flung herself at my feet and clung to them in respectful admiration. The Rakshasa women always fall in love with those who kill their father and brothers. In this land you must do that to win a bride. And there I was, with a powerful Rakshasi at my feet, wooing me,' said Bhima, again laughing gleefully like a boy who has won a prize. 'And Mother was all but dazed at seeing a fierce Rakshasi at my feet.'

'I am surprised that they accepted you as King of Rakshasavarta at once,' said Uddhava.

'Oh, no,' said Bhima, smiling to himself. 'They put me to a severe test.'

'What was the test?' asked Uddhava.

'A ceremonial feast was held before I was accepted as King,' said Bhima, 'They prepared all kinds of things and put them in a great heap before me. In front of me, a burly Rakshasa with a huge belly sat, ostensibly to see that I was not starved. He was one of their priests. After we had all started eating, he began to press me to eat more and more. He was a big eater himself, and for every morsel that he took he offered one to me.'

'Why did he do that?' asked Uddhava.

'I could see that it was not mere hospitality. It was a challenge to my kingship,' said Bhima chuckling to himself. 'Every Rakshasa was watching this combat between us; so I simply let myself go. He gave me a helping and I gave him one in return. This went on for some time. He was a big eater himself, I tell you, Uddhava. I had not seen the like of him and he had not seen the like of me either. You know, Uddhava, I ordinarily take what would more than satisfy four people,' Bhima smiled proudly, 'and once I make up my mind, I can fill one compartment after another of my stomach. So we went on feeding each other till the fellow could take no more. He was filled to bursting.'

'Oh, it was delightful to see him almost splitting, belching all the time, rubbing his hand over his fat paunch,' said Bhima laughing uproariously at the revived memory of that glorious event. 'There were tears in his eyes. He could eat no more. Now I reversed the hospitality. I went on feeding him, taking one morsel myself for one morsel pushed into his mouth. The other Rakshasas gave up eating themselves and stood around us, watching the competition. Then he could eat no more. But I would not let him say "no" and pushed a morsel into his mouth: he almost threw it out. I offered him another and began to take two morsels for every one which I offered him,' said Bhima gleefully, his eyes dancing merrily as if he was narrating a huge joke.

'He threw out whatever I gave him, though he tried to swallow it merely to maintain his prestige,' Bhima continued. 'Then he fainted; he rolled over, beating his stomach with his fists. The Rakshasas were surprised; they had never seen the fellow stop eating. I told them to take him away, for he could not get up by himself. And I continued to go on eating, as voraciously as before. They were dazed. They fell prostrate before me and gave roars of victory and called me what in the sacred language would be Raja Vrikodara. They had no doubt in their minds that the divine Virochana, had entered me' Then he added: 'I was no longer Bhima to the Rakshasas; I was Vrikodara—Virochana come to life. At that very moment they accepted me as their King by pricking their thumbs and painting my forehead with their blood.'

'What happened to the priest?' asked Uddhava.

'He died the next day,' replied Bhima.

'Well, I have never heard such a thing before in my life,' said Uddhava. 'What did you do then?'

'What did I do, you ask me? I made Hidimbaa my wife,' replied Bhima, as if it was the most natural thing to do.

'Oh, God of all gods! And what did Aunt Kunti and your Eldest say to that?' asked Uddhava.

'They made wry faces. Mother Kunti would not even look at my beautiful bride with bone necklaces and pointed teeth. Yudhishthira had religious compunctions. Arjuna and Nakula, in sheer disgust, kept their eyes turned away from me. Only Sahadeva came to my rescue. He said: "If we are to live hidden from this world, this is the best way in which we can do it". You know how wise he is. Then Mother agreed,' said Bhima.

'And so you were acclaimed their king?' asked Uddhava.

'Of course I was. Do you think I would have married Hidimbaa if I had not been invited to be their King? Then my difficulties began. According to their ceremonial rites, they chopped off Hidimba's head and wanted to roast his body for a ceremonial feast. I stepped in. I would not allow Hidimba to be roasted and eaten. I stood near the funeral pyre till all his flesh and bones were reduced to ashes, with the Rakshasas surrounding me, all unhappy at having lost an excellent feast. Two elders protested at what they said was a sacrilege. I brought their heads together and broke one against the other, and issued my royal commands: "Whoever eats human flesh will be suspended head downwards from a tree till all that he has eaten comes out. And any priest who performs the flesh-eating ceremony, will have his head broken",' said Bhima.

'So, they have now given up eating human flesh?' asked Uddhava.

'Most of them have. But as you have seen yourself some of them steal away into distant parts of the forest and enjoy a feast to their liking. They can't give up their craving for it', said Bhima.

'But why didn't Hidimbaa eat you up?' asked Uddhava.

'Oh, you don't know Hidimbaa. She is frighfully in love with me. Hidimba's skull was exposed to the sun and she insisted upon my hanging it at my waist. It was to be the insignia of my royalty. But I would not wear it. She insisted. I threatened to break her brother's skull to pieces. She cried piteously like a loving wife. "No", she said, "if his skull is not with you, his spirit will come and destroy you".'

'His spirit will destroy you!' Uddhava asked in surprise.

'You don't understand these people, Uddhava, Hidimbaa wanted the skull to be kept by me, but not out of love for her brother. She believed that if it was not kept under control, the spirit of Hidimba would rise and destroy me,' said Bhima.

'Then what did you do with the skull?' asked Uddhava.

'We came to a compromise—husband and wife. Uddhava, shall I tell you one thing? She makes a very fine wife. She is so loyal and affectionate. But I have a suspicion; if ever I fall ill or become weak, she will have me roasted alive and enjoy my flesh,' said Bhima.

'What was the compromise?' asked Uddhava.

'She keeps her brother's skull under her pillow, so that she can keep control over his spirit at night, lest I should be harmed,' said Bhima.

'And what do Aunt Kunti and the Brothers think about it?' asked Uddhava.

'Mother Kunti does not know whether to admire me for saving them all or to curse me for marrying a wicked Rakshasi. Yudhishthira thinks that this is a *tapascharya* (penance) which we must perform. Arjuna fidgets all the time. He tries to make bows and arrows out of the bamboos we have and shoots at high-flying birds. When he is disgusted with these feeble weapons, he makes reed pipes, plays on them, and whenever he feels safe from the voracious hunger of the Rakshasas, dances by himself. Nakula is equally unhappy. He tries to spend his time training deer, dogs and rabbits, though, before the training is complete, every one of them finds its way into the stomachs of my people. Sahadeva is the only wise man; he sees a deep meaning in all these trials of ours, and studies the means of avoiding our being harmed,' said Bhima.

'How do you feel?' asked Uddhava.

'I feel all right. I eat, drink, rule over the Rakshasas and make love to my Hidimbaa, though, by the way, the fibres that she puts on her hair are disgusting,' added Bhima in a whisper.

21

KING VRIKODARA MAKES A DECISION

*B*hima and Uddhava slowly made their way through the dense forest. Ultimately they came to a large clearing. On each of the surrounding trees a hut of grass and bamboo had been built.

'What are those nests for?' asked Uddhava, surprised at huts having been built on the tops of trees.

'Oh, that is where my Rakshasas live. Every night, each family goes up its tree and sleeps in its hut. You know, they dare not sleep on the ground, lest they should provide a feast for some enemy,' said Bhima.

At one end of the clearing, there was a grove of big trees, on each of which was a bamboo hut. Bhima proudly pointed them out. 'These are our palaces where Mother Kunti and the Brothers live. They rarely come down. I have told them not to when I am not present, for I cannot say when my Rakshasas may develop a craving for their delicious flesh. At times I have seen some of them looking at Mother's soft body with evident relish.' Then he pointed out a very big tree a little farther away, with sweeping branches, on which there was a spacious hut. 'That is my royal palace,' said Bhima proudly.

Standing in front of the huts, Bhima roared in his leonine way, this time not in anger, but in playfulness. Out of the openings of the huts appeared the familiar faces of Aunt Kunti and the four Brothers.

'Mother, here is Uddhava,' shouted Bhima in the sacred language of the gods. 'He has come to keep us company. Come down, all of you.'

Hearing his roar, Hidimbaa, from the royal hut, welcomed her husband with a loving croon. Bhima waved a huge hand at her with a hearty laugh. 'Hidimbaa,' he said in his broken Rakshasi, 'come down. We have been five brothers so far: now we are six.'

Uddhava could not shake off the feeling that he was still having a nightmare.

The afternoon meal of the community was over. The Rakshasas as usual took their meal before sunset and climbed up into their tree-top homes before it was dark.

Mother Kunti insisted that all talk should be postponed for the next day, as Uddhava needed a good night's rest. It was just like Aunt Kunti, thought Uddhava. She had seen that he was very weak and sleepy, and it was just as well that she did not allow the Five Brothers to ask him any questions.

Yudhishthira lived in a tree-top hut with Mother Kunti. The twins, Nakula and Sahadev, had a hut between them. Uddhava, therefore, paired off with Arjuna who had a hut to himself.

Each hut had a ladder of rope made out of fibres for the inmates to go up or come down. Mother Kunti was he only one who was carried to her hut on the houlders of one or other of her sons.

Uddhava found the Five Brothers living in an unnatural world. Except for Bhima, the Brothers, like aunt Kunti, lived in an isolated community by themelves, having practically no contact with the Rakshasa world. Yudhishthira had become grave, almost taciturn. Arjuna went about with his bow and flint-tipped arrows, oncerned only with the security of his brothers and mother. Nakula served Mother Kunti, kept her company and looked after her wants. Sahadeva, when he was not serving his elder brothers, was lost in thought during he day and gazed at the stars at night.

They talked among themselves; they did not care to earn the language of the Rakshasas, nor establish ontacts with them. They could never outgrow their repugnance to their habits.

Bhima was the only exception. He tried to keep his brothers and mother happy, looked after them with care, played husband to Hidimbaa, ate and drank, shouted at his chiefs, dominated the community, led them on expeditions and took part in their sports. His vital spirits overflowed the bounds of race, language and culture. He knew that his people considered the Rakshasas as aliens and the Rakshasas returned the feeling. But his zealous affection for his family and the reverence which he showed to Mother Kunti and Yudhishthira compelled he Rakshasas to treat his family with unquestionable though distant respect.

That night Uddhava slept like a log and got up only when the rays of the sun penetrated into his hut. Arjuna had already climbed down from the hut. Uddhava slipped down the rope ladder to the ground, where he found his cousin waiting for him.

'Brother Uddhava, hurry up. Take your bathe in the river. We are all dying to hear the news which you have brought.'

When Uddhava went for his bathe he saw Hidimba having hers in the same river a little way off with a few Rakshasi friends. She had taken off the wig of fibres which she always wore; the paint on her face had been washed away also. Uddhava was, therefore, surprised to find her a powerful but shapely and sinuous woman, more like a lioness than a human. No wonder Bhima was happy with her.

After his bathe and his morning *sandhya*[1], Uddhava joined the Five Brothers, who, accompanied by Kunti, led him to a knoll at a little distance from the settlement. Bhima, who had taken kindly to Nikumbha, set him to watch the forest path, with instructions to give a warning if anyone was found approaching them.

They all sat down in the generous shade of a clump of trees. Bhima, as was his wont, lay down on the grass sideways, leisurely listening to the talk, sometimes smiling to himself as some funny idea struck him.

'Now, Uddhava, tell us all about what happened after we left Hastinapura,' said Yudhishthira, in his quiet voice.

'But before that, tell us how Krishna is doing,' said Mother Kunti. 'And how are Grandfather Bhishma, the

Most Venerable Mother and Vidura, and of course, my Eldest?[2] Are they doing well?'

'Yes, tell her that first,' said Bhima, laughing at his mother's eager questions. 'Mother is more concerned with the health of her "Eldest" and his beloved sons than with all of us put together.'

'My son, don't wish ill even to your enemy,' said Kunti, mildly rebuking him. 'Some day the Great God will melt their hearts.'

'I wish them dead every moment of my life,' retorted Bhima, winking at Yudhishthira to convey that he was only teasing the mother.

'Now, Bhima will you listen to Uddhava?' said Yudhishthira, smiling indulgently. 'We must hear everything from him. He must also tell us how our elders are doing.'

It was a wonderful family knit in close affection—the mother, benign and good; Yudhishthira, sincere and dignified; Bhima, a huge naughty boy, in spite of his years, lying on the ground lazily; Arjuna sitting straight as a rod, all attention, his brilliant eyes turning from one speaker to another. Nakula sat next to him. Sahadeva sat a little farther away with his eyes fixed on the ground, Listening to every word, but cool, collected, and impassive. Uddhava could not help admiring Arjuna; he was so handsome, intelligent and alert.

Uddhava narrated all that had happened and all that he knew about Krishna. He also told them about Krishna's meeting the Most Venerable Mother,

Satyavati, and her concern about the Five Brothers; of how Krishna had been to see the Master; of how he himself came to the Land of the Demons and how he would have been roasted alive but for the timely arrival of Bhima. 'Krishna will soon be coming to Nagakoot from Kampilya,' he concluded. 'The Yadava chiefs will also arrive soon from Hastinapura. Krishna wants all of you to come with me and accompany us to Dwaraka. You must get out of this hell.'

Arjuna, fastidious as ever in spite of his long hair, untrimmed beard and fox skin shoulder-straps, grew flushed with joy. 'Oh, Uddhava, you are a messenger from the gods,' he said, and his cultured, well-modulated voice was unable to disguise his excitement. 'I hope we will soon get out of this infernal hole.' And he looked hopefully at Yudhishthira.

Yudhishthira, his eyes unsmiling, was lost in thought. All the others waited for him to speak, for the Brothers, in spite of their temperamental differences, were united in their respectful loyalty to the head of the family.

After a while Yudhishthira spoke, his voice low but clear. 'We accepted banishment because it was our duty. Grandfather and Uncle Vidura thought that it was in the interest of the Kurus and to our interest too,'

'It was in the interest of the Kurus all right, if by Kurus you mean only our uncle's sons', interjected Arjuna.

Yudhishthira, ignoring Arjuna's interruption, continued: 'We left Varanavata because Uncle Vidura who was the person who had our welfare most at heart, thought advisable that we should be supposed dead.'

'We are worse than dead,' commented Arjuna with a touch of bitterness.

'How can you be worse than dead when I am ruling over this land and my people have not yet eaten you up?' asked Bhima with an air of offended dignity, but also with a broad smile.

'If Krishna thinks that we should come to Dwaraka and proclaim to the world that we are alive, we ought to do so,' said Yudhishthira slowly. 'But we must first secure the approval of the Master, the Best of Munis, and Uncle Vidura.'

'We cannot always be guided by what Hastinapura thinks we should do,' said Arjuna, betraying impatience at the way his eldest brother looked at the situation. 'We cannot go on rotting in this wilderness till Duryodhana is pleased to suffer us to be "alive.' "

'Eldest, I would sooner train horses in Dwarka than sit here training rabbits, which generally find their way into the mouths of these subjects of Bhima's,' said Nakula in disgust.

'Then why not train a Rakshasi as I do?' interjected Bhima and chuckled as if he had cracked a mighty joke. When he made this characteristic remark, Mother Kunti looked at Bhima in indulgent disapproval.

Self-consciously Nakula glanced at his ugly fox-skin shoulder-straps, mentally comparing them with the fine silk which he always wore at Hastinapura, and said with a sneer: 'Not even The Great God, Shankara can train your Rakshasis!' he exclaimed 'Oh gods! What creatures!' He looked up to the sky to invoke divine help, and heaved a deep sigh.

Arjuna resumed his plea. 'I have made up my mind to go to Dwaraka and, in Krishna's company, perform deeds at which even the gods will tremble.' He paused a little and then said: 'I am sick of spending my days trying to shoot down flying birds with little bamboo sticks and being laughed at by the Rakshasas as a nincompoop who cannot decoy them by imitating their speech.'

'What more do you want?' asked Bhima.

'Oh, I know what I want. Every night I dream of my splendid bow, my shining silvery arrow-heads, and my magic strings which twang so musically,' said Arjuna reminiscently, and lapsed into a sullen silence.

Yudhishthira intervened in his quiet, decisive way. 'We should not go on lamenting over our present plight. The Great God is only testing our powers of endurance. We must stand the trial,' he said, and continued: 'What we have to decide is: should we go to Dwaraka as Krishna wants, or wait till we hear from Uncle Vidura?'

'Uncle Vidura is going to have to depend on the moods of King Dhritarashtra, I tell you,' said Arjuna impatiently. 'And the King's moods are not going to change, for he will never dare to do anything which his son, Duryodhana, disapproves of. He will never give us our due. We must accept Krishna's suggestion, go with him to Dwaraka or anywhere in the wide world and carve out our future for ourselves.'

Yudhishthira glanced at the irritated Arjuna in a mild though silent reproof.

'Imagine, Brother, the best bowman in Aryavarta spending his time shooting down birds', said Arjuna now in a chastened mood, and he pleaded almost piteously. 'Let us go, Brother. The gods will help us and we will carve out an empire for ourselves.'

'I have already won a kingdom for you. Why do you want more?' asked Bhima.

'Yes, a kingdom in which, every time your back is turned, we are afraid of being eaten up,' said Arjuna in contempt.

Yudhishthira raised a hand to stop this banter. 'We should not do what we want to, but what is right,' he said. 'I wish we could find out from the Master the proper thing to do in the situation!'

'When I met the Master, Krishna only wanted me to find out whether you were alive and safe,' said Uddhava.

'I agree that the Master loves us,' interrupted Arjuna, who had, again worked himself up into an excited state. 'So does Uncle Vidura; so does Grandfather Bhishma. But their only concern is to maintain the glory of the Kurus: we are only fuel to keep its flame burning bright. It does not matter to them if we are reduced to ashes.'

'You are very unfair to them. I cannot imagine that the Master has forgotten us,' said Yudhishthira.

'Am I unfair?' asked Arjuna with a touch of vehemence. 'Here are five of the best Aryas who ever wielded arms. Here is the noblest of women who ever bore a son. We are not to be happy; we are not to win fame. We must rot, rot, rot, in this wretched jungle.' Arjuna, carried away by indignation, permitted himself to speak a little defiantly.

Nakula nodded assent vigorously. Bhima patted Arjuna on the back with a laugh as if he had cracked a joke. Sahadeva alone sat silent, his face inexpressive.

Yudhishthira smiled indulgently in the manner of a wise parent. 'Arjuna, we cannot think of our own inclinations. We have to think what our Dharma is,' he said in his quiet, persuasive way.

'Is it not our duty to accept the advice of Krishna, who is the greatest champion of Dharma there can ever be? Should we not stand by his side to establish righteousness in the world?' asked Arjuna.

'Let us think patiently about it for a little,' said Yudhishthira. 'Which is the higher Dharma—to take a decision ourselves, or to wait for the decision of the elders—the Master, our Grandfather and Uncle Vidura?'

'———who have completely forgotten us, I am sure,' interrupted Nakula.

'It is not right to say that Nakula,' said Yudhishthira, 'It was the Most Venerable Mother (Satyavati) who charged Krishna with the mission of finding us, and I am sure Grandfather and uncle Vidura knew all about it,'

'But we must also try to help them by thinking for ourselves,' said Arjuna. 'Let us be the masters of our own lives.'

'I am willing to agree with you, Arjuna, if I can convince myself that to take a decision ourselves at this moment is our duty,' said Yudhishthira, and then turned to Sahadeva. 'Sahadeva, why don't you let us have your opinion? What would you advise?'

Sahadeva, the younger of the twins, who was listening intently with his eyes half closed, opened them wide and let a faint smile play upon his lips. Then he spoke slowly, precisely, weighing every word, and everybody listened to him intently, for he had the oracular gift of never speaking unless solicited. 'I have been watching the stars for a long time and I am sure relief will come to us from a person born under the constellation of Rohini. The only person associated with us who was born under that sign is our cousin, Krishna Vaasudeva.'

'That is why Uddhava has come from Krishna,' interjected Arjuna.

'Why didn't you tell us this before, you sly fellow?' asked Bhima.

'Did you ever ask me about it?' replied Sahadeva with a smile.

'Now I understand why every night you were peeping out of our hut and gazing at the stars,' said Nakula.

'——and losing all your sleep and growing thin,' commented Bhima.

'What do you advise us to do, Sahadeva?' asked Yudhishthira, who had the highest regard for his wisdom.

In a quiet, even voice, Sahadeva replied: 'Let Brother Uddhava go back to Krishna Vaasudeva. We ought to accept whatever he advises. If he advises us to go with him, we should. The planets will then be auspicious.'

'Thank you, Sahadeva. As usual you have rightly divined what the gods want us to do,' said Yudhishthira.

'Then it is a matter of days,' said Arjuna, transported with joy. 'Uddhava can go tomorrow and come back within a fortnight, at the latest within a month.'

'Yes, Uddhava must go back immediately,' said Mother Kunti.

Suddenly a crooning voice was heard in the distance. Bhima sat up, listened to the voice with a fond smile and let out a purring roar in reply.

The others were shocked at being interrupted by this animal love-making. Mother Kunti put her hands over her ears; she had not yet been able to avoid a shudder every time her son's wife crooned. Yudhishthira, as usual, smiled indulgently at the message which his brother exchanged with his wife Hidimbaa in the manner of the Rakshasas. There was a sneer on Arjuna's lips; undisguised disgust on Nakula's. Sahadeva had lapsed into impassivity.

Bhima brightened up, looked at his mother and brothers with a sly, defiant smile, and spoke to Uddhava: 'Brother, it is all too easy for you to talk about your going back. But there is an unalterable law of King Virochana's in my land. No human being who crosses into Rakshasavarta can ever leave it.'

'Oh, Bhima, please don't talk like this,' said Kunti.

'I will have to invoke the spirit of Virochana and get the edict changed for my beloved Uddhava's sake,' said Bhima with a laugh. 'But it will not be an easy matter.'

'Oh, I am sure you can do it, if you set about it,' said Yudhishthira.

'Yes. But one thing I tell you. Krishna or no Krishna, Master or no Master, we are not going to leave for about a year,' said Bhima.

'For about a year? What is wrong with you, Bhima?' shouted Arjuna almost in anger.

'Don't get excited, Brother. Everything is all right. Within five months, I am going to be a father, and I cannot leave Hidimbaa till our child is at least six months old. Everyone of us will have to wait till then.'

'Bhima, you are having a son!' said Kunti, suddenly forgetting her dislike of Hidimbaa, and transported with joy, 'He will be the eldest Kuru in his generation—the heir to *Chakravarti* Bharata's throne.'

'Of course, Mother,' said Bhima with a chuckle, 'unless your daughter-in-law plays a trick and gives birth to a daughter.'

'Don't say such inauspicious things,' retorted Mother Kunti.

∎

22

THE MIRACULOUS VICTORY

*W*hen Uddhava left Nagakoota, the twin Princesses broke down completely. Utterly miserable, they clung to each other in their distress. They had set their hearts on becoming the wives of Uddhava. Now he had gone to the Land of the Demons; he was never going to return, for he was going to be eaten up by the Rakshasas. They however decided to wait for his return till two full-moon nights were past; if he did not return by then, they would put an end to their lives.

What the twins could not understand was the significance of the last words spoken by Uddhava: 'Krishna wants me to go to Bhima.' If Krishna was a god as Uddhava claimed him to be, why should he send him to his death? Between themselves they came to the conclusion that, whatever Uddhava might say about his friend, he was a wicked fellow who had sent their 'husband' to the Land of the Demons.

Their parents and their brother were unhappy at the way the twins behaved. They would sit huddled in a corner, their arms around each other, sighing or shedding tears together. They would not be consoled.

They would not take their meals; they would sit in their usual seats, take a few morsels, burst into tears and go away. They would not attend the daily worship of Pashupati, nor would they take part in ceremonial dances.

Their mother Ravika sometimes scolded them, as others tried to give them such solace as she could. One day, feeling that the girls ought to regain a little control over themselves, she chided severely. 'Foolish girls, it is very stupid of you to go on weeping day after day and starving yourselves. Lord Pashupati is great. No harm is going to come to Uddhava.'

Maniman, their brother, was with them, nodding approval of what their mother was saying.

Pingala turned on her mother in an unfamiliar outburst of temper: 'Don't tell lies, mother. He is never going to return. He will be eaten up by the Rakshasas. Don't think that we are children.'

The other twin, Kapila, took up the thread. 'If you were so sure of his returning, why didn't you send your precious son along with him?' she asked and turning to Maniman continued: 'You great warrior, you think no end of yourself, but you are a coward. You shrank away. Why did you not keep Uddhava company?'

The mother tried to pacify them both. 'After all, Uddhava had to go because Krishna, his friend, asked him to do so. Why should Maniman risk his life?'

'That's it' shouted Kapila. 'Uddhava wanted to carry out Krishna's mandate, true, But this brother of ours never thought that his life was worth saving, so as to save his sisters' lives'.

'You are all selfish cowards,' Pingala said scornfully.

'Why should you be so foolish?' asked Maniman, deeply hurt by these taunts. 'If Uddava does not return, you will forget him in a year or two. Then you will get even better husbands.'

Kapila glared at Maniman in rage. 'Look at this future king of Nagakoota,' Pingala sneered. 'He has already started searching for new husbands for us. He has already assumed that Uddhava is not going to return.'

'My child,' said Ravika, trying to pacify her, 'don't get excited. We all know that Uddhava is not going to return; It is certain. Your brother is only thinking of your future.'

'We don't care what you think about our future,' said Pingala. We have already made our plans. We are waiting for two full-moons to pass; then we shall follow Uddhava.'

Kapila took up the thread. 'We will throw ourselves into the Ganga, or better still, we will go to the Land of the Demons and get ourselves eaten up as our lord was.'

Ravika was on the point of hitting the two girls, when Maniman intervened. 'Mother, don't upset yourself,' he said. 'I have already told father to persuade Grandfather to give a bit of his mind to these silly girls. Perhaps he has also told the venerable Master about their madness!'

'You are going to get the Master and Grandfather to talk to us!' exclaimed Pingala. 'The Master has already assured us that, if Uddhava does not return after two full-moons, he will take us away from this land of cowards. He will then let us do what we like with our lives.'

'The Princesses of Aryaka go to a foreign land!' exclaimed Ravika, horrified.

'Yes, we will go wherever the Master takes us,' said Pingala.

'We will even go to the other world—to anywhere where there are no cowards like the ones here', said Kapila, and added: 'This noble prince had not the courage to go with Uddhava. Cowards, cowards, cowards!' And the twins clung to each other and cried.

Maniman looked a little ashamed of himself. There was something wrong with him. He, the future lord of the Nagas, had not persuaded Uddhava to give up his mission, had not ventured to keep him company, and could not prevail upon his sisters to forget Uddhava. There was something about all the other three which was admirable and something in him which was not. He felt uneasy.

In a few days, however, the outlook for the twins became hopeful. Yadava warriors, with shining chariots and prancing horses, arrived at Nagakoota from Hastinapura under the command of Kritavarma in anticipation of Krishna's arrival, for, as originally arranged, he was to return to Dwaraka by way of Ekachakra Tirtha and Nagakoota.

Everyone in Nagakoota, except the twins, forgot
Uddhava and the boy Rakshasa, for no one had ever
before seen such chariots and horses, or such bows
and arrows. Their hearts also filled with pride when
they saw the stalwart Yadavas coming and
prostrating themselves before King Aryaka, the
maternal grandfather of their chief Vasudeva, Krishna's
father.

Prince Maniman, particularly, was in ecstasy. He
had heard of the swaggering Aryas who had harassed
his people, but had never imagined that there could be
such friendly warriors among them. He and their chiefs
were soon the best of companions. A ray of hope entered
even the hearts of the twins. This was Krishna's army.
If he had ordered Uddhava, to go to the Land of the
Demons, he would surely bring him back.

Then, he came, the friend of Uddhava, dark-blue
and handsome, with the peacock feather fluttering on
his diadem. The twins forgot their misery, and with the
other members of the family went to the outskirts of
the town to welcome him.

The Nagas were in a festive mood. They came out in
their gaudiest dresses with multi-coloured beads
hanging round necks. The women laughed and
chattered happily. Even Grandfather Aryaka had a smile
on his shrunken face.

Krishna prostrated himself before Grandfather
Aryaka and the Prince. The twins, full of admiration,
looked with open mouths at this friend of their
Uddhava's, who had figured so conspicuously in all he

had said. A conch, as if of gold, was suspended from his waist. On his left shoulder was strapped a shining weapon, circular and many-toothed, and his smile was sweet—sweeter than anyone else's, except of course Uddhava's.

As the people returned to the town, Krishna walked alongside Grandfather's litter, talking to him all the way. The twins were struck by manner in which this friend of Uddhava's talked, At first he was grave and reverential; then he was informal. When his smiling eyes, full of affectionate interest, rested on the members of the family one after the other as Grandfather introduced them, they kindled a smile even in the twins. Soon Krishna was no longer speaking reverentially, but informally. Including the whole family among his listeners, he talked playfully with mischievous eyes and an irresistible smile. The twins could not hear what he told Aryaka, but they saw, for the first time in their lives, the stern old man laughing uproariously. A wonderful man this, who could make Grandfather laugh!

Then the procession went to the shrine where Krishna worshipped Lord Pashupati. Later he was brought to the residence of the royal family. After the chiefs had gone, Aryaka's family gathered round him, curious to know all about Marishaa's famous grandson.

The twins were dying to meet the guest and tell him to go to the rescue of Uddhava. However, immediately the chiefs retired, Krishna himself enquired of Prince Karkotaka: 'Where is Uddhava? I don't see him here.'

The twins strained their ears to hear the conversation.

'He has left us,' said Karkotaka, his voice diffident.

'Where has he gone?' asked Krishna anxiously. 'He was to have joined me here to return to Dwaraka.'

Karkotaka felt a little confused. 'He has gone to Rakshasavarta, the Land of the Demons.'

'The Land of the Demons? Why?' asked Krishna.

'One of our chiefs captured a Rakshasa boy, who informed us that Sister Kunti and the Five Brothers were alive and in the Land of the Demons,' said Karkotaka.

'Are you sure?' asked Krishna.

'The boy was half mad, but that is what we understood him to say,' replied Karkotaka.

'So Uddhava himself went in searh of them?' asked Krishna.

'Yes, he said that you had asked him to do so,' said Karkotaka.

'That is just like Uddhava,' said Krishna with deep affection.

The twins could not help sobbing, and every eye was turned on them.

'What is the matter, sisters?' asked Krishna, sensing that their grief was somehow connected with what he had said.

Ravika intervened: 'Krishna, they are my daughters, Kapila and Pingala.'

'But why are you both crying?' asked Krishna in a voice full of concern.

Pingala threw decorum to the winds, and said with sobs and tears: 'Oh, Brother, he has been eaten up by the Rakshasas!'

'These cowards would not even go with him,' interrupted Kapila, looking at her father and brother angrily with tearful eyes.

Krishna looked at Karkotaka for an explanation of this outburst. The Prince told him the whole episode of the arrival of the Rakshasa boy and the departure of Uddhava. He concluded: 'Noble Vaasudeva, Uddhava went to the Land of the Demons, because, he said, you had asked him to do so. None of us could go with him. No Naga has ever crossed the boundary of Rakshasavarta. It is a terrible land from which no man returns alive.'

Krishna heard the confession of this doughty Naga Prince with a smile of compassion, 'I understand why none of you could accompany Uddhava,' he said with such an indulgent, forgiving note in his voice that every warrior in the family felt ashamed at having failed to do what he should have done.

Aryaka, who was listening to this conversation in his usual silent, observant way, turned to Krishna. 'If I had been young, I would have never allowed Uddhava to go alone,' he said, his large eyes showing a contemptuous disapproval of his people. 'The Naga warriors of this generation believe in oiling their hair and spending their time dancing at festivities. I wish I had been young,' the old man repeated helplessly with a sigh.

'It is no use shedding tears, Grandfather,' said Pingala. 'He will have been eaten up by now.'

'Did I not tell you, Grandfather, that they were cowards?' asked Kapila.

Krishna looked at the twins with a smile of appreciation.

'Don't worry, sister. I will go tomorrow to the Land of the Demons and bring Uddhava back. Please, Grandfather, cancel all the festivities for tomorrow. We shall hold them when I return with Uddhava, perhaps together with the Five Brothers,' he said, and rose from his seat.

'But he must be already dead and digested,' repeated Pingala. The twins could not be shaken in their conviction that Uddhava had already provided a meal for some of the Rakshasas.

Krishna smiled sweetly at them and said: 'Nothing shall happen to Uddhava so long as I am alive.' Then he turned to Aryaka, and, with a peculiar insistence on the inevitability of Fate, which he sometimes gave his words, added: 'Whoever tries to kill Uddhava shall not live.'

With a sweeping and decisive gesture, he threw his scarf over his shoulders, and followed by Satyaki and Shvetaketu, left the hall.

Suddenly Maniman, who was overpowered by a sense of shame at his own insufficiency, was moved to say: 'Grandfather, I am gong with Krishna to the Land of the Demons.'

Kapila burst out: 'Do you want to go now, you coward? You could not go when Uddhava went.'

King Aryaka's Nagas were anything but war-like. Their most useful weapon was the axe, which served them well for striking an enemy or occasionally turning a strip of forest into a passably tillable field. They could build clay houses in which they kept their pigs, goats and sheep, and the few miserable cattle which they possessed. Cattle-breeding on a large scale was an unknown art—an art of which the Aryas were the masters. They had donkeys in plenty; they had only a few horses, mostly bought from impecunious Aryas, more for show than for use.

The Nagas loved to settle on the banks of the Ganga and the Yamuna, for, with their small canoes, they could easily go up and down these highways. However, with the advance of the powerful Aryas into the valleys year after year, they sought security by retreating into the forest.

To these people, the arrival of a small contingent of Yadavas, whom they could feel to be at one with them, was an eye-opener. They were not like the Aryas of Hastinapura or Kampilya; they respected their chiefs; they did not clamour for land or cattle; they worshipped at the same shrine of Pashupati.

The Arya chiefs, Krishna and Uddhava, were not strangers. They were the children of 'their' Marishaa, the daughter of their beloved King Aryaka. With the Yadavas among them, they felt that they had a place in the big, wide world, dominated by the Arya warriors with their horses and chariots, their heavy maces and mighty bows.

Krishna's decision, to go to the Land of the Demons and bring back Uddhava alive, made a terrible impact on the Nagas. Till then, even the bravest of the Naga chiefs had shuddered at the prospect of meeting a Rakshasa. The very name of these terrible demons who came by night, made hideous noises, stole away their kinsfolk or cattle, ate raw flesh and cut open the vitals of the cattle with their bare hands, was anathema. A rumour, that a Rakshasa had appeared in a village, brought hundreds of Nagas with spears and axes to destroy the straying demon.

Now a new horizon had opened. Siguri Naga, their brave chief, had actually brought a Rakshasa boy as prisoner. Uddhava, their kinsman, had bravely gone to the dreaded land. Now Krishna, Marishaa's grandson, who had routed the Emperor Jarasandha and whose name was on everyone's lips as a wonder-worker, was going to rescue Uddhava from the Rakshasas.

A wave of courage swept through every Naga. The young chiefs got ready to accompany Krishna. Even the wisely timid Karkotaka summoned up the courage to express a wish to join him. Maniman's eyes had now been opened to new ambitions by the power and splendour of the Yadava chiefs. He had already taken a few lessons in wielding Uddhava's powerful bow and arrow, and was anxious to plunge into the adventure.

The Nagas gathered at the shrine of Pashupati. Their priests and Acharya Shvetaketu as the Arya priest, invoked the Great God to bless their venture. Even the twins, generally full of tears the whole day long after Uddhava had left, were now smiling.

Satyaki selected a hundred young Naga chiefs and gave a finishing touch to whatever little training they had had in the use of the crude arms. Five of these chiefs were attached to each of the twenty Yadavas who were selected for the expedition.

Krishna also took with him five of the best Garudas who were in the Yadava contingent. They were strange creatures, with artificial beaks fastened to their mouths, and creeched like eagles, and on level ground walked as if they were flying.

On a day declared auspicious by the priests, Krishna started for the frontier village with Siguri Naga as his guide. He was as cheerful as ever, joked to Aryaka, patted Maniman on the back, and smiled at the twins. He even made Ravika smile with the story of how she reminded him of his mother Yashoda who always used to punish him for stealing butter. His self-confidence was infectious. Everyone thought that he was going to return with Uddhava.

Aryaka in his litter accompanied them for half a day's journey. Prince Karkotaka came right to Lahuria, the frontier village, to await their return.

At Lahuria, Krishna took leave of Prince Karkotaka and the ladies of the royal family. The twins begged him to let them accompany him. Krishna laughed mischievously. 'If Uddhava has been eaten up by the Rakshasas, I will take you there to be eaten up too. Till then you must have patience,' he said.

'But why not take us with you now?' they asked.'

'Not now. Suppose you were eaten up and Uddhava was left alive, what would happen to him?' he asked smiling, and the twins laughed.

A sudden thought struck Pingala. 'Suppose Uddhava has been eaten up. What will you do?' she asked.

'Don't worry,' said Krishna, pinching her cheek. 'If anything happens to Uddhava, I will eat all the Rakshasas and give you some to eat also. But I am sure he is alive. He cannot die, and I will bring him back.'

Accompanied by Krishna, Siguri Naga led the party up the stony path. The rear was protected by Satyaki, followed by some retainers who carried their rations.

When they came to the craggy heights, Krishna began to sing the war-song of the Yadavas. The other Yadavas took it up. The Nagas also, in high spirits, joined in though without understanding a word of the song. But their courage rose with the rising notes and they began to climb the heights rapidly.

When they reached the top of the precipice, Krishna took his *Sharnga* and lifted his conch *Panchajanya* and blew a victorious note on it till the forest echoes multiplied. Everyone looked with awe at this challenge delivered to the whole might of the Rakshasas.

As if in obedience to his command, Uddhava emerged from the densely-wooded valley with a joyous shout, the limping Nikumbha running by his side. They could see behind them several shadowy forms half-concealed by the dense forest, which no sooner sighted Krishna's presence and heard the *Panchajanya* than they threw the load which they were carrying on their shoulders to the ground and scampered away.

It was a strange sight. Uddhava, alive and safe, emerged from the mysterious hell at Krishna's command. This was indeed a god!

Krishna hailed Uddhava with a joyous shout and ran down to the valley to envelop him in his arms. The others still awestruck by the strange miracle worked by Krishna came down the steep craggy slope of the hill, shouting 'Victory to Krishna and Uddhava!'

'Are the Five Brothers alive?' asked Krishna in a whisper to Uddhava.

Uddhava nodded in the affirmative, but by a glance warned Krishna against pressing his query in the presence of others. Then he loudly and firmly said so that everyone could hear: 'Noble Vaasudeva, King Vrikodara, the mighty king of the Rakshasas, is highly pleased with the friendship of King Aryaka of the Nagas, and has sent these presents to him as tokens of the peace estabhished between the Nagas and the Rakshasas.'

Krishna pointed at the bundles which the Rakshasas had thrown on the ground before they disappeared, and asked: 'What are these presents?'

'They are fox skins,' said Uddhava pointing to the bundles.

'Are these the presents sent by King Vrikodara to Grandfather Aryaka?' asked Krishna.

'Yes. And now there will be peace between the Nagas and the Rakshasas. King Vrikodara has promised that hereafter no Rakshasas will ever eat any Naga who is the subject of the great King Aryaka. In token of this friendship, King Vrikodara will send every month a present of fifty fox skins,' said Uddhava, and smiled. 'And as the representative of King Aryaka, I have promised—and I hope the promise will be kept by the great King—to present in return fifty heads, of goats and sheep to King Vrikodara. This young Rakshasa,' said Uddhava patting the head of Nikumbha, who smiled happily, 'who has now picked up our sacred language fairly well, will attend to the exchange every month on the night of the full-moon.'

The Nagas were jubilant beyond description. The fact that they need no more be afraid of the Rakshasas came to them as a relief from a nightmarish fear.

After a joyous feast, all turned to climb the hill on the return journey. When the others proceeded ahead, Krishna turned to Uddhava. 'I am glad you have come back alive. How did you escape the Rakshasas? Did you get any news of the Five Brothers?'

'They are all safe—Aunt Kunti and the Five Brothers', replied Uddhava with a smile. 'King Vrikodara is no other than our brother Bhima.'

'Bhima!' exclaimed Krishna in surprise. 'How did he come to be the king of the Rakshasas?'

'It is a long story which I will tell you presently. But Bhima, alone of all the mortals, could have performed this feat,' said Uddhava. 'However, they are not prepared to come to Dwaraka just now.'

'That is what I want too. I want them to remain where they are till the month of Margashirsha next year. The *swayamvara* of Drupada's daughter, Krishnaa, is going to take place at Kampilya in Paush,' said Krishna.

'*Swayamvara!* I thought she was going to be wedded to you!' said Uddhava.

'I seem to elude everyone who wants to marry me,' said Krishna with a smile. 'We have decided that she is to choose a husband in a *swayamvara,*'

'And will you enter the *swayamvara* contest?' asked Uddhava.

'Do you think I am likely to? I want Arjuna to do it. That is why I want them to come to Kampilya only in Paush next,' said Krishna.

'That will exactly suit Bhima,' said Uddhava. 'He will not come out for a year, and they have all decided that they will come out only when you ask them to.'

'I am glad that they are reconciled to being where they are for a year', said Krishna.

'Reconciled? Even elephants would not be able to drag them out till next year. King Vrikodara is going to have a Crown Prince born to Hidimbaa, his Rakshasi queen. He will leave his kingdom only when he is six months old,' said Uddhava.

Krishna laughed. 'You can never say what miracles Bhima may perform next,' he said.

When they came to Lahuria, a messenger from King Aryaka was awaiting them. 'Hasten home, all of you. The Nagas have been invaded by a wicked king.'

Every one was surprised, because there had not even been a rumour that there was the possibility of an invasion. But the spirit of the party was high and only rose higher at the prospect of giving battle to the invader.

'Uddhava, a new trial faces us,' remarked Krishna.

23

THE LAST WISH OF ARYAKA

$\mathcal{T}$he news, that the Naga territory on the north bank of the Yamuna had been invaded, did not dampen the ardour of the conquering party, which returned to Nagakoota with drums beating and pipes playing. On the way, wherever it halted, the villagers gave it a hearty welcome with songs and dances, and were eager to see the presents sent to their beloved King by the King of the Rakshasas. And the announcement, that no longer would any Rakshasa eat a Naga, sent a thrill of relief through every heart.

Uddhava, however, was not quite happy. When he told the story of his adventure to Karkotaka and Ravika, his eyes sought the twins in vain. Somehow or other, they invariably slipped away as soon as he began to talk about himself. This was unexpected, and Uddhava felt that there was something wrong. The twins would not evade him in this noticeable way without some reason.

Uddhava took Maniman—who by now was feeling like a warrior in his own right—into his confidence. 'My brother, what is wrong with Kapila and Pingala? Why do they shun me? Are they still very angry?'

Krishna, who was talking to Prince Karkotaka at the time, overheard this whispered conversation and turned to Uddhava: "Uddhava, the twins piteously begged me to bring you back alive. They came here all the way to welcome you. Can't you guess why they are angry?'

'Angry with me? What have I done?' asked Uddhava pentiently.

'You! You have done nothing but offend them all the while,' said Krishna with a mischievous smile.

'What have I done?' insisted Uddhava.

'You are their husband—at least they have accepted you as one. They expect you to seek them out. They want to hear all about your heroic adventures, not in a crowd, but by themselves alone. When will you be a good husband?' asked Krishna, laughing at Uddhava's surprised look.

'I, a husband! Even you, Krishna, want me to marry the twins?' asked Uddhava helplessly.

'The twins have already married you and also won you by their devotion. Uddhava, when women are bent on winning husbands, there is no escape. If I were you, I would yield with a good grace', said Krishna, and turned to Maniman. 'Maniman, will you take Uddhava to the twins when there is no one else present? And don't stay there yourself. The twins want an opportunity to cry to their heart's content when Uddhava tells them how he was on the point of being cooked alive and eaten by the Rakshasas, and how at that very moment his last thought was of them.'

'How do you know I thought of them then?' asked Uddhava.

'You did, didn't you? How I came to know of it is my secret,' said Krishna, as he laughingly walked away.

When the party reached Nagakoota it was received ceremoniously by King Aryaka, though everyone was agitated over the news of the invasion. The same day, festivities were held to celebrate the victory over the Rakshasas. The Nagas and the Yadavas danced till most of them could stand on their legs on longer, and ate and drank till the early hours of the morning.

Next day, messengers brought the details of the invasion, Chekitana, the Yadava King of Pushkara, had been attacked by Duryodhana, the Crown Prince of the Kurus. Instead of surrendering, the Yadava Chief, with his people, had crossed the Yamuna and, in his turn, had been driving the Nagas out of their settlements and appropriating their possessions. In the skirmishes which had followed, many Nagas had been killed. Unable to resist the powerful Yadavas, the Nagas were fleeing into the interior of the forest.

It was very disquieting news. So far the Aryans had respected the Yamuna as the boundary between themselves and the Nagas: now they were crossing over in large numbers.

There was panic when the news spread among the people. King Aryaka, deeply perturbed, convened a meeting of the chiefs, to which Krishna, Uddhava, Satyaki and Shvetaketu were also invited. All the chiefs were highly agitated. They talked of sending a large contingent of Nagas to the rescue of their people living on the banks of the Yamuna.

When Aryaka sought Krishna's advice, he said quietly: 'Venerable Grandfather, I sense something sinister behind this move of Duryodhana's. Chekitana is a Yadava chief: he stands guard over the highway between Saurashtra and Hastinapura, Duryodhana may have captured Pushkara to prevent us going northward. Chekitana, unable to resist, must have crossed the Yamuna in order to find an asylum in your territory'.

'He is not seeking an asylum', said Aryaka, a little impatient at the way Krishna was looking at the situation. 'He is destroying our settlements and killing our people.'

'I agree that is all wrong', said Krishna. 'But, once there is a war, people go mad; they cannot see what is wrong and what is right. If you permit me, I will make a suggestion', he added, folding his hands.

'By all means, do. We want your advice', said Aryaka.

'Noble Grandfather, if I am right in my guess, it would be wise to extend hospitality to Chekitana and his people during the rains,' said Krishna with quiet persuasiveness.

'What if he takes advantage of our hospitality and destroys us?' said Karkotaka. 'We have had enough experience of the Aryas; in war they are merciless; in peace they are deceitful.'

'You are right, Uncle', said Krishna with a disarming smile. 'We have a bad record as conquerors, particularly against weak people. But, if I give you my word that

Chekitana will leave your territory at the end of the rainy season, will you still insist on driving him out by force?'

Karkotaka clearly showed in his face that he had no confidence in what Krishna was saying. He looked at his father to enquire what he would say.

'Uncle, please do not place confidence in me', said Krishna. 'You know Uddhava well; he will soon marry the twins. If he stays in your midst and promises to drive Chekitana out of your territory in case I am unable to induce him to leave it, will you then feel confidence in me?'

Aryaka looked at his son. Karkotaka was watching the chiefs who, he noticed, mistrusted Krishna.

'Grandfather, by all means send an army to drive out Chekitana, if you are so minded. Uddhava will go with it, and, if necessary, Satayaki also. And you will win the war, I have no doubt', said Krishna and continued: 'But it will mean war—killing, plundering, burning settlements and raping women.' Krishna paused for a while for effect. 'On the other hand, if you accept my suggestion, you will have given Chekitana by way of hospitality only what he can now extract from you by force. And then I will see that he leaves your land', he added with earnest insistence, 'And what I have promised shall come to pass', said Krishna in tone of finality.

The Naga chiefs, who had already been hypnotised by Krishna's miraculous feat in overcoming the Rakshasas without striking a blow, were impressed by the transparent sincerity with which he gave the promise.

Aryaka raised himself from his litter, closed his eyes for a moment and said firmly: 'Lord Pashupati is great Krishna, my son, my people will extend hospitality to Chekitana. But you will have to see that our territories are vacated after the rains.'

The next day, when Krishna came to meet King Aryaka at his invitation, he was shocked to see the change in the old man who was shaking in every limb, his eyes having lost their glow.

Krishna prostrated himself before his father's maternal grandfather, folded his hands, and said 'Grandfather, give me you commands.'

'Krishna, I want to talk to you in confidence', said the old King, his voice low and faltering. With a wave of his feeble hand, he commanded Karkotaka and the chiefs to leave them alone. When the others had gone, Aryaka added pathetically: 'Krishna, give me your hand'.

Krishna gave his hand to the old man.

'Krishna,' the old man said in a tremulous voice, 'the news which we received yesterday has given me a great shock. I would never have thought that an Arya king would cross the Yamuna to harass my people. I am distressed—very distressed', he added, as tears trickled down his cheek. 'Listen to an old man's story— an old man who has only a few days to live. You are my Marishaa's grandson. I have a claim on you, Krishna.

Krishna patted the hand of the old man affectionately, and said: 'Look upon me as you look upon Maniman, Grandfather. I am all yours'.

The old King paused for a while. Then, trembling

with emotion, he continued in his usual crisp voice: 'The advice that you gave us yesterday was wise. I would never have expected it from a young man like you. May Lord Pashupati give you the strength to fulfil your promise!'

'Don't worry, Grandfather. It is for the Great God to protect us. But, even at the cost of my life, I shall try to fulfil my pledge', said Krishna.

'Krishna' my son, I fear that a grim future awaits my people', said Aryaka.

'Why should that be so, Grandfather?' asked Krishna, his voice expressing sympathy.

'When I was young, we Nagas laughed at the Aryas who came riding in chariots, with bows and arrows in their hands', said Aryaka in a weak voice, reminiscently, I then thought that we were a powerful people whom none could oust from our domain. But your grandfather's people—the Yadavas—came and converted our forests on the other bank of the Yamuna into settlements for themselves. The lands on the banks of the Ganga were also part of our heritage; slowly the Kurus and the Panchalas came and settled there. My people invariably had to retreat into the forests before them.'

The old man was silent for a little while. Then, with a long sigh, he continued: 'My people are good-natured, easy-going and peace-loving. They like petty skirmishes, but hate to fight wars; in fact, they cannot stand them. They do not easily take to the ways of your people, to bows and arrows, to horses and chariots, to rearing cattle and cultivating lands. We are stuck in our old,

old ways. If things continue as they are, the Nagas wil
disappear from the earth.'

Krishna was moved by the grief which the old man's
voice betrayed, and went on patting his thin, trembling
hand. 'I am thinking, thinking, thinking, all the the
time: What is it that is driving us into the interior o
the forests?' His voice was almost inaudible. After a
moment's silence, he continued: 'Karkotaka is not equa
to the fight. My other brave sons are all dead. Manimar
is very easy-going. We cannot match the Aryas ir
strength, skill or vigour.'

Aryaka paused for breath, while Krishna admired
the old King's wisdom. 'When I saw Uddhava and you
come into our midst, I felt that Lord Pashupati had
answered my prayers to save my people', continued the
King. 'I consulted our priests; they agreed with me tha
you had come at the behest of Pashupati to save us. Ir
a few days you have breathed a new life into my people
A spirit of adventure—may be short-lived—has come to
them. The peace with the Rakshasas has given them a
new hope'.

'I am so glad that our coming has helped you all'
said Krishna.

'So far I have been opposed to my people taking to
the Arya ways of living. I thought that, if my people are
peaceful, nobody would attack them. But during the
last week, I have been thinking during the day, during
the night, thinking, thinking, I have now decided tha
my people should take to the Arya way of living, forge
arms and fight, rear cattle and horses, and grow barley
and rice, as your people have been doing. Though ou

people love their old ways, they will listen to you. They think of you only as Marishaa's grandson. And, moreover, they are not afraid of you. They believed that you do not want to enslave them or be their king', said the old King.

'I can assure you, Grandfather, that I have no ambition to be the king of the Nagas or of the Aryas either. More than once I was offered a kingship, but I refused', said Krishna. 'Once you are a king, the hearts of the people are closed to you. I want them to come to me with open hearts, so that I can enter them.'

'Help me, Krishna, help me', said Aryaka. His trembling hands made a futile attempt to take Krishna's hand as the tears rolled down his shrunken cheeks. 'Lead my people from helplessness to strength'.

'Venerable Grandfather, it is easy to think of horses and chariots, but it is not easy to acquire them', said Krishna.

'Why? I do not understand', said Aryaka.

'Horses and chariots, bows and arrows, are weapons of war, they are costly; they require experts to handle them. Rearing horses requires labour, skill and money, Whatever is needed for them must come from the fertile earth, from multiplying cattle, particularly from cows which are the mothers of plenty, and from hard, very hard work. You cannot have the one without the other,' said Krishna.

'How did you manage to obtain them when you took your people to Dwaraka?' asked Aryaka.

'When we marched to freedom through the deserts, we passed through a fiery ordeal, and from this ordeal, we emerged as a tough people. That was our making. We had taken our horses and cattle to Saurashtra. We were adepts in tilling lands and rearing cows.[1] So we were able immediately to turn Saurashtra into a land of plenty. Besides, the Great God gave us ports—Dwaraka, Prabhasa and Sabar Kathha.[2] They have been pouring unlimited wealth into our lap. So we did not require, like other kings, to wage wars, or levy tributes to maintain our strength', said Krishna.

'You are lucky, God has blessed you with wisdom, Krishna. What would you advise me to do?' asked Aryaka.

'If you want your people to survive, let them keep to such of their ancient way as are needed to maintain their self-respect, and adopt the Arya ways where they are lacking in strength', said Krishna.

'Show me the way, please, my son', besought Aryaka pathetically, 'I do not want my people to sink into slavery. I want to save them'.

Krishna paused for a while. 'Grandfather, the first thing is to open your people's eyes to what is happening outside.'

'Oh, I know that can never be', said Aryaka.

'It can be. If you invite a *rishi* to establish an *ashram* here, it would be a home of learning and love, where your people could learn the ways of Dharma and *Tapas*', said Krishna.

'But what about getting strong—strong enough not to be overwhelmed by the Aryas?' asked Aryaka.

'That means that the Nagas must give up their easy

ways and take to stern *Tapas*. Shvetaketu will train them to our ways of war; above all, train your people to breed horses. The Aryas are all powerful because they worship the horse, the divine winner of all battles, from whom all strength flows'. Then he added: 'The Nagas will have to learn how to win wars. I hate bloody wars. I have never fought them except in defence of righteousness. But every man should be ready to fight for Dharma, and, if necessary, to die for it.'

'But what do you want me to do?' asked Aryaka, unable to follow the implications of what Krishna was saying. 'Do not speak to me in riddles.'

'I will speak plainly', said Krishna. 'Satyaki can go and meet Chekitana. I can send an invitation to Dhaumya *rishi* to take a few promising boys into his *ashram* at Utkochaka Tirtha. I will place at your disposal the twenty-five horses and ten mares which King Drupada presented me with. I can also send him a request to present you with a hundred cows, rich in milk, for the *ashram* in the first instance. Guru Sandipani perhaps can spare an expert in arms to instruct your people in the use of the latest weapons', said Krishna.

'But without you, my people will not take to the new ways easily, I know how reluctant they are', said Aryaka.

'I cannot stay here indefinitely', replied Krishna. 'I must go to Avanti where Guru Sandipani is waiting for me. But after Uddhava's marriage with the twins, he can stay here for a whole year, in fact till I come back in the month of Paush of next year.'

'Are you coming back in Paush next year?' asked Aryaka.

'Yes. I will also bring some Yadava warriors with me. We are going to attend the *swayamvara* of King Drupada's daughter. And, if I can get King Drupada to invite Maniman, he can attend it too. He is deeply attached to Uddhava', said Krishna.

When Karkotaka and the chiefs, and also Shvetaketu, Satyaki and Uddhava were recalled, the old King lay for some time with closed eyes. The others sat around silently, wating for him to open them.

When he did so, there was a glow in them. 'Karkotaka, chiefs, the prophecy which Lord Pashupati inspired our High Priest to make, has come true. Krishna has promised to befriend us.' The old man's mouth was twisted into a vague semblance of a smile. 'Krishna will lead you to victory. Give me your hands and swear that you will obey him implicitly.'

Karkotaka, Maniman and the chiefs gathered round the litter, and each gave his right hand to the old man, who, with a feeble movement, placed it in the hands of Krishna. The old man's large eyes grew larger.

'Krishna, my Marishaa's grandson, keep your promise to me. Befriend my people', said the old man.

Krishna, overwhelmed with emotion, bent his head low over the outstretched hand of Karkotaka and the other chiefs. For a while no one spoke.

Tears ran down the hollow cheek of Aryaka. 'I can now die happily', he whispered and threw back his head, a smile frozen on his twisted lips.

24

THE BOY WHO WAS A GIRL

𝒟ronacharya, the great military leader of the Kurus, sat in his usual seat in front of his mansion in the *Yuddha shala* of Hastinapura. A frown was on his brow, and his brilliant eyes were lit with displeasure.

Before him stood Duryodhana, the strong, handsome Prince of the Kurus, the elegant master-bowman Karna, the King of Anga, and also his own son Aswatthama. They had come to their teacher to tell him of the great victory they had won over Chekitana, the Yadava King of Pushkara, but had been reproved for their impetuous, thoughtless action.

'I told you, Duryodhana, to make a friend of Chekitana and bring his son to be educated here. And what did you do? You went and overwhelmed him. There was no sense in the Kurus crushing a small fly like that. And you drove him across the Yamuna,' said Dronacharya.

'He was obstinate, Master. He did not acknowledge defeat,' said Karna hastily, his fine face flushed in indignation. 'He had therefore to be driven out of his kingdom.'

'He was a brave man; that was why I wanted to make a friend of him,' replied Dronacharya, showing his displeasure by the way he spoke. 'Who will now guard that highway? The Yadava chiefs are settled all along the highway to Pushkara.'

'But you approved of our marching on Chekitana, father,' said Aswatthama, with ill-concealed dislike of the rebuke.

'He would never have been our friend, Gurudeva,' said Duryodhana peevishly.

'I wish you sometimes applied your mind to making friends,' said Dronacharya.

'He can never be our friend,' insisted Karna emphatically. 'And he must be uprooted like a poisonous plant.'

'But how can you destroy your enemies without any friends?' asked Dronacharya.

'With Pushkara in our hands, we can look after both Virata and Krishna. The whole highway between Saurashtra and Hastinapura will be under our control,' said Karna.

Dronacharya looked at his pupils with contempt. 'If the Yadavas and Virata combine against us now, we will have our hands full with them. Then who will stop Drupada from marching on Hastinapura?'

'And I have asked Vikarna to take charge of Pushkara,' said Karna.

'But where will you find the Kuru warriors to settle in a wilderness—with hostile Virata on one side, Shalva on the other, and the Yadava chiefs gathering round

Chekitana? Well, now go, my blessing. I will discuss the matter with Grandfather and see what we can do,' said Dronacharya.

After the three youngsters had left, Dronacharya was wrapped in thought. Duryodhana was as headstrong, self-willed and impetuous as ever; he would never take to statesmanship and could never follow advice implicitly.

His plan had failed. He wanted to strengthen the frontier against Shalva and even the Yadavas, by making a loyal friend of Chekitana. Now his puplis had made him an implacable enemy. Would Krishna go to his assistance and recapture Pushkara?

Krishna had become a major problem, thought Dronacharya. He was now in Kampilya, possibly soon going to marry Drupada's daughter. With Chekitana, the Yadava, driven out of his domains, Krishna and his father-in-law were likely to declare war on the Kurus, particularly now that there was disaffection among the Kuru chiefs on account of the death of the Five Brothers. It was not a very happy prospect. Hasty, short-sighted, obstinate fools these, Dronacharya muttered. How long will it take them to realise that a mere exhibition of strength is not valour?

Dronacharya was so lost in thought that he forgot to indulge in his favourite pastime of throwing grams to the fish and the tortoises. Even his assistant, with four new cadets wanting to join the *Yuddha shala*, did not catch his eye for a long time.

'Yes, Shankha,' said Dronacharya when he awoke from his reverie, 'did you find these boys fit to join us?'

Shankha, a middle-aged disciple who was in charge of selecting new entrants to the *Yuddha shala*, stepped up to the Guru and whispered: 'The boy who came yesterday is more of a girl than a boy.'

'Turn him out', said the Guru severely. 'I will not take a pupil who is more of a girl than a boy.' he added with a decisive sweep of his hand.

'He will not go, Gurudeva. He refuses to take his food till you have met him yourself,' said Shankha with his hands folded.

'What about the others? Call them,' ordered the Guru.

Two boys between the ages of twelve and fourteen came forward, led by Shankha. 'These are the sons of the Kuru chief Subahu from Uttarakuru. He is also here,' said Shankha, pointing to the chief who stood near his sons.

'I do not want the father. I want the sons,' snapped the Guru. Then he turned to the boys. 'You are twelve— and you, fourteen?'

'Yes lord,' muttered the boys, frightened at the severe mien of the Guru.

'What have you been doing all these years?' asked the Guru with a frown. 'Your father ought to have known that the age for joining the Guru, as enjoined by the Shastras, is eight.'

The boys looked down and stood rooted to the spot. Their father stepped forward and, unnerved by the severe demeanour of the Guru said: 'Their mother would not part with them at an early age.'

'And wasted four years? All right,' said the Guru. 'Boys. I will take you as my pupils, but you will have to work hard. Are you ready to face it, both of you?' he asked and his eyes suddenly became paternal.

This encouraged one of the boys, who said with joined but trembling hands, 'Yes Gurudeva.'

Dronacharya called them nearer him, smiled and patted them on the back. 'If you work hard to learn, I shall also work hard to see that you learn.'

The boys were overwhelmed at this gracious gesture, and fell at the Guru's feet. After receiving his blessing, they left.

Then a hefty boy, his face full of ill-concealed pride, came forward. 'Angaraka is from Kamboja, venerable Sir,' said Shankha, introducing the young candidate. 'He is related to the noble Princess Bhanumatidevi.'

'What is you age?' asked Dronacharya with narrowed eyes.

'Sixteen,' said the boy with superior smile.

What have you been doing all this time?' asked the Guru with a note of disapproval in his voice.

'Wrestling, riding, hunting,' said Angaraka, setting out his qualifications with self-confidence.

'Then, what do you want to come here for?' asked the Guru.

'Father insisted that I should come here. He says that you alone can teach me how to be a good warrior,' replied the boy.

'Have you got it in you to be a good warrior?' asked the Guru in a voice of contempt.

The boy was in no way disconcerted by the Guru's attiude. He smiled and said: 'Father thinks I am already on the way to be a warrior.'

'What do you think, my boy?' asked the Guru.

The boy smiled. 'If you ask me, I am as good a warrior as any.'

A smile flickered on the lips of the Guru. 'I see,' he said. 'Perhaps you are right. But we must find out.' Then he called Shankha. 'Shankha, prove him in a contest—will you?—in hunting, riding, mace-combat and body-combat with Sukarna.' Then turning to Angaraka, he said: 'He is only thirteen. You must beat him if you can.'

'I will beat him hollow,' said Angaraka with a grin.

'Then you do not need any more training,' said Guru quietly.

'And suppose he beats me?'

Drona laughed outright for the first time. 'Then you will not join my *Yuddha shala* boy;'

'Not join it? Why?' asked Angaraka.

'Because you lack the humility to be a good student,' said the Guru, and in an authoritative manner, waved him away.

After Angaraka was dismissed, Shankha brought forward the fourth boy who was dressed as an anchorite and whom Shankha had described as more of a girl than a boy. He was a lovely boy with a silky skin, beautiful eyes and a sweet mouth. He walked slowly and hesitantly, with an imperceptible feminine grace. His locks, matted at the top of his head were long and soft, and his hips, below the antelope skin, had tell-tale curves. Yet he was vigorous and strong, and bore himself like a boy. He prostrated himself before the Acharya with the easy grace of a well-born Arya.

Dronacharya was interested in the strange personality of the boy, who might as well have been a girl. The boy, conspicuously well-mannered, stood with folded hands, waiting to be spoken to.

'You are the boy who came to the *Yuddha shala* two days ago?' asked Dronacharya in a kindly manner which he seldom adopted towards strangers.

'Yes lord'.

'What is your name?'

'My name is Shikhandin; lord. I am the boy who came two days ago by boat.' The voice, which the boy tried to make firm and vigorous, was sweet, almost feminine.

'And you refused to take food till you saw me yourself?' asked the Guru.

'Yes lord,' said the boy, bending his head gracefully over his joined hands.

'Why?'

'To be your pupil is the only aim of my life. If the aim is not fulfilled, I have nothing to live for,' replied the boy modestly.

'What is your *gotra, brahmachari?* asked the Guru.

'I am not a Brahman. I am a Kshatriya of the Kaushika *gotra*, Lord.

'Have you been initiated into the studies of the Vedas?'

'Yes, lord,'

'Archery?'

'Yes.'

'Mace-combat?'

'I want to learn it at your worshipful feet,' said the boy, lowering his eyes modestly.

'What is your age?' asked the Guru, feeling interested in the boy.

'Sixteen, lord' replied the boy.

'But you look twelve,' remarked the Guru.

'That is my misfortune,' said the boy.

'Have you learnt the elements of body-combat?'

'No, lord.' The boy's face was red with confusion. Almost inaudibly, he added: 'No teacher would teach it to me.'

'Why?'

Shikhandin felt confused. Then he summoned up courage to say: 'My teachers suspected that I was a girl.' It was said so modestly that the Guru could not help smiling at the boy's confusion.

'I do not teach girls either,' said the Guru.

'You would, I am sure, lord, if you knew how unfortunate I am,' said the boy in a choking voice.

'Where do you come from and who are your parents?' asked the Guru.

The great military leader, ordinarily severe and authoritative, in his dealing with men, looked at the girlish boy with an indulgent smile.

'My mother was the Princess of Kashi,' said the boy,' and then paused as if his throat was stopped. Then he cleared it and said: 'My father is your enemy, the noble Drupada, King of Panchala.'

Dronacharya was taken aback. The smile disappeaerd. 'Then what rumour says is true. You are the daughter of King Drupada, whom your mother brought up as a boy at her father's house?' he asked.

'Yes, lord,' replied Shikhandin, lowering his eyes, 'I was brought to my father after my mother's death when I was ten.'

'All along you were passed off as a boy?' asked Dronacharya.

'Yes. Father wanted me to be what I really was. But I resisted stubbornly. I wanted to be a boy, to learn the art of war, to take my rightful place as the brother of noble Dhrishtadyumna and Satyajit. Father was angry,' said the boy.

Dronacharya's suspicions were then aroused and he wanted to go to the bottom of this mysterious appearance of Shikhandin in his *Yuddha shala*. 'Why?' he asked.

'Father thought that it was dishonest for me to pass myself off as a boy,' came the straightforward reply. 'I was in distress beyond words. My tastes, upbringing and training—all were those of a boy. I wanted to be a warrior like my father and brothers.'

'Did you never feel that you would like to be a girl?' asked Dronacharya.

'Sometimes I did,' replied Shikhadin. 'My heart

invariably revolted against harshness, cruelty and wickedness. Often I felt attracted to boys, in a way which had nothing boyish about it. I was sensitive and felt worked up on occasions. But I crushed that part of my nature. I tried to be a boy.'

'When was it discovered that you were a girl?'

'No one knew that I was a girl, except my father, my brothers, my sister and the minister Udbodhana, but they all kept it a secret. Many people suspected that I was not a boy. My teachers, out of caution, would not teach me body-combat and mace-combat, for if I had insisted, I would have been discovered for what I was,' said the boy.

'But I have heard that you were married to the Princess of Dasharna even before you came to your father's court,' said Dronacharya.

Yes. An offer was made and father accepted it. When we were married, the princess was six years old. And now King Hiranyavarma insists on his daughter being called to Kampilya. That is why I have run away,' said Shikhandin frankly.

'Or, rather, your father sent you to me?' asked Dronacharya. He had a feeling that Drupada was trying to plant his daughter on him as a spy.

'No,' said Shikhandin, and looked up with courage. 'My father does not know that I have come here.'

'No? Do you want me to believe that you, a royal princess, came away without your father's knowledge?' asked Dronacharya.

'Yes, I did. I stole away at night from Kampilya. I

had to run away or drown myself before my wife came to me.'

'But why come to me?' asked Dronacharya.

'I was told that in the three worlds there was only one guru who could make a great warrior out of a girl,' said Shikhandin almost piteously. He began to fear that Dronacharya would not accept him as his pupil.

'He must be a fool if he told you that I take girls as my pupils,' said the Guru a little impatiently.

'No, lord,' replied Shikhandin. 'The man who told me was the finest being I have come across in my life.

'Who is he?' asked Dronacharya.

'Krishna Vaasudeva.'

On hearing the name, Dronacharya, startled, sat up and caught his breath. Krishna Vaasudeva was weaving a magic web around him. He was in Kampilya. He was going to marry the daughter of his enemy. Now here he was sending his enemy's daughter to his *Yuddha shala*. It was all clear to him now. And he decided to beat Krishna at his own game. Does Vaasudeva know that you are a girl?' he asked.

'I told him so,' replied Shikhandin.

'What sort of a man is he?' asked Dronacharya.

'He is a wonderful man, lord,' replied Shikhandin, moved by deep admiration. 'He came to Kampilya, and its cloudy atmosphere became joyous. Every one of us felt different—even father.

Dronacharya was now all attention. His alert mind now wanted to know all about things in Kampilya. 'Has he accepted your father's proposal to marry your sister?' he asked.

'You already know about it?' asked Shikhandin raising his eyes. 'Do you want to know what Krishna Vaasudeva said to the proposal? He has declined to wed my sister Krishnaa. He said that he would not wed a princess to become the instrument of her father's wrath.'

For a moment Dronacharya felt as if he was hearing the words in a dream. He could not believe his ears. In spite of the transparent honesty of Shikhandin, he thought that he was only trying to deceive him. 'How do you know that Krishna declined to marry your sister?' he asked.

'I overheard him when he told my father so,' replied Shikhandin.

Dronacharya felt that the boy was telling the truth, and a change came over him. 'How was it that Vaasudeva advised you to come to me?' he asked.

'About the time he came to Kampilya, my father-in-law's message had come. My wife was to be sent for. This created a terrible situation for father, for me and for the whole of Panchala. The moment she came, I could be found out and my family would be exposed to ridicule. Father, who is so honest, would be charged with deception in passing me off as a boy and getting me married to the Princess of Dasharna.'

'Yes, what then?'

'Then I made up my mind to run away or to die,

before my secret was discovered. But, curiously enough, when I saw Vaasudeva a new hope was born in me,' said Shikhandin.

'How? What hope did he give you?' asked Dronacharya.

'Vaasudeva did not give me any hope. But, wherever he moves, he brings the breeze of hope with him.'

'You have lost your heart to Vaasudeva, it seems,' said Droncharya with a smile.

'No, I have seen the miracle. The breeze blew on father, on Dhrishtadyumna, on my sister Krishnaa and on me. All of us in our own ways found a fresh way of looking at things.'

Dronacharya was lost in thought. He could not understand the mystery of this Vaasudeva. The whole atmosphere appeared to be charged with it ever since the day when Krishna arrived in Hastinapura. 'What did Vaasudeva do to you all?'

Shikhandin was so full of Vaasudeva that he was led to express himself with eloquence.

'He did nothing in particular,' he replied. 'He spoke to us in an affectionate voice as if he knew all of us intimately. He looked at us and we felt different. His eyes were so flattering; whenever he looked me I felt that there were only two persons in this world—he and I—and the two of us shared the truth. He seemed to see into the very depth of my heart and stirred it to a new intensity. This was a challenge to me. Oh, I cannot, describe it, but I felt as if I was born afresh.'

Dronacharya could not help wondering at the impact

which Krishna seemed to make on every one. 'So, you decided not to die?' he asked.

'No, I decided to tell him all that I had felt and suffered and was suffering. I begged his friend, Acharya Shvetaketu, to take me to him at night, so that no one should know that I was going to him,' said Shikhandin.

'Did you see him?' asked Dronacharya.

'Yes. He came out of the mansion in which he was housed, and took me for a walk in the grounds.' Shikhandin could not help bursting into praises of him. 'Yes, he was so kind. I began to tell him of my unfortunate life. He heard me with patience. He encouraged me to confess the unexpressed anguish of my heart. I told him how I had wanted to be a man all my life and how at every step I was being smothered by my sex. I told him of the frustration of which I was the victim, of the approaching arrival of my wife and of my desire to put an end to my life.'

'What did Vaasudeva say to that?' asked Dronacharya.

'He heard me with such understanding that my difficulties began to disappear even as I told him my tale of woe. I cried as I spoke of my misery. He smiled sweetly and sympathetically as he alone can. He pressed my cheeks as if I was a little child. Then he spoke, and his voice was like the life-giving drops of rain on parched soil,' said Shikhandin.

'What did he say?' asked Dronacharya.

'He said something like this "My boy, never give up life so long as there is a chance to live it in Dharma.

You have borne you trials bravely. Now do not give up courage." I replied that I had no courage left. He laughed and said, "Do you want to die of cowardice?" I replied "No". Then he said, "If you have courage to face death, I will show you the way to die courageously". He said it with such confidence that I felt that I had seen the end of my troubles.'

Dronacharya looked at this boy with a new interest— an interest in the miracle-worker who could give hope to a dying heart 'What then?' he asked.

Shikhandin continued: 'Vaasudeva said: "Do you want to be a man, a real man, vigorous, brave and noble?" I said: "Yes, lord". Then he put his hand on my shoulders, looked into my eyes, and said: "Go to Guru Dronacharya. Be his pupil. He alone can make a man of you. He is the greatest living Acharya. Even clay becomes gold in his hands".

Dronacharya began to experience what Shikhandin said he had felt when he saw Krishna. His heart was full of unexpected joy and pride.

'Did he say exactly that?' he asked.

'Yes, lord. I have not forgotten one word of what he said, for each was a drop of nectar to me. But I was taken aback at what he proposed. I said that father would never permit me to go to you, his greatest enemy,' said Shikhandin.

'Am I so bad?' asked Dronacharya, for the first time laughing without restraint. He himself was now feeling very happy.

'You know the reason, lord.'

'Yes, I know,' said Dronacharya. 'What was Vaasudeva's reply?'

'He said: "Shikhandin, you want to die like a coward without your noble father's consent. You can equally well be brave and go to become a man without his consent. And if you return alive as a hero, your father will welcome you."

'What did you say? asked Dronacharya.

'I asked him: "If the venerable Dronacharya refuses to accept me as his pupil, what shall I do?"'

'What did Vaasudeva reply?' asked Dronacharya.

'He replied: "He is a great teacher. As a true Brahman he will never say 'no' to a deserving aspirant who wants to learn. But, when you approach him, remove every vestige of hatred from your heart. Be frank and honest with him. Serve him as a loyal son, as if you were more his son than your father's. But this thing I know, Shikhandin," he continued, "if anyone in this world can make a man of you, it is Dronacharya."' Shikhandin said this in a moving tone, and Dronacharya, usually self-possessed, was moved himself.

'Did you agree?' asked Dronacharya.

'There was no question of my agreeing. I fell at his feet. He had been a saviour to me. I immediately changed my dress for a *brahmachari's*. Acharya Shvetaketu took me to a boat in the dead of night and by slow stages I came here,' said Shikhandin.

Dronacharya felt strangely attracted to this boy.

But he could not help expressing his doubts. 'Why should I not take you for your father's spy planted on me by Vaasudeva?'

Shikhandin folded his hands. 'Keep me with you, lord, and try me. If in thought, word or deed, you find me a fraud, I will lay down my life at your feet. You are my spiritual father.'

For a moment Dronacharya sat quiet, thinking. 'Shikhandin, do you want to be a man, a real man?' he asked.

'I want to be a man. But that is impossible,' replied Shikhandin.

'Suppose I make the impossible possible, are you ready to go through the necessary austerities?' asked Dronacharya.

Shikhandin's face flushed with joy. 'I will, I will Please, lord, make me a man.'

'I know a Yaksha, Sthoonakarna. He has knowledge of the magic which can change a woman into a man. But you will have to go through fearful torture for months. Are you ready to go to him?' asked Dronacharya.

'I will obey the master in everything. Do with me as you please,' replied Shikhandin.

25

INVITATION TO THE SWAYAMVARA

A frown on his brow, Dronacharya got into the waiting chariot with a slow, decisive movement which was characteristic of him. Though apparently self-possessed, he was in a rage.

The rains had come and gone. The roads were now open to traffic, The Ganga was no longer a roaring, muddy flood, but a placid highway.

Only the day before, boats coming from Kampilya had brought a delegation of learned Brahmans headed by a minister to invite the Kuru princes to the *swayamvara* of Draupadi, the daughter of King Yajnasena Drupada, which was fixed for the first day of the bright half of the month of Chaitra.

The report, that delegation had come with the invitation to the *swayamvara,* spread like wildfire in Hastinapura and reached the ears of the Acharya. That very morning, Princess Bhanumati, wife of the Crown Prince Duryodhana, had also come to him with it.

The Acharya loved this beautiful Princess of Kamboja as if she had been his own daughter. Impulsive, sprightly and possessive, she brought sunshine into the warrior's life, dominated as it was by the lust for power. He was her father's great friend and had brought about her marriage with Duryodhana after her eldest sister, his first wife, had died.

In her effusive, child-like way, Bhanumati worshipped her big, self-willed husband. She gloried in his exploits and gave him complete loyalty. At times she even exercised a soothing influence over him, and he found comfort in the arms of his doting and admiring wife.

She felt there was a rift in this happy world of hers when she heard that her husband had decided to go to the *swayamvara* to win Draupadi. Very much shaken by the situation, she came to the Acharya to tell him of the impending calamity, and beg him to intervene.

The news shocked the Acharya. Poor, sweet Bhanumati! Such a loving wife, wasted on this irrepressible Duryodhana. And what time and energy had he himself not wasted in trying to make a hero out of him? The Acharya sighed. If only Arjuna, his devoted pupil, had been alive!

The Acharya would have certainly liked one of his pupils to inflict a defeat on his bitterest enemy, Drupada, and exact the hand of his proud daughter as a tribute. But, for Duryodhana to go as an ordinary suitor and seek her hand was intolerable. It was a blow to his prestige and pride.

Immediately on hearing the news, the Acharya made up his mind. He would not allow Duryodhana to go to the *swayamvara*. Grandfather Bhishma, he was sure, would not think of permitting the Kuru Crown Prince to suffer such a humiliation.

As his chariot was being swiftly driven to the royal palace, the Acharya's mind went back to Krishna Vaasudeva. Vaasudeva was not his enemy, as he had once thought he was; he was a friend who held him in great admiration. He had the perception to acknowledge him, Dronacharya, as the greatest of military leaders, able to make a man out of a woman. He was a splendid fellow, this young cowherd, Vaasudeva. What a pity, he got no opportunity to meet him when he visited Hastinapura!

Again his mind went back to the folly which Duryodhana was ready to commit. If, against his advice, his pupil went to the *swayamvara*, he would leave the Kurus. He was an unrivalled warrior, a pupil of Parashurama, and a Brahman who would not stoop to gain position or wealth at the cost of his self-respect. If Duryodhana married Draupadi, he would leave Hastinapura.

The *Rajasabha* had already been considering the problem when the Acharya arrived. Grandfather Bhishma sat on his throne, tall and straight and as stern as ever. The blind King, Dhritarashtra sat on a throne by his side turning his blind eyes from one person to the other, his mouth often sagging—a pitiable embodiment, the Acharya thought, of the great power which Bhishma and himself had built up.

Duryodhana, the Crown Prince, sat near his father, his eyes showing truculence. Next to him sat his brother Duhshasana, lean and hungry-looking, his shifty eyes watching everyone warily. There was their uncle

Shakuni too, the Prince of Gandhara and the King's brother-in-law, fat and unctuous as ever, a deceptive image of good nature, his deep-seated, small eyes beaming mischief.

Karna, the charioteer's son, sat next to him, his brilliant eyes flashing disapproval of the lengthy discussion of a matter which, in his view, was capable of an easy, straightforward solution. And by his side sat his own son Aswatthama, now Duryodhana's right-hand man.

The Acharya was surprised to find that the saintly Vidura, who enjoyed Grandfather's confidence, was not among the ministers present. However, old Kunika, the astute minister, was there, his eyes dim with age and twitching. His own brother-in-law, Kripacharya, who had already arrived before him, was seated next to him.

Folding his hands before Grandfather and the blind King, the Acharya, as a learned Brahman, gave them a blessing from the hallowed Vedic mantras, suited to the occasion. And as he did so, he could not help thinking of what a different *Rajasabha* it would have been had his favourite pupils, the Five Brothers, been alive and present.

For a moment, regret shot through his heart: it was a foolish impulse which had prompted him to help Duryodhana to put Yudhishthira out of the way. Then he had thought that, with Duryodhana as Crown Prince, it would be easy to dominate the scene in Hastinapura. But his judgment had been at fault, perhaps for the first time. It would have been easy to guide a man of reason and virtue; it was impossible to deal with an egregious fool.

When the Acharya had taken his seat, the King informed him of what had been going on before he came.

'Respected Acharya, we have to take an important decision. Should we accept the invitation of King Drupada and send our Princes to the *swayamvara* of Draupadi?' he asked,

Turning his blind eyes helplessly towards Duryodhana, he added: 'It is a matter of high policy for us. We ought not to come to any hasty decision. The King of Panchala, as we all know, is hostile to us. To bring his daughter into our family might mean endless intrigues and ultimate disaster.'

The Acharya tried to fathom the intentions of Grandfather whose eyes were fixed on the blind King, but the old man, mechanically moving his hand over his flowing beard, sat as inscrutable as ever.

'Kunika, will you please tell the Acharya what you told us?' the blind King asked.

Kunika, the old minister. his eyes twitching ceaselessly, folded his hands and, with sententious loquacity, said: 'As the noble lord commands. With Grandfather's permission, I will repeat what I stated. Panchala has been a thorn in our side. It has prevented us from making any conquests in the east. King Drupada is a very determined king and has been preparing for a war with us for a long time. He looks upon Guru Dronacharya, our great military leader, as his enemy. His son, Dhrishtadyumna, is a highly trained warrior and very ambitious and also unforgiving. Reports also have it that Krishnaa, the Princess, is a very strong-minded woman, with all the faults of her father. The affairs of Hastinapura, so zealously looked after by the venerable Grandfather, will be seriously affected if she enters the royal family of the Emperor Bharata of sacred memory. As was said by the ancient Manu, 'Before selecting a wife, look at the ways of her parents." And there is a blot on the family too. One of the sons of Drupada is neither a man nor a woman. Noble lord, he was married to the Princess of Dasharna. When she was to be brought to live with her husband this prince or princess—as you choose —was hurried away by King Drupada to hide the disgrace which would follow if it was found out that what had been passed off as a man was really a woman.' Having delivered himself of this speech, Kunika again joined his hands together ceremoniously.

The Acharya was highly amused at the way Shikhandin's disappearance was being explained away by the world. Kunika did not know that it was he, Dronacharya, who was making a man and a hero out of Shikhandin.

Duryodhana, for a moment, looked angrily at Kunika, and interjected. 'You think that the Kuru Princes are such weaklings that they can become the playthings of their wives?'

'I crave forgiveness of the Crown Prince,' said Kunika who, brought up in a very old tradition, would never address any member of the royal family except with ceremonious courtesy. 'No man and no family can escape from the clutches of a daughter-in-law. As the ancient proverb has it, "a wife, however docile, invariably ends by taming the husband and his family." Then what about a strong-minded wife?'

Dronacharya could see what was passing through the mind of Duryodhana. Bhanumati was right; he had made up his mind to win Draupadi.

Now the king's eyes were turned towards where Shakuni was sitting. 'Prince of Gandhara, what have you to say?'

The Acharya could not suppress a look of contempt. He hated this villain who exercised such a baneful influence on his pupil and filled the Court of the Kurus with interminable intrigues.

Shakuni laughed and said: 'I cannot match the wisdom of the learned and respected minister Kunika. But he is not fair to the royal house of Bharata of glorious memory.' And he looked triumphantly at Duryodhana and Duhshasana. 'The Kuru Princes are lions. If the Princess of Panchala weds any one of them, how can she be anything but his devoted slave?' He winked imperceptibly at Duryodhana, and again in his half-sarcastic and half-mocking vein, continued: 'With Grandfather as the guardian of the Kurus, Duryodhana as the Crown Prince and minister Kunika to give sage advice, and with the great Acharya to win our wars, what could a princess do?'

Duryodhana took up the thread impatiently. 'Venerable Grandfather, we must go to the *swayamvara*. One or the other of us is sure to win Draupadi. Who

:an compare with us?' Then he turned to Kunika and
idded: What greater humiliation can we inflict on
)rupada than carrying away his daughter by the
strength of our arms?'

The Acharya saw an imperceptible smile creeping
over Grandfather's stern face. The old man was definitely
on his side, he thought.

'Suppose none of you are selected by the Princess.
Then it will be a humiliation for us, won't it?' The King
aised the doubt, his blind gaze fixed on Duryodhana.

Uncle Shakuni laughed loudly, rolled his body, folded
his hands and in a mocking voice said: 'Noble King a
swayamvara is a sacred occasion hallowed by ancient
radition. There is glory if you win the bride. There is
no disgrace if you lose her, for,' he continued laughingly
is if it was a huge joke, 'a bride can marry only one
prince...'

The stern look of Grandfather arrested Shakuni's
mocking speech. Then in his guttural voice, Grandfather
isked: 'Acharya, what do you think about this matter?'

The Acharya folded his hands before Bhishma and
spoke in a solemn voice: 'Venerable Grandfather, noble
King, I am pained at the attitude of Duryodhana. It
vould be a humiliation for a Kuru Prince to go to
)rupada's Court to seek the hand of his daughter. I
vould expect him to destroy the power of Drupada once
ind for all and carry away his daughter as the price
or leaving him in peace. How utterly I have failed to
nspire my pupils with the noble pride which goes with
neroism!'

'Do you doubt our courage, Acharyadeva?' asked Karna. He would never let anyone doubt his bravery.

Grandfather raised a hand to stop the conversation flowing into irrelevant channels. 'Acharya, it seems you are against our Princes attending the *swayamvara.*'

'Venerable Grandfather, it is difficult for me to reconcile myself to our Princes attending the *swayamvara.* I do not know what you would like to do in the matter. But this thing I do know: Neither Duryodhana nor Karna, nor even my son Aswatthama is likely to bring strength to the Kurus if they go. If any one of them wins Draupadi, the Kuru power will be torn by factions. If none of them wins her, our prestige will have gone. In either event, our strength is sure to be shattered. And let me for my part make this clear: I...

Before, however, the Acharya could complete his sentence and deliver his ultimatum renouncing his office if Duryodhana went to the *swayamvara,* Vidura came into the hall, approached Grandfather and whispered something into his ear. Everyone silently watched this whispered conversation which must have been of great importance, interposed unceremoniously as it was into the middle of a grave consultation.

The Acharya watched the face of Grandfather, whose eyes, as he heard Vidura, grew interested and then shone with a momentary glow. When the conversation was finished there was a distinct smile on Grandfather's lips.

As Vidura finished the conversation, he received nod from Grandfather, giving him silent permission to

;o ahead. Vidura turned to the King with folded hands and said: 'Noble King, Uddhava, the son of noble Devabhaga of the Shooras, has brought a message which has a bearing on what the noble lord is going to decide. He is waiting outside. Is it your command that he should be brought in?'

Everybody was taken aback and looked at Vidura in surprise. The Acharya glanced at everyone present to discover what this development meant. Evidently, Vidura, in spite of his saintliness, had an unfathomable way of doing things.

'What is the mission which brings Uddhava, son of Devabhaga, here?' asked the king.

Grandfather slowly went on moving his hands over his beard, his attitude now completely detached.

'Uddhava came suddenly this morning and sent me word from outside the city gates that he would like to stay with me,' said Vidura. 'I went and received him with appropriate honour. He has brought an urgent message from the Best of Yadavas, Krishna Vaasudeva.'

'Krishna Vaasudeva!' exclaimed Duryodhana. There was a scowl on the face of Karna. Aswatthama glared angrily at Vidura.

Disregarding the interruption, Vidura continued: But before bringing the message to Grandfather, Uddhava wanted to pay his respects to the Most Venerable Mother. So I took him to her, and, after the interview was over, brought him here to meet the noble lord. I have already sought Grandfather's permission.'

'Krishna Vaasudeva!' Duryodhana again interjected
in excitement. 'We were already in the midst of important
deliberations. Why should we make our deliberations
more difficult by allowing Krishna Vaasudeva to
intervene in this manner? Why can't Uddhava wait?'

The guttural voice of Grandfather cut into
Duryodhana's speech. 'Any message which the Best of
Yadavas, Vaasudeva, chooses to send, is welcome to
the Court of the Kurus. Vidura, please request the son
of Devabhaga to come in. We shall be glad to meet him,'
be said authoritatively.

Dronacharya's mind was in a whirl. Vidura's coming
into the hall had prevented his delivering his ultimatum.
Normally he would have liked to deliver it before
Uddhava came, but, at the mention of Krishna
Vaasudeva, a thrill passed through his body. Was
Vaasudeva going to intervene miraculously?

26

BHANUMATI'S DEVOTION

*D*ronacharya was fully satisfied with himself when he returned to the *Yuddha shala*. From being in a difficult situation, he had emerged as the powerful and indispensable defender of Kuru policy. His decision to go to Pushkara was right. Things were indeed changing fast. Duryodhana, left to himself, would never be able to maintain the dignity of Bharata's house. He had no eyes to see that Krishna Vaasudeva's star was rising on the horizon and that he was emerging more powerful than a king. And, the Acharya smiled to himself, he was friendly to him.

When the Acharya came to the *Yuddha shala*, he found Princess Bhanumati, wife of Duryodhana, impatiently waiting for him, her face inflamed, her eyes tear-laden, her fresh beauty enhanced by the shadow of misery which clouded it for the moment, She immediately fell at his feet and asked piteously: 'What has been done, Acharyadeva? Is my fate sealed?'

Kripaadevi, the wife of the Acharya, stout, dignified and maternal, sat next to her with a consoling arm round her shoulders.

Dronacharya placed his hands affectionately on the head of Bhanumati and said: 'My blessing. Nothing will happen to you, my child.'

'Has Aryaputra given up his intention of going to the *swayamvara?*' she asked with trembling lips.

'No. He is going to attend the *swayamvara,*' said the Acharya. 'But don't you worry. He is not likely to win Draupadi. Curiously, almost miraculously, Krishna Vaasudeva came to our rescue.'

'Krishna Vaasudeva, is he here?' exclaimed Bhanumati, a new light glowing on her face. 'I would like to meet him.'

'You are mistaken, child. He is not here. But he sent a message which changed the face of things. Do you know how your husband drove Chekitana out of Pushkara? Vaasudeva sent word that it should be restored to the Yadava King,' said the Acharya.

'Aryaputra will never agree to do so,' said Bhanumati. 'I know him.'

'But you don't know me, Bhanumati,' said the Acharya with a smile. 'It has been decided to hand it back to King Chekitana. I am going there myself to do it and receive Krishna and Balarama, who are going there on their way to the *swayamvara,*' said the Acharya. Then his brow was furrowed for a moment as he had a sudden inspiration. He turned to Bhanumati with a smile. 'Bhanumati, you told me months ago that, when Vaasudeva was here, he adopted you as a sister.'

'Yes, Acharyadeva.' replied Bhanumati, blushing,

as the memory of that fearful night at the shrine of Gouri, the Mother Goddess, came back to her. 'He was so very, very kind. If he had not been there, I would have had to drown myself in the Ganga.'

'Well, then, will you come with me to meet him at Pushkara?' asked the Acharya.

'To meet Krishna Vaasudeva! Aryaputra will never permit it. He is not happy about Vaasudeva,' said Bhanumati.

'Do you want to make sure that Duryodhana does not win Draupadi?' asked the Acharya.

'I wish I could, Acharyadeva,' replied Bhanumati.

'Perhaps, if you could secure a promise from Krishna Vaasudeva, he would help you,'

'How can he help me? He cannot stop Aryaputra from going to the *swayamvara* and winning the bride.'

'I do not know,' said the Acharya thoughtfully as if speaking to himself. 'The stories that Krishna can work miracles, which we have heard so often, may be true after all. I cannot shake off the feeling that, in the matter of Pushkara, his intervention was miraculous.' The Acharya did not tell the Princess that the intervention affected his personal fortunes also. Then he added: 'I will tell you what to do. Go to the Most Venerable Mother. Tell her how Krishna has adopted you as his younger sister and how, as a sister, you would like to greet him. She may perhaps give you permission to come with me. If necessary, get the help of Vidura. He has geat influence with the Mother. When there, it will be up to you to secure a promise from Krishna that he will do all in his power to prevent Draupadi from choosing Duryodhana.

'How can he give such a promise?' asked Bhanumati.

'This much I know. If you succeed in getting him to give you promise, he will keep it', said the Acharya.

'He won't give such a promise,' said Bhanumati.

'Then, his adopting you as his younger sister is a joke,' said the Acharya with a smile.

'I know, Acharyadeva, that he is a man of his word.'

'Well, then, child, it would be best to go to the Most Venerable Mother and get her consent. If she gives you the permission, Duryodhana will not venture to stop you from coming with me,' said the Acharya.

'I will try. But I do not think Krishna Vaasudeva will help in this matter.'

'If he really is what he is reported to be, he may make the impossible possible,' said the Acharya.

When Bhanumati took his leave, there was a smile of triumph on the Acharya's face. Things were going his way.

Bhanumati was exultant. The Most Venerable Mother had consented to her going to Pushkara with the Acharya. She was going to meet Krishna again — Krishna, who had played the flute and attracted the cowherdesses of Vrindavan, and of whom the ballad-singers of her father's court had sung so enthusiastically.

Now he was no longer a cowherd, but a powerful man whom most people respected. Even her husband, Duryodhana, who had scant respect for most people, had told her to win his goodwill. Now she would secure his help. She was sure that he would somehow dissuade Draupadi from choosing Duryodhana as her husband at the *swayamvara*. Then she would be happy as the favourite wife of her husband whom she loved, and become the future Empress of Hastinapura.

She could not contain her happiness. Walking along with an almost dancing step, she confided all her secrets to her favourite parrot, whose cage hung by her side. It was a fine parrot with a fresh green body, which always responded to her by saying: 'Bhanumati, all is well.'

Her husband, as usual, had gone to uncle Shakuni's to gamble. He would return late at night as he always did. Then she would tell him of her proposed visit to Pushkara.

As was usual with her, she did not go to sleep before her husband returned home, and sat up late till he came. He was tipsy, and, when she held out her hand to receive his diadem, he glared at her, and gnashed his teeth, foaming at the mouth. Then, by an effort, he steadied himself and, instead of the usual endearments with which he accosted her, caught her hand in a vicious grip. Rolling his eyes fearfully, he asked her in an angry, broken whisper: 'You slut, you went to Acharyadeva today, didn't you?'

Bhanumati was taken aback. Her happiness ebbed

away. She was frightened at the attitude of her husband and tried to pacify him with a smile. 'Yes, you know I go to him almost every day.'

This reply exasperated Duryodhana all the more. He shook her by the shoulders. 'You liar,' he shouted. 'You went there to conspire against me. You wanted him to oppose my going to the *swayamvara*. I know what you are up to, you wicked woman.'

Because of the violence with which her husband was shaking her, Bhanumati almost fell to the ground. She went pale.

'Come on, speak. Why did you go?' Shall I tell you? Uncle Shakuni told me about it. The Acharya is to take you to Pushkara,' shouted Duryodhana.

She should have known that uncle Shakuni had his spies all over Hastinapura. With some diffculty, she murmured: 'The Most Venerable Mother has permitted me to go to Pushkara with the Acharya.'

'The Most Venerable Mother!' exclaimed Duryodhana, gnashing his teeth again. 'Oh, you went to her too to get her permission?' You never even asked me about it. You wanted to meet Krishna, didn't you?'

Bhanumati lost her nerve. She broke down and whined: 'You told me to make a friend of him and you were quite happy when he said I was his little sister.'

Duryodhana took his hand away from her shoulders, and stood before her with arms akimbo, as frightening as before. 'Little sister, little sister! And why does the little sister want to see the big brother?'

Bhanumati was now sobbing. With great difficulty, she managed to say: 'What is wrong in my going to pay him my respects?'

'Shall I tell you why you are going? You liar! said Duryodhana slapping her in the face. 'You liar! You are going to ask him to poison Draupadi's ears against me. The little sister wants help from her big brother to become the empress of Hastinapura, doesn't she? Come, speak the truth.'

Bhanumati collapsed on the bedstead. She did not know what to say, not being in the habit of telling lies.

Duryodhana stepped forward and stood over her like an avenging angel, caught hold of her arms and twisted them. 'Tell me the truth. What did you want to go there for? You think that some day you will come to be the Empress of Hastinapura? Don't you worry! Draupadi or no Draupadi. I shall see that you never become that, you slut!'

'Oh please, please, lord, you are hurting me,' cried Bhanumati, as Duryodhana continued to twist her arms.

'I don't care if you die,' he shouted.

The pain was intolerable. Bhanumati summoned up her dying courage, and looked defiantly at her husband. 'Yes, kill me, kill me,' she cried in a choking voice. 'Then you will have killed your son.'

It took Duryodhana a moment to realize what she was saying. Then he understood the significance of her remark, took away his hands and rubbed his eyes for a little while, The remark had a marvellous effect on him. In a moment he became sober.

'Are you with child?' his voice changed. His first wife, Bhanumati's elder sister, and her child, had both died at its birth. He had been married to Bhanumati for the last two years and he was awaiting a son, but the son had been slow in coming. 'Are you sure?' he asked her.

Bhanumati, shaken though she was by Duryodhana's violence, looked down modestly and in a trembling voice said: 'It is true.'

'Why didn't you tell me before?' asked Duryodhana with a touch of impatience, for his anger had now disappeared.

'How could I tell you before I was sure?'

'Are you sure now?'

'Of course, I am,' replied Bhanumati.

Duryodhana, prompted by a protective instinct, put his arm around his wife. 'Don't cry. It will do harm to the child. But why do you do silly things? Going to Krishna Vaasudeva to prevent the Princess of Panchala from choosing me as a husband?'

With the change in Duryodhana's attitude Bhanumati summoned up courage. She looked down again in modesty and, clinging to Duryodhana with a helpless gesture, whispered: 'I want your son to be the Emperor of Hastinapura.' She said it with such childlike simplicity that Duryodhana took her into his arms.

'Your son will be the Emperor of Hastinapura, Draupadi or no Draupadi. Don't you worry. He will be the first among the Bharatas. But I must win Draupadi. Do you know, if I wed the daughter of Drupada, I will be ten times more powerful than I am?'

Bhanumati could hardly restrain a sob. Her fate was sealed. Whatever Duryodhana might say now, once Panchala's Princess becomes his wife, Duryodhana would become a different person. But she accepted the inevitable; she loved her husband and would not do anything to incur his displeasure. 'Aryaputra, I will obey your wish. I will not go to Pushkara.'

For a moment Duryodhana smiled. Then a doubt struck him. 'But you have obtained the consent of the Most Venerable Mother. What will she say to this?'

'I will tell her that I did not feel fit enough to travel to Pushkara. She will undestand.'

Duryodhana got up from the bed-stead and, as usual, handed his diadem and his ornaments one by one to Bhanumati, and waited till she had deposited them in a secure place where they were generally kept.

Neither of them spoke for some time. Duryodhana could not hide his pride and satisfaction at the prospect of Bhanumati's becoming the mother of his first-born son. It was a good omen, this, for every one in the royal family of the Kurus was anxious to see an heir born to the throne of *Chakravati* Bharata. And, with tender affection, he wiped her tears before they laid themselves down to rest.

Bhanumati, in her childlike simplicity, forgot her misery. It did not matter to her whether she met Krishna or not, nor did it matter whether Duryodhana brought another wife of a higher rank than her own. She wanted her husband to love her; she wanted to sleep always in his arms; there was no other happiness which she prized more. And in a few minutes, she was sound asleep.

A little later she was shaken out of her sleep by her husband. She saw him sitting straight up and saying: "Devi, I have thought over the matter. You must go and meet Krishna Vaasudeva.'

Bhanumati, thinking that she was in a dream, closed her eyes and turned on her side. Then he repeated: 'Devi, I do want you to go to Krishna.'

Bhanumati woke up again, understood what he was saying, sat up, rubbed her eyes and looked, at him in surprise. 'Why should I go? I am happy as I am,' she said finally, clinging to him with a fond gesture.

'Don't you want to make me happier? Go to Krishna. I wish you to go to him,' Duryodhana insisted.

'But what should I go to him for?'

'Go and convey him my best greetings and pay him your sisterly respects,' said Duryodhana smiling.

'No, I won't go. I don't feel like going,' said Bhanumati. 'There is no sense in my travelling all that way.'

She could not understand why he wanted her to go

to Pushkara after having shouted at her for wanting to. Perhaps he was trying to make up for his rudeness to her. But she had not minded his rudeness. She was familiar with his stormy moods which passed off as quickly as they came. She did not want to do anything which would displease him, and, if in his heart he did not want her to go, she would never think of doing so. She turned away from him as if she was sleepy, and closed her eyes.

'You are an obstinate, foolish woman,' muttered Duryodhana. 'Don't you see how important it is that you should go to Krishna?'

Bhanumati neither opened her eyes nor responded.

Duryodhana heaved a deep sigh. 'I am born under an unlucky star—in the morning Acharyadeva, at night my wife! Whenever there is a chance for me to make headway, even those whom I consider mine turn against me.'

He put his hand to his forehead and sat, a disconsolate figure, for a considerable time. Again he muttered under his breath: 'Why is it that there is no one to stand by me?' He sighed again and laid himself down to sleep, with his face turned away from Bhanumati.

Bhanumati could not sleep any more. Her husband's sighs tore at her heart. In spite of her inexperience, she had sensed that, somehow or other, at every step, his path was being obstructed by unseen, imponderable forces. Anyway, she knew he felt it that way, and when that feeling obsessed him he became a prey to stormy moods. She knew that some of the elders in the family disapproved of his ways; also that his ambition had often been thwarted by some member or the other of his own family.

She had also shared his bitter feelings when, for no fault of his own, he had been superseded by Yudhishthira, in the office of Crown Prince. It was a grievous wrong, she had then felt, that he should be punished for his father having been born blind. Now he wanted to win Draupadi to become, in course of time, a powerful monarch. Evidently Gurudeva was barring the way. So was she. She had even enlisted the Acharyadeva in this conspiracy to frustrate his plans. She had been thinking of gaining Krishna's support. He was perfectly right. He was alone and friendless, this big husband of hers, so protective and loving in spite of some of his uncertain ways.

He had his friends, true—Karna and Aswatthama, who encouraged his moods rather than restrained them. There was his uncle Shakuni, an evil influence, scarcely a desirable person. His father doted on him far too foolishly. His mother never gave him sympathy when he really needed it, though she loved him. She, his wife, was the only person who could give him warmth and support in his solitary struggle against fate. But she had been found wanting!

Bhanumati heard Duryodhana sighing repeatedly in his sleep. She could not bear it. What did it matter whether she went to Krishna or not? She could not keep quiet any longer. She got up, placed her hand tenderly on Duryodhana's shoulders and shook him awake. 'Aryaputra, I will go to Krishna if you want me to', she said.

Duryodhana got up. He was in a wretched mood. 'What did you say?' he asked her.

'I am sorry I did not agree to abide by your wishes. I will go to Krishna if you want me to', said Bhanumati.

'Will you really go?' asked Duryodhana. He shook his head as if trying to awaken himself from a fantastic dream.

'Yes, I will, Aryaputra', said Bhanumati, clinging to him, 'I will do whatever you wish. Will you tell me what you want me to do?'

'Then, go and meet him. Ask him to be my friend. He has become a powerful man. His alliance will be very useful to me', said Duryodhana.

'Yes, lord, I will do it.'

'And will you do one thing more, will you do it?' asked Duryodhana.

'What?'

'Ask him to arrange for Draupadi to choose me at the *swayamvara*', said Duryodhana.

Athough she was in his arms, Bhanumati was shocked at the selfishness implied in the question. She bit her lips and was inclined to withdraw from his arms. And get away from the bedstead. He was asking her to pander to his fancy for the Princess of Panchala. For a moment she could not speak.

Duryodhana asked her anxiously: 'Tell me, Devi, that you will do it. Do it for my sake. It will not affect your position. But my future depends upon it.'

Bhanumati made up her mind. 'If you are happy, I don't care for my position, even for my life. I will go to Pushkara and do my best to persuade Krishna to help you to win Draupadi.'

'You are so good, beloved,' said Duryodhana, effusively embracing her, overwhelmed by her generosity.

Bhanumati clung to him and suppressed a sob, hiding her head against his chest. She was being asked to sacrifice her position, her prospects, the future of her sons, her very life. Well she would do it if that made him happy.

'And also', Duryodhana added, 'you need not go with Acharyadeva alone. I shall ask uncle Shakuni to accompany you.'

Resentment choked her. Her husband felt no confidence in her. Her effort to win it had gone in vain. He was sending uncle to spy on her.

'Yes, lord, if you so wish', she said, and, suppressing a sob, lay down to spend a sleepless night.

∎

27

UDDHAVA'S MISSION

*T*he *Rajasabha* agreed to allow Duryodhana to go to the *swayamvara* because of the opportune arrival of Krishna's message brought by Uddhava.

Uddhava, handsome and self-possessed, came to the *Rajasabha* with a smile on his face, and, with easy courtesy, prostrated himself before Grandfather and the King. After saluting the others, he gave an additional touch to his courtesy by prostrating himself before Dronacharya also, in recognition of his great position as an outstanding Brahman warrior and a disciple of that source of might, Parashurama.

'Welcome, Uddhava, son of Devabhaga. We are glad to see you again in Hastinapura. Take your seat,' said Grandfather.

'Are your people well?'

'I do not come from Dwaraka, Venerable Sir. For the last few months, I have been living with my father-in-law, the Best of Nagas,' replied Uddhava.

'Then it is true that you have married the Naga Princesses?' asked the King.

'Yes, I have, lord,' replied Uddhava.

'Are the noble lord of the Nagas, King Karkotaka, and his people well?' enquired Grandfather.

'Yes, Grandfather,' replied Uddhava.

'Vidura tells me that you bring us a message from the Best of the Yadavas, Krishna Vaasudeva,' said Grandfather.

'Yes, Venerable Sir', replied Uddhava. 'And also a message from King Chekitana of Pushkara, and another from the lord of the Nagas. They all prostrate themselves before Grandfather and greet the noble King.'

'And what are the messages that you bring?' asked Grandfather.

'The Best of Yadavas, Krishna Vaasudeva, sends you this message,' began Uddhava in his most persuasive voice. 'He and Balarama are coming north to attend the *swayamavara* of the Princess of Panchala. Several Yadava *atirathis* are also coming with them. On their way, they want to spend a few days at holy Pushkara.'

'They are welcome,' said Dhritarashtra.

'Vaasudeva was sure that you would make them so, lord,' replied Uddhava. 'But he begs of the noble lord and Grandfather to right a grievous wrong. Last year, King Chekitana was driven out of Pushkara by the Kuru forces. It was an unjust war, entirely unprovoked. King Chekitana and his people therefore had to find an asylum with King Karkotaka across the Yamuna. Krishna Vaasudeva seeks this favour: Restore him his lost territory so that he can play host to the Yadava warriors at Pushkara.'

'What?' interjected Duryodhana. his brow gathered in sudden anger. 'Pushkara was won by the force of our arms and we will retain it with all the might of the Kurus.' As he said these words, he almost jumped from his seat. Karna instinctively clutched at his sword, while Aswatthama threw a fierce look at Uddhava.

Uddhava turned to Duryodhana with an apologetic smile and continued unperturbed: 'Noble Prince, let me complete Vaasudeva's message that I am commissioned to deliver to Grandfather and the noble King. Ultimately it will be for them to decide what to do.'

'Great God, this Vaasudeva is working a miracle,' muttered Dronacharya to himself as a wave of warm friendliness for him surged up in his heart. Here was a strange drama being set in motion by this miracle-worker, which was surely going to end as he wanted it.

'To this message,' continued Uddhava, 'King Chekitana has added one of his own.'

'What is it?' asked Grandfather.

'His message is: "Grandfather Bhishma, you are the very embodiment of Dharma. As King of Pushkara, I was very friendly to the Kurus. Without any provocation, my territory was invaded, and I and my people had to take refuge with the noble King of the Nagas. With your famed righteousness, noble Grandfather, you should restore it to me and my people. If Krishna Vaasudeva and Balarama, the noble sons of Vasudeva, come to Pushkara, I must be there to play the host".'

Duryodhana, irritated by the courtly ways of

Uddhava, said, his face red with anger: 'Grandfather, this is too much.'

Grandfather did not heed Duryodhana's interruption and, turning to Uddhava, asked him: 'Son of Devabhaga, what message do you bring from King Karkotaka, the Best of Nagas?'

'The Best of Nagas has also sent a similar message: "My son Maniman, before he goes to the *swayamvara*, would like to join King Chekitana in receiving the Vaasudeva Brothers and bringing them to Nagakoota on their way to Kampilya".'

'These are strange messages,' commented the blind King.

'Father, they are commands,' broke in Duryodhana. His blood was boiling at what he considered to be impertinent demands which, but for the decorum required to be observed in the presence of the elders, he would have rejected forthwith.

'It is an insult!' exclaimed Karna in indignation, as his hand unconsciously went again to the sword hanging by his side.

'We will not surrender Pushkara,' said Duryodhana.

Grandfather raised his hand to silence the indignant protests of the youngsters.

'Noble Grandfather, Krishna Vaasudeva has also sent word by me to convey to you, Venerable, Sir, that the Yadavas are not coming to fight with the Kurus. After halting at Pushkara, we will all go to the *swayamvara* of Draupadi. King Chekitana is invited; he is also coming with us. So is Maniman, Prince

Karkotaka's son and my brother-in-law. Naturally we do not want a war over Pushkara on the way,' said Uddhava.

Shakuni, with a broadly benevolent smile, said, spreading out his fat hands: 'If that is your wish, the best way is to accept our hospitality at Pushkara. The noble King would not like to reject the request of Krishna Vaasudeva altogether, inspired as it is by a spirit of friendliness.'

Grandfather looked indulgently at Shakuni and turned to Uddhava, expecting a reply.

'Noble King, there would have been no necessity to send these messages if all that was wanted was mere hospitality,' said Uddhava.

'Then we will have to reject the request of Vaasudeva,' said Duryodhana impetuously.

Uddhava turned to the King. It is open to you, noble King, to turn down the request. Vaasudeva had that possibility in mind and begged you not to do so. Satyaki, with the Yadava *atirathis,* will already be on the way. King Chekitana and Prince Maniman are prepared to cross the Yamuna.'

'Do you threaten the Best of Kurus with war?' asked Duryodhana angrily.

'We do not want a war,' replied Uddhava. 'We want the Best of Kurus and Grandfather, the defender of Dharma, to right the wrong done to Chekitana.'

Duryodhana turned to Grandfather and said:

'Venerable Grandfather, we cannot be dictated to by Vaasudcva.' Then, turning to Dronacharya, he added: 'Acharyadeva, let us march to the defence of Pushkara.'

Dronacharya looked enigmatically at his pupil and said with a smile: 'Duryodhana, you wanted to go to the *swayamvara* to win the bride. So do the Yadavas; so do King Chekitana and Prince Maniman. You cannot have a war with the parties going to the *swayamvara*, if you want to win the hand of Draupadi,' he added with a paternal smile, but with a sarcastic emphasis.

'I don't care what happens at the *swayamvara*. Chekitana cannot have Pushkara back because of the threats of Vaasudeva. We must reject his demands,' concluded Duryodhana, slapping his hand on his thigh.

Dronacharya said in the authoritative tones of a Guru to a pupil: 'There is no heroism in winning unrighteously. There is no humiliation in yielding to Dharma.' The Acharya's face was full of dignity. 'I had already told you that it was wrong to have driven Chekitana out of Pushkara. It was wrong politically because you converted a friend into a foe. It was wrong militarily, for Pushkara is surrounded by kings who could easily combine to take it over. And now it is unwise to disregard the friendly advice of Krishna Vaasudeva, a great hero. He gives us an opportunity not only to right a wrong, but to make a dignified escape from an untenable position. I would, humbly request Grandfather to grant the request of Vaasudeva.'

'You won't fight?' asked Duryodhana rather rudely.

'You can fight if you want. But I will have nothing

to do with it,' said the Acharya coolly, 'I am sure, noble Grandfather is of the same mind.'

'What you say is right, Acharya,' said Grandfather, after raising his hand, as was his habit, to call attention to his remark. 'We cannot depart from Dharma. We cannot go to war for an unrighteous cause. Uddhava, please convey my blessing to noble Vaasudeva. Tell him that we will hand over Pushkara to King Chekitana and even join him in receiving Krishna and Balarama, the noblest of Yadavas, with due honours. Acharya, you yourself said just now that there must be no war between the Princes going to the *swayamvara*.' Grandfather exchanged a significant glance with Vidura. 'Now that there is going to be no war, please agree to Duryodhana and the other Princes attending the *swayamvara* of Draupadi. Who knows what the great God has in store for us? I feel that, with His blessing, things are going to turn out well.'

In a momentary flash, Dronacharya reviewed the situation. It was necessary to teach Duryodhana a lesson. With the Yadava *atirathis* going to the *swayamvara* in such strength, it was not likely that a Kuru Prince would win the bride. Even if Krishna Vaasudeva did not accept the bride himself, with Balarama, the master mace-wielder in the whole of Aryavarta, and Satyaki and Kritavarma, who were spoken of as great archers, there was little chance of Duryodhana's doing so. If Duryodhana failed to win the bride it would be no humiliation for him, Dronacharya, for he had objected to Duryodhana's going to the *swayamvara*.

With Duryodhana as Crown Prince, the power of the Kurus was sure to decline. Another power was rising. Krishna Vaasudeva was acquiring ascendancy over the kings of Aryavarta. With the Yadavas welded into a compact alliance under his leadership, with Jarasandha bottled up in the east, Drupada pledged to him in friendship, and Bhishma supporting him as an embodiment of Dharma, there was no saying how far he would go. And judging by the way Krishna had behaved towards him, he deserved to go far. He might end by being an uncrowned *Chakravartin*, in which case nothing would serve his purpose better than to make friends with Krishna Vaasudeva.

He flashed a smile of contempt at Duryodhana, turned to Grandfather respectfully and said: 'If Pushkara is to be handed over to King Chekitana, and Krishna and Balarama are to be received with due honours, will the venerable Grandfather permit me to go there and play the host?'

'Certainly you can do so, Acharya,' said Grandfather.

As the *Rajasabha* was dispersing, a chamberlain came in. 'Sir, the Most Venerable Mother is free from *puja* now. You can bring Uddhava,' he said to Vidura.

Vidura exchanged a significant glance with Uddhava. Both of them hurriedly left for the mansion of the Most Venerable Mother.

The Most Venerable Mother, the grandmother of Dhitarashtra, was on her usual seat—the very image of the placid dignity which nature gives to those who enjoy a beautiful old age.

With a graceful wave of her hand, she welcomed Uddhava and Vidura. This was the second occasion in his life that Uddhava had had the opportunity of meeting this great woman, who had a charm as wonderful in her old age as she was reputed to have had in youth. Besides, she was as kindly as the Mother Goddess in her most propitious mood.

As he prostrated himself before her, Uddhava's imagination was fired with vivid pictures of the life of this strange woman, once a fisher-girl, now a divinity, and was overwhelmed by the privilege of having her *darshan.*

'Son of Devabhaga,' said the Empress in a voice still melodious, 'are you well? I understand you come from Nagakoola. Are your father-in-law and the others all well?'

'They are well. The Princesses of King Karkotaka prostrate themselves humbly before you and seek the blessing of the Most Venerable Mother,' said Uddhava.

The old face was lit by a sweet smile. What mysterious power that smile must have held, Uddhava thought, when it swayed the heart of the Emperor Shantanu in the years gone by!

'Have you any news?' she asked significantly.

'Yes, Venerable Mother,' said Uddhava almost in a whisper, 'You must have received my message which I sent you before the rains. The Five Brothers are living in Rakshasavarta, where nobody can find them.'

The Empress looked on all sides to see that no one

was within ear-shot, and said: 'Yes, Vidura told me about it. I am so happy. I wish to see them take their proper place in life. Then I can spend my last days happily.'

'That is why I am here, Venerable Mother,' said Uddhava. 'Vaasudeva wishes that they should come out of that terrible Land of the Demons in the month of Margashirsha, about the time the *swayamvara* of Draupadi is held.'

The old Empress smiled again. 'Everyone seems to be anxious to win Drupada's daughter—Duryodhana also, and even Karna and Aswatthama, I learn. What was decided at the the *Rajasabha*, Vidura?'

Vidura folded his hands and respectfully said: 'Venerable Mother, they decided that the Princes should accept the invitation of Drupada.'

'How did Drona come to agree to this?' asked astute Empress.

Vidura laughed. 'It was a surprise indeed. I think he was happy to undo the mischief that Duryodhana had done by driving Chekitana out of Pushkara. Perhaps he thought that Duryodhana would fail to win the bride, and learn a lesson,'

'He is a difficult boy to deal with, this Duryodhana of mine. The Great God alone knows how things are going to shape when he rules over Hastinapura. Now, Uddhava, what is the latest news of my sons?' the Empress turned to Uddhava.

'The situation is impossible,' said Uddhava. 'Vaasudeva wants them to go to the *swayamvara*. He thinks that that would be an appropriate occasion for them to return to life in the presence of the assembled kings. It would be a great opportunity to restore them to their position.'

'Then, what is the difficulty?' asked the Empress. 'Won't they come out?'

Uddhava lowered his voice, cast his eyes on all sides of the room to see that no one else was present, and said: 'Yudhishtira will not come out till the Master gives the word; he says it is his business to tell him what to do. Arjuna wants to come out of Rakshasavarta at once, even if he has to go with us to Dwaraka: he is discontented with the life he is leading in Rakshasavarta, but he will not come out unless all the brothers and Aunt Kunti agree to do so.'

'I know they are wonderful brothers—five flames of the same fire. I have not seen such affection and confidence among brothers in all my life. Dwaipayana is here; he landed this morning. He might agree to Yudhishthira coming out,' said the Empress.

'But that is not all. Bhima says he will not come out at all, and the others say that they will not come out without him,' said Uddhava.

'But surely he does not want to bury himself in the Land of the Demons?' asked the Empress.

'He is the King of the Rakshasas, Venerable Mother, and now he has a Crown Prince,' said Uddhava.

'What?' asked the Empress in surprise. Even Vidura could not help opening his eyes wide.

'He has got a giant of a son, who, even though he is only six months old, roars like a lion. Bhima claims that he himself is the first descendant of the Emperor Bharata who has won a kingdom without the help of his ancestors and that he has a son who is the eldest heir to the glory of the Bharatas,' said Uddhava.

The Venerable Mother's face brightened into a broad smile. 'Yes, it is true. He will be the heir-apparent to the empire of Hastinapura some day. Why does not Bhima bring him here?'

'The Queen of the Rakshasas, Hidimbaa, will not part with her son.'

'Then bring her also, even though Bhima is the first Bharata to have married a Rakshasi. I hope she is not in the habit of eating men!' said the Empress.

'King Vrikodara,—that is what Bhima is called there—Mother, has issued an edict that no Rakshasa must eat human flesh, and Hidimbaa, like a loyal wife, has given up eating it, though I am afraid sometimes she feels like doing so. But the situation revolves round Ghatotkacha,' said Uddhava.

'Ghatotkacha! What a name!' exclaimed the Empress.

'Yes, that is the name of Bhima's son,' replied Uddhava.

'But why Ghatotkacha?' she asked, unable to restrain her impulse to laugh at the funny name.

'The Rakshasas call him Virochana. Bhima has

named him Ghatotkacha, because he is as hairless as
the bottom of an earthen pot,' replied Uddhava, joining
in the laughter. 'But the boy has created immense
difficulties. Hidimbaa will not leave her people. Her
people will not allow her to leave. She will not allow
Ghatotkacha to be taken from her. Bhima will not leave
the boy behind. The Brothers will not leave without
Bhima. And we do not know what to do. Vaasudeva has
sent me a message that I must see that the Five
Brothers come to the *swayamvara* without anyone
knowing it. How can I achieve the impossible? That is
why I came to you, Venerable Mother.'

The Empress thought for a little while. 'This is indeed
a difficult position. Vidura, can't you go and persuade
them?'

'It is beyond me, Mother,' replied Vidura. 'I can
persuade everyone else in the world except Bhima once
he is in an obstinate mood.'

The Venerable Mother placed her wrinkled though
shapely hand on her brow, as if she had suddenly seen
the light. 'I see it now. That is why Dwaipayana arrived
unexpectedly this morning. When I heard that he has
come, I was sure that something important was going
to happen. He turns up every time we need him,' said
the Empress, her face glowing with maternal pride. 'Do
you know, Uddhava, that Dwaipayana is great as a Sage,
but greater as a son? I do not know what I would have
done but for him. Vidura, will you go and see whether
he has finished his midday *sandhya?* If he has, will
you ask him to come up?'

Vidura left, and the Empress began to enquire of Uddhava about what was happening in Nagakoota.

A heavy step and a hearty laugh were heard. Uddhava rose from his seat with joined hands as Veda Vyasa came, his broad face beaming with an affectionate smile. In spite of his heavy body, the Master prostrated himself before his mother, taking the dust from her feet and applying it to his eyes.

The Empress stroked the magnificent, snow-white head of the Sage as if she was patting the head of a small child.

'Mother, are you well?' asked the octogenarian son.

'As well as a very old woman can be,' said the Empress, and smiled, 'I need you badly Krishna.'

The Sage smiled broadly in response, 'I somehow knew that you want me here at this time.'

'How did you know it, my son?'

'I do not know how. But an insistent voice in me— the Great God's perhaps—told me: "Go to Mother" and I obeyed. Perhaps your unexpressed wish comes in the form of His mandate.'

'My son, we are facing a very difficult position. You know the Five Brothers are living in hiding in Rakshasavarta. Bhima seems to have become the King of the Rakshasas and married a Rakshasi. He has also got a son. Now Krishna Vaasudeva wants them to come out. He thinks the appropriate time to return to life would be the *swayamvara* of Draupadi. But Bhima will not

Leave Rakshasavarta, and so the others, as you can easily imagine, will not think of leaving without him.'

'Why?' asked the Master.

'These things are all bound up together, Krishna. Bhima will not leave his son behind him. The Rakshasi—what is her name, Uddhava?—will not part with her son or come away with her husband either. What is to be done?' asked the Empress.

'Mother, she is perfectly right,' said the Master quietly. 'You have not lived among the Rakshasas as I have. She would find our customs—or rather the way in which we live—rather unnatural. She would immediately wither away if she came to live with us.'

'Then, how can you get the Five Brothers to come out? Perhaps such an opportunity for their re-appearance will never reoccur,' said the Empress.

'If the mother does not give up her son to the father, the father has to sacrifice his son to his duty. Remember, Dharma is tied up with the triumph of the Five Brothers,' said the Master. 'Perhaps it is even best for the boy to be with his mother. Unlike your son, he may not prefer to go with his father,' he added and laughed loudly, as he reminded his mother of how she had parted with him when he was an infant to his father, Sage Parashara.

'And I was right and the Rakshasi is wrong,' replied the Empress, as the memory crossed her mind of that unhappy moment when she had handed over little

Krishna Dwaipayana to Muni Parashara. 'A child's place is with its father. That is the only way to preserve the tradition of a righteous family. I would have never deprived you of your father...

'....Unless you had happened to be a Rakshasi', said the Master, and again laughed heartily. 'A Rakshas would sacrifice her husband and, if need be, devour her child too.'

'Don't tell me that there are such demons, Krishna,' said the Empress. 'But what is to be done about Bhima? Once he makes up his mind, he is as obstinate as he alone can be. Krishna, my son, suppose you go to Rakshasavarta yourself and meet them. You will be able to persuade him. I am sure.'

The Sage laughed—for his age, a very boyish smile. 'I now know why I was wanted here—to untie yet another knot. Yes, I will go. They are my children, and your wishes are commands, Mother'

'My son, you are such a comfort,' said the Empress, and her smile was proud.

∎

28

THE MASTER IN RAKSHASAVARTA

$\mathcal{I}$t was a great occasion. The orders of King Vrikodara had gone forth. Everyone must get ready to receive his grandfather.

Every Rakshasa went to work, cutting paths through impenetrable jungle growth; renovating their tree-top homes and adorning them with fresh leaves; building a hut for the guest on the ground—an unthinkable proposition so far; and surrounding it with sacrificial gardens, which Yudhishthira insisted should be prepared according to the appropriate ritual.

There was cleaning and washing in the whole settlement, such as had never been seen since the divine ancestor Virochana created Rakshasavarta. Women were busy preparing new fibre wigs, men cutting new chips for their lips. Foxes were hunted to provide new shoulder-straps. The Rakshasis were also ordered to prepare some kind of covering—garlands of leaves, if nothing else could be found—for their ample bosoms.

All sorts of rumours spread all over Rakshasavarta about King Vrikodara's grandfather: he was not a human being; he had the spirit of Virochana himself. Wherever he went, people went mad with joy. He could also make the dead live again. The elder Rakshasas shook their heads, but the younger ones readily believed the rumours.

There were more Rakshasas in the community who, at some time or other, had strayed beyond the frontiers of their land. They had seen this grandfather with his long, white beard going up and down the river, meeting crowds of people and curing them of their diseases.

One old Rakshasa corroborated this fact. Once he had been dying; hearing of the grandfather's coming, he had taken the chips from his nose and joined the crowds who had gone to meet him, and he was cured. With this corroboration, the ailing and the maimed among the Rakshasas awaited the Sage's arrival almost breathlessly, for they acquired new hope.

Only Hidimbaa was disturbed. With a woman's instinct, she had a premonition of the coming disaster. Though her husband had the spirit of Virochana in him and made her happy, she was not unconscious of the fact that her mother-in-law disapproved of her ways. As the Queen of the Rakshasas, she was accustomed to receiving loyal admiration, and the way her mother-in-law treated her, smarted. More than that, she had sensed an unexpressed intention on the elder woman's part to take her husband away—and perhaps her son also—from her if she could possibly do so. And if this grandfather also dispproved of her and her people, the situation would be terrible. Kunti was then sure to take them away from her.

When the appointed day came, a large party of Rakshasa men, women and children, led by Nikumbha, started for the frontier. There they camped for the night, and early next morning Bhima started with twenty-five

Rakshasas to cross the craggy boundary of Rakshasavarta to receive and bring back the Master.

Siguri Naga had already arrived announcing that the Master would be waiting for them soon after the morning sacrificial session. Bhima was literally dying to see the old ritual performed by the Master.

Siguri Naga led them back to the frontier village of Lahuria. It was the first time such a large number of Rakshasas had crossed the frontier of their land in open daylight. This, at first, had frightened the Nagas, but their fright was replaced by curiosity when their guests behaved harmlessly and in a way which was not consistent with their reputation. Their strange looks and behaviour delighted the Naga children, and they came flocking in high spirits when they found that King Vrikodara himself roared at them in mock ferocity and then laughed with boyish glee.

The Master had just finished the sacrifice and the last *mantras* had been chanted by him, Jaimini and the four pupils who were accompanying him. When the chant was finished, Bhima approached the Master and took the dust from his feet and applied it to his eyes. The Sage hugged him heartily.

The Rakshasa retainers did not know exactly how to pay homage to their King's grandfather. In trying to follow his example by prostrating themselves, many of them tumbled to the ground, to the hilarious merriment of the Nagas. However, they were highly impressed when the Master patted each one of them on his head and spoke to him—though clumsily—a few words of greeting in the Rakshasa dialect, of which he knew a little.

Then followed the usual ceremony. Every one was

given a pot of milk. It had to be goat's milk, for cow's milk was not available in plenty. The Rakshasas looked at the pots of milk with great suspicion, for they never drank milk; they preferred the dripping flesh of goats torn by their strong, steely nails.

Each one came to the Master, who put into the pot a small leaf from the bundle carried by Jaimini. The Master blessed it as each one took it away. The Rakshasas, though suspicious of drinking such unfamiliar stuff in the beginning, could not help following their King's example.

Vedic chants followed. And suddenly, as each one got up to pay his respects to the Master, there was a cry of jubilation from the ailing and the maimed who suddenly felt healed.

The Rakshasas did not know what to do but they followed the rest in a group suspiciously as if at some ceremony of witch-craft. And when the Master blessed them, some of them felt a sudden influx of energy, and, to the delight of all, performed a war-dance.

The ritual over, the Master, Jaimini and the pupils were each accommodated in cages formed of tough fibres. The cages were then slung on poles which the Rakshasas carried on their shoulders.

With steady steps, the Rakshasas, trained to the rough and craggy terrain, carried the Master and his pupils. The great Sage for the first time in his life swung between earth and heaven as the Rakshasas jumped from crag to crag. The Rakshasas had thought that the white-bearded grandfather would grow frightened. But all they had from him was a broad, encouraging smile and hearty compliments: 'Well done, my sons, well done.'

They crossed the craggy barrier, came down the slope and crossed the streamlet. With tears of respect and relief, Yudhishthira, Arjuna, Nakula, Sahadeva and Mother Kunti rushed to prostrate themselves before the Master, who, coming out of his swinging cage, embraced each one and breathed in the scent of their hair with affection.

Hidimbaa and the Rakshasas looked on sullenly, holding themselves aloof a few steps away. The Master looked at them, waved them to come nearer, turned to Kunti and asked: 'Kunti, where is my daughter-in-law? Oh, yes, I see her there. And that is Bhima's son.'

He stepped forward to where Hidimbaa was standing with Ghatotkacha in her hands, looking open-eyed at the strange way in which her husband and his brothers were receiving their grandfather. Hidimbaa could not conceive that such abasement could be the normal conduct on the part of a human being. She was only accustomed to see victims cringing before those who were ready to kill them.

Bhima whispered in her ear: 'Fall at the Master's feet'. She did not know what to do, and, in trying to bend her knees fell flat, throwing the body to the ground. He roared lustily. The Master hastily put a hand on the head of Hidimbaa, murmured a blessing, and took up Ghatotkacha with almost motherly tenderness.

It was a giant boy, though six months old. It had the Master's dark colour, a huge head absolutely hairless, bright, big eyes and rounded, fat legs, with which it kicked, showing restless energy.

The Master took the boy in his arms, making a cradle

of them, swung him till he ceased to roar and began to smile. Then Ghatotkacha, gazing steadfastly at the strange face in front of him, caught the beard in both his hands and purred with joy, putting some hair in his mouth. Everyone enjoyed the sight.

The Master then turned to Hidimbaa with a paternal smile and in his broken Rakshasi dialect said: 'Hidimbaa, you are the luckiest woman in the world. You are the mother of the heir apparent to Bharata's mighty throne.' And, with an affectionate gesture, he rubbed the hairless head of Ghatotkacha repeatedly till the boy, pulling again at the white beard, which appeared very attractive to him, laughed loudly.

And the crowd which had surrounded them was in an ecstasy over the friendship which Ghatotkacha felt for his great-grandfather.

The Five Brothers had been anxious to see that the susceptibilities of the Master should be respected and that his ritual should not be seriously interfered with. They, therefore, had secured large collection of fruits, roots, nuts, wild, coarse grains and honey, to make up for the lack of milk, curds and ghee which were unknown in the Rakshasa community. To the Aryas, a religious ceremony without milk, curds and ghee was unthinkable, for the Sage had said that ghee was life and curds were strength, but the Rakshasas had never heard of them. On the way back to King Vrikodara's headquarters, sacrifices and ritual, therefore, had to be performed only with coarse grains, nuts and fruits which grew in plenty in the forest.

■

29

KING VRIKODARA RELINQUISHES
THE SCEPTRE

*O*n the evening of the next day, as they sat around the sacrificial fire, the Master told the Five Brothers and Mother Kunti that the time had arrived for their leaving Rakshasavarta as early as possible. Only Bhima hesitated; he liked to be a king in his own right; he loved Hidimbaa and Ghatotkacha, and did not like leaving while his son was still an infant. All the others were ready; they had been dying to leave the forest all the time.

The Master, however, impressed upon them how important it was for them to come back to life at the *swayamvara,* where most of the kings of Aryavarta were likely to gather. If they did so, the occasion might compel Duryodhana to welcome them in the presence of the kings. Bhishma and the Venerable Mother were all the time awaiting their return.

'And Vaasudeva also wants you to come,' continued the Master, 'and I would hesitate to disagree with him. He is perhaps the best friend you have.'

It was past midnight. All of them were sound asleep around the sacrificial fire, which was fast sinking into embers. In spite of a strong breeze which was whistling through the forest, Arjuna, whose senses were extraordinarily sharp, woke up with the feeling that something unusual was happening. He listened and heard a faint thud. It was followed by another similar noise; then again a third one.

It could not be the noise of a fruit falling to the ground from a tree, he was convinced, for none of the trees in the settlement bore such fruits. It could only be the sound of Rakshasas dropping one by one from their tree-top homes. The Rakshasas coming out of their homes one after the other in the dead of night was ominous. Such things happened only when they wanted to gather stealthily to go on some murderous expedition.

Arjuna sat up and tried to peer into the darkness which surrounded them, faintly lit up by the sacrificial fire. Under the open sky, the Master was sleeping soundly near the sacrificial pit, in which the embers were dying: A little beyond that, Mother Kunti was sleeping; next to her, the Eldest, Yudhishthira; Nakula and Sahadeva by his side. Jaimini and the other pupils of the Master were sleeping a little farther away. Farthest of them all lay Brother Bhima, the rhythm of whose stentorian snore testified to his sleeping the sleep of the innocent, if not of the just.

Arjuna had been conscious of the dangers of sleeping on the ground. In this strange land no one was safe at night if he did not climb up to his hut on the tree. But the Sage would not have dreamt of climbing up a tree even to save his life. So every one had decided to sleep in the open near him. That was a chance for the Rakshasas if they wanted one.

Arjuna opened his eyes wide and sniffed the air. Every few moments, a Rakshasa could be heard dropping from his hut. Evidently something was happening, of which King Vrikodara was kept in ignorance.

To make himself doubly sure, Arjuna woke up Sahadeva, who also agreed that the crackling of dried leaves indicated that the Rakshasas dropping from the tree-tops were going to some prearranged gathering. They wondered what the object of these sinister movements could be. Possibly it was to attack them. The Rakshasas gave loyalty to Vrikodara because he was all-powerful and believed to be possessed with the spirit of their God, Virochana. But they had not reconciled themselves to his brothers or mother, who to them were complete aliens. Perhaps the arrival of the Master had awakened some suspicions in their minds and led them to a decision to kill the strangers in the dead of night.

Arjuna, on all fours, crawled over to where Bhima was sleeping and woke him up. It required some shaking to induce King Vrikodara to deprive himself of the happy slumber in which he was wrapped. But no sooner had he woken up, than he grasped the significance of what was happening. He took hold of his heavy bludgeon and got ready to meet any attack.

'But, Brother, there seem to be many of them. I wonder how many they are,' whispered Arjuna.

Sahadeva applied his ear to the ground. 'It must be a crowd—perhaps more than fifty,' he said.

'Arjuna, are your bow and arrows ready?' asked Bhima. 'You can easily shoot in the dark.'

'I know, I can', replied Arjuna. 'But I can do little with arrows which have tips of flint and against such a crowd too. And it is quite likely that in darkness our skulls may be broken before we know where we are'.

'What are you talking about?' came the voice of the Master, as he sat up, rubbing his eyes.

'Master, the Rakshasas are preparing for some expedition without Bhima's orders—which is very unusual for them. Possibly they intend to attack us. And whenever they go on an expedition in the dead of night, they are very murderous,' said Sahadeva.

'If they intend to attack any one of us, it can only be me,' said the Master with a smile. 'But, I am a very harmless person'.

'Why should they attack you, Master?' asked Arjuna.

'As you say, they regard Vrikodara as the incarnation of Virochana. Normally they would not like to hurt his grandfather', said the Master. Then he paused for a moment and listened attentively as the smothered sound of whispering men was distinctly heard coming from a distance. He added: 'I understand the reason. They think that I have come to take Ghatotkacha away from them. Perhaps my saying that he is the heir of Emperor Bharata's empire has roused their suspicions.'

'They are very sensitive on that point, Master,' said Arjuna. 'They are fiercely attached to the family of Hidimbaa. They believe that Ghatotkacha is a god and they would do anything to prevent him being taken away.'

'Well, let them come,' said the Master placidly. 'I have faced many such situations before and the Great God has always protected me. I will die only when I will it—that is what the Great God has assured me.'

'They cannot attack us while I am here,' said Bhima.

'Brother, you are too confident about your hold over your people,' remarked Arjuna with a wry smile.

The ominous sound of men moving cautiously in the dark at a distance could now be heard distinctly. 'Bhima, there is only one way to save the Master—and perhaps all of us', said Arjuna. 'You must bring Ghatotkacha here. Then we will all be safe.'

'How can I bring Ghatotkacha from the arms of his mother?' whispered Bhima, shaking his head. 'If I try to do it, their suspicion that we are kidnapping the boy will be confirmed. But, if you like, I will drag Hidimbaa here.'

'Please, don't,' appealed Arjuna. 'That would rouse the whole settlement to ferocity.'

'Brother', intervened Sahadeva, 'what Arjuna says is the right thing to do. Bring the boy here.'

'Come, Bhima, there is no time to lose,' said Arjuna. 'No use waking up Mother, Yudhishthira or Nakula. I can hear where the sound comes from. Come with me.

We must get Ghatotkacha at any cost before they come here.'

Bhima threw up his hands in despair at the absurdity of this proposal, but allowed himself to be dragged along by Arjuna. The giant was happy to perform deeds of valour, but he hated going about stealing babies in the dark. But he knew that Arjuna was resourceful and could think of all sorts of devices which were beyond him.

The Master looked at them and said quietly: 'Don't worry about us. Nothing will happen unless the Great God so wills.'

'We would prefer to do our best to save ourselves,' said Arjuna.

'Sahadeva, will you wake up Jaimini?' asked the Master. 'I want to light a fire in the sacrificial pit,'

'Not for some time,' said Arjuna. 'Let us bring Ghatotkacha here under cover of darkness.'

The two brothers—Bhima and Arjuna—went out into the darkness. They could guess righty the direction from which the whisperings were coming, though in the breeze they were very indistinct. With his uncanny gift of finding directions even in the dark, Arjuna led Bhima towards Vrikodara's hut, holding his hand lest they should lose each other. Walking warily, making a detour, running wherever possible, sometimes stumbling, they reached the three trees with intervening branches, on which the comparatively large hut of King Vrikodara was built.

'We shall have to climb the tree, Bhima,' said Arjuna. 'The ladder has been rolled up on the top.'

Bhima sighed. 'I am so heavy. If I try to climb the tree, Hidimbaa may wake up,' he said.

'Don't worry. I will go up the tree and drop one end of the ladder for you,' said Arjuna.

'But if she comes to know that you are there, she will eat you up,' said Bhima.

'But it is our only hope, isn't it?' said Arjuna.

Arjuna had an agile body, kept in sinewy trim by constant exercise. As he prepared to climb the tree, he added: 'After you come up, lift Ghatotkacha from the side of his mother. If she wakes up, tell her that you came back because you felt unhappy without her. I will wait outside. On some pretext or other, come out of the hut and hand over the boy to me. Then you can spend the rest of the night with your wife.'

'I never thought that you were so clever at stealing babies, Arjuna,' said Bhima, suppressing an inclination to laugh at what he thought was a delightful prank.

Holding his breath, Arjuna climbed the tree softly. When he reached the top, he could sense the place where Hidimbaa was sleeping in the hut from the direction from which her breathing came. He unwound the ladder of ropes and lowered its lose end to the ground. Bhima caught hold of it, fastened it to the trunk of the tree and climbed up as softly as he could.

He crept through the small door of the hut and directed his steps towards the place where Hidimbaa was sleeping on a bed of fox skins. He felt for Ghatotkacha who was lying by her side, lifted him and handed him to Arjuna at the door. Then, silently laughing to himself in the dark, he slipped into his wife's bed. Hidimbaa felt the presence of her husband without opening her eyes, clung to him ardently and whispered: 'Oh, you have come back!'

'Of course,' replied Bhima, taking her in his arms. 'How can I get to sleep without you?'

'Oh, you are a wonderful husband,' she remarked.

'And, you are a wonderful wife,' said Bhima. chuckling to himself.

Their bodies mingled. In the storm of passion which followed, Hidimbaa forgot all about the child.

Arjuna took Ghatotkacha fondly in his arms. In spite of his dislike of the Rakshasas, he liked this bald-headed baby giant nephew of his. Luckily the boy was sound asleep and remained undisturbed by being carried by Arjuna.

On the way, however, Ghatotkacha opened his eyes and muttered something. As a boy, Arjuna had played the part of a girl in many extemporised theatricals, and could imitate a woman's voice. His soft mutterings quieted the boy.

As fast as he could, Arjuna made a detour to escape the crowd which, from the sound, appeared to be moving towards the Master's hut. Once, in a hurry to reach the hut, he stumbled and almost fell, but he clung to Ghatotkacha and prevented him from falling to the ground. He was a marvellous boy, this nephew of his. He opened his eyes, held on to Arjuna and laughed. He appeared to be enjoying the adventure.

When Arjuna arrived at the Master's hut, the Rakshasas could be heard coming nearer on padded feet, pushing through the jungle growth. The Master, however, sat quietly in front of the sacrificial pit, with Yudhishthira and Kunti on one side, Nakula and Sahadeva on the other, and Jaimini and his pupils behind him.

The impending danger had affected all of them, except the Master who was his benign self awaiting events with complete indifference. But his self-composure was infectious. No one spoke.

Breathlessly, Arjuna ran into the sacrificial compound and handed over Ghatotkacha to the Master. The Master took Ghatotkacha in his hands very softly. 'Jaimini, you can bring some fuel. Also offer an oblation to the God of Fire. Let us seek His protection.'

Jaimini lighted some firewood and threw it into the sacrificial pit and poured on handfuls of coarse grain. The flames leapt up, lighting the scene.

Ghatotkacha opened his eyes and looked at the Master. The Master made a fond clucking sound, at which he gurgled with pleasure. The boy avidly licked the honey which the Master gave him, played with the long white beard, and, having had his fill, closed his eyes and went to sleep contentedly.

The crowd, armed with the shoulder blades of wild animals, on murder bent, emerged out of the thicket into the circle of light thrown by the sacrificial fire, and stopped, stupefied. In their dim minds, the Rakshasas had thought that they would break the skulls of the Master and his companions while they were asleep. But here was a wonder of wonders. The old man with the white beard sat in front of the fire, wide awake. In his arms was Virochana Incarnate. Not knowing what to do and looking very foolish, they halted.

The Master waved his hand to invite them to come nearer and spoke to them in a kindly voice: 'My sons, why do you stand there at a distance? Come near. Sit by my side. But don't disturb Ghatotkacha; he is sound asleep.'

The Rakshasas were puzzled. They could not understand how Ghatotkacha come to be there. In the evening, after they had settled the matter of the expedition with Hidimbaa, they had seen her climbing to her home with the boy in her arms. How had he come here?

One by one, the Rakshasas, unsure of themselves, came up to the sacrificial fire and began to take their seats around the Master. With his finger on his lips, he continued enjoining silence upon them. And the Rakshasas themselves were not inclined to disturb the sleep of the royal descendant of their mighty ancestor.

Hidimbaa got up in the morning and found her husband sleeping peacefully by her side. She was thrilled. He had come back to her unexpectedly at night; he could not do without her. They had spent a wonderful night together. She was also very glad indeed that no harm had come to him; it would have been possible for him to have injured himself defending his people against the planned attack. Then she looked for the child in the cradle, missed him and let out a piercing wail. She plucked off her fibrous wig, tore her hair, shook Vrikodara awake and beat her breasts. Her Virochana had disappeared.

Bhima put on an air of being shocked at the sudden disappearance of Ghatotkacha. He ferociously swore that he would kill everyone who had a hand in kidnapping him.

They climbed down from their home and went about making enquiries, Hidimbaa crying hysterically, Bhima roaring in feigned anger. Suddenly he stopped, put a finger on his forehead and said: 'Look here, Hidimbaa, we must ask the Grandfather where Ghatotkacha is. You know, he knows the past, the present and the future. He can tell us exactly where he may be.'

'Your grandfather! But he may not be there himself!' exclaimed Hidimbaa in excitement, forgetting for the moment that she was not supposed to know the fate which was to have overtaken the Master.

Bhima looked at her with an air of innocence and asked maliciously: 'What could have happened to the Master? Where may he have gone? If he has gone, perhaps Ghatotkacha may have gone with him.'

Hidimbaa moaned. 'Oh, my little Virochana, where are you?'

'Don't worry, Hidimbaa,' said Bhima, patting her on the back 'let us go to Grandfather .'

As they proceeded towards the Master's hut, they made enquiries of the Rakshasas they met on the way. None of them had seen Ghatotkacha. Everyone was shocked to learn of his disappearance, and joined in the search. Very soon there was a crowd surrounding them, shouting, gesticulating, groaning, and looking around for traces of the boy.

When they came near the Master's hut, Hidimbaa was struck dumb, her mouth open, her hands on her throat as if she was choked. There was the Master as alive as ever, coming up after his morning dip in the nearby stream with Ghatotkacha, who had evidently enjoyed his early morning bathe, in his arms. The Master took his seat in front of the sacrificial fire and began chanting the Vedas to the accompaniment of the boy's delighted chortle.

Hidimbaa shouted with joy: 'He is there! How can he have come here?' she asked and ran towards him.

'You don't know the Master, Hidimbaa. He can make an infant run. Ghatotkacha must have walked all the way himself,' said Bhima with a solemn face.

The chanting came to an end. People took the consecrated offerings of grain, nuts and roots blessed by the Master. Some of the maimed, who recovered the use of their limbs, danced for joy.

When Bhima and Hidimbaa made their way through the crowd and stood by the Master, he smiled at her and told Ghatotkacha with a hearty laugh: 'My son, here is your mother.'

Hidimbaa extended her hands to take her son. In

reply, Ghatotkacha roared at her, turned away and clung to the Master. The Master laughed, hugged the boy and then tried to hand him to his mother. Everyone joined in the laugh that followed at Ghatotkacha's efforts to get away from his mother.

'But, Master, how did he come here in the night? Who brought him here?' asked Hidimbaa.

The Master laughed. 'Why not ask Ghatotkacha himself?' he said and extended his hands to the little boy. The boy crawled over to him, and stood on his lap, holding himself upright by his beard. The Master fondled the boy and asked: 'How did you come here?'

Ghatotkacha roared in reply.

'Look here. He refuses to tell me who brought him here. Well, son, do you like your great-grandfather?' he asked the boy.

Ghatotkacha danced for joy and roared again. The crowd burst out laughing.

It was now broad daylight. Suddenly Hidimbaa became conscious that she was without her wig and paint—an unforgivable lapse of decorum on the part of the queen; without them she felt what an Arya woman would feel without clothes. She saw that her subjects were now staring at her in amazement. A deep sense of shame overcame her. She put her face in her hands and sobbed at the loss of her queenly dignity.

Mother Kunti immediately saw the predicament in which Hidimbaa found herself. She moved closer to her daughter-in-law, put a friendly hand over her shoulders and pulled her head to her lap. So far Kunti had never been reconciled to her son's marrying a Rakshasi. She had maintained only nominal contacts with her. But, in the predicament in which she found the queen, she could not restrain her motherly instinct to befriend her. Kunti took the downcast Hidimbaa to the Master's hut, away from the gaze of her people who were shocked at her impropriety. For the first time, since they had first met, mother-in-law and daughter-in-law were united in mutual concern in defence of womanly propriety.

After everyone in the crowd had been fed in the usual way, the Master blessed them and spoke in a kindly voice: 'My children, I am going to leave you—if King Vrikodara permits it—the day after tomorrow.'

Everybody was surprised. Some felt sorry; others felt relieved.

'Master,' said Bhima looking with malicious delight at Hidimbaa, who now had her wig and paint, 'Hidimbaa thinks that you are going to take Ghatotkacha away with you. Do you mean to do so?'

Everybody waited to hear what the Master would say. He laughed aloud and said: 'Ghatotkacha, my great-grandson, is the descendant of two heroes—the divine Virochana, the Lord of the Rakshasas, and the mighty Emperor Bharata of Kurus. How can I take him away from his people? If all of you agree I will request the venerable priests to invoke God Virochana for his blessing and install Ghatotkacha as King, the day before I go.'

The people hailed the announcement with joy. Hidimbaa looked on, with her eyes wide open at this unexpected event.

'But, Master, if Ghatotkacha becomes King. where do I stand?' asked Bhima who was now reconciled to leaving the land of demons.

'You are wanted elsewhere, my boy,' replied the Master. 'After Ghatotkacha becomes King and when the new moon rises, you, with you brothers and Kunti, will leave Rakshasavarta for your own land.'

'King Vrikodara to leave us!' exclaimed a few leading Rakshasa chiefs. 'He must remain with us.'

'His people are awaiting him,' said the Master.

'Oh, but what shall we do without King Vrikodara?' asked Kumbha, the father of Nikumbha.

'Who will protect us from the evil spirits and our enemies.' asked the priests.

'Nothing will happen to you. I leave you my blessing,' said the Master. 'Hidimbaa as Queen Mother will watch over your welfare till Ghatotkacha becomes old enough to rule himself.'

'But, Master, why should the King leave us at all?' asked Hidimbaa, joining her hands in the way her husband did, for the first time feeling nervous at having to rule over her people without Bhima. 'Let him remain here.'

'My child,' said the Master, as he patted her hands as if she was a little child, 'Vrikodara has not only to fight for the Rakshasas, but also fight for Dharma. Dharma, you know, is greater than life. All life depends upon it. But I assure you of this. Whenever Rakshasavarta is in danger, you have only to remember him, and he will appear in person. I will make a suggestion. When Bhima leaves your land, you appoint Kumbha to look after your welfare. Then, every year select the strongest amongst you and appoint him as the guardian of Ghatotkacha with a proper ceremony. When you do so, I promise you that the spirit of Virochana will enter him for the year. During that year he will look after you.'[1]

The priests, happy at having little Virochana as their King, went into conclave and invoked Virochana, who entered into the body of one of them. Then the mandate came: Ghatotkacha should be installed as the King of the Rakshasas.

Next day, high festivities were held. Rituals were duly performed. Ghatotkacha, standing impatiently on the lap of his mother, was crowned King, his forehead and arms ceremoniously anointed with human blood— no more from a human victim, but from the fingers of the priests who, in duty bound, had to make a symbolic sacrifice.

Before dawn on the third day, the Rakshasas gathered to accompany the Master to the frontier. He blessed the ailing and the maimed. Those who had been cured, clung to his feet in gratitude.

At the frontier, when the Master parted, he called the Five Brothers aside and told them; 'My sons, do not forget that you are believed to be dead. You, as sons of Pandu, should so remain till the time comes for you to take your proper place in the world.'

'But how are we to know when we should appear in the world?' asked Yudhishthira.

'Krishna Vaasudeva wants you to attend the *swayamvara* of Draupadi without your being known as the sons of Pandu. Go forth from here as Brahmans. Tie up your long hair in the manner of ascetics. Vaasudeva will decide what is the most appropriate time for you to reappear in the world as the sons of Pandu,' said the Master.

'As the Master commands,' said Yudhishthira.

'Before you go to the *swayamvara*, go to Utkochaka Tirtha and appoint Dhaumya Rishi as your *purohit*. No Kshatriya can be true to his duties unless guided by a *tapaswin*. The king who neglects the life of the spirit does not deserve to rule. And remember one thing: You are five brothers in one—five fingers of the same hand; do not part from one another. My blessing to you all. And Kunti, may you and your sons be happy.'

With these words, the Master stepped into the cage of ropes slung on poles and was carried by the Rakshasas to Lahuria, where King Karkotaka's chiefs were awaiting him.

KRISHNA IN A PREDICAMENT

*W*hen Krishna returned to Dwaraka, he was troubled at the situation he found there. During his absence, the Yadavas had grown indolent and pleasure-loving. The neighbouring kings had become friendly. The more powerful ones had been subdued. The danger of war had receded. There had been no urge to lead a strenuous life and no one to inspire discipline.

Partly, this was his own fault, he thought. In going North, he had removed from their midst the steel-frame of tried friends which maintained the structure of the Yadava power. In close association with him, the Yadavas had developed a sense of identity with all that he did and all that he lived for. The most prominent among them were Uddhava, unflinching, reliable, moved by the same passion for Dharma as himself; Satyaki, loyal, brave, ambitious, impatient to perform deeds of glory; Kritavarma, stolid, understanding, with a rare power to organise men; Charudeshna, the wise, shrewd and resourceful warrior, who had been installed as King of Agravana, to guard the frontier against Shalva, and Chekitana, the proud, impulsive, but tireless fighter who had been in charge of Pushkara, but had had to withdraw across the Yamuna to escape defeat at the hands of Duryodhana.

The other Yadava *atirathis,* who had been left behind in Saurashtra, were brave men, skilled in the arts of war, no doubt. They looked up to his leadership with loyalty and admiration but were not centres of self-generating strength themselves, not having a clear grasp of the mission to which he, Krishna, had dedicated himself. In his absence they had been easily influenced by the general atmosphere prevailing among their people.

Several other factors had also contributed to easy living among the Yadavas. Their cattle had multiplied. The earth had been yielding in plenty. The three ports—Dwaraka, Prabhasa and Sabar Kaccha[1]—received ships laden with foreign luxuries—gold, diamonds, pearls, and sandalwood. Prosperity had brought luxury; luxury, ostentation. Drinking and gambling, which the Yadavas were always fond of, now absorbed most of the energy of the well-to-do young men.

It was s serious situation, Krishna felt. All his plans in the North were based on the Yadavas, strong in peace and war, sharing his desire to vindicate Dharma. The widespread epidemic of pleasure-huntings however had sapped the heroic spirit which they had developed when he had led them into Saurashtra and got them to build up both strength and prosperity.

His group of friends headed by Satyaki and Kritavarma, who had returned with him, were ready to co-operate with him. As before, they began going to the sea-shore every morning to keep their skill in martial arts in perfect trim. But other young Yadavas stood aloof. The young and the gay among them looked with unconcern at these strenuous exercises even if they did not dare to sneer at them. The blight of the unheroic was on them.

How was this situation to be saved? In this evergrowing avidity for pleasure, Krishna saw the end of the Yadava power and the eclipse of his own mission.

At first Krishna discussed the matter with the leading elders—among them, King Ugrasena, now the ghost of his former self; his father Vasudeva, good-natured and placid as ever; and his saintly uncle Akrura. Krishna described the dangers which confronted them. Chekitana had been deprived of Pushkara by Duryodhana. It was likely that Draupadi might be induced to marry Meghasandhi, the grandson of Jarasandha, who in alliance with Drupada, the sworn enemy of Dronacharya, was sure to overwhelm the kings of Aryavarta. Now Mathura was without Yadava rule and Pushkara in the hands of Duryodhana; Charudeshna would be isolated at Agravana; Shalva, whom they had forced into inaction, could easily force a war on them. Frontiers were to be defended by unflagging readiness, not by complacent sef-confidence, he added.

The King had grown feeble. He heard Krishna with patience, and, as was usual with him, did not feel like taking a decision himself one way or the other. He left it to the council of the Chiefs to take it. Vasudeva and Akrura, in spite of their great confidence in Krishna, discouraged the idea of the Yadavas undertaking what they thought was a grandiose venture to dominate Aryavarta. It would be hazardous, unsettling their lives again. They had had enough of trials and misfortunes. Luckily they had survived them. Now the time had come to cry halt, to strive for peace without the aid of arms and gather its harvest.

Disappointed in the elders, Krishna turned to his brother Balarama, whose affection for him had remained unshaken throughout life. His talks with his Big Brother, however, were even less satisfying. Balarama was happy and contented. He had developed a dislike for strenuous living. He preferred to spend his time among his boon-companions, drinking and gambling, bossing over everybody, and living on the memory of his heroic deeds which he loved to recount over and over again. He had no doubt in his mind: No one would ever again quarrel with the Yadavas.

Balarama was forthright. Govinda had remained the same as when he was young, trying to work miracles all the time. He himself, however, had had enough of them. If Govinda was very keen to go to the *swayamvara*, he could go; Balarama would accompany him if he wanted, but in no event enter the contest. He did not want to be burdened with an additional wife who would bring a war with the Kurus as her dowry.

Also, Duryodhana was his favourite pupil, said Balarama. He liked him immensely. The poor man had

had a run of bad luck having been born to a blind father and deprived of his royal inheritance. And Chekitana or no Chekitana, he was not going to deprive Duryodhana of the fruits of his victory, by taking over Pushkara. If Chekitana had lost, he had lost; he could return to Dwaraka and be content with being a Yadava Chief, who was no whit inferior to the king of a forest principality. In a war all could not win; someone must lose. And surely the Yadavas could not keep going all over the world righting the wrongs of other people. Having given a bit of his mind, his Big Brother left Krishna to make the best of the situation.

Krishna met with stubborn resistance when the Chiefs assembled in council. He explained the whole position. Pushkara had to be wrested from Duryodhana and restored to Chekitana, the Yadava King. The honour of the Yadavas demanded it. If they failed in their duty, they would lose their hegemony over the Yadava princelings of the North. The time had also come when Mathura, their patrimony, had to be rehabilitated. If they rebuilt their native city, they would, with a formidable outpost, emerge as a power in the North.

It was of still greater importance, he urged, that Jarasandha should be prevented from entering into a matrimonial alliance with Drupada. Such an alliance would mean the end of Drupada as a great power. The independent Arya kings would be turned into the vassals of Magadha. Homes of learning, now flourishing in Aryavarta, would be destroyed or left to wither away for want of support. Jarasandha had been the bitterest enemy of the Yadavas, unforgiving and implacable. He could best be checkmated at the *swayamvara* if a friendly warrior, supported by the formidable might of the Yadav *atirathis,* won the bride. He himself had decided not to enter the contest, but some of the *atirathis*—Satyaki; Kritavarma and Gada, his step-brother—were master bow-men; any of them might win the contest.

All Krishna's powers of persuasion could make no impression on the group of chiefs led by Satrajit, who was very influential. He owned several ships and vast properties. He was reputed to possess *Syamantaka,* the magic jewel, which turned whatever it touched into gold. He led a life of ostentatious luxury and had become a patron of the pleasure-loving section of the rich Yadavas.

The opposition of Satrajit to Krishna's suggestion arose from his deep-seated distrust of him. From the time he had returned as a disgruntled refugee to Mathura after Kamsa's death, he had sensed the danger of the Yadavas being led by a restless, resourceful and influential young Chief with wild dreams of establishing Dharma over men. He had long perceived that if Krishna had had his way, the Yadava would be committed to a hazardous life of corporate adventure lasting for generations in a vain attempt to dominate the whole of Aryavarta. He, Satrajit, was not interested in Aryavarta.

Satrajit had a firm conviction that, after everything was said, the Yadavas had no business with other people's affairs. Personally, he was interested only in leading a good life and enjoying high prestige in his community. Nothing that did not make him prosperous could be Dharma. He did not believe in living for others.

Satrajit laughed at the whole plan as propounded by Krishna. It was no business of the Yadavas to look after the kings of Aryavarta; they had not come to their rescue when Jarasandha was bent on annihilating them. The powers in the North should be left to fight their own battles. The Yadavas would profit immensely by remaining uncommitted.

If Drupada gave his daughter to Jarasandha, said Satrajit, it would no doubt put an end to the power of the Panchalas, and was, therefore, for Bhishma of Hastinapura—not for them—to take up the challenge of Magadhan power. In fighting each other, these powerful rivals might conceivably destroy each other. There was no sense in the Yadavas being concerned with the fate of either.

Satrajit then expatiated on the blessing which peace had brought. They had won prosperity and comfort. Their concern should only be for increasing them, and for that non-involvement in the affairs of rival powers was needed. The Great God had not given life to the Yadavas in order to waste it on other people's quarrels, wound up Satrajit.

Krishna's plea that the Yadavas had pledged themselves to uphold Dharma, not merely in Saurashtra, but the whole of Aryavarta, had little appeal. Most of the Yadava Chiefs felt that there was no reason why the young Yadava warriors should be sent to be killed in somebody else's war.

Even such of them as had so far been willing to accept Krishna's suggestions, were now for accepting the solution favoured by Balarama. Duryodhana's occupation of Pushkara should be gracefully acquiesced in. Krishna, with Satyaki, and Kritavarma, should go to the *swayamvara,* but not enter any contest. Draupadi was not worth winning at the cost of inviting Jarasandha's wrath or making Drona an enemy.

Krishna came away from the council in deep distress. His well-laid plans had come to naught. The Yadavas had sorely disappointed him. Blind to the new developments in the North, they were only interested in their immediate well-being. He was the saviour only in so far as he served their ends. Now that they were happy and prosperous, they were no longer concerned with what he thought their mission was. His aim that the Yadavas should institute a righteous way of living throughout Aryavarta was to them no more than a foolish dream. They had not the wisdom to see that their own good was bound up with the good of the Aryas.

They could not enter into his burning desire to right the wrong done to Chekitana by Duryodhana or to arrest the triumph of *adharma* which was sure to follow if Jarasandha's attempt to dominate Aryavarta succeeded. Still less were they interested in removing the bitter hostility between Drona and Drupada which might one day be the source of innumerable woes and for which the arbitrative might of the Yadavas was necessary.

Naturally, the Yadavas did not know anything about

his attempt to bring the Five Brothers back into the world at the *swayamvara*, and, if possible, see to it that Arjuna became the husband of Draupadi. Nor could he tell them about it. Even if he had, they would have laughed at the very idea. At best it was a gamble. Something might prevent Arjuna from attending the *swayamvara*. Being Drona's pupil, he might not be chosen by Draupadi. The assembled kings might break up the *swayamvara* in a frenzy of disappointment. Jarasandha might even kidnap Draupadi.

All his hopes and promises had been on the certainty that the Yadavas in all their strength would restore his kingdom to Chekitana and keep the ring clear for Arjuna to win the bride. Every hope he had had now lay in the dust.

For the first time in many years, Krishna faced a crisis in his self-confidence; he did not know what to do. In his difficulties, he had nobody even to talk to. Uddhava was away. Satyaki, being such a loyal friend, did not shirk the heavy responsibility of training the group of young Yadava warriors ready to accept his leadership, but in his heart of hearts he had his doubts about taking the risk of such a mighty adventure.

Mother Devaki and his wives, Rukmini and Shaibya, instinctively sensed the struggle which was going on in his heart and they each reacted in her own characteristic way.

Mother Devaki, loving and protective, saw to it that the trials through which he was passing did not cast their shadow on the affectionate relations which subsisted between him and the members of the family. Living in a dream-world revolving around her darling Govinda, she was convinced that he was a God and that there were no grounds for anxiety about the future.

Rukmini, the Princess of Vidarbha, more beautiful than ever, now that her curves were rounded by mother-hood, had absolute faith in her husband. He could never fail. He had been born to re-establish Dharma. Difficulties only came his way to make his triumphs more effective. And in her fascinating way she contributed a true woman's hope and faith—man's strongest ally.

31

"WHAT IS DHARMA?"

*Sh*aibya, the princess of Karavirapura, being wise and ever watchful, could see the heroic tumult raging in the heart of her lord. She knew that he was great only because he could grapple with difficulties as no one else could. She had seen him involved in a grim struggle, needing swift action against overwhelming disaster, and knew what miraculous strength he had to overcome a crisis, however ominous. She spoke little, but followed every mood of Krishna's and by a glance, word or gesture, encouraged his faith in himself.

Krishna deeply appreciated the loving faith which his mother and wives had in him and maintained his usual self-composure and his cheerful smile. At heart, however, he was deeply perturbed. He had an insistent feeling about what the true situation was. The Yadavas had proved a broken reed. The hope of securing a swift triumph for Dharma, which he had conceived and planned, was well-nigh gone. All that was left to him was to attend the *swayamvara* and do his best. But his presence would no longer invest the *swayamvara* with the majesty of irresistible Dharma. He would only be one amongst the distinguished guests. In the assembly of kings every one would see that the Yadavas as a whole were not behind him. And if the mission of Uddhava failed—and there was no saying whether his appeal to Bhishma's sense of justice would prevail—the Nagas, led by Uddhava, might not be able to take Pushkara by force. If Pushkara was not restored to Chekitana, he would have failed hopelessly, and the glamour of irresistibility which he had been invested with would fade away.

If the Five Brothers did not make their appearance on the stage of the *swayamvara* in a spectacular manner, as he had planned. they would sink as before into helpless dependants of the Kuru royal family. The fratricidal conflict might recommence—or nothing might happen at all—for Duryodhana would completely dominate Hastinapura. In addition, Jarasandha—the sworn enemy of the Arya way of life—might carry away the Princess of Panchala. The pursuit of the ways of *Satya, Yajna* and *Tapas* at the *ashrams* of the *rishis,* on which Aryadharma flourished, would wither away for want of protection and without support.

The more he thought of the predicament, the more he felt that he had missed something. They had called him a God; he was only a bundle of weaknesses. They thought that he was a miracle-worker; he had only been a clever man with a rare run of luck.

His friends carried a general impression that there was Dharma wherever he was and that Dharma brought victory. He had won many victories, it was true, but did he bring Dharma wherever he moved? If he did, why did not his kinsmen see Dharma in what he was convinced was the right thing to do? If he could not get them to follow its path, how could he overcome *adharma* in other kings for generations to come? And how was Dharma to be re-established and protected? How could he become Dharma-*gopta*, the protector of righteousness, not in his time, but for eternity?

He was led into a labyrinth of intricate puzzles. What was his Dharma for which he was fighting? And how could he protect it and inspire others with it in every situation in face of the vast passions and weaknesses released by man?

It was a stormy night—rain, thunder, lightning, the sea lashing in giant waves against the embankment, the rain falling on the roof as if in a shower of rocks.

A cry suddenly tore the air: 'What is Dharma?' The cry shattered Krishna's sleep and stirred his dream-world. 'What is Dharma?'—reverberated all over the earth and in the heavens.

Scenes—vague, confused and shapeless—came before him. Men floated by, rising, mingling and vanishing. Vrindavan, with its leafy trees, grinning monkeys, dancing peacocks. And he abandoned Radha, fresh like a *kunda* flower, whom he loved as his life, to a lonely fate.[1] Was this Dharma?

The royal wrestling ground at Mathura. Men, women and children shouting, straining their eyes, gesticulating. He was pounding the bloody face of the tyrant, Kamsa, dragging his dead body along the ground, the people hailing him as a saviour. But he had killed his maternal uncle.[1] Was that Dharma?

Big Brother and himself were running away from Mathura, finding safety in Gomantaka across the barren hills of Sahyadri. They were afraid of Jarasandha's destroying the Yadavas because of them.[2] Was it cowardice? Was it Dharma?

At the foot of the Gomantaka Hill Balarama was ready to smash Jarasandha's skull. He intervened and stopped Big Brother's mace in mid career, and thus saved the life of the emperor, the source of all *adharma* in Aryavarta—to the undoing of many righteous kings, closing of numerous homes of learning and piety, and the ruination of thousands of families.[2] Was that Dharma?

On the outskirts of Kundinapura, he lifted Princess Rukmini into his chariot, kidnapped her, inflicted wounds on her pursuing brother. The *swayamvara* became an occasion for the gnashing of teeth and wailing of women. The heart of the good-natured Bhishmaka was broken. Rukmi was driven into self-imposed exile.[2] Was that Dharma?

Hastinapura. He threw his weight against Duryodhana struggling to right the wrong done to him. He came in the way of Karna, the unfortunate man, wronged by his mother at the moment of his birth and by men, who braved his misfortunes with noble fortitude, retrieving the gold of skill and status out of the dust by sheer ability and character. Was that Dharma?

The Palace of Kampilya. Drupada and his children opened their hearts to him. He accepted their confidence, but refused to take the risk of fighting the Kurus, planned a spectacular *swayamvara* which was likely to end in complete failure. Was that Dharma?

Krishna shivered in his sleep. Opening his eyes he saw the loving eyes of Rukmini fixed on him. He tried to smile and fell asleep....

Again he saw men and women coming in endless processions, shouting, grimacing, praying, wailing, talking of Dharma, waiting to know what it was, himself unable to give a satisfying answer. He heard himself asking these men and women: 'Do you know Dharma?'

'Yes' said one, 'I know it'. And he was a profit-mad skinflint. He had the face of Satrajit, but a little twisted and much more sinister. 'I buy Dharma,' he said, 'from the Brahmans, even from the gods. I feed my family. I worship at the shrines. For I alone know how to gather riches and to give them.'

'Your Dharma is the child of greed. I know you not', Krishna heard himself saying, and let him pass by...

'I know Dharma,' claimed another, marked with the emblems of sanctity. 'I am pious. I have shrunk from the ways of sin, never murdered, never stolen, never whored. My way is the only righteous way.'

'Your Dharma is the child of fear. I know you not,' said Krishna and let him pass by...

The third came, a dare-devil. 'I know my Dharma,' he said, 'I have destroyed my enemies, for whoever opposes me is of the seed of sin. I perform sacrifices, give in charity and thereby proclaim my victory to the world. I feed the Brahmans and my praises are sung by them.'

'Your Dharma is the child of vanity. I know you not,' said Krishna and let him pass by....

Then there came before him one who was meek and resigned. 'I know Dharma. no one else does,' he said. 'It is humility. Unresisting, I suffer wrongs cheerfully. I bear hunger, thirst, cold, even misfortune. That is the privilege of the meek in spirit. Theirs is the glory of Dharma.'

'Your Dharma is the child of the slave mind which does not know the divinity within him. I know you not,' said Krishna and let him pass by....

Then came another, sly as a fox, and said: 'I know my Dharma. I stand away from risky action and the dens of lions, and walk the path of safety, which comes of peace and fearing the wrath of the gods.'

'Your Dharma is the child of cowardice. I know you not,' said Krishna and let him pass by.....

Yet there came another, who said: 'I know my Dharma. It is to peddle the favour of the gods to those who open their money bags to me. I offer the hope of salvation to those who have one. Drunk with it, they dance with joy.

'Your Dharma is the child of fraud. I know you not,' said Krishna and let him pass by.....

Still another came, who said with an air of superiority: 'I know my Dharma. It is to escape the snares of life, to repress the longings of the flesh. I scorn human weakness in myself and in others, and revel in stern detachment. I avoid contacts with men and live apart and superior to them.'

'Your Dharma is the child of arrogance. I know you not,' said Krishna and let him pass by....

And yet another came, satisfied with himself. 'I know my Dharma.' he said, 'I lend money to the gods, by giving alms to the poor. I enter what I give in a ledger, which Chitragupta, the divine accountant, will open when I appear at my death before the throne of Dharma. I will then present my bill and collect my dues with compound interest and live in comfort thereafter.'

Krishna said: 'Your Dharma is the child of commerce. I know you not,' and let him also pass by....

And yet another came and his manner was unctuous, and he said: 'I know my Dharma. I do not care what I do—I murder, steal, avenge. But I chant the glories of the Great God and turn my sin into a song. I know He will forgive me, however wicked I am. My God is merciful,'

'Your Dharma is the child of deceit. I know you not,' said Krishna and let him pass by....

And then came another with the mien of wisdom and the words of a saint. 'My Dharma is not to resist evil. I shall suffer in silence and shall inherit the kingdom of heaven. Let the wicked seek their foul destiny. They are no concern of mine. My martyrdom will win me glory.'

'Your Dharma is the child of inaction. I know you

not,' said Krishna with a sigh, and he let him pass by....

Then another came with his body fragrant like the lemon leaves, with smirking lips and well oiled hair. 'All Dharma is illusion. I eat, drink and enjoy myself as I like. My body is my only shrine. The pleasures of the flesh are my rituals of worship. Beyond them, there is nothing; after me, there is nothing.'

'You are the child of a demon. I shall never forgive you,' said Krishna, and in disgust he turned his back on him...

Suddenly the procession vanished.

Krishna awoke, his heart pounding wildly. Then he smiled to himself. His dream had told him how men looked upon Dharma. But he also had known Dharma.

He knew the Dharma of the rulers of men like Bhishma and Drupada. It was to defend their people, to feed the starving, to help the helpless, to foster learning, to uphold the ancient ways of godly living.

He also knew the Dharma of the family. It created the beautiful bond which Drupada had woven between himself and his children; it knit the Five Brothers together so that they lived for each other and for their mother; it made Rukmini and Shaibya parts of him; it led his Mother Devaki to see all in her child and her child in all.

He also knew the Dharma of the Master, who lived only to understand all who came to him with sympathy and who, by the love he bore them, inspired them to be better than they were.

All this was Dharma, no doubt. But so also were the Dharmas of all those others whom he had rejected. It gave each of them something noble to live by—ladders built out of weakness of the heart so that they might climb to a higher Dharma, always feeling better than before with each rung they climbed. Men were differently made, and each needed his own ladder. But for that, they would have been demons with smirking lips and a self-satisfied air, as that one in the procession was, whose body was his shrine, and whose only rituals of worship were the pleasures of the flesh.

Thunder-claps shook the halls of the mansion, Lightning rent the air. The sea-waves lashed angrily at the embankment.

Whilst the flashes illumined the room in which he lay, an inner light seemed to come to him as well. He saw clearly, distinctly—what he had been groping for so long. Life—sinful, wretched, noble, inspiring—was one and indivisible. In accepting the mission for fighting of its ennoblement, he had embraced, not a part of life, but the whole of it.

Unwittingly he had been struggling to fulfil the expectations of all—as a son, as a friend, as a husband, as a brother, as a warrior, as a leader, as a defender of the righteous way—at all times feeding the hunger of men and women for someone to love, to cheer and to inspire; and they had learnt to gauge the excellence of other men by comparing them to him. This was the secret of why he had moved many who, but for him, would have remained stagnant.

That was why, in their ecstasy at finding him what

they had hungered for, many had called him 'their' Govinda; others, a redeemer; some, even a God.

Mother Devaki and uncle Akrura, deeply religious souls, in their overflowing love of him, had looked upon him as Vaasudeva, not the son of Vasudeva, the Yadava chief, but VAASUDEVA, That is All, as many ardent worshippers called the Great God.

He would like to be VAASUDEVA, That is All, the Great God, if he could, he mused. Then he would find a place in every heart. Then his Dharma would inspire all men in all ages at all times. But what was this Dharma?

He laughed to himself. He did not know it even at this critical moment when the fabric of his life was crashing round him.

He opened his eyes. He found Rukmini looking at him with anxiety. 'Has your sleep been disturbed?' she asked.

'No, I am only thinking.'

'What are you thinking, lord?' she again asked.

'Vaidarbhi, what do you think your Dharma is?'

Rukmini smiled the smile of the happy and devoted wife. 'My Dharma! That is very simple. To live in you so that you can live in my heart.'

Krishna pressed her hand and closed his eyes.

He dozed off, and in the twilight of a half-sleep, resumed the chain of his broken thoughts. Dharma is not merely a hope. Nor speculation. Nor rituals. Nothing which is inspired by anger, greed or fear....It is the will to shape oneself, men and situations, by rising above weaknesses.

No, that was not enough; Dharma for each one is, to weld the vision, the will and the deed—they are not three, but one—so that he may strive, each in his own way, to live in All—VAASUDEVA—so that All may live in him.

The next morning, Satyaki and Kritavarma came to him, heart-broken. They did not know what to do. In a whisper, Satyaki asked: 'Lord, what shall we do now? The Yadavas have no faith in what we are going to do.'

There was a new light in his eyes. He smiled the smile of one to whom light had come. 'Don't blame them, Satyaki. They have not failed. It would be truer to say we have failed them.'

'But what shall we do? It looks as if the three of us are going on a fool's errand!'

'Satyaki, they will come, if we live in faith ourselves'. said Krishna.

'How can we do that?'

Krishna smiled. 'We shall give them faith, Satyaki, if we take Pushkara, find a bridegroom for Draupadi and heal the hatred between Drona and Drupada. For the moment don't think of what will happen. Let us make things happen.'

32

"DHARMA HAS SEIZED ME"

$\mathcal{T}$he rains had gone. The sea was now calm. Ships began to ply. The morning breeze began to bring its refreshing vigour.

A delegation from Kampilya brought Drupada's invitation to the Yadava King, Ugrasena, and all the Yadava *atirathis*,[1] to attend the *swayamvara* of Draupadi on the eleventh day of the bright half of the month of Paush. The Council of Chiefs expressed by a formal decision the views it had already formed. Krishna, Satyaki and Kritavarma, the best of the Yadava *atirathis*, should proceed to Kampilya to attend the *swayamvara*, but not to participate in any contest.

Krishna accepted the Council's decision with an inscrutable smile, leaving Satrajit and his enemies to gloat over his defeat. He and his two friends, Satyaki and Kritavarma, kept their own counsel. To all appearances they were reconciled to the behest of the King.

However, Satyaki could not conceal his disappointment. He felt like a race-horse which had been arrested in mid-career. This attitude of the Council's he said, was cowardly. Without much effort.

he himself could have taken Pushkara. With his expert bowmanship, he stood a fair chance of winning Draupadi; it was his life's opportunity.

He could not understand exactly why Krishna accepted the decision. But he knew his friend well; there were many more things passing in that mind than he could fathom. With frenzied zeal, therefore, he spent his time in perfecting his own skill in arms and in training all the bands of *maharathis* and *rathis*—his, Krishna's and Kritavarma's—in body-combat, mace-wielding, archery, chariot-driving and all the other arts of war, shouting at every one who failed to come up to his expectation.

The Yadava chiefs, other than his friends, laughed at Satyaki for wasting his time in this manner; they knew that there was no reward in store for him. Often they sneered at him. "Whatever you do, Satyaki, there is not going to be any Draupadi for you". At such remarks, Satyaki would fly into a temper and. many a time, an exchange of hot words, and sometimes even blows, would follow.

In the month of Kartik, Kritavarma, with his own band of *maharathis* and *rathis*, left Dwaraka with the appropriate equipment. He carried Krishna's message to Charudeshna, King of Agravana, to invite the Yadava princes of the surrounding area to assemble at his headquarters and join Krishna in celebrating a festival which fell on the eleventh day of the bright half of the month of Margashirsha. He also carried a special message for Uddhava.

Most of the Yadava chiefs took little notice of the

unusual activities of Krishna's friends. As Krishna had accepted the decision of the Council of Chiefs, they were sure that he would abide by it. If he did not want to do so, he would have submitted the matter to the Council again.

The impatient Satyaki shouted, cursed, stormed, and worked all through the day getting the bands ready for tough fighting. It was announced that he, with his band, would leave Dwaraka a fortnight in advance of Krishna.

The crafty old Satrajit, however, watched Krishna's activities with a wary eye. He knew the unfathomable ways of young Krishna better. The young Chief was a master of surprises. The very fact that he had unhesitatingly accepted the decision of the Council showed some mystery lay behind these active preparations.

If they were going to the *swayamvara* merely as guests, what was the sense of Satyaki and Kritavarma training their bands in the way they were doing? If Satyaki was not going to contest at the *swayamvara*, why did he practice so assiduously at perfecting his skill in archery? If war was not in view, why give such intensive training to their horses? Why this sudden decision to make new chariots, new and more powerful maces and formidable bows for themselves and their lieutenants?

All things indicated one thing and one thing only; a desperate bid to capture Pushkara, Satrajit thought. And when he heard that Satyaki was going in advance of Krishna to Agravana to meet some of the Yadava princes, his suspicions were confirmed. Satyaki was the strong arm of Krishna. He was preparing to take Pushkara and win Draupadi. There was no other explanation of his mystifying conduct. This sinister move had to be met, for it meant the Yadavas were going to war.

At one time Satrajit had liked young Satyaki. He was handsome, brave and well-mannered. His father was a distinguished Chief of the Yadavas. He had a sunny temper. Though turbulent at times, he was marked out for greatness.

Satrajit had even thought of giving his daughter Satyabhama to Satyaki. Satyaka, his father, however, had turned down the offer. Satyaki himself would not listen to it; he was too far committed to Krishna's adventures to think of marrying. This had hurt Satrajit's vanity. The aristocratic Satyaka and his son had spurned a matrimonial alliance with him!

The only way to prevent a commitment to war, he thought, was to frustrate Krishna's plan by depriving him of his fiery, trusted and powerful comrade. It was an object worth accomplishing at this crisis when his, Satrajit's influence over the Yadavas was growing.

Satyaki, with his contingent now swollen to three times its normal strength, had decided to leave Dwaraka for Agravana on the early morning of the auspicious first day of the bright half of Margashirsha. Everybody knew that Krishna was to leave a fortnight later. His contingent was already getting ready to proceed on their journey.

Before the morning star had risen on the appointed

day, Krishna, with his principal *maharathis,* proceeded to the place outside Dwaraka where Satyaki. and his contingent would take their leave of him.

When he reached the spot, Krishna was surprised to find that there was no sign of Satyaki, though his comrades were impatiently waiting for him, ready to start. The warriors, who so far had been proud of the indomitable leadership of their chief, were almost broken-hearted at his delay in joining them. Had the impetuous Satyaki lost confidence? That was unthinkable. Or had he been taken ill? That too was difficult to imagine. Above all, what would Dwaraka, which was already laughing at them for making unrewarding preparations, say if their journey was not undertaken because they had been abandoned by their chief?

Leaning out of his chariot, Krishna asked Ahuka, the principal *maharathi* of Satyaki: 'Where is your master?'

Ahuka jumped down from his chariot, came to Krishna, folded his hands and whispered in his ear: 'Lord, the master is not to be found.'

'Did you enquire at his mansion?' Krishna asked anxiously, unable to understand this new development.

'Yes. He did not return there last night. His chariot has been waiting for him all the time,' whispered the unhappy second-in-command.

'I am surprised,' said Krishna, puzzled. 'He left me last evening to go to his maternal uncle's. But he was not going to spend the night there.'

'The charioteer told me, lord, that the master went to his maternal uncle's house and dismissed him saying that he would walk home.'

'It was just like Satyaki.' Krishna muttered under his breath. 'Did you enquire at his maternal uncle's?' he asked Ahuka.

'Yes, lord,' replied Ahuka. 'The gate-keeper said he saw the master leaving the house to go to his own mansion.'

Krishna thought for a while. Time was passing. The auspicious moment for the contingent to start was approaching. Surely something must have happened to Satyaki. He could not have over-slept. He was never in the habit of being late.. He would never, never shirk his duty. Something had to be done and it must be done now.

'When do you start?' asked Krishna.

'We are to start one ghatika[2] after the sun rises,' replied Ahuka. 'The Brahmans are already here to bless our departure. I don't know what to do.'

Krishna, his eyes flashing, turned to Ahuka: 'Get ready to start at the appointed moment.'

'But, lord, how can we start without the master? What will the Yadavas think if he does not join us in time?'

Krishna saw the light. His Dharma had presented itself to him. He said with firmness: 'Your master's reputation is dearer to me than my life. You must start at the very moment when your master wanted you to.'

'But who will lead us?' asked Ahuka.

'I will,'said Krishna quietly and turned to Gada, his principal *maharathi*, who was in charge of his band, 'Gada, I am going for my arms and will return before the sun rises. How long will you take to get our contingent ready to follow me with the equipment?'

'Two days at the least, lord,' replied Gada.

'No,' said Krishna decisively. 'Gather our contingent and catch me up by tomorrow night.'

'As the lord commands,' said Gada.

Krishna pushed his charioteer Bahuka aside, took the reins in his hand, lashed out at the horses and returned home at a flying speed. The gate-keeper was surprised to see the master returning in such breathless haste.

Krishna went up to Rukmini and woke her up. 'Give me my Sharnga, Vaidarbhi. Help me tie up the *Chakra*. Bahuka, carry my mace *Kaumodaki* to the chariot.

'What is the matter?' asked Rukmini, almost in a panic at the precipitate way in which Krishna was preparing for departure.

'What has happened?'

'Satyaki has disappeared. He must have been kidnapped; otherwise I can't understand why he is not with his band. And there is no time to lose; his band must start immediately and I am going to lead it.'

'But why this hurry?' asked Rukmini.

'It shall not be said that Satyaki's band could not start at the auspicious moment for want of a leader. If his band returned home after all the preparations we have made, we would have accepted defeat,' said Krishna.

As Bahuka was helping him to put on his weapons, Krishna turned to Rukmini. 'Vaidarbhi, did I not tell you that some day I would tell you what Dharma is?'

'Yes, lord,'

'I will now tell you what it is. Go and tell Big Brother: "Satyaki has disappeared. I suspect foul play. I have made a promise to Chekitana that I will restore Pushkara to him. I have promised King Karkotaka that the Yadavas shall leave the Naga territory. I have promised King Drupada that his daughter's *swayamvara* shall be a success. I have promised Draupadi that I will help her to choose a brave young warrior".' Then his voice sank into a solemn whisper: 'And tell him— and for his ears only—that I have promised the Empress Satyavati that the Five Brothers shall come to life at the *swayamvara*. The Yadavas have failed me, but I cannot, fail those to whom I stand pledged; my word shall remain true.' His eyes were as of one inspired, 'For a long time, I only tried to grasp hold of Dharma, but now Dharma has grasped me. And if the Yadavas betray their Dharma. I must find others who will stand by it.'

Rukmini, overwhelmed, fell at his feet. Krishna lifted her up, caressed her head and left.

33

BIG BROTHER IS ANGRY

$\mathscr{R}$ukmini was very agitated. She rushed to Shaibya who was sleeping, and woke her up. 'Shaibya, the lord has gone!' In a voice choking with distress, she narrated to her what had happened between her and their lord.

Shaibya had greater self-command. She also understood the significance of what Krishna had done. She told Rukmini to go to Balarama and give him the message. She herself would go and inform Mother Devaki and Father Vasudeva, she said.

Forgetting to change her dress or to adjust her hair, Rukmini, in wild impatience, rushed next door to wake up Revati. 'I want to see the Eldest, Revati. I must see him immediately; The lord has gone. And I have a message from him to deliver,' she said.

Revati at first hesitated to awaken her husband so early. He rarely got up before the sun rose high, for he had to sleep off the effects of the previous night, the best part of which he always spent sipping wine with tipsy Yadavas and playing dice. But Rukmini was insistent and Revati awakened Balarama.

The giant roused himself with a considerable effort. Half-asleep, he was sluggish and in a bad humour, his nose red and swollen. He shouted at Revati for disturbing his slumber. He was going to turn on his side and close his eyes again, when, between slumber and wakefulness, he caught Revati's repeated warning: 'But, lord, Govinda gone!'

The significance of these words sank little by little into the giant's half-sleeping mind. He got up, shook his head, opened his eyes wide and growled. 'What nonsense are you talking?'

'Here is Rukmini, lord, wanting to speak to you.'

'So early! What is the matter?' His own shouting had fully woken him up now.

'Govinda has gone!' said Revati.

'Where to?' asked Balarama.

'Suddenly he left for Pushkara, because Satyaki had disappeared,' said Revati.

With a lumbering gesture. Balarama hoisted his huge body out of the bed. 'Call Rukmini,' he shouted. 'What is all this trouble about?'

Rukmini came into the room and narrated what had happened. As she spoke, bitterness crept into her voice and manner. With tearful, indignant passion, she exclaimed: 'The Yadavas—you all—have failed the lord. You have forsaken him. He has gone to keep his word,'

'But, why? Why? Why?' shouted Balarama, still confused.

'He came to me before leaving and asked me to convey a message to you,'

'What is the message?'

'He asked me to convey to you this message, 'Eldest: I have promised Chekitana to restore Pushkara to him; promised King Karkotaka that the Yadavas shall leave his territory; promised King Drupada that his daughter's *swayamvara* shall be a success; and promised Draupadi herself that I will help her to select a brave young warrior",' said Rukmini.

'Why does he go on making such wild promises?' asked Balarama. Then, having regained his good humour, he added: 'And why does he leave it to his wife to bother me with those promises when it is time for me to enjoy early morning sleep?'

Then he looked at the forbidding look which the two women cast at him for his ill-timed remark, and becoming serious, asked:

'What else did he say?'

Rukmini looked all round to see that no one besides the three was present. 'He told me to convey a secret to you. He has promised the venerable Satyavati, Empress of Hastinapura, that the Five Brothers shall come to life at the *swayamvara*.'

'And has he gone to fulfil his promises?' asked Balarama, opening his eyes wide in surprise.

'You would not help him. The Yadavas would not help him. What else could he do? He is not a back-slider,' said Rukmini with a touch of anger.

'So, he has gone to sacrifice himself?'

'He has left us for ever,' said Rukmini in a voice of despair. 'I know him.'

'But why should he leave us for ever?' Still the Big Brother could not understand what all this meant.

'Do you know the last words the lord said to me? He said: "I cannot fail those to whom I stand pledged. My word shall remain true". Then he added: "For a long time I only tried to grasp hold of Dharma, but now Dharma has grasped me. And if the Yadavas betray their Dharma, I must find others who will stand by it". He has gone. He is never going to come back to you. And you, of all others, have sent him into the wilderness.' Rukmini broke down. 'Oh, what will happen to the lord? I know he will never again return to you, for you have failed him, you have rejected him,' she continued. 'You, you, his Big Brother, whom he worshipped, have driven him out.' Overpowered by her emotions, Rukmini broke into hysterical sobs and fell fainting to the ground.

As Revati tried to revive Rukmini, the Big Brother got up, took a pot of cold water and poured it over his head to drive away the remaining fumes of intoxication. Then he shook his leonine head, and with his unkempt beard looking like the bristles of a porcupine, shouted at Revati, 'Why did Satyaki run away? I do not understand.'

'Rukmini is right. Satyaki would never have run away. He must have been killed or kidnapped,' said Revati.

'Who would dare do that?' the Big Brother asked himself.

The extraordinary event of a young Yadava chief, only next in precedence to the cadets of the families of Ugrasena and Vasudeva, being killed or kidnapped in

Dwaraka itself, was like a sacrilege. Then suddenly Govinda's departure made its full impact on him. He opened his eyes wide and set his lips firmly. 'Rukmini, you are right. It is all my doing. Govinda has left us because I failed him.' And his voice was hoarse with self condemnation.

Balarama sat down on his bed and placed his hands over his eyes for a while then he shook off his mood by a physical effort, like that of lion rousing himself to spring. He got up from his bed, his eyes flashing wildly, tightened his *dhoti*, put on his scarf, took his huge conch, and, going out on to the terrace, blew on it a terrific blast. The blast echoed all over Dwaraka.

The chiefs rose from their beds, startled at this, extraordinary happening. Balarama's conch on its fiercest note! Something cataclysmic must have taken place, for the Big Brother rarely blew his conch and had never done it so angrily.

Every one of them got out of bed, put on such clothes as were available and rushed to the courtyard of the royal palace, where it was the practice of the Yadava Chiefs to congregate on important occasions. There came King Ugrasena, trembling all over with excitement; Vasudeva, in an unusually agitated mood; Akrura, his brows furrowed with anxiety. And they found Big Brother, his huge head thrown back defiantly and gesticulating wildly.

Before the Big Brother's mind pictures were floating—of the sweet little toddler, whom he had taught to walk; of the cunning companion who had led him into a hundred pranks, of the young hero who had rushed into the wrestling ground to kill the tyrant Kamsa; of the comrade who looked after him in Gomantaka, always treating him with respect; of the redeemer who had led them into the wilderness to reach the heaven of Dwaraka; of the miracle-worker who in a few months' visit to Aryavarta, had come to dominate it. He had gone. And he, Balarama, had let him down! It was wrong, all wrong. He was guilty of having proved untrue to his beloved Govinda. He was a big fool to have rejected his suggestions.

The implications of Govinda's last promise also dawned on him. Govinda had promised the Empress Satyavati that he would bring back the Five Brothers to life at Draupadi's *swayamvara*. He was not a fool, so he would not have made a vain promise: he must have been working towards some definite end. And if Govinda could bring the Five Brothers to life and the Yadavas could restore them to their high position in imperial Hastinapura, they would have performed a superhuman feat, acquiring ascendancy over Aryavarta; a miracle which the god-like Govinda alone could perform. It would be the greatest adventure of their lives—no, in the annals of men.

Govinda was wonderful—growing ever more wonderful, Big Brother was thinking. How could Govinda bring back to life the Five Brothers who had been burnt to death and then ceremoniously cremated? It was an inconceivable thing. But Govinda could always make the impossible possible. That was it! Now he understood why Govinda was eager to go North.

Oh, if Govinda had only told him before that he was going to bring the Five Brothers back to life, he would never have thought of staying away. Now he must go and help him to work this miracle. And suddenly, with the extravagant volatility which characterized him, his mind swung over and he was appalled at the demoralization to which the Yadava had sunk— gambling, drinking, living in luxuries, unwilling to undertake heroic acts.

Govinda was right. Too much prosperity was a wicked thing. The Yadavas must take to their austere ways once again. And he thought of Satrajit living in wealth and luxury, his ships bringing in gold and pearls, his house always crowded with gay parties. He himself had seen the luxurious ways of that man, his corrupting ways. Only yesterday night he had been a guest at one of those parties. And Satrajit also had the *Syamantaka* jewel, which turned everything into gold, buying the loyalties of the Yadava chiefs as if they were slaves for sale. What was the use of this gold, so Big Brother's thoughts ran. All that it produced was the cowardly behaviour of the Yadava chiefs in rejecting Govinda's suggestion! No, the Yadavas must be saved from themselves, he thought, and he, the Big Brother, was going to save them.

Balarama lashed out with a tongue of fire at the Yadavas who had rejected Dharma as seen by Govinda.

'You cowards!' he addressed the bewildered chiefs when they gathered together, 'You traitors to your Dharma! You have failed Govinda and he has left you!' In his expansive way, he was moved to the very depth of his being. He had also completely forgotten that he was one of the first to reject his younger brother's suggestions.

Big Brother's burning words lacerated every heart. Suddenly it dawned on them how precious Govinda was and how they had failed him.

'Noble King' the flood of Balaram's eloquence flowed on, 'no busy body shall meddle in this affair. No coward shall tell me to think of consequences. Such men are hogs who wallow in the dirt of luxury.' For the moment Balarama was forgetting how he was living himself. It had simply become as clear as daylight to him that everything was all wrong. 'Cowards! They want luxury, comforts, prosperity, drinking, gambling. They do not want Dharma. I will have none of it. Noble King, call the Council, if you like. But I have made up my mind. Every *atirathi* shall get ready as early as possible to march with me to Agravana. Krishna's promises shall be kept—I swear by the Great God, Somanatha. Pushkara shall be recaptured. The *swayamvara* of Drupada's daughter shall be a success. And we will bring back Govinda triumphant in our midst.' Then he hesitated a little; a flash of introspection followed; he looked around in proud defiance. 'And I make a vow; listen, noble lord. Till Govinda comes back, I will not touch drink. If he is not in our midst, life is not worth living.'

'What about my son?' asked Satyaka, who was perturbed at the disappearance of his son. 'What can have happened to him?'

'What can have happened to him!' the Big Brother turned to Satyaka. 'He would never have shirked his duty. He would not have left Govinda to go by himself. Someone and—I can guess who he may have been—

must have played him foul.' He looked at the chiefs as if he knew who was guilty.

'He disappeared while he was coming from his maternal uncle's house to our mansion. Someone must have kidnapped him,' said Satyaka.

'Don't worry, uncle Satyaka. Whoever has kidnapped Satyaki, he and his people shall pay for it with their lives if need be, I swear by the Great God,' said Balarama.

All the Yadava Chiefs were as much surprised at Govinda's departure as they were dismayed to learn of Satyaki's disappearance. Everyone was swayed by Balarama's fiery words.

Someone said: 'Let us call the Council.'

'What can the Council do?' roared Big Brother. 'Discuss, deliberate, decide—utter nonsense! Govinda was to have started a fortnight hence with his band. In his place, I am going to start with all our *atirathis*. I would like to know who wants to stay behind.'

Working himself into a towering rage, he looked all round fiercely. He turned to the King. 'Noble lord, we are going to stand by Govinda. Wherever Govinda is, there Dharma is; and where Dharma is, there victory is. That will come true. Give us your blessing. And I want you,' he added, 'to give me your word that the man who has killed Satyaki shall not live.'

The Chiefs, hypnotized by the torrential flood of angry words, shouted: *"Sadhu, sadhu."*

34

THE CHARMING KIDNAPPER

*W*hen Satyaki had left Krishna the previous night, he was in a happy mood.

Since he had thrown in his lot with Krishna years ago, he had helped his friend in most of his adventures. Now a glorious opportunity was before him. Uddhava was far away in the North and it was left to him to restore Pushkara to Chekitana.

At first he had found it difficult to surrender himself to Krishna's leadership. But as they worked together, he discovered that his own personality blossomed under his friend's guidance, and he became easily reconciled to the role of a trusted lieutenant.

He was high-spirited; by temperament, appropriative. Sometimes. therefore, he grew jealous of Uddhava. All the same he was generous enough to realise that Uddhava could anticipate Krishna's unexpressed wishes, while he himself could not. Uddhava was also shrewd and self-restrained, while he was impulsive and outspoken. It was, therefore, all for his good, he admitted to himself, that Krishna did not share some of his secrets with him.

He was happy at the thought that next morning he would proceed to Agravana. Once there, as planned, he would lead the assembled kings to make a surprise assault on Pushkara, some days before the long-awaited festival which the Yadavas were expected to join. The festival of victory was actually to be celebrated at Pushkara.

When Krishna joined them at Pushkara, they would all proceed to the *swayamvara*. He was in the secret: the contest for Draupadi's hand was confined to archery. As Krishna had decided to stand out of contest, there was more than a fair chance for him to win the Princess. If a woman was worth marrying, he said to himself, she might as well be a princess of one of the foremost royal houses in Aryavarta. He smiled to himself.

When he arrived at his maternal uncle's house, he sent away his chariot, instructing his charioteer to present himself at his own mansion ten *ghatikas* after midnight. Then he joined his uncle's family at their meal.

When he started to walk home, the streets were deserted. At sundown, the Yadavas usually returned home, had their meal and retired for the night soon after; only the gay young men, who made up the gambling and drinking parties, stayed late at the house of some opulent chief or other.

The moonlight was fascinating. The dark shadows of the mansions which stood on both sides of the street melted into one another across the narrow streets, looking like giants huddled together in sleep.

Satyaki had only two streets to cross before he

would reach his own mansion, when, at the turn of a dark street, someone accosted him: 'Noble Satyaki, what are you doing here at this time of the night? It does not befit a warrior like you,'

It was a mocking voice which Satyaki recognised as that of Jayasena, the rowdy young chief with whom he had had a quarrel only a few days ago.

'I am not in the habit of gambling or drinking', said Satyaki. for he did not like the familiarity with which Jayasena accosted him.

'Going to your mansion, Satyaki?' asked Jayasena the thick-set stalwart young man, as he joined steps with him. 'I am also going that way,' he added.

Satyaki gave him no reply. He did not like keeping company with Jayasena, but he could not reject his friendly gesture.

'What do you gain, Satyaki, by going on such foolish adventures? Your place should be with us, as our chief,' said Jayasena with sarcastic emphasis.

'I know where my place is,' said Satyaki politely, as they entered a very dark, narrow lane.

'You know your place, do you?' asked Jayasena with a loud laugh, familiarly placing a hand on Satyaki's shoulder.

Before Satyaki could shake off Jayasena's hand from his shoulder, he was tripped up. His companion took to his heels.

As Satyaki struggled to regain his feet, a gag was pushed into his mouth. Several hands closed on him; a sack was thrown over his head, muffling whatever sound he might have made. His sword was taken away from him and his arms and legs were deftly tied. Immediately he was lifted off the ground by sturdy men, who began to carry him at a running pace.

Satyaki ceased to struggle when he found that the odds were against him. He had to wait for a possible opportunity to escape.

With running steps, his kidnappers carried him, he felt, along winding streets. After a little while, he was placed in a ramshackle chariot, which shook from side to side. As it rattled along, he was able to notice that the chariot, drawn by miserable ponies, was being driven towards Mount Raivataka.

He was familiar with the roads which led to the foot of the hill. He, therefore, could easily trace the route which his kidnappers were taking.

Clearly he was kidnapped. But by whom and to what intent? Before he could pursue the thought, the chariot halted at the foot of the Mount. He was lifted into a palanquin, which was soon carried up the hill. About eight or ten people carried or accompanied the palanquin: their presence could be sensed by their rhythmic steps and hard breathing. Two of them appeared to be the leaders, for they gave orders in whispers. He could not identify any of them.

Now they came up to a little height. The path was uneven, for some of the porters stumbled now and then. The palanquin then came to a halt. Evidently they were before one of mansions of the chiefs, which stood in the citadel which the Yadavas had built on Mount Raivataka.

Some of the men were whispering to the gate-keeper. The doors were heard being flung open. He was lifted from the palanquin and taken inside the house. Those who carried him crossed three or four rooms and began to climb down a sort of stairs. There was no fresh air and yet it was cool. Evidently he was going to be taken to some subterranean cave, possibly to be left to die.

What a fate, he thought, for the hero who, at that very moment, was expected to lead his contingent to victory! And what would Govinda think of him, disappearing when he was most needed!

After going down a little, those who bore him on their shoulders lowered him on to the ground and untied the knots of the rope with which they had bound him. The patter of their feet showed that they were climbing the stairs hurriedly. Then a trap door was closed with an ominous sound.

As soon as he felt that he had been left alone, Satyaki shook himself free from the rope and threw off the sack which covered the upper part of his body.

Darkness was all around him. Satyaki could not discover whether the cave in which he found himself was large or small, or whether it had any opening for air and light. Insects were all around him, trying to crawl over his body.

He sat up. When his eyes grew accustomed to the darkness, he could see that one end of the cave was lit by a streak of light.

Lest he might hit his head against the roof of the cave, he crawled on all fours towards the streak of light. There was no doubt what it was; moon-light was penetrating through a crevice in the rock.

It was a grim prospect that faced him. He was not sure whether he was going to be starved to death or just kept in confinement for a time. He could not imagine who was interested in his being kidnapped. Jayasena's group—not very influential—though ready to stage an open quarrel, would not have ventured upon a hazard which would certainly bring down upon them the wrath of the King and the powerful families of Vasudeva and Satyaka.

Who then could be interested in his not going on Krishna's great adventure? It must be someone very powerful who wanted to frustrate the whole adventure, bring disgrace upon him and prove that Krishna was not the miracle-worker that he was supposed to be. Was Satrajit at the back of this plot?

He thought of his blighted prospects: of people thinking that he had run away from the adventure; of Krishna charging him with having betrayed his trust; of the loss of the glory which would have been surely his had he captured Pushkara; of losing the chance of winning Draupadi.

For a moment he felt crushed as he lay, looking up at the moon-lit crevice, and hitting out at the insects which harassed him. 'Govinda, Govinda, you are a miracle worker. Why don't you work a miracle and rescue me from this terrible plight? I have always thought that you were a god. If you are one, why not come to my rescue?'

Time passed on dragging feet. The moon-lit streak

turned white. It was dawn. He was to have started on his journey at sunrise. Now his contingent would return to Dwaraka, shamefaced, betrayed by its leader, the laughing-stock of all the Yadavas. His family would be disgraced. Krishna would wonder how he had disappeared. He was sure to try to find him. Perhaps he might organize a search party. But how long would it take to find him in this wretched cave?

The light of the dawn turned rosy, then sunny. The sun had risen. He turned his eyes to where he thought the sun's rays must be striking the rock above, and offered prayers to the God Surya. He cried: 'Accept my prayers, God. I have not taken bath, it is true I have no water to give you an offering. But you are the Lord of Light, Set me free!'

No one came. The cave was full of vermin. In a corner lay a broken mud pot which might once have served to provide water for some unfortunate man like himself.

He went up the steps leading to the trap-door, tried to lift it, but failed. The *ghatikas* passed slowly, one by one. The sun was now overhead, for now a direct ray fell on the floor of the cave. He went and stood beneath it, reviving his drooping spirits.

Food or no food, water or no water, he would survive at least for a few days and by then Krishna was sure to come to his rescue. Perhaps Balarama would help him too.

The King, Vasudeva, Akrura, his father and the elders would not permit such barbarous treatment of one of the most prominent young chiefs. They would move heaven and earth to find him out. But who could say when they would do so? Whose prisoner was he? It must be someone very powerful. Who could it be? Had Satrajit become strong enough to raise his hand against Satyaka's son and Krishna's comrade?

A little after mid-day, he heard a noise coming through the trap-door. He went and stood near the stairs. Someone was removing the heavy stone which had been placed over the trapdoor. He waited. Possibly someone was coming to give him food and water. Then he would know who had kidnapped him. And if he ever became free, he would destroy the kidnapper—him and his family, leaving no trace of them in Dwaraka.

Slowly the trap door was lifted. Satyaki thought that possibly someone was coming not to give him food, but to murder him. He stepped back, and placed himself against the wall ready to defend himself.

The trap door was lifted, but no one came down. Someone was peering through it to see where he was. Satyaki waited impatiently to face the visitor.

Then he heard delicate armlets jingling. A woman had kidnapped him! It was a ridiculous situation. Satyaki, the great hero, kidnapped by a woman!

Satyaki approached the stairs and looked up. A fair, beautiful face was looking at him. Two eyes gleamed with mischief. A soft, rounded arm, with jingling armlets, was waving towards him.

A soft, sweet voice invited him: 'Satyaka's son, come up, Don't be frightened of women. I am not going to run away with you.'

Satyaki was surprised almost out of his senses. He

had heard the voice somewhere, some time. 'Who are you?' he asked, trying to recognize the face.

'Come out of the darkness and have a look at me,' said the melodious voice, suppressing mischievous laughter.

Satyaki went up the steps and crawled out of the trap door. His eyes, blinded by the darkness so far, could not see, in the twilight which pervaded the upper part of the cave, who the fair captor was. He could only see beside her two tall women attendants standing a little away.

He came out of the trap door, brushed himself a little, crushed a loathsome insect or two, and asked: 'Who are you? And why have you brought me here?'

'Follow me quietly. There will be time enough to talk when we leave this dirty hole,' said the laughing voice.

In the twilight, Satyaki could see a small, plumpish young woman, glittering in gold and diamonds; she wore a richly bejewelled girdle, its tiny golden bells jingling over dancing rounded hips.

He thought that he was dreaming: the young woman, he was sure, would vanish in a moment and he would find himself once again in the vermin-ridden cave. Or, was it a murderous phantom coming to lure him to his death?

As he climbed another stair, carved out of the rocks, to an upper chamber, Satyaki could not help admiring the seductive grace with which his kidnapper walked. She had plump, but shapely contours, a graceful neck and a wonderful head covered with flowers.

He followed the phantom to an upper chamber which led into a large one. The sun-light, coming from a large aperture, flooded it, lighting stone jars, large pots of clay and little niches in which lay heaps of gold nuggets, pearls and diamonds. It had seats covered with bearskin mattresses and pillows. Jugs. which looked suspiciously like containing wine, and tempting food were placed near them.

In a large niche in one of the walls, a lighted wick floated in a small ghee lamp made of gold, casting a glow upon a small image of Lakshmi, the Goddess of Wealth. In front of the divinity was a large jewel — larger than any that Satyaki had ever seen — scintillating flamelets of all the colours of the rainbow.

Satyaki thought that his imagination was playing him a trick, bringing him from the vermin-ridden cave in which he was confined to die of starvation, into this well-furnished room in a stone mansion littered with gold and precious stones. His eyes were dazzled by an impossibly large jewel, and he had been guided by a phantom maiden. The tricks of fate were very cruel.

Suddenly the young woman stopped in the middle of the room, suppressed her laughter and turned towards him. 'Son of Satyaka, sit down. Clean the dust off your body. Eat and drink, and then we will talk,' said the young woman in a friendly voice. She flung herself with charming abandon on to a seat covered by bear-skins.

35

THE KIDNAPPER'S SECRET

*S*atyaki placed his hand on his forehead. He was going mad. The round beaming face, the dainty body, the laughing eyes, the rebellious hair which refused to be confined into flower-strung tresses, the henna-painted palms, shapely as pink lotuses, the mocking melodious voice—this was a dream of beauty. He gasped. He recognised the young woman.

'Satrajit's daughter! It can't be!' he exclaimed, in spite of being in her presence. But there was no doubt about it. The coruscating jewel before the Goddess could be no other than the famed *Syamantaka* which Satrajit was reputed to possess!

'Satyaki, don't go on blinking as if you were not wide awake. I am Satyaa, Satrajit's daughter, in flesh and blood—not her ghost. I am not dead yet. So saying, she laughed uproariously at the confusion which was evident on Satyaki's face.

Satyaki thought that he understood the situation. Satrajit had kidnapped him. He was inflicting a humiliation on him by exposing him to his daughter's ridicule—a daughter whose hand he had rejected. Indignation surged up in him.

'What are you laughing at?' he demanded in an angry voice.—'Your father did not want me to accompany Govinda, did he?' Then he continued bitterly. 'Your father is a wicked man. He has prevented my leaving Dwaraka. He has destroyed the prospects of my leading a great adventure. He has made me a laughing-stock— ruined my life. And you, his daughter, are now enjoying my discomfiture.'

'Now, Satyaki, don't get so excited,' she said with a smile. 'Will you sit down? Drink a little water. It will cool you down,' she added peremptorily, without being in the least perturbed at Satyaki's outburst.

Satyaki knew that he was indignant almost to boiling point, a state which would put him at a disadvantage in this situation. He sat down on a seat and drank water from a jar which stood near him.

'Now, listen, Satyaka's son', said Satyabhama as if chiding a naughty boy. 'My father is not so wicked as you think. He is a very kind man.'

'Your father is a demon. I hate him. He has ruined me,' said Satyaki bitterly.

The only response was sparkling eyes, laughing lips and hands raised in mock protest.

'Satyaki, don't be unfair. I got you kidnapped, not my father,' said the young woman with a touch of bravado.

'What? You got me kidnapped! I refuse to believe it.' Satyaki could not repress his fury, and glared at the callous young woman who had the effrontery to confess that she had got him kidnapped.

'My father does not even know that you are here. I had to employ experts to do this job so well", she said coolly.

'You took your revenge for my rejecting you, did you?' asked Satyaki contemptuously. 'You think that you can win me by confining me in a cave or that you can tempt me with all these riches? Or frighten me? Bribe me? I shall never, never accept you, even if I have to die!'

'You foolish young man,' said Satyabhama smilling impudently. 'You think that you are so fine that I must be dying for you. After your father rejected my father's offer, I almost forgot your name.'

'Then why did you bring me here, you wicked woman?' Satyaki shouted angrily.

'Because I wanted to save you from Jayasena and his gang. They had decided to fall upon you—kill you, if possible—as you were leaving your house early this morning to join your contingent. I wanted to remove you before the gang carried out their sinister design.'

'Lies, lies, lies!' exclaimed Satyaki. 'Why were you interested in saving me? Oh, I know, only to prevent me from going with my friend, Govinda.'

'Again wrong, wrong, utterly wrong,' replied Satyabhama, laughing. 'I kidnapped you, Satyaka's son, because I wanted you to be saved for the sake of Vaasudeva.'

Satyaki opened his eyes in wide surprise at what Satyabhama said with such self-composure.

'If I had not kidnapped you, you would have been either killed or mortally wounded by the gang. I wanted you to be by Krishna's side when he was taking such enormous risks. I do not want him to be left alone,' said Satyabhama. There crept into her voice a strange note of anxiety.

Satyaki's anger subsided. There was some truth in what Satyabhama said. If the gang had decided to attack him soon after midnight when he was leaving his house, he could have been overpowered, wounded or killed. But why was this daughter of Satrajit—who was hostile to Krishna—interested in helping him?

'You wanted to help Krishna? I can't believe it,' said Satyaki, beginning to feel again that he was dreaming.

'Why did I kidnap you then? For the fun of having a look at your face which you imagine is very handsome! And that too after your father treated my father so shabbily!' she said mockingly.

'But why are you interested in Krishna? Your father has always opposed him and tried to frustrate every venture of his,' said Satyaki, puzzled.

'And like a dutiful daughter, I have tried to frustrate every plan of my father's,' she said. 'Kritavarma had been supplying you with horses, chariots and gold. He is not a rich Chief himself. Do all these come from him? Or from his partner? Don't forget that he is the son of my mother's sister. Satyaki, you are just a child. You don't understand women,' said Satyabhama.

Satyaki was staggered. 'Do you mean to say that you have been supplying horses, chariots and gold to Kritavarma?'

Satyabhama laughed. 'I don't supply them. They are my father's property; I only steal them from him!' she said coolly. 'He cannot discover the theft because we have got so much gold!' Then she flourished her hand to show the gold and jewels lying all around. 'Rooms and rooms full of it. No one can find out what is missing. And we have so many fine horses that a few more or less will make no difference.'

Satyaki was dumbfounded. He did not know whether to admire or to hate this young woman. 'You have been helping us in our preparations for this venture? And you kidnapped me! Why? why? I don't understand you, Satyaa.'

'No one should try to understand women; they are unfathomable,' said Satyabhama with her characteristic effrontery. 'That was how the Great God, Shankara, was outwitted by Mother Parvati.'

'But what have you to do with our adventure?' asked Satyaki.

Immediately she lowered her voice and whispered: 'Will you promise me to keep it a secret? I will tell you, because I want a friend in the enemy's camp,' and her eyes danced mischievously.

Satyaki's curiosity was roused. 'Yes, I will keep it a secret.'

'From Govinda even?'

'Yes, so long as I am satisfied that you are honest in helping him,' replied Satyaki.

'I am honest about helping him. Otherwise. do you

think that it would be worth my taking all this trouble in kidnapping you?' she asked with mock contempt.

'Tell me, why are you interested in us?'

'Don't say "us". I am only interested in your friend Govinda—not in you,' she corrected.

'Why are you, Satyajit's daughter, interested in him? Come, tell the truth,' Satyaki insisted on asking.

'Shall I tell you frankly?' Her voice was low, but carried the poignancy of long-suppressed feelings, and her beautiful eyes were full of dreams. 'Since I was a child, Father and all our people have hated Krishna, and I have liked him immensely. So I had to defy them all. As a young girl, I dreamt of becoming his wife. I was very angry with Rukmini and Shaibya when they married him. I still think that those proud, cold women cannot give him what I could have, had I married him.'

Satyaki smiled at the conceit of this young woman, who thought that she could be a better wife to Krishna than Rukmini or Shaibya. 'Would you still like to be his wife?'

The young girl audaciously glared at Satyaki, her face flaming. 'And why not?'

'He will never marry you.'

'That is my business. But in the meantime. I want him to be not only a redeemer of the Yadavas, but a saviour of Aryavarta. I want him to be worshipped as a god. Then some day'—and she hopefully looked into the future— 'some day, he will be mine—and I will give him joys which the *gopis* of Vrindavan, of whom people talk so much, could never have given him.' She spoke almost in an inaudible whisper, her glowing face blushing crimson. 'You know, whenever I see him, my heart jumps—very wildly.'

Suddenly Satyaki was lost in admiration at this determined young woman, understood her motive in kidnapping him and was dumbfounded.

Quickly, Satyabhama underwent a change of mood. "Satyaka's son, don't sit there like an idiot. Come with me. I have got a well-equipped chariot ready for you, and my brother was good enough to steal the best horses from our stables for you. His trusted charioteer is ready to take you to Krishna. Get up. Here are some fruits; before you come with me, eat your fill of them.'

'Satyabhama, you are wonderful. I shall never forget it.'

'Men are so forgetful,' she said with a mocking sigh. 'Remember that, when I want you to help me in winning Krishna.'

'That is madness', said Satyaki.

'It is only a mad woman who gets the husband she likes,' she retorted laughing. 'A wise woman gets one who is liked by all, except her. What a calamity I escaped when your father refused to let you marry me!' she added, putting out her tongue at him.

Suddenly Satyaki was thoughtful. 'Satyabhama, if I go away like this, everybody will say that I ran away from my duty. The Yadavas will continue to laugh at me. Krishna may understand me when I explain everything to him, but nobody else will believe the strange story of how I was kidnapped by Satrajit's daughter and rescued by her at the same time.'

'You are so distrustful, Satyaki,' Satyabhama thought for a while, and her forehead was puckered up very charmingly. Then she added: 'Can you not rely upon me? I will straighten out the whole thing myself.'

'But I can't keep Govinda in ignorance of how I could not lead my contingent'.

'Govinda has already joined your contingent. He must be far away by now, speeding towards Pushkar,' She was thoughtful for a moment.

'What!'

'Yes, when you were not to be found, he immediately took charge of your contingent and left Dwaraka.'

'That is all the more reason why I should explain to the noble King and venerable Vasudeva that I did not forsake Govinda'.

'You are a tiresome young man, Satyaki', she said with a frown. Then she got up, her mind made up. 'Come along, I will take you to them myself and confess to them why and how I kidnapped you. Do you know that things have changed since the morning? Big Brother has taken a hand in the venture. He has called upon all the *atirathis* to get ready to go North to help Krishna redeem his promises'.

'What! That is marvellous, Satyabhama'.

'I am only speaking the truth. Every *atirathi* is getting ready to follow Balarama to the *swayamvara* of

Draupadi'. Then she laughed deliciously. 'You have still a chance left to become the King of Panchala's son-in-law. Then I will have the pleasure of gloating over the Princess of Panchala's misfortune in selecting my rejected suitor as her husband. I will then feel very superior. Come along, hurry up'.

'Where shall we go from here?'

'We will go straight to Big Brother. You know, he called Father this morning and threatened him that if Satyaki was not found by the end of the day, he would have Father branded as a traitor'. Then Satyabhama laughed. 'I am a good girl. I may save my father as well. Poor father, he does not know how wicked his daughter is—and sometimes so helpful to him. Come, let us go to Big Brother. But keep my secret. I want your Govinda for myself. Not a word to anyone— least of all to Govinda himself.'

It suddenly struck Satyaki how his friend worked miracles—he was rescued from possible death and certain infamy through the medium of this charming 'instrument' who loved Krishna without his knowing it.

36

DHARMA WINS

$\mathcal{D}$harma had grasped Krishna. It was in haste, and so was Krishna.

He led Satyaki's chariot warriors at breakneck speed. The horsemen, grooms leading relay horses, servants on foot and a train of bullock-carts carrying equipment and provisions followed as fast as they could.

On the third day, Gada, Krishna's *maharathi*, joined him with his contingent. He gave his master the heartening news of what had happened in Dwaraka after he left. Balarama had shaken off his lethargy and was now going to lead all the Yadava *atirathis* to the rescue of Pushkara. Satyaki had not been killed; he had been saved by Satyabhama, the daughter of Satrajit, from assassins and would now be accompanying Balarama. Satrajit had surrendered to the popular mood in Dwaraka and was giving every assistance in preparing for the adventure.

As usual. riders went in advance of Krishna's party to inform the leaders of the villages on that sparsely-populated route, of his arrival. His name had already become a legend and they never missed an occasion to offer him worship whenever he happened to pass that way. On this occasion also, they turned out in holiday mood, with drums beating and horns blowing, to give him a hearty welcome.

The route skirted Shalva's territory. Once a bitter enemy, this crafty king, not yet recovered from the stunning defeat which Krishna had inflicted upon him, sent his courtiers to extend him ostentatious hospitality. Krishna had no time to accept a ceremonial reception. He only halted for the night, partook of the hospitality and started again early next morning. He was anxious to reach Pushkara as fast as the contingent he led could make it.

The meeting at Agravana, which everyone had been talking about, was only a feint. In fact, Kritavarma had already carried a secret message from Krishna that the Yadava chiefs and the Naga *yuvaraja* Maniman were to assemble at a place within two days' chariot journey from Pushkara in order to make a surprise assault.

On the way, therefore, Krishna sent a message to Charudeshna, Kritavarma and Maniman at Agravana that he himself had come very much in advance of the appointed date and that all should join him as early as they could. When Gada delivered the message to the Yadavas and the Nagas at Agravana, they came in high spirits and decided not to wait for Uddhava's return from Hastinapura.

By forced marches, the chiefs reached the appointed place to find to their surprise that Krishna, with his contingent, had already arrived two days before them. The next day, spies brought the news that Dronacharya, the great military leader of the Kurus, had arrived at

Pushkara, ready to take the field against them. They were, however, not sure whether any of the Kuru Princes had come with him. The warriors pulled at their moustaches, exercised their muscles and sharpened their arrows.

At dawn on the third day, they came within sight of the fort of Pushkara, situated on a vast lake, the margin of which was studded with hamlets. And when the news reached the hamlets that Krishna Vaasudeva of legendary fame was coming, the inhabitants came to have his *darshan* and offer him flowers and fruits.

Under instructions from Krishna, the Yadavas camped there. It was his fight, he said, and he alone would see it through. Chekitana begged to be allowed to join him, but Krishna was adamant.

'Chekitana, I asked you to take charge of Pushkara and guard our route to the North,' he said with a kindly pat on his friend's shoulder. 'When you were driven out of Pushkara, I gave you a promise that I would restore it to you. I must redeem that promise myself. If I fail, you will all be there to give the Kurus a taste of Yadava valour; by then, perhaps Balarama will join you. But then it would be a general war between the Kurus and the Yadavas, and I do not want that. I only want to teach a lesson to Duryodhana'.

Disregarding the advice of his friends, Krishna sallied forth from the camp, driving his chariot, with his personal escort following him. If Dronacharya or Duryodhana had decided to fight him, it was just as well that he should accept the challenge individually; for the code of honour, which the Arya warriors generally honoured, required that when an *atirathi* was pitted against another the combat should be confined to them alone.

When Krishna came near the gates of the fort, an extraordinary sight met his eyes. There were no warlike preparations, not even a single archer was on the walls. On the contrary, men and women, standing on the walls and gaily dressed, were awaiting him, and no sooner was he in sight than they shouted, 'Victory to Krishna Vaasudeva!'

Krishna halted his chariot a little away from the gates of the fort and blew his *Panchajanya* on a ringing note, clear and friendly.

The gates opened. Three chariots issued forth.

Krishna, standing in his chariot, saw that the chariot in front was flying a flag bearing the sign of a waterpot embroidered in gold. This was the emblem of Acharya Drona, the redoubtable teacher of the martial art. The next to follow was a Yadava chariot flying the flag of Uddhava. Krishna's eyes grew moist; his loyal friend had worked wonders. The third one was flying the flag of Shakuni, the Prince of Gandhara, the maternal uncle of Duryodhana.

Gada, who had accompanied Krishna at the head of the escort in his own chariot, was taken aback when he saw that Dronacharya and Uddhava were coming together. Krishna smiled to him, 'Gada, unstring your bow. Pushkara will be restored to Chekitana without your having to take any trouble'.

Gada simply could not understand what was happening. 'Are they not going to fight, lord?'

'No. The Grandfather of the Kurus is righting a wrong; he is restoring Pushkara to Chekitana. This is

Dharma. Go and ask Chekitana, Charudeshna and the others to come,' said Krishna.

The three chariots halted in front of Krishna's chariot. From the first one alighted Dronacharya, dressed in costly silks, his mien commanding, his eyes bright, his smile winning. 'Noble Vaasudeva,' he said with a friendly smile, 'you have taken Pushkara without even stringing your bow. You alone could do it. King Dhritarashtra and Grandfather have sent me to welcome you and Chekitana.'

Krishna stretched out his arms to his charioteer and stepped down from his chariot. With the humility which always characterized him, he was going to prostrate himself before the great Brahman warrior, when Dronachraya took him in his arms. The Acharya had heard his name for years; thought of him for months waited to see him for days. But what he actually saw transcended whatever he had imagined—a figure of grace, a boyish smile of admiration and transparent sincerity, which invited affection, and above all, a presence which evoked the best in him.

'Vaasudeva, my eyes are blessed today, for they have seen you!' exclaimed the seasoned warrior in an outburst of admiration. But no sooner were the words spoken than the astute Brahman pulled himself up and became his usual circumspect self.

Uddhava, with a smile of triumph, fell at Krishna's feet and was enveloped in his arms. 'Uddhava, you have worked a miracle.' whispered Krishna.

'It is your name that always works miracles, Govinda', replied Uddhava.

As to the third chariot, Uncle Shakuni descended from it, or rather, rolled out of it, the very embodiment of comfortable living. He approached Krishna with unctuous courtesy and said: 'Noblest of the Yadavas, my humble salutations. I bring a message from *Yuvaraja* Duryodhana, who sends you his blessing.' And he smiled ingratiatingly. 'What the noble Kuru has won by force of arms, he is happy to give you back as a tribute to the wisdom which you embody.'

'I knew that the Crown Prince was always generous,' said Krishna and smiled. 'Is he in good health?'

Dronacharya excelled himself in hospitality. He could be as gracious as a host as he could be irresistible in war.

Krishna and the other leaders were housed in tents. The rest spread themselves out under the groves of trees which fringed the lake, each beside his own chariot, with the horses tied nearby.

The Yadava chiefs who had accompanied Krishna, in spite of their disappointment at not winning a sensational victory over the mighty Kurus, were amazed at what Uddhava had achieved. However, they felt happy at the thought that Dronacharya must have decided not to fight only when he learnt that the formidable Yadava warriors were there to give him battle.

As Dronacharya sat talking to Krishna in his tent listening to the highly expressive voice of his guest and watching his mobile features, his mind was running along two distinct currents. One was how to win the confidence and loyalty of this young man who had shot up into power and influence so early in life. The other ran cautiously, afraid of being diverted to a course which might interfere with his own ambitions by his guest's fascinating personality and uncanny statesmanship.

Putting on his most charming smile, the Acharya asked: 'How was it, Vaasudeva, that you came alone to Pushkara to fight the power of the Kurus? Did you expect us to hand it over to you so peacefully?'

Krishna smiled. 'That is my secret, Best of Brahmans. But I will tell it to you, if you so desire.'

'But, suppose we had decided to fight you?' asked the Acharya.

'Acharya, I thought that the best way was to have the fate of Pushkara decided by a fight with Duryodhana alone. It was scarcely worth launching into a war between the Kurus and the Yadavas for the sake of a small principality,' replied Krishna. The Acharya smiled at his guest's perspicacity. 'Why did you imagine that Duryodhana would have sallied forth to fight you alone?'

Krishna smiled in response. 'As your pupil, he would not forswear the code which requires an *atirathii* to fight another singlehanded in a combat.'

'Did you hope to vanquish Duryodhana, Vaasudeva?' asked Dronacharya.

'Best of Acharyas, I have neither hopes nor fears', said Krishna modestly. 'I do the duty which is before me. If I thought of all the possible consequences of what I am doing, I would not survive for a moment.'

'Sometimes it may be rash to do one's duty. Don't you think so?'

'Those who have faith are never rash, and I had

faith in you and in Grandfather,' said Krishna with a disarming smile.

'That is why I sent Uddhava to Hastinapura. And you see, my faith was justified.'

Dronacharya gave up his cautious approach for the moment and smiled happily at this compliment. 'Was it also because of this faith that you sent Shikhandin to me?'

'Would I have done it, had it been otherwise?' countered Krishna. 'How is he?'

'Oh, he is being looked after by the Yaksha, Sthoonakarna. He is on his way to becoming a man,' said Dronacharya proudly. Then his suspicious nature got the better of him. 'Why did you think, Vaasudeva, that I would accept Drupada's son as my pupil? You know that he is my enemy.'

'Because you are a Brahman in the grand tradition of Bhagavan Parashurama. I was sure—enemy or no enemy—you would never turn away a pupil who came to you in humility,' said Krishna with a flattering smile.

'You know how to play on human weakness, Vaasudeva,' remarked Dronacharya, laughing happily at being compared to his Guru who had already come to be regarded as God on earth. It was difficult to distrust this young man for long.

'No, Acharyadeva, I trust the best instincts of men. And scarcely ever have I been disappointed,' said Krishna. 'As to Shikhandin, I put him into your charge; now I want him back.'

'But he has not yet fully recovered. He is very weak.'

'All the same, I want him at the *swayamvara* in Kampilya. I will leave Uddhava behind, who will take him there, surrounding him with every comfort.

Dronacharya's cautious nature immediately took up arms. 'Why are you so interested in Drupada?' he asked.

'He is a noble king. If he overcomes bitterness, he will be a pillar of Dharma.'

Dronacharya laughed. 'And if I overcame my hostility, I would also become another, would I?'

'Noble Acharya, Dharma cannot stand on one pillar alone,' said Krishna with an equally hearty laugh.

'Vaasudeva, you talk so much about Dharma that it seems you know it,' remarked Drona. 'What is it.'

'That is what I have come to learn from you,' Krishna promptly answered. 'But I know it when I see it. I saw it when you, in spite of you hatred for Drupada, accepted his son as your pupil, because you are a true Brahman. I also saw it when, in spite of your love for Duryodhana, you came here to restore Pushkara yourself.'

The Acharya's reserve was dissolved. He was full of genuine admiration for his guest. 'You know how to flatter, noble Vaasudeva. But I warn you,' he continued, 'I will never accept Drupada as a friend. It will never be a part of my Dharma.'

'But you have consented to Duryodhana winning Draupadi at the *swayamvara*. If he wins her, you will have to be friends with the noble King of Panchala,' remarked Krishna.

Dronacharya knit his brows. He would have resented

such a remark from anyone else, however highly placed. But he found his guest so charming and so sincere in his utterances that he could not find it in him to take offence. He paused for a moment and said deliberately: 'I was against Duryodhana's attending the *swayamvara*. He has disgraced himself by deciding to attend it; I would never have expected it of a pupil of mine. Drupada himself, I understand, did not expect that the Kurus would accept his invitation. But Duryodhana has gone mad over Drupada's daughter,' said the Acharya in disgust. 'He wants to win her at any cost.' Then he narrowed his eyes and looked keenly at Krishna to fathom his thoughts. 'Perhaps you will be asked to win Draupadi for him.'

Krishna evaded a direct reply. 'Why are you so opposed to Drupada's daughter? Drupada may have offended you, but Draupadi, like any other princess, would certainly prefer to serve her husband's interests rather than her father's.'

'You don't know Drupada and his family,' said Dronacharya. 'They are all proud, vindictive, and revengeful. If the Princess comes to Hastinapura, I will have nothing to do with the Kurus', added the Acharya in a firm tone.

'But, surely, surely, the Princess coming into the family will not alter your position in Hastinapura.'

'Vaasudeva, I don't leave it to others to decide what position I shall hold,' said Dronacharya. His voice was now a little detached, almost severe. 'If Drupada's daughter comes to Hastinapura, I will leave it.'

Krishna thought for a while and looked at the

change that had come over Dronacharya. 'Best of Brahmans, whatever you decide will surely be right.'

Dronacharya's lips were set in firmness. He was not prepared to discuss the matter any further. 'Well, Duryodhana is going to do his best to win Draupadi. Let us see what happens. Perhaps he will win her with your assistance,' he said sarcastically.

'I have no influence either with Drupada or his daughter.'

'But would not Drupada feel an insuperable objection to giving his daughter to a pupil of mine?' asked the Acharya.

'I fear Duryodhana's acceptance of the invitation must have upset many people's calculations. I cannot say how things will shape.'

'In spite of you!' said Dronacharya with a meaningful smile.

'I can only do what seems to me right. It is for the Great God to decide what is right and wrong,' said Krishna, and then added as if he was thinking aloud: 'But *Chakravarti* Bharata's house is not likely to betray Dharma so long as you, the Best of Brahmans, are its military leader.'

Dronacharya could not help smiling at this splendid compliment which he was happy to appropriate. It was true that he was a great restraining influence. 'I can only do my best,' he said, assuming an air of modesty which ill concealed his self-confidence that his "best" would always be the best.

37

BHANUMATI SECURES A PROMISE

$\mathscr{N}$ext day Bhanumati, Duryodhana's wife and Princess of Kashi, slim, small and graceful, came to Krishna's tent accompanied by Shakuni and his wife. She was pale and hesitant. There was a shadow of fear in her eyes every time she glanced at her husband's maternal uncle. Bending lithely, she touched Krishna's feet with her right hand, as a younger sister might, and received his blessing.

'Princess Bhanumati is very anxious to meet you, noble Vaasudeva. She is your sister, you know, and you are always so good,' said Shakuni in his unctuous way, squatting on the seat placed for him, with one fat leg crossed over the other. 'And who would not like to be adopted as a sister by the Best of the Yadavas?' added Shakuni in fulsome adulation.

Krishna turned to Bhanumati. 'How is the_Yuvaraja? Is he well?'

Bhanumati nervously glanced at Shakuni and then looked down—a gesture which did not escape Krishna. 'Aryaputra is doing well,' she said in a low voice. 'He sends you his blessing.' She turned to Shakuni as if to receive an assurance that she was playing her part well, and added: 'Aryaputra was good enough to permit me to come here to pay my respects to my noble brother.'

'That was very good of him', said Krishna politely.

'Oh, yes,' added Shakuni heartily. '*Yuvaraja* Duryodhana holds you in great regard, Vaasudeva. He would have come to meet you himself, but you know he is very busy with affairs of the State. He has also sent a message which Bhanumati will give you,' he added, trying to get Bhanumati to play her part.

Bhanumati's lips trembled. Krishna could see that she was no longer her gay self. She had been tutored to say something which she found it difficult to say.

'Little sister, don't feel shy,' said Krishna encouragingly. 'Tell me whatever you want to say frankly.'

Bhanumati made an effort to control herself and said in a weak voice: 'Aryaputra would like you to help him win Draupadi.'

Not to embarrass her any further, Krishna turned to Shakuni.

'Noble Prince of Gandhara, what can I do in such matters? A *swayamvara* is a *swayamvara*: the choice of the bridegroom lies with the bride.'

'But Drupada, I am sure, holds you in great regard— also Princess Draupadi,' said Shakuni. 'If you press Prince Duryodhana's suit, his purpose will be achieved. Will it not, Bhanumati?' Then he smilingly added: 'In that way, the hostilities between the Kurus and the Panchalas would also become a thing of the past.'

Krishna paused a little before replying. 'I am rather embarrassed at the request you make. Is it not a curious request, noble Shakuni? In one breath, Bhanumati says that I am her elder brother: in the next, she wants me to find another powerful wife for Duryodhana who might supersede her.' He laughed in his fascinating way. 'Bhanumati, what ought I do?'

Bhanumati lips trembled. 'Aryaputra's wish is my wish. He is bent on winning Draupadi, and what better choice can the Princess of Panchala make than the noble Crown Prince of the Kurus? I shall certainly welcome her as my sister,' added Bhanumati in a weak voice.

This transparently honest young woman would never make a good liar, thought Krishna.

'You, Princess of Kashi, are the most devoted of wives,' said Krishna. 'Why does Duryodhana want another Princess of a higher rank for his wife?'

Shakuni interrupted. 'It is not a question of superseding the Princess of Kashi. Who knows better than you, Vaasudeva, that political alliances are of great importance to princes?'

'Oh, I do understand the ways of kings, though I am not one myself,' said Krishna with a laugh. 'But I would prefer a wife who wants me than one who is only a political instrument,' he added with disarming frankness.

'Oh, you are different, noble Vaasudeva. You are wonderful. We all know that you have rejected the offer f Draupadi. You alone are capable of such a noble acrifice,' said Shakuni in his fulsome way.

'I shall be very, very unhappy if Aryaputra does not ecure Draupadi, I would do anything to make him 1appy. Please, please, brother, don't make me unhappy,' :ntreated Bhanumati.

'Don't I know that?' asked Krishna enigmatically. And would I not do anything to make you happy?'

'Yes, yes, Bhanumati, don't you worry,' said Shakuni, waving his plump hands. 'Noble Vaasudeva vill do anything to make you happy. He will promise to ecure Draupadi for *Yuvaraja*.'

'Please, don't misunderstand me,' Krishna turned o Shakuni. 'I cannot promise to secure the Princess of ?anchala for Duryodhana. All that I can do is to help vou to press Duryodhana's suit.'

'But, if you help, she is sure to select Duryodhana,' ;aid Shakuni.

'...unless the *swayamvara* is not left to her choice, 1s is usual,' added Krishna. 'If a test is prescribed, :hen Duryodhana will have to win it.'

'Is a test going to be prescribed for the *swayamvara?*' 1sked Shakuni.

'No one knows what King Drupada will do,' said Krishna.

'Duryodhana is an irresistible warrior and will be uccessful, whatever the test,' remarked Shakuni.

'I hope he will, if a test is prescribed,' said Krishna.

'But you will do your best, won't you?' piteously

pleaded Bhanumati, again furtively looking at Shakun who was watching her with suspicious eyes lest she might betray her real feelings. 'Promise me that you will do your best,' she added with folded hands.

'Little sister, I will do my best,' said Krishna with an enigmatic smile. 'The Prince of Gandhara, however, is doubtful whether I will or not. I can only assure you of this. I will myself take him to Princess Draupadi. Is that enough? Of course, if she insists on a martial test, it will be in the hands of Duryodhana himself,' added Krishna.

Shakuni smiled. He had complete confidence in his own persuasive powers. 'If you are good enough to take me to her—and also put in a word for *Yuvaraja* yourself—everything will be all right. Bhanumati, Vaasudeva is very kind, very generous and very noble. *Yuvaraja* cannot have a better friend than him. Vaasudeva, the happiness of your little sister is in your hands.'

'Her happiness is the concern of *Yuvaraja* Duryodhana first. Though, as a brother, it is my concern too,' said Krishna looking at Bhanumati with affectionate protectiveness.

'This is most good of you, most good of you, Vaasudeva', said Shakuni as he placed his hands on the ground to lift himself to a standing position. Having made his salutation, he swung his way out, followed by his wife and Bhanumati, who while leaving, looked at Krishna with her eyes full of tears.

When they had gone a few steps, Krishna rose from his seat and said: 'Litter sister, I am growing forgetful of my obligations. Come here. I must give you a present.'

Bhanumati hurried back. Krishna unclasped a wristlet from his arm, came a step forward, and lifted Bhanumati's arm, to fasten it on. As he bent down to reach her arm, he whispered; 'Don't you worry. I will keep my promise, but Duryodhana will never have Draupadi.'

When the wristlet was fastened, Krishna straightened himself. Bhanumati's face was flushed with joy as she lowered her eyes in mute gratitude.

Two days before the full-moon day, Balarama arrived with a mighty force. Many Yadava warriors and Naga chiefs also came with him. They had come in high hopes of capturing Pushkara by might, but were disappointed to find Chekitana ruling over it, and Krishna enjoying Dronacharya's hospitality.

There were shouts of victory on both sides, the triumphant notes of conches and the beating of drums, besides embraces and the mutual exchange of garlands.

In the evening bonfires were lighted. Dances were held. Bards sang heroic songs.

Two days later, all the Yadava *atirathis*, led by Balarama and Krishna, and the Naga warriors led by Prince Maniman, started on their journey to Kampilya to attend the *swayamvara* of the Princess of Panchala.

As Dronacharya watched them depart, he felt no doubt that Krishna held the future of Aryavarta in his hands.

38

HOW TO WIN THE BRIDE

A city as splendid as Amaravati, the home of the gods, had sprung up on the bank of the Ganga to house the royal visitors to the *swayamvara* of Draupadi.

It was a city of tents, shamianas and huts, adorned with banners, buntings and the particular flags of each royal house; a city crowded with chariots and elephants, horses and bullock-carts, about which men walked about briskly, though some lay lazily on the sands.

Several kings had opened free kitchens where, besides their retainers, Brahmans and the poor were provided with food. Each king's generosity was a measure of his importance.

The *srenis* or guilds of traders had set up improvised fairs to tempt customers. To amuse the large crowds which gathered all day long, acrobats, jugglers and wrestlers vied with each other. Astrologers went about telling the fortunes of others so as to make their own. Learned Brahmans and ash-covered ascetics drew the homage of the crowds, as they were escorted to the distinguished visitors who were awaiting their advice or blessing.

In a large shamiana, Duryodhana, the Crown Prince of Hastinapura, lay on a mat, clothed only in his wrestling straps. He was having his muscular body rubbed with oil by the two wrestlers who always attended on him. An expert warrior, he made a point of keeping his limbs in perfect suppleness, ready at a moment's notice to wrestle in body combat, wield the mace or shoot an arrow.

Patiently though he lay under the deft fingers of the wrestlers, his mind was restless with impatience, thinking of the *swayamvara* which was to come off two days later. His whole future depended on winning Drupada's daughter as a wife.

No one in Kampilya appeared to have expected that the Kurus would accept the invitation. King Drupada, his host, was cool, though correct, in his reception of him. But there was nothing surprising in that, in view of his known hostility towards the Guru of the Kurus, Dronacharya.

When they had arrived, huge crowds had gathered to see what he and his brothers were like, and his name was whispered from mouth to mouth. Their arrival had created a sensation, and that was all he wanted.

Duryodhana's party had been one of the largest to arrive and the most imposing. It consisted of about thirty of his brothers and his four maternal uncles, the Princes of Gandhara, all of whom, except Shakuni, the eldest, were stalwart and fine-looking.

Karna, his closest friend, driving his chariot with

god-like grace, as usual, had also attracted universal admiration with his handsome face and dignified bearing.

His friend Aswatthama with his matted locks and fierce mien, the son of Dronacharya, the arch-enemy of Drupada, had drawn the greatest attention of them all. Unable to restrain their curiosity, people had rushed to see for themselves the warrior son of a warrior father. But his arrogant manner had done little to create a favourable impression. Many, he could see, cursed the unwelcome guest under their breath.

For the first time, the dark night of frustration which had been his life so far, was opening into a new dawn, thought Duryodhana, as he was kneaded by the expert hands of his massagists.

All these years he had had to suffer in silent agony, a victim of cruel, evil planets, cribbed and confined within the walls of discipline. True they had been raised, long before he was born, by his stern and terrible Grandfather and by the imponderable stifling influence of that deathless woman—the Most Venerable Mother.

For a moment Duryodhana's mind dwelt on this ancient great-grandmother whom he only saw on formal occasions as a distant divinity of sinister might. He had never ceased to wonder how she, who never went out and saw only a few people, could inspire so much awe or exercise so great an influence.

As Duryodhana looked back on his past, he could not help wondering how things had conspired to make him look wrong every time he tried to do the right thing.

All his frustrations, he could see, arose from his father having been born blind. According to the ancient canons of the Aryas, Dhritarashtra was, in consequence, barred from the throne, which barred him also. Though he was in every way fit to be a king, kingship had been beyond his reach.

Again, the gods had dealt him another mean blow. In his childhood, when, in spite of the bar, he was expected to be Crown Prince, his future had been marred. His Grandfather and the invisible Mother had brought the Five Brothers into the family and accepted them as the heirs of his uncle Pandu, the late Emperor.

The Five Brothers were handsome, charming, and brilliant each in his own way; but so was he. Yet they stole the affections of all in Hastinapura, even his own mother's. His Grandfather and the Venerable Mother were openly partial to them.

Of these brothers, Duryodhana could never forget that he hated Bhima, the second one, the most. He had been the curse of his life. In spite of his best efforts he could never excel him in strength; the bully never missed an occasion to overcome him and humiliate him by jibes and taunts.

The Five Brothers had no business to be where they were, Duryodhana was convinced. Palace gossip had it that they were not his uncle's legitimate sons. He believed that they were not. In trying to deprive them of their position, therefore, he was only restoring the scales of justice—nay, defending Dharma itself. But for a long time all his attempts to eliminate them had gone wrong.

He was, however, lucky in his friends—the brave, handsome and skilful Karna, the charioteer's son, vied in charm and skill with Arjuna, the third of the Five Brothers; and the brave Aswatthama—which meant that Aswatthama's father, Drona, the great military leader, was bound to him too. His uncle Shakuni, the great master strategist, was more than a match for all the other diplomats of the court put together. His younger brother Duhshasana was an extremely resourceful and energetic young man ready to carry out his plans.

At first, nothing had been of any help to him against those Five Brothers for a long time. Once, in a diving competition in the Ganga, he had pressed Bhima down in the flood choking him to death, but curiously enough the fellow had walked into Hastinapura a few days later, hale and hearty, to be greeted by everyone.

Ultimately he had been driven to plan their assassination. He had employed a gang whose loyalty he had secured by spending large sums of money. But Vidura, that saintly hypocrite, had discovered the conspiracy; and the terrible old man had intervened. All that had happened was that the Five Brothers were banished to Varanavata.

Then it was that he had to make the most fateful decision of his life. His face lit up with a smile. How wonderful the plan had succeeded!

Thanks to the ingenuity of his uncle Shakuni and

he skill of the Yaksha, Sthoonakarna, a mansion of ac and sulphur was built at Varanavata to house the Five Brothers. They had lived in that palace and it had been burnt down over their heads, thanks to Purochana, hough, loyal man that he was, he himself had been burnt of death in discharging his duty.

Duryodhana had been appointed *yuvaraja* in the place of Yudhishthira. He had thus successfully taken the first great step in his life.

But even then his ambition remained unfulfilled. His path as *Yuvaraja* became thorny. He was distrusted by many. His wishes were thwarted. His plans went wrong. Even his Guru, Dronacharya, was not invariably helpful. The other day, he had deliberately humiliated Duryodhana by restoring Pushkara to Chekitana, thus converting his great victory into a foolish adventure. Why he had done this was more than Duryodhana could imagine.

He had indeed been waiting despairingly for a new chapter of his life to be opened. In some of his many bitter moments he had even offered prayers to Yama, the God of Death, to take away Grandfather and the Venerable Mother to the Land of the Manes, and his own father too!

Unexpectedly the great opportunity of his life came to him. King Drupada invited the Kuru Princes to the *swayamvara* of his daughter. Straightaway he decided to accept and win Drupada's daughter—without the approval of Dronacharya, if need were.

If he won her, of which he had no doubt, Grandfather or no Grandfather, he would immediately emerge as the uncrowned king of Hastinapura. He might even get his father to retire. He would then assume royal status.

The path to Chakravartiship would then be opened before him. He would follow it up with an Aswamedha sacrifice on a grand scale, as his great ancestor Bharata had done before him.

The planets turned propitious. The obstinate Acharyadeva yielded. Even his wife, generally so ineffective, helped him to win the friendship of Krishna. The cowherd, undoubtedly a powerful factor in Aryavarta, would now be on his side.

He smiled at his own cleverness. If the Five Brothers had been alive, what would they not have done with the help of their cousin Krishna?

He had no doubt that the Princess of Panchala would choose him as her husband. What better lot could Drupada's daughter have than to be the consort of *Chakravarti* Bharata's heir. the Crown Prince of Kuru's vast Empire?

Duryodhana's thoughts wandered off to his wife Bhanumati. She had extracted a promise from Krishna that he would see that things were made easy for his uncle, Shakuni, to press his suit. She was a fine woman, this little wife of his. Even after he married Draupadi, he would never forget her—he promised himself.

But, would Krishna keep his promise? There he was, as difficult to understand as ever. He loved his cousins, the Five Brothers, and no doubt suspected him, Duryodhana, of having got rid of them. But he had a reputation for keeping his word. He would not, therefore, break the promise which he had given to his adopted sister, Bhanumati. It was really very, very clever of his wife to have won the affection of so astute a person.

Time passed. The wrestlers continued to massage his body. But his impatience grew. Why had not Uncle Shakuni returned by now? Was the cowherd playing a trick on him?

He listened for footsteps. Here he was—his long-awaited Uncle. Those steps, as heavy as ever, could only be his; so was the familiar loud breathing. It was curious how Uncle grew fatter day after day, and with it cleverer and cleverer.

With a smile, Duryodhana greeted his fat uncle with his waddling bulk and small cunning eyes and the ingratiating smile which could never conceal the craftiness behind.

'What did he say?' asked Duryodhana, as he dismissed his attendants and sat up, his body glistening with oil.

'He is ready to keep his promise to take me to Draupadi. But he thinks that it will be difficult to persuade her to choose you,' replied Uncle Shakuni, rubbing his hands almost gleefully at the cloud of disappointment which came over his nephew's face.

'Oh, is he up to his tricks again, the cowherd? Why would it be difficult for him to help?' asked Duryodhana.

'Now, Duryodhana, how many times have I to tell you to keep your tongue under control? He is not a "cowherd",' said Shakuni with emphasis. He is Krishna Vaasudeva, the mighty among men. Kings by the dozen are crowding to pay him respect. Take a vow, my boy, never to refer to him as a cowherd.'

'But he was a cowherd once. And what else is he now?' said Duryodhana contemptuously.

'Dear boy, make up your mind once and for all whether you want him as a friend or an enemy. He is the rising sun. Begin offering prayers to him,' said Shakuni with the broad smile of an indulgent teacher talking to a stupid pupil.

'I am sorry I let the word slip out,' said Duryodhana penitently. 'I will try not to call him a "cowherd". Now tell me, why is it difficult for Draupadi to choose me?'

The small, beady eyes in the plump face were serious. 'She might not be acceptable to Guru Dronacharya' said Shakuni, as with a fat hand he smoothed his silky beard. 'Noble Vaasudeva thinks that that would be Draupadi's objection,' he added with an ironical emphasis on the word 'noble' to impress his advice upon his sister's son.

'Acharyadeva has to accept her,' Duryodhana remarked truculently. 'He has given his consent to my coming to the *swayamvara*, hasn't he?' he added and smiled.

'The Acharya's consent to your coming to the *swayamvara* does not mean friendliness toward

Drupada; if you marry Draupadi, he might leave Hastinapura—so Vaasudeva thinks,' said Shakuni. 'She is likely to demand a pledge that the Acharyadeva would welcome her.'

'This cow...—this Krishna—is now creating unnecessary difficulties,' said Duryodhana impatiently.

'Vaasudeva also thinks that, as you are a pupil of the Acharyadeva, you might side with him if there was a conflict between him and Drupada,' said Shakuni.

Duryodhana slapped his thigh, 'Uncle, you should have told him straightaway that I have made up my mind. Go and tell him that I will always side with my father-in-law—Acharya or no Acharya.'

'My son, the Princess of Panchala appears to be a difficult young woman. She may not be prepared to take your word; she may insist—so Vaasudeva thinks— that Aswatthama should take a vow that even at the cost of his life, he would prevent his father leaving the Kurus if she comes to Hastinapura,' said Shakuni.

'Is not my word enough?' asked Duryodhana indignantly.

'You know, my son, that you are not among the trusted ones of the world,' said Shakuni with a smile. 'Vaasudeva says that she might not accept your assurance.'

Duryodhana's face flushed with anger. 'A cowherd doubts the word of a descendant of Emperor Bharata!'

'Sh....sh....sh.....,' interrupted Shakuni, putting his

finger to his lips. 'Again that word! Forget it. These Yadavas are more powerful than many kings. And here he dominates the whole galaxy of kings,' he added.

'All right, all right,' said Duryodhana, nodding his head in mock submission. 'I swear not to speak the truth hereafter. It is a strange world in which an upstart can command kings. What does he want?'

'He wants Aswatthama to take the vow,' said Shakuni.

'All right, all right. I will get him to agree. Please ask some one to call him,' said Duryodhana as he lay down on the mat again, and, by a gesture, called in the wrestlers who were waiting outside, to resume the massage.

39

HOW TO CARRY OFF THE BRIDE

$\mathcal{T}$he camp of Jarasandha, the Emperor of Magadha, was perhaps the largest, though it lacked the refinement of the camp of the Kurus.

The feudatory kings of Magadha—and several of them had come—like their Emperor, took pride in being rough in their manners and overbearing in their behaviour. They scorned the graces which characterized the behaviour of the Arya kings; in fact they held those kings in contempt for what they thought was their degeneracy.

Most of these princes were experts in body combat only, and, as their habit was, went about the camp barebodied in complete disregard of the susceptibilities of the Panchalas who were accustomed to see their princes decked out in silks and ornaments and diadems.

In a tent in the centre of the camp, guarded by heavy-bodied mace-bearers, Jarasandha, still vigorous in spite of his years, sat surrounded by his principal feudatories.

His son, Sahadeva, sat on his right. Next to him sat his grandson, Meghasandhi. Both were younger editions of the Emperor—heavy and muscular, their faces full, their eyes bold though they lacked the cunning which characterized those of the Emperor.

'Sahadeva, go to Drupada,' said Jarasandha in a blunt, jerky, and peremptory voice. 'Tell him I want him to understand why I have come. After Meghasandhi is married to Draupadi, we shall discuss the plan of campaign'.

'But, Father, if his intention was to give Draupadi to Meghasandhi, why did he hold a *swayamvara* inviting all these princes here?' asked Sahadeva who, though a man, always lived in boyish terror of his dominating father.

Jarasandha laughed contemptuously. 'These Arya kings think that their daughters are goddesses. They want them to be married before an assembly of kings. Vain fools!' he said.

'But, lord, are we sure that the Princess will carry out her father's wishes? I am told that she has a very strong will,' said Sahadeva.

Jarasandha knit his brow. 'I hate these *swayamvaras*. At the last moment, these Arya girls go wild and choose anyone they like.'

'What if Draupadi does so on this occasion?'

Jarasandha's eyes widened in surprise. 'I will not suffer the humiliation of Drupada's daughter rejecting Meghasandhi.' Then he slyly winked at his son and said in a low tone: 'Anyway the horses of Magadha are swift—*swayamvara* or no *swayamvara*. They can bear Drupada himself to Rajagriha if it comes to that.' And the feudatories who were present laughed as if this was a great joke.

For a few moments, they held a consultation in a whisper.

'I have the report,' said Meghasandhi in a low whisper. 'There will be a good opportunity when Draupadi is proceeding to the *swayamvara mandap* from the *Yajna shala*, the shrine of the sacrificial fire. Then she will be unguarded, accompanied only by a few priests and some princesses. It will be easy to break up the procession and carry her off.'

'My son, swift action and surprise are the requisites of success,' said Jarasandha with an encouraging smile. 'You may take two or three of our best men with you. But once you act, do not hesitate,' Then after a little pause, he added: 'We will all be at the cross-road then on our way to the *swayamvara mandap.* The moment you blow your conch, we will join you on the road to Magadha.'

As the Emperor was giving these orders in a whisper, King Vidanda and his son, Danda, feudatories of Magadha, came into the tent. The Emperor fixed his eyes angrily on Vidanda. 'Why are you so late, Vidanda? We reached here quite a while ago.'

Vidanda stood before the Emporor, folded his hands and said apologetically: 'Huge crowds barred our way.'

'What was happening?' asked the Emperor.

'The Yadavas, Balarama and Krishna Vaasudeva, were returning from the royal palace to their camp, accompanied by all the Yadava *atirathis,*' said Vidanda.

'Krishna!' exclaimed the Emperor, frowning 'Why, is the cowherd here? He is not a king.'

'Lord, he attracts more attention than any king. Even many kings—Virata, Sunita and Bhoja for instance—have gone to greet him; some Kuru princes too. Huge crowds surround him wherever he goes. Many people prostrate themselves before him as if he was a god and seek his blessing, shouting. "Victory to Krishna Vaasudeva!" said Vidanda.

'Where is his camp?' asked Jarasandha.

'At a certain distance from here. I understand that about twenty Yadava *atirathis* have come with him,' said Vidanda.

'Oh, so many?' asked the Emperor in surprise. 'What is the cowherd up to?'

'It is difficult to say, but he dominates the scene.'

'Did Drupada receive him at the city gates?' asked Jarasandha.

'No, lord,' replied Vidanda. 'Vaasudeva had sent word to King that he must not go to the trouble of receiving the Yadavas himself. So, the Princes, Dhrishtadyumna and Satyajit, received them. And the first thing the Yadavas did on their arrival was to go on foot to pay their respects to the King.'

'Is he hoping to win Draupadi?' Jarasandha asked himself. A shadow of anxiety crossed his brow.

'Your noble lordship knows that he has already rejected Drupada's offer of the Princess's hand,' said Vidanda.

'I don't believe it,' said Jarasandha. 'Anyway, Sahadeva, go to King Drupada and make sure that the Princess chooses Meghasandhi. If she does so, we shall be saved a lot of trouble.'

'I am not sure, lord, but Vaasudeva seems to have come to an understanding with the Kurus. I hear that they have handed over Pushkara to Chekitana, a relative of Krishna's. It must have been the price paid to win him over to Duryodhana's side,' said Sahadeva.

Jarasandha, his eyes wide with surprise, thought for a while. Krishna Vaasudeva here again! There was a fatality which brought the cowherd into his life every time he made an attempt to extend his hegemony over Aryavarta.

A series of incidents passed before his mind. The cowherd had killed his son-in-law, Kamsa, his most powerful instrument for dominating the Arya world[1]. Inflicted the most terrible blow to his prestige, at Gomantaka. Frustrated his plans to cement an alliance with the Kings of Chedi and Vidarbha. Kidnapped the Princess of Vidarbha before his very eyes, so to speak[2]. Every time the fellow had turned up and ruined his well-laid plans.

To teach the Arya kings a lesson, he had burned down Mathura over the heads of their Yadava kinsmen. But even there he had failed. The Yadavas had escaped to Saurashtra, and the thoroughness with which he had taken his revenge on Mathura had only recoiled on him. Krishna had emerged a hero, while he himself had acquired a reputation as a blood-thirsty savage.

As a result of that costly adventure, he had had to

retire to his native Magadha and lord it over a few miserable princelets ruling a people who lived in swampy lands which remained flooded half the year.

But he had made use of those barren years with great skill and self-restraint. He had encouraged Drupada to nurse his hatred of Dronacharya. His future success, as he saw it, lay in fomenting a conflict between Kampilya and Hastinapura.

He had pursued a policy which would culminate in a marriage between his grandson Meghasandhi and Drupada's daughter—an idea which he had skilfully promoted. It would lay the foundation of a grand strategy for weakening, if not destroying, the power of the Kurus. It was his last chance to dominate the heart of Aryavarta—an ambition which had lured him all his life.

Drupada, however, had been slippery. He had gone on negotiating, never finalising the alliance, though all the time expressing his willingness to enter into it. The emperor, therefore, had been shocked when he heard that Draupadi was being offered to Krishna Vaasudeva, his enemy. But soon there had followed a report that the offer had been rejected. Naturally the cowherd was not prepared to invite another conflict with him, the Emperor had thought.

So, when the pressing invitation came to him from Drupada to attend the *swayamvara*, he promptly accepted it. He had no doubt that this was one of the strange ways of an Arya king cementing a matrimonial alliance. They—these Arya kings—believed in going through the gesture of leaving the choice of a husband to their daughters at a spectacularly-staged *swayamvara*. Much as he disliked them, he had to deal with them and was prepared to humour them like little children.

All the same what was Vaasudeva here for? Did he expect to be chosen by Draupadi before the assembly of kings? Then, why had he rejected the offer previously made to him? Yet the cowherd was made that way. He was fond of spectacular triumphs.

At Kundinapura, King Bhishmaka had declined to give him a seat among the Kings, but he had contrived to obtain a more than royal reception. Then he had been only an insignificant chief. Now he had waxed mighty—this cowherd—this inveterate enemy of his. He enjoyed a prestige almost as great as an emperor's, and the ridiculous part of it was that he had no empire. He was talked about by kings in the same breath as himself, Bhishma and Drupada. To the common people he seemed even greater—he attracted their devotion.

A nameless fear came over Jarasandha. He stared vacantly. His mouth sagged. His mind grew dim. In the dimness he saw the naked ascetic with a garland of skulls as he had stepped out of Mathura when it was in flames. The ascetic's words rang out in his ears: 'You will never conquer Aryavarta till you offer a sacrifice of the heads of a hundred kings.' He shuddered. He had then felt his guardian god, the Mighty Rudra, the God of destruction, speaking to him.

This mood lasted only a moment. Soon he was his old self. He looked at his son Sahadeva and others, who appeared to be shocked at the change which had come over the Emperor. Unconscious of it, he could not understand why they looked at him in that strange way. He muttered under his breath: 'What can a cowherd do?' He cleared his throat and resumed the conversation at the point where he had left it.

He told his son to deliver an ultimatum to Drupada. 'Draupadi dare not choose the cowherd as her husband at the *swayamvara*. If she does, the Emperor will see that the *swayamvara* is broken up.'

At the same time, he saw the utter impracticability of any such attempt. The Kuru princes had arrived in strength. So had the Yadava warriors. The Panchala warriors were many and mighty. Many kings would stand by Krishna and Drupada. If they all combined, his attempt to break up the *swayamvara* would fail hopelessly. There was only one way. If Drupada did not give the promise he required, he would leave Kampilya at once—and *with* the Princess.

Thrusting his chin forward, he looked at Sahadeva. his mind made up. 'But Drupada dare not play me false.' he said. Then he added: 'Sahadeva, tell King Drupada— and take no nonsense from him—that if the Princess does not choose Meghasandhi, he will have to deal with Jarasandha.'

Karna, King of Anga, and Aswatthama, son of Dronacharya, occupied a smaller camp near Duryodhana's.

Strict in his religious observance, Karna had taken his bathe in the sacred Ganga and offered prayers to his guardian deity, the Sun God, first thing in the morning. He was now seated under a banyan tree, distributing food to the poor, for one of his vows was never to take food himself till the poor had been fed.

As he gave food to the poor, his handsome face wore a friendly smile, and his noble brow was creaseless. His eyes shone with sympathy particularly for the blind and the lame who approached him with piteous appeals.

Aswatthama, with his matted locks and knotted beard, came up from Duryodhana's camp, a frown upon his face, and waited impatiently till Karna had finished distributing food to the hungry. Then they sat down to their meal.

Karna could see that Aswatthama was ready for an outburst.

'Karna, there is no end to the selfishness of Duryodhana,' said Aswatthama in a voice charged with righteous indignation.

'What's the matter, Aswatthama? Something has made you very, very angry. What is it?' asked Karna with a friendly smile.

'Do you know why Duryodhana called me just now?' asked Aswatthama. 'He wanted me to take a vow. Oh, the absurdity of it, the selfishness of it!' he exclaimed, smarting under a sense of injustice and finding it difficult to swallow the food he was taking.

Karna smiled. He was accustomed to these outbursts of his friend's which often bordered on the volcanic. 'Keep a little calmer and tell me what the matter is.'

'Duryodhana had sought the help of Krishna

Vaasudeva to secure Draupadi for himself,' said Aswatthama, his throat almost choking. 'And the Yadava will not help him unless Duryodhana assured him that Father will give up his hostility to Drupada. As if Father was a little child!' he exclaimed.

'But what have you to do with that?' asked Karna indulgently as if he was talking to an angry child.

'Don't be impatient,' shouted Aswatthama, who was the very image of impatience himself. 'He wants me to make a vow that, if Draupadi comes to Hastinapura, I will see, even at the cost of my life, that Father does not leave the Kurus.'

Karna smiled at his friend's indignation and could not help teasing him with the question; 'Then, why don't you make the vow?'

'I make that vow! I risk my father's wrath so that Duryodhana may marry the daughter of his enemy! Why should I? If I were sure of securing my father's consent, I might as well marry the Princess myself,' said Aswatthama.

Karna laughed heartily. 'Seriously, friend, do you want to marry that Princess of Panchala yourself?'

'Why not? The son of the great Acharya—and an expert in arms as I am—is as good a husband for Draupadi as any king. It would not be the first time that a king's daughter had been married to a Brahman. But there are so many royal diadems ready to beg for her hand that my matted locks would have no chance,' said Aswatthama, contemptuously looking at Karna as if he was the symbol of royalty. 'Now Duryodhana wants me not only to forgo Draupadi, but secure her for him. This is the gratitude he shows for all that I have done for him.'

'Aswatthama, don't be angry with Duryodhana,' said Karna persuasively. 'He has set his heart on winning Draupadi. He has long been deprived of his due and this marriage would be a step forward for him towards imperial status, even during his father's lifetime. We are his best friends. We owe him everything. We should not grudge him fulfillment of his ambition.'

'If he has helped us, surely we have also helped him in return,' said Aswatthama, looking angry at Karna's reaction to his own ambitious idea. 'Don't you aspire to win Draupadi for yourself?'

'Who would look at me, with so many kings wanting to win her?' asked Karna with a modest smile.

'But you are the handsomest king here and the finest archer. If she has to choose a good-looking and valiant husband, there is no one to compete with you,' said Aswatthama, carried away by his grudge against Duryodhana.

'But I will never compete with Duryodhana,' said Karna. 'When he lifted me out of obscurity and made me king of Anga, I pledged myself to be always loyal to him. And I will stand true to my word, whatever befalls him or me. If I were you, I would certainly oblige him. Also, don't forget: Nobody will choose us in preference to the Crown Prince of the Kurus. If he wants peace between the Kurus and the Panchalas, why should we stand in his way?'

'Suppose there is an archery test, who but you could win it?' asked Aswatthama.

'I think I could,' said Karna with a touch of resignation. 'But I also know that, being a charioteer's son, I should not take part in it. If I enter the contest at all, it will be to show the kings of Aryavarta that Duryodhana has at his command the finest bowman in the three worlds.'

'Karna, you can never forget that you are a charioteer's son. That is the trouble with you. You do not know to aim high,' said Aswatthama.

'I am a charioteer's son; that is a fact; and it is unforgivable to forget a fact. I also know what is due to friendship,' said Karna. 'Duryodhana gave me all that I possess when I had nothing. I cannot be ungrateful to him and neither can you,' he added.

Aswatthama glared at Karna for a while, shook his head, passed his hand over his sweating brow and said: 'You are right, Karna. If I were not to give Draupadi the promises Duryodhana desires, it would be ingratitude.'

'I hope you will give the pledge that he requires,' said Karna in a coaxing tone.

'All right. If that is what you all want, I will do it. But it will be the last time I will oblige Duryodhana', said Aswatthama.

'Dear friend, we will have to stand by him, I don't know how many more times. He has a knack of running into difficulties. We have to save him from himself,' said Karna.

Prince Maniman, son of King Karkotaka of the Nagas, felt elated when he arrived in Kampilya in the company of Uddhava and was ceremoniously received.

He was no longer the ease-loving Naga prince that he had been before. Thanks to his brother-in-law Uddhava, he was now as skilful a warrior as any—so Uddhava had assured him. He had taken part in the march on Pushkara. He had the privilege of always being favoured by Krishna and Balarama. He had spent days and nights with mighty Yadava *atirathis* who had taken very kindly to him as Marishaa's grand-nephew.

Now he was happy to be among the vast gathering of Arya Kings and surrounded by his own well-equipped Naga warriors. But it did not matter to him who chose Draupadi. He loved the sweet, free ways of the Naga damsels. He had no desire to marry this high and mighty Arya princess; there was no likelihood of her choosing him either, he knew.

By acquiring a place amongst the Arya kings, he had made his people secure against Aryan incursions, and he was happy.

Siguri Naga, his favourite chief, came to see him.

'Could you find any trace of the Five Brothers?' the Prince anxiously asked in a whisper.

Siguri Naga shook his head. 'I have been to all the camps.'

'Oh, Lord Pashupati, what will Vaasudeva say?' Maniman exclaimed and got ready to go to Krishna.

40

DRUPADA'S DILEMMA

$\mathcal{A}$ s the sixteen-day ceremonial proceeded, and the eleventh day of the bright half of Paush, the day of the *swayamvara*, grew nearer, Draupadi became uneasy.

Everytime she went up to the terrace, she found that Kampilya was being transformed. The tents with gaily fluttering banners; the chariots, elephants and horses crowding the streets: the crowds of kings and princes arriving with an air of festivity; the Ganga covered with numberless boats and canoes full of laughing, singing and cheering men, women and children, celebrating her coming nuptials—everyone and everything showed enjoyment, except herself.

Doubts continued to assail her. Would the *swayamvara* secure her a husband who would fulfil the aim of her father's life? Was this a proper way of choosing a husband? Would she have sufficient loyalty and charm to inspire her husband to redeem her father's pledge?

Her life and her father's aim in life, both were in the balance, she thought. Oppressed by this uncertainty as she was, she would have preferred to be left alone. But her days and half the nights were crowded. She had to take part in endless rituals after being decked out in a style befitting a royal bride. Elders, relatives and friends came to congratulate her in continuous succession. The emissaries of royal guests brought presents after these had been accepted by her father— presents which were in the nature of an advance price paid for her, she thought.

She wished her father had announced to the guests the fact that a suitor would have to pass a severe test, decided upon by Guru Sandipani, before she would marry him. So far they had been left under the impression that she was to choose the bridegroom in the open assembly after the suitors had exhibited their skill, each in the arms favoured by him.

The test, she knew, was going to be very hard; perhaps no master bowman could pass it. Anyway she would not have been content with an easier test. She wanted to marry only the best bowman in Aryavarta.

Krishna's promise that the *swayamvara* would make her father the most outstanding king in Aryavarta had almost come true. Certainly it would be fulfilled. But it would also create enormous difficulties if no one was found equal to the test.

It was funny, thought Draupadi, how kings wanted wives only to help them to enter into political alliances. She laughed to herself—she was an exception. She was going to select her husband because she wanted him to serve her father's purpose.

Krishna stood in a class by himself. Though he called himself a cowherd, his nature was loftier than that of all the kings she knew. But he would not marry her, Draupadi, to serve her father's hatred. He had, however, kept his promise. He had brought to Kampilya all the famous Yadava chiefs who, led by Balarama, Akrura and himself, were more impressive as men and warriors than most kings.

From her balcony, she had seen the Yadavas when they came to greet her father on the steps of the palace. Balarama was there, a giant of a man, towering over the other chiefs, and carrying himself with dignity; Akrura, quiet, self-possessed, the image of elderly dignity, walking with deliberate steps; and Yuyudhana Satyaki, the son of Satyaka, tall, lithe and sinewy, graceful in body and noble in bearing. Even among them Krishna stood out as the most distinctive figure, radiating noble power, his skin shining with the deep-blue colour of the heavens, his peacock feather waving gaily as ever, bearing himself with grace and simple dignity, and his smile as irresistible as ever.

The Kuru Princes had also come—Duryodhana, Duhshasana and their brothers; the King of Anga, Karna, the charioteer's handsome son; even Aswatthama, the fierce-looking son of Dronacharya. To see them come to seek her hand had annoyed her father very much and complicated things, though their arrival had added importance to the occasion.

She had got up early that day, gone through the ceremonial bathe with turmeric, saffron and musk, and subjected herself to being decked out by friends in gold and glittering diamonds. Her long glossy hair had been woven into braids with flowers by expert flower-women. She was being got ready to play the part of a goddess.

And she had more than a suspicion she looked every inch a goddess—majestic and radiant.

Then she had gone and prostrated herself at her father's feet—a daily form of worship which she had invariably performed in earnest since her childhood; to her, he was more than a god. Doing so, she had felt distressed to see his face so grim bearing the traces of unhappiness. Yes, he was very, very unhappy.

Then she and Dhrishtadyumna, her elder brother, had received Duhshasana, the brother of Duryodhana, the Kuru *Yuvaraja* who brought presents which in richness were beyond compare. He had been accompanied by a learned Brahman from the court of Hastinapura who, as was customary, eulogised the Crown Prince of the Kurus in an epic recital fulsomely describing his lineage as well as his valour, charm, high resolve and noble life. He also sang the praises of Karna, the heroic and generous master bowman of Aryavarta, and of the brave Aswatthama, son of Dronacharya, at which she felt like turning away her head.

After the emissary had gone, Dhrishtadyumna had said; 'Krishna Vaasudeva wants to bring you Duryodhana's uncle, Shakuni, the Prince of Gandhara. He told me that Duryodhana's wife, Bhanumati, who is like a younger sister to him, had extracted a promise from him that he would arrange a meeting between you and Duryodhana's uncle.'

Draupadi had been shocked. Duryodhana was Drona's favourite pupil. Apart from this insuperable objection, he had a lurid reputation. By his restless intrigues, he was reported to have poisoned the atmosphere in Hastinapura. He also had his cousins banished and sent to their death in the burning palace at Varanavata. He had himself been banished by his grandfather for riotous living. And now he was using his wife to win her, Draupadi. She would die a thousand times rather than place her hand in his in holy wedlock before the sacred fire.

'Vaasudeva helping Duryodhana to press his suit— and that too at the request of his wife! And of all people to meet—that too, on an auspicious day—Shakuni, the villain, who contrived the death of the Five Brothers! What does he think of me?' she exclaimed angrily.

'What is the harm in receiving Shakuni?' asked Dhrishtadyumna. 'Krishna is very keen that you should do so.'

'Am I to marry a pupil of Dronacharya's?' Her face was red. 'What has happened to Vaasudeva? Is he playing double?' Then she added: 'I wish Father would announce that there is going to be a test soon. It would put an end to this stream of importunate go-betweens.'

'Don't get excited, Krishnaa,' said Dhrishtadyumna quietly. 'Krishna knows that the man whom you choose has to pass the test. But somehow he seeks to keep up the illusion that you are free to choose the bridegroom youself.'

'Sometimes I don't understand what Vaasudeva is doing' said Draupadi in irritation. 'Every time, he contrives to talk us into submission. Father surrendered his judgment to him. You and I did the same also. We now have the *swayamvara* on our hands.

He knows that there is going to be a test and still he wants me to suffer the humiliation of hearing the praises of Duryodhana whom I will never marry', she continued, shaking her graceful head in disgust. 'He gave me a pledge that he would stand by me. Is this the way he keeps his promise?' Her voice was filled with bitterness. 'What has Father to say about it?'

'Father is very disturbed about the whole matter. He never expected the Kurus to accept the invitation. It needed all the self-control he possesses to receive them with due ceremony. He also thinks that Krishna is playing double,' replied Dhrishtadyumna.

'Let us go and consult him,' said Draupadi. Then in excitement, she almost shouted: 'Must I marry Duryodhana, Drona's pupil, who murdered his cousins?'

Dhrishtadyumna smiled at his sister's outburst. Krishnaa, I find it difficult to distrust Vaasudeva. Talk to Shakuni if Father permits it. There is no harm in talking. Then, when you are alone with Vaasudeva, tell him what you feel about this. You can quarrel all right, I know.' Then he dissolved into a broad smile. 'I wish he had married you. Then we would all have been saved your outbursts.'

About the same time, on one of verandahs of the palace overlooking the river, King Drupada was sitting, rocking himself furiously on a swing suspended from the ceiling by gilded chains. Whenever he was in an angry mood, he did this; it enabled him to regain control over himself.

Drupada looked like a trapped lion. His brow was deeply furrowed. His eyes glared with almost murderous rage at the rays of the afternoon sun as they fell on the ripples of the river. One of his hands was clenched.

He wore no diadem; it lay by his side. His scarf had slid from his shoulder on to the ground; his sword, unfastened, also lay at his side—all symptoms of agitation in a king who was so very meticulous about the way he handled the insignia of royalty.

The *swayamvara,* no doubt, had improved his status among the kings of Aryavarta, who had gravitated to Kampilya as if to offer their homage to a *Chakravartin.* With them had come valour, pomp and splendour. Also learned Brahmans had come and venerable ascetics, guilds of traders and endless crowds. He was thus placed on the top of the world.

However, everything had gone wrong. Drona's pupils had come and his son too. Duryodhana, the Kuru *Yuvaraja,* whom report branded as the murderer of his cousins, was an able warrior and likely to win the contest!

He had to summon all his self-command to offer garlands and coconuts to them, particularly to Aswatthama. That they should have come at all was an unpleasant surprise to him. The wicked Drona must have managed it only to humiliate him the more. But never, would he give his daughter to Duryodhana—no, never.

Krishna Vaasudeva—that cunning, plausible, sweet-spoken Yadava chief—had contrived to put him in this impossible position, practically trapping him. He had rejected the offer of Draupadi's hand for himself and induced him to hold a *swayamvara,* from which it was impossible to exclude Drona's pupils.

Now spies had reported to him that Uddhava, Krishna's friend, had visited Hastinapura and extracted a price from the Kurus. Pushkara had been restored to the Yadava chief, Chekitana. Why had Bhishma and Drona paid this price to Krishna? Was it to join them in humiliating him, Drupada, before the kings by making him give his daughter to Duryodhana? Or was it to help the Kuru Prince to carry Draupadi away by force, as was common at *swayamvaras*?

It was difficult to believe that Vaasudeva, who looked so noble and righteous, was capable of such betrayal. And for what? No, it was impossible. He had brought all his Yadava warriors as he had promised. Guru Sandipani and Acharya Shvetaketu, who had worked hard to prepare the *swayamvara*, had implicit confidence in him. He himself had paid him, Drupada, respect with the transparent affection of a son.

But then, for what sinister bargain had the price of Pushkara been paid? Krishna must be playing some deep game. If he wanted to see Draupadi married to Duryodhana—that murderer of his cousins and their mother, almost a matricide—he was going to be disappointed. Would he submit to this indignity? No never. If no one else upheld the Arya code of morals, he at least would not swerve from it. In his fury, the King stopped swinging himself.

Udbodhana, the old Minister, came to report that the arena where the *swayamvara* was to be held had been completed and he wanted the King or Prince Dhrishtadyumna to inspect the target for the test which was ready to be installed. The invitation brought no pleasure to Drupada and he asked the Minister to take the Prince with him.

The chamberlain came to announce that Sahadeva, the Crown Prince of Magadha, wanted to pay his respects to the King. Drupada's irritation grew at this unexpected and inopportune visit, but controlling himself, he put on his diadem, fastened his sword on and went to meet the Prince of Magadha.

As he reached the throne room, a question arose in his mind. If Krishna was bent on double-crossing him, could Jarasandha be induced to enter the contest? He was a great archer and might win it.

'Noble King, *Chakravarti* is pleased to send you an urgent message,' said Sahadeva rather bluntly, after he had been received with due courtesy.

'What message does the noble son of Brihadratha send?' asked Drupada, annoyed at the peremptory tone of Sahadeva.

'My noble father came to Kampilya because you sent him a pressing invitation. He takes it that your daughter will choose my son, Meghasandhi, at the *swayamvara*, and seal the alliance between Magadha and Panchala,' said Sahadeva with the superior air of a conqueror laying down the terms of an alliance.

In the mood in which Drupada was, his annoyance increased at the tone and content of Jarasandha's message, and his face became unusually stern.

'Father has asked me to convey to you his assurance once again,' continued Sahadeva, as if delivering a royal command. 'If Meghasandhi is married to Draupadi, our two armies will work together under your command. It will then be for you to decide against whom to march.'

To Drupada, courtesy was the soul of human intercourse. His sense of delicacy, therefore, was outraged by the blunt way in which the Magadha Prince suggested the bargain.

'Please convey my salutations to the noble Emperor,' replied Drupada, keeping strict command over himself. 'I am his friend as I have always been. I would consider myself very fortunate if I could ally myself to him,' said Drupada.

'What is the difficulty then?' asked Sahadeva, finding that though Drupada's words were friendly his tone was scarcely so.

Drupada was sick of these blatant overtures. He thought that the time had come to reveal the secret. 'Noble Prince, my daughter has taken a pledge that she will wed only the Prince who wins the test prescribed by her.'

'What? Have you provided a test?' asked Sahadeva in surprise.

'Yes, I was going to announce it this very evening, now that all the guests have arrived. Whoever wins the test in archery prescribed by Guru Sandipani shall wed Krishnaa.' Then he saw the look of annoyance on his guest's face and added: 'I hope it will not come in the way of our alliance.'

Sahadeva could not conceal his disappointment. 'This puts us on the same level as the other Princes,' he said indignantly.

Self-control now came easy to Drupada as he saw how annoyed Sahadeva was. 'You know the sacred canons which govern a *swayamvara*. Draupadi's choice is final,' said Drupada.

'But then our alliance is in jeopardy,' said Sahadeva reproachfully. 'Meghasandhi can never win the test; he is not as expert marksman.'

'That is rather unfortunate,' said Drupada coolly.

'Like all of us, he excels in mace-combat,' said Sahadeva.

'But the Emperor is a reputed bowman. Could he not enter the test himself? asked Drupada quietly.

Sahadeva eyed Drupada suspiciously. Was the King mocking the great *Chakravarti?* 'You want the *Chakravarti* to enter the test! Do you want to humiliate him before the kings?' he asked offensively.

Drupada, with a great effort, maintained his courteous behaviour. 'Noble Prince, Drupada has never gone back on his word and never will do so. Whoever wins the test shall be my son-in-law, whatever his age, and whatever his royal status.'

'But, if more than one king wins the test, or if all fail?' asked Sahadeva, sorely puzzled at the rules which seemed to fetter all straightforward marriage dealings.

'Then, according to the sacred canons, my daughter will choose whomsoever she likes from all those who have succeeded or, if no one has, from all the kings,' replied Drupada, anxious to put an end to this horse-trading.

'What if a Kuru Prince wins the test and no one else?' asked Sahadeva. 'They are your enemies. I hear your enemy Drona has sent them here to carry away your daughter.'

Drupada felt the blow. He could not conceal his feeling any longer. 'My daughter shall never marry Duryodhana or Drona's son,' he said firmly. 'Noble Prince, that is why I want your father to help.'

'In what way do you want us to help?' asked Sahadeva.

Drupada sighed. 'Noble Prince, I am in a great difficulty myself. I cannot deny the test by contest to my daughter. But I don't want her to be married to any of the Kurus or to Drona's son.' Then his voice sank to a whisper. 'If your father wins the test, I shall be glad to give my daughter to him,'

'You want the *Chakravarti* to lose the test and be the laughing-stock of all the kings?' asked Sahadeva. Then he angrily added: 'You seem to have decoyed us into an impossible position. We will not be your playthings. But we will save ourselves all this worry. noble King. We know how to.' With this scarcely veiled threat, he rose to leave.

Drupada understood what Sahadeva implied and faced him with blazing eyes. 'No one shall dare to treat my daughter as a Rakshasi,'[1] he said in a peremptory tone. 'I shall uphold Arya Dharma. My promise to the kings shall be kept. The test shall be held.'

For a moment there was silence. Then guest and host parted without a word, each measuring the other with angry glances.

■

41

A GIFT FROM THE ENEMY

$\mathscr{D}$raupadi, Dhrishtadyumna and Satyajit found their father on his return from the interview with Sahadeva, highly agitated. Disregarding the rules of courtesy which enjoined the young of the family to keep a respectful distance from their elders, they sat down by his side on the swing. It was not infrequent for them to sit like this. To the unity of their hearts, they sometimes added the warmth of physical proximity.

For some time Drupada sat rocking the swing in silence, his forehead contracted in tension. Dhrishtadyumna looked at his father protectively. Draupadi's eyes were fixed on the ground, her shapely flower decked head bent gracefully. Satyajit, perplexed, kept on looking at his father, expecting an outburst.

'We are trapped,' Drupada broke the silence, his gruff voice echoing the suppressed excitement. 'We thought that the *swayamvara* would enable me to destroy Drona. But our object is frustrated. Vaasudeva has played a trick.'

Drupada continued to stare at the ground.

'Are you sure, Father, that Vaasudeva has been playing with us?' asked Dhrishtadyumna, trying to retain a sense of fairness.

Drupada, surprised at the doubt expressed by his son, stopped rocking the swing. 'Yes,' he said at last. 'He always talked of bringing about a friendship between the Kuru and the Panchalas. He wants to secure it by my humiliation,' he added bitterly.

After a little pause, he continued: 'As you know, my son, I sent the invitation to the Kurus only because royal courtesy demanded it. But I did not expect that Drona would let his pupils accept it.'

'They have even been sending presents, as you know. How can we help it?' asked Dhrishtadyumna.

'We cannot prevent them from entering the contest or from winning it,' said Drupada in the same vein of bitterness. 'That means Krishnaa will be carried to Hastinapura as the bride of that fratricide, to be the slave of that revengeful Brahman.' He took a short breath and exclaimed: 'Humiliation will be heaped upon humiliation!'

'Are they all master-bowmen, Father?' asked Draupadi. 'How will they stand in relation to others in the contest?'

'Krishnaa, Duryodhana is a master-bowman, so is Karna and so is Aswatthama,' said Drupada. 'Among the Yadavas, the marksmen, apart from Vaasudeva, are Uddhava, Satyaki and Kritavarma. Among the warriors of Magadha, there is no one who can come up to them, except perhaps Jarasandha. Virata, however, is a famed archer and so is Shishupala, the King of Chedi.'

'Of all of them, Karna is said to be the best,' said Dhrishtadyumna. 'But he is base-born.'

'If any of the pupils of Drona wins, I will not accept him,' said Draupadi firmly, her beautiful eyes flashing.

'How can you escape it? That's what worries me,' said Drupada, gazing at the distant waters of the Ganga as if expecting them to give an answer. Then he turned to Draupadi. 'We are trapped. I have given my word to the kings of Aryavarta that you shall be given in marriage to the winner. I cannot break my word.'

'But, Father, if more than one prince wins the contest, surely Krishnaa can select whomsoever she likes from among the winners,' replied Dhrishtadyumna.

'She can,' said Drupada.

'And if no one wins the contest?' asked Draupadi.

'Then you are free to choose whomsoever you like,' answered Drupada. 'But it will mean a break-up, a fight between kings—as has happened many a time—and perhaps kidnapping.'

'The contest is going to be very difficult. Father,' said Dhrishtadyumna. 'No one is likely to win.'

Drupada knit his brow and spoke in a helpless tone: 'My children, when *swayamvara* begins, I shall be in the high heavens. When it ends, I shall have fallen to the very depths. Krishnaa will be led to a butcher's house like a sacrificial goat. I wish I had not placed faith in Vaasudeva's words.'

'What was the message from Jarasandha? Is he creating difficulties?' asked Dhrishtadyumna, anxious to know what had passed between his father and Sahadeva. 'Does he insist upon Krishnaa being given to his grandson, Meghasandhi?'

Drupada flared up. 'Do you know what an insolent message Sahadeva brought? Jarasandha insists that Krishnaa must be married to Meghasandhi. Failing it— I suspect—he would like to kidnap her,' he said and his voice quivered in suppressed anger. 'O! the wickedness of it! To break my word to all the kings of Aryavarta or see her kidnapped!' He could no longer control himself and gave vent to his fury. 'The Princess of Panchala to be kidnapped like a Rakshasi! Had I not been his host, I would have struck Sahadeva.' Then Drupada lapsed into silent fury.

'Father, are you quite sure that Vaasudeva wants to humiliate you?' asked Dhrishtadyumna to divert his father's attention from the affront that had been offered. 'Why should he?'

Drupada turned to his son and laughed in bitterness. 'He still assures me that the *swayamvara* will vindicate my honour.'

'But, why does he think that Duryodhana will not win the contest?' asked Dhrishtadyumna. 'Does he think that Uddhava or Satyaki can succeed?'

'Uddhava is one of the finest young warriors I have come across. Satyaki is a quivering flame of valour. But if Vaasudeva had either of them in mind, why did he send Uddhava to Hastinapura?' asked Drupada, 'Oh, it's all so difficult to understand.'

'There may be some other mission which he has been asked to perform,' said Dhrishtadyumna.

'No. I learn that he was present in the Kuru Raja Sabha when it was decided to accept our invitation.

Clearly Vaasudeva wants Krishnaa to be married to Duryodhana,' replied Drupada.

'Can we not improve upon what Vaasudeva himself did at Kundinapura?' asked Dhrishtadyumna hesitatingly. 'Select one of the warrior kings and help him to kidnap Krishnaa from the *swayamvara*?'

Drupada looked at his son in surprise. 'My son', he said sternly, 'I have lived in Dharma all my life. I will not swerve from it. I will not be a party to fraud, whatever happens. And Vaasudeva's case was different. Rukmini herself ran away with him. It was a Gandharva marriage—sanctioned by ancient custom among the Kshatriyas.'

'Krishnaa too can escape', said Dhrishtadyumna.

'No, never', said Draupadi with emphasis. 'I will fulfil Father's pledge. I will have as my husband whoever proves to be the best archer in the contest'.

'I know, Krishnaa, I know. You are a wonderful daughter,' said Drupada, placing his hand on her head with fondness. 'But it will be the greatest calamity of my life if any of the Kuru Princes or Aswatthama wins the test.' He heaved a sigh.

'Don't think about it that way, Father. Trust me. I will never fail you,' said Draupadi, as tears of affection sprang into her eyes. 'Your pledge shall be honoured ever. Drona shall not triumph.'

Drupada looked with pride at the flushed face of his daughter. Then he shook his head. 'My child, our world of men is different from what you think it is', he said.

'I shall make a new world, Father,' said Draupadi, smiling through her tears.

The chamberlain came hurriedly and said unceremoniously: 'My lord, my lord, Prince Shikhandin has come!'

Drupada and his children suddenly jumped off the swing.

'Shikhandin!' they all exclaimed at the same time.

'Here he is, lord'.

Young Shikhandin walked in, almost a ghost of his former self—frail and lean, grown perceptibly taller, walking with tottering steps, with a fuzzy growth of hair above his lips and on his chin. Drupada and his three children stood speechless. They looked as if they had seen a ghost.

Walking feebly, Shikhandin fell at his father's feet.

Drupada took him in his arms, but as a matter of form. Krishnaa wiped away her tears of joy. Dhrishtadyumna smiled. Satyajit shouted with joy.

'Shikhandin, where have you been all this time?' asked Drupada coolly. This son of his had always been a problem and Drupada was annoyed that he had come now to complicate an already over-complicated situation.

'Father, I went to remove the blot on our family', said Shikhandin almost hysterically as he laid his head on his father's shoulder. He awaited a parental pat of joy, which, however, was not forthcoming. 'I am no longer a woman', he added in a whisper.

'What!' exclaimed Drupada, his eyes opening wide in surprise.

'Yes, the Great God had blessed me with manhood', said Shikhandin with a frail smile. 'You can now send a message to King Hiranyavarma to send his daughter to Kampilya to live with her husband', he added in a trembling voice.

Drupada's eyes grew moist as he realized the significance of what Shikhandin had said.

'Is that a fact, my son?' he asked, unable to believe his ears.

'Yes, Father', replied Shikhandin with a look of happiness. 'With the blessing of my Guru, I have been transformed in body and mind. You have no longer two daughters, you have three sons.'

'Who was the Guru who gave you the blessing?' asked Drupada.

'Father, you will be surprised. It was Dronacharya', replied Shikhandin, anxiously looking at his father's face for his reaction.

Drupada's face was transformed into a raging volcano. His eyes blazed with anger. 'Dronacharya? The Acharya of the Kurus? He made you a man?' shouted Drupada in a voice which sounded like a hissing torrent of lava. Then he pushed Shikhandin away. 'Woe unto me! You have received the gift of life from my bitterest enemy!'

Everyone present was aghast at this outburst. The King drew himself up, and looked at Shikhandin with almost murderous eyes. 'I would rather have seen you dead first', he said foaming at the mouth and, restraining an impulse to strike his son, he stamped out of the room.

To Shikhandim his father's outburst came as a shock. His already pale face became almost bloodless. His lips trembled. He groped for support and would have fallen had not Draupadi taken him in her arms and, with a tenderness like a mother's, made him lie down on the swing.

Dhrishtadyumna followed his father who needed all the support he could give, out of the room, Satyajit hurriedly brought water and sprinkled it on the face of his unconscious brother.

Then Shikhandin was carried by servants into an inner apartment and placed on a bed. Satyajit stood by his side. Draupadi sat near him, her chin on her hands, anxiously watching the death-like pallor which had spread over her brother's face.

It was a terrible situation, thought Draupadi. Shikhandin appeared to be dying. The *swayamvara*, instead of being an occasion for joy, was developing into a ghastly tragedy. Jarasandha might kidnap her. It would mean a bitter, bloody conflict between the Panchalas and the Magadhas. If Duryodhana won her in the contest, she would never marry the fratricide, and her father's honour would be lost.

Now Shikhandin had come, almost re-born, as a present given to his father by his greatest enemy.

The cup of humiliation was complete. Draupadi did not know what to do and continued to bite at one of the gold chains she wore on her neck. She felt as if she were going mad. She looked at Shikhandin or rather the brother who had been her sister, once, the cause of this humiliation. The dust of the road he had travelled on had covered his face and coated the scabbard of his sword. Evidently, he had travelled very far to reach Kampilya in time.

True enough, he was no longer the delicate girl that he had been. He had a pale, emaciated face, from which the graceful, delicate lines had disappeared. The brow was no longer transparent. The chin had become tough. There had been a real transformation.

After a little while, Satyajit poured some water into his mouth. Then he opened his eyes, recognized his sister and younger brother and tried to smile apologetically.

Draupadi looked affectionately at his face, tanned and roughened by wind and sun. In spite of the disgrace that he had brought on the family, her heart was drawn towards her sister who was now a brother. But she knew that his presence here on this occasion would make everyone unhappy, even more unhappy than they already were. She turned wearily aside and drew the chain between her young lips in a gesture of despair.

Shikhandin got up. 'Krishnaa. Even you have become angry with me?' he asked desperately. 'I thought that at least you would have understood. You were always a mother to me.'

'But how did it all happen, brother?' asked Draupadi. 'I still cannot understand what you have been saying. We all thought that you had drowned yourself in the Ganga.'

'I was going to drown myself in the Ganga', said Shikhandin in a feeble voice. 'But a God crossed my path. He advised me to go to Dronacharya. The great

Acharya received me affectionately, though I was his enemy's son'.

Shikhandin looked at his sister and brother to see how his words were received. He saw a frown on the faces of both and sighed. He continued in a timid voice: 'The Acharya sent me to a Yaksha. Between them they began to work a miracle. For four months I was in torture. I was denied food and kept on herbs and water. My body was pounded. I was bled. Sometimes I felt as if I was being cut to pieces. I remained unconscious for days. When I woke up, I found myself in the grip of Yama, the God of Death. But I knew the Great God had worked a miracle. I was a man'.

Shikhandin's voice was choked with emotion, There were tears streaming down his cheeks. He gave expression to his feelings. 'Even though I was in feeble health, I rushed here. I wanted to be present at your *swayamvara*. And I thought you would all be happy to see me.' He broke into sobs. 'But you have turned against me. Father wants me to die. None of you needs me. I went through the torture at the hands of the Yaksha to remove the blot on our family and prove to the world that King Drupada had a real man as his son'.

Shikhandin was now sobbing like a little girl. 'I wish I were dead. I have brought misery upon you all. I have nowhere to go. None of you needs me.' And with his face in his hand, he continued to sob piteously.

Draupadi could not help placing an affectionate hand on his back. Satyajit, who felt the misery of his brother, took one of his hands in his own affectionately.

'Shikhandin, my brother, you have come at the wrong moment', said Draupadi. 'We are already enmeshed in the coils of Duryodhana.'

'How? I can't believe it.'

'He is going to inflict upon us an even greater humiliation than the one we suffered at Ahichhatra. In giving you manhood, the wicked Brahman has played his hand with uncanny skill. For he has so arranged things that the day after tomorrow, one of his pupils will carry me away to his land.'

Shikhandin had by now recovered. 'Krishnaa, you are unfair to Acharyadeva', he said. 'He could have sent me away. Then I would have died and he would have got rid of his enemy's son. But he accepted me. He never raised the question of his enmity with Father. Oh!' he broke down again. 'Why did he not leave me to die?'

'How did you go to him? You said a God sent you', said Draupadi.

Shikhandin wiped his tears and a faint smile played upon his lips. 'Yes, Krishnaa, a God came to my rescue.'

'Who was this God?' asked Draupadi. 'Tell me frankly, Shikhandin. Whoever sent you to him must have intended to hurt Father.'

'No, no', said Shikhandin indignantly. 'You remember the day on which a mission arrived from my father-in-law. It brought a message that my wife must be invited here. It would have disgraced Panchala's royal family if Drupada, the righteous King, had been found to have passed off a girl as a boy and had her married. Then he came to my help, this God.' There were tears in his eyes again. 'He was very kind. He wanted to save our family's honour. He sent me to Dronacharya. Had I not carried his message, the Acharya would have never accepted me as a pupil'.

'Who was this strange God of yours?' asked Draupadi skeptically.

'You know him, Krishnaa. He has promised to stand by you and yet would not accept you as his bride', said Shikhandin.

'Krishna Vaasudeva!' exclaimed Draupadi, amazed.

'Yes', said Shikhandin. 'He stood by me when all of you and the whole world were my enemies.'

'Oh! Great God!' exclaimed Draupadi, catching her breath. 'Again, Krishna Vaasudeva! Father is perfectly right. He has entrapped us. That is why he is forcing us to accept you as a gift from our enemy.'

'Dronacharya was very friendly. Where is the harm in reciprocating the friendliness?' asked Shikhandin.

'You are speaking with the voice of Vaasudeva', said Draupadi.

'It is my own voice, Sister', said Shikhandin, 'And it is none the worse for saying what Vaasudeva also feels.'

Draupadi looked at her brother angrily, her face flushed. 'You meddle in matters which you do not understand, Shikhandin. Father and I have to face the *swayamvara* the day after tomorrow. Jarasandha would kidnap me if he could. Duryodhana is bent upon having me, but I would sooner die than marry him. I have made up my mind that whomsoever I marry will have to fight Dronacharya. Your Vaasudeva would not enter the contest. He has broken his word to stand by Father and me.'

A deathly pallor spead over Shikhandin's face. His hands trembled. 'Why do you blame Vaasudeva for your plight? I owe him my manhood. The *swayamvara* will put Father at the head of the other kings. Vaasudeva has won over even the mighty Dronacharya, who himself came to receive him at Pushkara.'

'Have you become Krishna's slave?' asked Draupadi with bitterness in her voice.

'I am the slave of no one, neither Krishna nor Dronacharya', said Shikhandin. And with a touch of pride he added: 'I am Drupada's son. I will not be a party to bringing humiliation on him. It is the Great God who has sent Vaasudeva to us to save us from our difficulties and the bitterness which has obsessed us all these years'.

Draupadi rose and walked with quick short steps from her seat to the open window. 'You say that because your mind is full of Vaasudeva', she said. Her voice was husky.

'He is like no other man', said Shikhandin.

'I am tired of hearing that', said Draupadi as she turned as if she wanted to hit him and controlled herself, biting her lips. Shikhandin could see this. In spite of everything, he could not help launching into a fervid panegyric of Krishna. He told her how Krishna had conquered the Demons; brought about peace between the Nagas and the Rakshasas; helped the Nagas to become a warrior race; conquered Pushkara without striking a blow and even induced the formidable Dronacharya to receive him with respect. 'And yet, Sister', he continued, 'he is gentle and wise. I will never forget how he came to my help when I was in the depth of despair. The very sight of him gave me hope—.' Shikhandin got no further.

Draupadi's face was pale with fury. She tore at her gold chain till it snapped. 'Enough of your Vaasudeva! A God indeed! He is a cunning man who has trapped us into an impossible position. You will have to choose between him and Father.'

Shikhandin had also gone pale. 'I will not listen to this, Krishnaa, much as I love Father', he cried angrily.

'Listen you shall', Draupadi's voice quivered with passion. She faced him, her figure as stiff as a spear. 'This very hour you must decide to end your allegiance to Krishna and Drona. Otherwise, we shall never meet again.'

Shikhandin did not speak, but with some effort got up from the bed and stood gazing at the emptiness beyond the balcony. Then his face became as stubborn as hers was. 'You don't know what you are asking, Krishnaa. You want me to forswear my saviour and my manhood.

'Choose between your father and the cowherd', insisted Draupadi. Shikhandin looked at her with steely eyes, tossed his head, and, without a word, turned and slowly left the room.

∎

42

"SHARE MY BURDEN WITH ME, KRISHNAA"

*D*raupadi looked at the retreating figure of her brother Shikhandin. She had no power left in her to move. After her fury had spent itself, she was left with a void. She stood there absent-minded, her eyes vacantly fixed on the door through which he had passed. Then the sound of a departing chariot was heard; it told her that her brother had left the palace.

She listened to the sound till it faded away. Then she sank all limp on the bed and began to cry. There was wrath in her sobs, and bitter self-pity. An immense dreariness had taken possession of her. Was there ever, she asked herself, a more unfortunate Princess?

She had been so sure of herself till Krishna Vaasudeva came into her life. She had decided to marry him to fulfil her father's pledge. She would have made him a good wife. The Yadavas and the Panchalas between them would have made him mightier than the mightiest *Chakravartin*.

The tragedy, however, began when he came, worked himself into their hearts and hypnotized them into submitting to his wishes. Now they were landed in the

toils of ambitious kings and the superhuman cunning
of a man whom even her brother called a god.

At the chagrin of this new experience, she sobbed.
So far she had luxuriated in the sense of mastery which
her father had built up round her family. Her family,
she had come to believe, was a thing set on a pedestal
of glory. Pride in her father had burnt fiercely in her.
Now its whole fabric had collapsed. Something had to
be done to save it. 'Oh, Great God, come to our rescue',
she cried.

Suddenly she heard the tramping of many horses
and two or three chariots coming to a grinding halt.
Torches were seen moving in the forecourt. Someone
had come—someone who rode in a chariot with four
horses. Only a few among the guests rode in this way.
There were also shouts of welcome as if a great king
had arrived. An unexpected visitor at this hour of the
day!

In a few moments she knew who he was. A huge
crowd collected near the palace. There were vociferous
shouts of "Victory to Krishna Vaasudeva!" She all but
collapsed.

Her father, in his present mood, was going to have
to face Vaasudeva! She had half a mind to run to his
rescue. Then she restrained herself. Her father was not
a weakling who needed her support in an hour of crisis.

Time passed. Satyajit came in bubbling with
excitement. Krishnaa, the noble Vaasudeva has come
to meet Father. Father says that he is not well and

wants you to see him instead. He leaves everything in your hands.'

Her blood boiled at this unexpected intrusion. Her first impulse was to send word that she was not ready to receive him. But her father had left no choice to her.

The Minister Udbodhana appeared on the door-step, ceremoniously ushering in the visitor. From beyond the door came the familiar voice—cheerful and affectionate. 'Noble Princess, won't you give me a welcome as you did before?'

She hurriedly got up, adjusted her dress and came forward. In the flickering light of the numberless wicks which floated in the perfumed oil in the lamps, she saw the figure which she had never forgotten—the smiling face, the flashing eyes, the peacock feather—the very image of affectionate understanding. Oh, the cunning of the man!

With some difficulty, she suppressed her inclination to run away from his presence. 'Noble Vaasudeva', she summoned up sufficient self-command to say, 'Father has sent word through Satyajit that I must see you; he is not well.'

Though she spoke these words in apparent self-possession, she was dying to explode with indignation. But she found it difficult to do so when she saw Krishna approaching with his irrestistible smile.

'My blessing, noble Princess', said Krishna in a voice of concern. 'I have been longing to see you', he added, as he took the seat to which Satyajit had invited him.

The attendants who had followed Krishna lighted

more oil lamps, fixed on the walls, and withdrew. Udbodhana also respectfully retired. Satyajit was too excited to take his seat and stood with all too evident admiration, hoping that his sister would not let her temper get the better of her courtesy.

There was a strange weariness about Krishna which Draupadi found difficult to associate with him.

'Satyajit, help me to get rid of this harness', said Krishna, turning towards the youngster as if he was his younger brother. 'I am tired', he added.

'You, tired!' exclaimed Satyajit, surprised at this strange confession from a man whose superhuman feats had become a legend. 'They say that you never get tired, that you never need sleep.'

'Satyajit, I am sick—sick of seeing so much misery inflicted for no purpose', said Krishna in a sad voice as if speaking to himself.

Draupadi sensed an indirect reproof in the words and was going to flare up, when Krishna, with a gesture of weariness, unfastened the scarf from which his sword was suspended and dropped it on to the ground. Satyajit picked it up and put it aside.

Before she knew what she was doing, Draupadi, her annoyance for the moment forgotten, had taken the diadem from Krishna's hands and placed it on a low table.

With a merry laugh as if at his own expense, Krishna untied the shining Chakra and placed it in the hands of Satyajit, who reverentially looked at this famed weapon of miraculous destructiveness.

'How is your Father? Is he vey unwell?' asked Krishna, and then added: 'I wish I could have seen your noble Father. Has he closed his heart against me?'

Draupadi did not like this direct question and her brow became clouded again. 'He is not well', she replied tersely.

'Now tell me, Draupadi, how have you fared these days? Are you ready to face the *swayamvara*? And how many suitors have you been thinking about?' asked Krishna, trying to help Draupadi to overcome the annoyance she felt.

Draupadi's irritation increased, because she felt that Krishna was mocking her, her father and her family. 'What do I feel!' she burst out with a touch of anger. 'Don't you know everything?'

'I wish I did', replied Krishna with a smile.

'You got Father to hold the *swayamvara*, advised him to invite all the kings and fixed the test. And now we are trapped. Anyway, Father feels that way', she hastened to add.

'Why? What is wrong with the *swayamvara*?' asked Krishna.

'What is wrong! Everything is wrong. If Duryodhana or Aswatthama wins the test, I shall be dragged to Hastinapura as a slave to fall at the feet of Drona. If Jarasandha wins the test or kidnaps me, I shall be worse than a slave in Girivraja', said Draupadi.

'What you say is perfectly true', said Krishna quietly.

His tone irritated Draupadi even more. 'You won't accept me. You won't enter the contest', she continued bitterly. 'And as if that was not enough, you stole my brother and made him a slave of Drona.'

'Oh, you have come to know that, have you?' said Krishna with a smile. 'Yes, I met him on the way. He was lying huddled in the chariot, crying like a child, heart-broken and disconsolate'.

'You seem to like him very much', she sneered.

'He is a brave boy. He passed through every torture cheerfully to make his noble father and all of you proud of him', he added and sighed. His eyes, fixed on Draupadi, were reproachful.

Draupadi's anger was rising. 'You have made friends with our enemy and extracted a price from him. He delivered Pushkara into your hands—a price paid, the Gods alone know for what.' Her face was aflame. 'The ballad-singers sing that you were false to the *gopis.* Now you have been false to us.'

Satyajit, who was listening intently to every word his sister spoke, wished she would be less vehement. He turned to Krishna, expecting an angry retort, but was surprised to see that he only continued to look sadly at her, his eyes serious.

After Draupadi had finished her passionate outburst, Krishna replied in a low, sad tone: 'Forbear, noble Princess. I do not heed the abuse of men, but a woman's taunt hurts me, particularly when she is a sister whom I cherish dearly.' He leaned back in his seat as if in utter helplessness.

Draupdi felt that he was feigning frustration, and steeled her heart against his blandishments.

After a pause, Krishna said: 'You have had your say, sister. Let me have mine.'

'Have it by all means', said Draupadi with a sneer.

'I was happy, very happy, when your Father, you and your brothers placed your confidence in me', he continued in a quiet voice without a trace of resentment. 'Strong in your faith in me, for a whole year I have been trying to transform this world of ours. I thought I had done it, but now I know that I have failed.'

Draupadi looked at him with questioning eyes, confounded by the despairing ring in his voice.

'Now none of you have faith left in me, I see', he continued. 'I am weary of men who do not see the magic of faith, nor hear its music. And the time is so short—only two nights and a day.' He paused. 'The work of the whole year—perhaps of my whole lifetime—is being undone. Oh, ye immortal Gods, why can't mortals save themselves?' Krishna was now looking at her with infinite kindliness and pity.

Draupadi found her anger ebbing, as a strange warmth stole into her heart. This hero, of whom everyone talked with admiring humbleness, was begging her to give him the gift of her faith! He had none of the diplomat's wiles, nor the sorcerer's art. His trustful eyes beamed with affection, upbraiding her for playing him false.

Draupadi made a last effort to resist, repeating to herself that he had played them false. But she could not help feeling sympathy for the figure of infinite sadness before her.

Satyajit looked at him with eyes wide open and heart throbbing, as Krishna closed his eyes and placed his hands on them.

The next moment, as he removed his hands, he looked straight at Draupadi. 'Draupadi, have you lost faith in me?' he asked her. 'If you have, how shall I work the miracle? You must be by my side.' Now his voice was firm as if he was claiming what was his own.

No one spoke. 'Draupadi, don't turn away from me,' he said with irresistible sweetness. 'Tell me, please, tell me frankly. Have you anyone you would choose among the kings assembled here? Let me know his name and you shall wed him—*swayamvara* or no *swayamvara*.'

The question brought Draupadi down to earth. 'I wanted to choose, but you denied that to me. I have now no choice but to be the wife of the warrior who fights for my father's honour' she added.

'Would you be prepared to sacrifice your life for anyone who wins the contest, as Savitri of yore did for Satyavan?' asked Krishna with insistence.

'What else is left to me? I will do it, so long as my father is not humiliated,' replied Draupadi, steeling her heart against yielding.

'Can we not vanquish Drona without going to war?' asked Krishna.

The question, took Draupadi by surprise. 'Without going to war! How?' she faltered.

'We can convert hatred into Dharma', replied Krishna quietly.

'I want to follow Dharma as I see it', said Draupadi, regaining her old spirit, 'My father's pledge is my Dharma.'

'Draupadi, you are a woman, strong and true, but brought up in royal pride. You may find it difficult to see Dharma as I do', said Krishna.

'How do you see it?' she asked with a sneer.

'I cannot see Dharma as the instrument of pride and hatred', said Krishna, with a far-off look. 'I am trying to see it as life itself. It sweetens the cowherd's gruel and gives to the meanest beggar the dignity of a highborn king. But what does it mean?' Then he turned towards Draupadi and looked straight into her eyes. 'Do you want to know what it is? It is the will of the Great God—not the God we see in the shrines, but the Great God Vaasudeva, That is in All and in Whom we all live.' He now spoke slowly as if inspired. His face was lit up and a stillness seemed to surround him.

Satyajit, open-eyed, gazed at him with awe. Draupadi held her breath and listened to the beating of her heart. He appeared to be so distant and yet so near.

Draupadi continued to look at him breathlessly. She saw that his face was surrounded by a dazzling halo, and a strange power flowed to her from his eyes. She seemed to be floating in a sea of radiance—not alone, but with him. She found his words difficult to follow, but somehow she felt that she understood him and he understood her. A bond sprang up between her and him.

She trembled from head to foot. She felt as if she was on the edge of a world of which, in all her life, she had never dreamt—a world of beautiful and terrible things. She forgot herself in wonder and spoke in an inaudible whisper: 'Vaasudeva That is in All! And who are you then?'

Krishna's attitude and mood both changed. He laughed a low warm laugh. 'I am you brother who wants to share his burden with you.'

'What is your burden? You are in the happiest position in life', she asked almost in spite of herself.

'A heavy burden lies on me. Do you want to know what it is?' It is to purge man of *adharma*', replied Krishna.

'And what is *adharma*?' she asked almost mechanically.

'I cannot describe it. I feel it. It is to deny that Vaasudeva is in all of us,' said Krishna.

Draupadi was confused. She did not know what to ask him. It was so difficult.

'I want to see Dharma crowned in Panchala and Hastinapura and in all the kingdoms of Aryavarta. That is why I never rest', he added. 'Will you help me?' he asked and again looked into her eyes. His eyes were almost begging her to say 'yes'.

'I do not know how I can help. I do not know myself what I want', said Draupadi evading the question.

'My sister, you are hungry for faith, But you do not know how to satisfy the hunger', said Krishna with an indulgent smile.

Krishna's eyes were no longer those of a tired man, nor of a radiant Vaasudeva; they were—she found— those of a mother—very wise and very tender. Her mother had died so long ago that she scarcely remembered her. A rush of longing came over her for something she had never known. She was almost inclined to lay herself at his feet and weep. It was true that she had lost her faith in everything and that she was hungering for it.

Draupadi felt humbled. She bent her proud head. 'What must I do?' she cried piteously.

Krishna smiled. 'Shall I tell you? You are very beautiful, Draupadi. And to most women, to be beautiful is to be happy. But you are not. You have in you a hunger for seeing righteousness prevail. But pride and bitterness have spoiled your appetite',

'I am rotten, I know', she muttered, as she realized how pride and bitterness had made her family miserable for years.

'Don't be unfair to yourself, Draupadi; you have it in you to fight for Dharma—not to be proud of worthless things', said Krishna.

She was now humble. 'I know, I know, what you say is true', she said. 'I have cherished a wicked pride, and a wish to see my father take his revenge. So I have been afraid to be myself. But that price I must pay as his devoted daughter. I wish I had not been born into a royal family.' Draupadi's tragic eyes looked up only to find Krishna laughing in kind, gentle merriment. She flushed.

'Krishnaa', he said, addressing her for the first time by her personal name, with an affectionate emphasis, you are rightly proud of your father and of your family. If harnessed to Dharma. kingly power is a great thing. I know how hard I had to struggle for the want of it.'

'But you are happy', said Draupadi.

'I am happy because I try to live in Dharma every moment of my life', said Krishna.

'I am unhappy. Perhaps because I cannot live in Dharma as you do. I do not know what is to live in Dharma. Show me my Dharma, Govinda.' She now felt a bond which entitled her to call him by the name which those nearest to him used.'

'Each man must find his Dharma for himself, for the ways of Dharma are many', replied Krishna.

'What is my Dharma for the moment?' asked Draupadi.

'It is to go through with the swayamvara, having faith in your heart. Select the best archer in Aryavarta; follow his footsteps wherever he goes. And by your devotion to him, create an empire of Dharma', said Krishna.

'What about my father?' asked Draupadi.

'If you follow your Dharma, Krishnaa, your father will triumph. Drona will suffer defeat—not in battle which only ends life, but in Dharma which ends pride, wrath and hate', said Krishna.

'What would you do if you were my father?' asked Draupadi hopefully.

'I would teach Dronacharya a lesson which he would never forget—make him conscious that he fell from the highest estate of Brahmanhood when he humiliated your father,' said Krishna.

'Drona will never admit defeat,' said Draupadi shaking her head.

'Why are you so sure?' asked Krishna with a laugh and then changed the subject. 'But let us come back to what faces us at the moment. I ask you again: Have you any warrior in view?'

'I have no choice', replied Draupadi humbly. 'I will choose the one that you choose for me.'

'Then listen, Krishnaa. As I begged of you before please share my burden with me,' said Krishna. 'How can I do that?' asked Draupadi.

'Don't be afraid of Jarasandha. He can never win the contest. He can never kidnap you.'

'How do you know?' asked Draupadi.

'With his age and lumbering body, he can never win the test.'

'But he can kidnap me', she said with a shudder.

'He will do so only over my dead body', replied Krishna with firmness, 'and over the dead bodies of all the Yadava *atirathis*.'

Draupadi felt grateful for this assurance which, given with the inevitability of destiny, carried conviction. 'What if Duryodhana wins the test?' she asked,

'That is the heaviest burden I have to bear. Do not ask me any more', said Krishna. His face was suddenly strained with a great sadness again.

It was Draupadi's turn to be the comforter. 'If you cannot tell me, I will not ask you, Govinda.'

'Believe me when I tell you that I want you to be the wife of a man who lives in Dharma, the mother of heroic sons. a mighty queen who shall live in the memory of men as upholding a vast empire of Dharma', said Krishna.

There was silence for a moment. Something in Draupadi melted. She felt compassion for this god-like man. Her heart became suddenly warm, as if sunshine had flowed into a closed room. 'Govinda, I place myself at your disposal completely. But see that my father is not humiliated. That is all I beg of you.'

Krishna spoke slowly, distinctly and firmly. 'I will stand by you and your father, whatever happens. Just now I cannot promise you anything more. So ask me no questions.' Then he repeated 'Take the *swayamvara* as part of your Dharma and mine.'

'I shall, Govinda,' said Draupadi in a spirit of complete surrender.

'Then, I want you to suffer one indignity for my sake. Shakuni and Aswatthama, the son of Dronachaya, want to see you', said Krishna.

'Drona's son!' Draupadi's voice was again full of annoyance, 'You want me to drink a cup of poison.'

'Yes. I am bringing them to you because that is what I have promised Bhanumati, wife of Duryodhana. Aswatthama will give you a pledge: if you choose any of the Kurus, including him, Dronacharya's son, he will prevent his father from leaving Hastinapura, even at the cost of his life,' said Krishna.

Draupadi's brow was contracted. 'And if I do not chose a Kuru?'

'The choice will always be yours', said Krishna.

'But what if Duryodhana wins the contest?' asked Draupadi reverting to the one fear which oppressed her ceaselessly.

Krishna laughed. His eyes danced. 'The Mahadevi of the Kurus can humble Drona as no one else can.'

He was the fascinating cowherd again. Draupadi vainly tried to understand the significance of this mocking remark, and remained quiet.

Then Krishna lowered his voice and continued: 'If it is any satisfaction to you, I will tell you a secret: I have assured Bhanumati, who is a little sister to me, that she will not have you as the second wife of Duryodhana. Is that enough?'

For a moment Draupadi blushed. Then she folded her hands in helpessness. 'You want me to accept a promise from Aswatthama as if I were going to be a Kuru's wife. You have promised Bhanumati that I shall not marry Duryodhana', she laughed. 'I cannot understand you. What is your real nature?'

'Whatever you think it to be—so long as you do not lose faith in me', replied Krishna.

'Am I to undergo this humiliation so that you may fulfil your promise?' asked Draupadi.

'Yes. It will bind you to me as nothing else will', said Krishna.

'Very well, let things be as you wish them. Is there anything more?' she asked.

'Nothing more.'

'You are a sorcerer. I am not sure whether I might not consent to marry Duryodhana if you asked me to do so.'

'I may even ask you to do that if your Dharma demands it', said Krishna laughing.

Draupadi opened her eyes wide at the inscrutable ways of Krishna. 'You can never speak except in riddles, Govinda.'

'I am a riddle myself. And you are another. But there is no time to solve riddles just now. Shall I send you Shakuni and Aswatthama?' asked Krishna.

'I will see them if you so wish', she said. 'But let me ask Father's permission first. Can I assure him that you will never do anything which will hurt Father?' asked Draupadi.

'Do so. As I said before, I will stand by you and your father even if it costs me my life itself', said Krishna.

43

SHIKHANDIN INTERVENES

*W*hen Krishna left her, Draupadi felt as if she was in a dream. His face, glowing with a strange light, and his look of infinite tenderness lingered before her eyes. She continued to hear his voice, so convincing, asking her: 'Krishnaa, won't you have faith in me?' and also her own, answering: 'I have faith in you; I shall abide by what you say.'

She was no longer unhappy at what the *swayamvara* would bring her the next day. It was no concern of hers, she felt. She would go through with it, not only for the sake of her father, but for his sake, to lighten the burden that he was bearing.

When she went up to her father, he was lying in bed with a tormenting headache, his eyes closed. The heart of the proud, strong man was bursting with bitterness. She told him—unwilling listener though he was—of the talk she had had with Krishna. He, Krishna, would never let him down. The *swayamvara* would be a success. Jarasandha would not dare to kidnap her. Duryodhana would not win her hand. Drona's pride would be broken.

'Words, words, words,' said Drupada in a tired voice. 'Vaasudeva will say anything.' He shook his head dolefully. 'I am bewildered. How he is going to do all that?'

'Father, how he is going to do it all is no concern of ours.' she replied with a smile. 'I don't feel any more anxiety. I have transferred everything on to his shoulders.'

'My child, he has bewitched you. He is playing a trick on us,' said Drupada, unable to convince himself that Krishna had been serious in what he had said.

'To what end, Father?' asked Draupadi in a soothing tone. 'He is so dedicated to Dharma. What can he gain by humiliating us or conspiring with Drona against us?'

'I cannot understand him,' said Drupada pathetically, adding in self-disgust, 'and I don't know why we are so stupid as to listen to him.'

'As Vaasudeva puts it, we must take the course that Dharma dictates to us for the moment', remarked Draupadi. 'We should face the *swayamvara.*'

The roles were reversed. Now the daughter was the stronger of the two.

'There is nothing else that we can do,' said Drupada in despair, holding his splitting head in his hands and staring vacantly at the ceiling.

Then, for the first time, he noticed the change that had come over his daughter. He looked at her attentively and added: 'Krishnaa, you seem to have become different suddenly. You appear to be intoxicated. Has Vaasudeva's talk gone to your head?'

'I am more than intoxicated, Father. I am delirious with joy,' said Draupadi with a laugh.

'Why? Why? I can't understand it.'

'I have left everything to him,' said Draupadi smiling, as she put her hand on her father's brow.

'Have you gone mad?' asked Drupada. 'Tell me again what he told you. My head is swimming and I did not understand the full significance of what he promised you,' he added with a sigh.

'He said many things, Father,' she replied. 'He said that he would stand by us; that Jarasandha would not dare to kidnap me; that I would not have to marry Duryodhana; that Drona's pride would be broken.'

'They are a gambler's promises,' said Drupada desperately.

Draupadi laughed cheerfully. 'He is a mighty gambler. He has staked his fame, his future, his very life on this *swayamvara* of mine.'

'He may gamble for himself as much as he likes. But why does he do it with my honour and your future?'

'He is not gambling *with* you and me, Father, but *for* you and me,' said Draupadi.

'Why are you so sure? You seem to have changed altogether.'

'Father, don't you worry,' said Draupadi persuasively. 'He showed me the right way—my Dharma. For the moment, it is to go through with the *swayamvara* having a song in my heart, and I am going to do it.'

'I can't understand the change in you, Krishnaa,' said Drupada.

'I don't understand it myself, Father.'

'All right. If you have confidence in Vaasudeva, I

have nothing more to say. But how does he propose to break the pride of Drona?'

'He begged me not to ask any more questions.'

'And you are content?'

'Yes, content to leave everything to him. Father, somehow I am convinced that he can enter all hearts and fulfil all wishes.' Then she smiled sweetly. 'Anyway he appears to have entered mine.'

Drupada looked at his daughter as a new understanding dawned on him. 'My child,' he said with a pathetic helplessness, you have been to me a greater comfort than all my other children. You have shared my humiliation, my thirst for revenge, my hatred for Drona. Just now I can't see my way clearly. You are a wise woman. I leave the *swayamvara* in your hands. If it miscarries, I will not be able to survive the humiliation. You know that, don't you?'

Draupadi looked into her father's eyes with tender affection. 'Father, have I not suffered seeing you unhappy? Have I not always watched over you?'

'You have, you have, Krishnaa,' said Drupada as he patted her hand.

'Then, please share my faith in Govinda.'

'Oh, the Great God has left nothing else for me to do! The sorcerer has been at work,' said Drupada, and a smile broke over his unhappy face. 'We have all been victims of his sorcery. If you have made up your mind to submit to what is going to happen, I will submit too, for I don't see any other way out of it.'

'Father, Vaasudeva wanted a favour from you,' said Draupadi, as she saw that her father was in a receptive mood.

'What is it?' asked Drupada, his suspicions aroused. 'It must be something which Vaasudeva wanted you to extract from me.'

'He wanted you and me to meet Shakuni, the maternal uncle of Duryodhana, and Aswatthama, son of Drona,' replied Draupadi.

'Son of Drona!' Drupada flared up again. 'Have I got to make him a promise too?'

'No. Govinda wants you to accept a promise from him. A promise to the effect that if I ever marry a Kuru Prince, he will, at the cost of his life, see that his father Drona does not leave Hastinapura,' said Draupadi.

'What is this nonsense?' exploded Drupada again, as he sat up in bed. 'In one breath he gives you a promise that he will see that you do not marry Duryodhana; in the next, he wants to secure you for a Kuru prince. What new absurdity is this?'

'I can't make any sense of it either, Father, I confess,' said Draupadi frankly. 'I don't know why Govinda wants Aswatthama to give the promise. But I beg of you to do as he says, Father. There is something behind all this, which we cannot fathom.'

'He is a riddle, this Govinda of yours,' said Drupada, emphasizing the familiar name by which she had begun to refer to Krishna.

'He himself admitted that he was a riddle,' replied Draupadi with a smile.

Drupada's mood changed. He said laughing, 'I don't like making decisions tonight. Do what you like but consult Dhrishtadyumna. I have no doubt that you will do the proper thing.'

'Even if I have Shikhandin brought back to the palace?' asked Draupadi mischievously.

'Shikhandin! why?'

'Father, Govinda saved him from committing suicide. He helped him to become a man, thus removing the blot on our family. He brought this almost newborn brother to us, and we rejected him,' said Draupadi.

'I will never forgive the boy,' said Drupada.

'Father, think for a moment,' urged Draupadi, again placing a soft hand on his aching brow. 'He went through endless torture to make you proud and happy. He had hoped that we would welcome him. Instead, we drove him out into the wilderness.'

'But why did he have to come at this time?' asked Drupada.

'I wish I knew. Possibly he wanted to join in the festive occasion of the *swayamvara*. I cannot forget his wan, piteous, hope-bereft face as he left me,' replied Draupadi persuasively. 'When he went back to Krishna's camp, he was crying like a child—so Vaasudeva told me.'

Drupada stared vacantly at the dim light burning in his room. He was evidently wrestling with himself.

Draupadi added: 'Would it have been better, Father, had Drona, the enemy, left him to commit suicide? On the contrary, he forgot his enmity, took Shikhandin under his care and gave him new life. Possibly he was sent back to be helpful to us in the *swayamvara*. Please, Father forgive him. I shall not feel happy till he comes back.'

A doubt arose in Drupada's mind: Krishnaa had changed; Shikhandin had changed; perhaps Drona himself had changed. Was he the only one to nurse a meaningless hatred? He gave up struggling with himself.

'Krishnaa, do what you like,' he said like a sick child.

Then, staring at the ceiling, he repeated: 'Do what you like.'

Suddenly he moved his head impatiently as if to shake off an incubus and, rising from his bed, he said: 'Let me know when Shakuni and Aswatthama come. I will meet them. It shall not be said that Yajnasena Drupada had not the courage to face Drona's son.'

Draupadi came out of her father's room, happy at the idea that his attitude towards Shikhandin had changed. When she met Drishtadyumna who was just returning from the *swayamvara mandap*, she told him what had transpired at the interview she had had with Drupada.

'Dhrishtadyumna, Father is willing to receive Shikhandin back into the family. I want him back tonight. I don't want to go to the *swayamvara* in an unhappy frame of mind. I shall immediately ask Satyaji to bring him back,' said Draupadi.

'But, why have you so suddenly changed, and Father too?' asked Dhrishtadyumna in surprise.

'I don't know how the change had occurred, but occurred it has.' Then she paused for a while and looked appealingly at Dhrishtadyumna. 'Brother, have we not allowed the memory of an old humiliation to poison our hearts for too long?'

'Why do you ask that?'

'Evidently Father was asking that same question to himself when I left him.'

Dhrishtadyumna was taken aback. 'Krishna has worked a miracle in the interview he had with you,' he said.

Draupadi smiled happily. 'If Krishna can work a miracle, so can we. If he can transform the hatred of kings into the amity of Dharma, why cannot we?'

Shakuni and Aswatthama, when they arrived at the palace, were received by King Drupada in the throne room, which was brilliantly lit by brass lamps in each of which a hundred wicks had been lighted. Near him, in respectful silence, stood Dhrishtadyumna and Satyajit, and also, a little behind them, Shikhandin, happy to have been reconciled to his family, but pale, weak and supporting himself by leaning against the wall. Draupadi stood near him.

Drupada, seated on his throne, invited the guests to take their seats in front of him. Shakuni, after prostrating himself before the King, rose with a considerable effort and lowered his bulk into the seat with elephantine deliberation.

Aswatthama walked up, and, in conformity with his status as a Brahman, extended both his hands towards the King in blessing, with the formal words: 'May you live a hundred autumns.' As he took his seat, his eyes fell on Draupadi, and he could not take them off her, so fascinated was he by her beauty.

After all these courtesies had been exchanged, there was a moment of uncomfortable silence. Then, Drupada, wan and tired, but exercising great self-restraint, asked the guests politely: 'To what do we owe the pleasure of your visit at this time of the day?'

Shakuni smiled unctuously, rubbed his hands, shifted his position, and in an ingratiating voice said: 'Best of Kings, we come from the valorous *Yuvaraja* of the Kurus. Vaasudeva must have told you about our coming.

The King nodded. 'Yes, Prince of Gandhara, Vaasudeva conveyed your message to Draupadi that you urgently wanted to see us.'

'Yes, yes,' said Shakuni, with an oleaginous smile. 'The *Yuvaraja* sends his salutation to you, noble King. He wants to secure your princely friendship by seeking the hand of the noble Princess, the crown jewel among maidens.'

'The Princess, my sister, is no longer a free agent,' said Dhrishtadyumna, taking upon himself the burden of the conversation. 'An archery test has been fixed; it is already announced. Have you not heard about it?'

'No, we have not,' broke in Aswatthama, irritation writ large on his face.

'My sister shall wed only the master bowman who passes the test in archery prescribed by our Father,' said Dhrishtadyumna.

The guests were taken aback and exchanged glances. The next moment, Shakuni, overcoming his surprise. replied with a broad smile; 'If that is your wish, my noble lord, things will be easy indeed. The *Yuvaraja* is the best marksman in Aryavarta. Aswatthama will bear me out. It would have been better, however, had the Princess chosen the *Yuvaraja* without a test.'

'The test has been prescribed already,' said Drupada briefly. It was only with some difficulty that he could overcome his disgust at the ingratiating manner in which Shakuni spoke.

'We have heard, that the *Yuvaraja* is a perfect marksman,' said Drishtadyumna, resuming the thread of the conversation.

'Oh, yes,' said Shakuni with a smile. 'The valorous *Yuvaraja,* is indeed an incomparable bowman. He is sure to win the test.' His small, round eyes beamed confidence.

'Then there is no need for you to press his suit,' said Dhrishtadyumna and, in a voice tinged with irony, asked: 'But Karna, the King of Anga, is reputed to be the best bowman in Aryavarta, is he not?'

Shakuni laughed contemptuously. 'Noble *Yuvaraja,* people will say anything. But we know the might of our *Yuvaraja,*' he said.

Drupada could not help asking: 'Is it not true that the only bowman who could outstrip Karna was Arjuna, son of Pandu, who met his death at Varanavata?'

The King spoke these words with an air of innocence, but the barb was deadly.

Both the guests were taken aback. But Shakuni quickly recovered his poise and his face became comically grief-stricken, as he said with a deep sigh: 'Alas, alas, the Five Brothers are no more. They were the noblest of men. And Arjuna was a great warrior, just like our *Yuvaraja*. Our *Yuvaraja's* heart was broken when he heard that the Five Brothers had lost their lives in Varanavata. But who can defy fate?'

His eyes were full of the unshed tears which he could always call forth when required.

Aswatthama was impatient to take up the thread of the conversation.

'Noble King, Karna is out of the contest,' he said. He is a charioteer's son. And, to tell you the truth, often even I have done better than he.' His attempt to sound modest was not very successful.

'Then your *Yuvaraja* is sure to win the contest,' remarked the King.

'I have no doubt about it in my mind,' said Shakuni with the ingratiating smile which never left his face. 'If I may say so, the valorous Duryodhana would be the fittest warrior to marry the beautiful Princess. I am lucky to have such a nephew. In course of time he should be a great *Chakravartin*.'

Drupada was irritatingly silent.

'We must heal the old wounds,' Shakuni continued. 'And we are here to do it. Is that not so, Aswatthama?' He looked at Aswatthama, inviting him to speak.

'Yes, I have come here to give you a solemn promise, noble King,' said Aswatthama.

'What is the promise that you propose to give me?' asked Drupada.

'Some doubt is felt—so the noble Vaasudeva says—as to whether my venerable father, the Best of Acharyas, may not leave Hastinapura if the *Yuvaraja* weds the Princess. I am here to give you a firm promise: If the noble Princess marries a Kuru Prince, my father will not leave Hastinapur. I will back the promise with my life,' affirmed Aswatthama with a solemn air.

King Drupada heard the promise in silence. It was, however, broken by a husky, tremulous voice, asking: 'Are you sure, noble Aswatthama, that the venerable Acharyadeva would accept my sister as the Crown Princess of the Kurus?'

Drupada turned towards his children with a frown. How could one of his children be guilty of discourtesy in speaking uninvited before him and in the presence of strangers?

All turned towards the place from which the strange voice had come. Dhrishtadyumna and Satyajit made way and slowly Shikhandin came forward, his large eyes fixed on Aswatthama, his face flushed with excitement.

Shakuni was taken aback. Aswatthama glared at the interrupter angrily, as if trying to destroy him by his very look.

When he looked at his son, Drupada forgave the lapse, and, grasping the significance of the question, turned to Aswatthama, expecting a straight reply to a straight question.

Aswatthama recognised Shikhandin. The boy was a disciple of his father's! But he was puzzled. An anchorite there and now in a dress befitting a prince! He was also surprised at the boy's temerity in interrupting the conversation. 'You, you, you! The anchorite who was in the *Yuddha shala!*' he exclaimed, unable to believe his eyes.

'He is my son, Shikhandin,' interrupted Drupada, not displeased at Aswatthama's arrogant self-confidence being shaken.

Shakuni realized the situation and recovered his self-possession.

'Noble Prince, you are mistaken,' he said. Rubbing his hands, and smiling, he turned to the King 'Acharyadeva loves his son more than you, my noble lord, think. He will never let a solemn promise given by his son be broken.'

Drupada thought that the time had come to end the interview. 'It is very noble of you, Aswatthama, to give this promise,' he said, rising to indicate that the interview was at an end. 'Evidently you are a generous friend to the *Yuvaraja.* If the occasion arises, I will hold you to your promise,' he added.

'I shall certainly keep my promise, whatever happens,' said Aswatthama, as he rose to depart.

'We will take leave of you now, noble King,' said Shakuni. 'I look forward to welcoming the noble Princess in our camp tomorrow evening as the bride of our valorous *Yuvaraja.*'

Drupada coolly acknowledged the salutations as Shakuni and Aswatthama left the room.

When the visitors had departed, Drupada beckoned his children to follow him to the bedroom. He gave his diadem to Satyajit, sat down on the bed and looked at Shikhandin.

'Shikhandin, what did you mean by your question?' he asked.

'Noble Father, please excuse my rudeness in interrupting your conversation,' replied Shikhandin with his hands joined, and added:

'But I could not contain myself when Aswatthama was giving a pledge which it will not be possible to keep.'

Drupada looked at his son who was still troubled at having seemed rude to his father, and smiled. 'Don't look so crestfallen, my boy. You did the right thing to prick the bubble of that conceited fellow. But what did you intend to suggest by your question?' he asked.

'Bhanumati, the present Crown Princess, is almost a daughter to Acharyadeva. He will never allow any other princess—much less Draupadi—to be the Crown Princess and take her place,' said Shikhandin, offering an explanation.

'Did I not tell you, Father, that I would not have to marry Duryodhana?' asked Draupadi with a merry twinkle in her eyes.

'I would not like it either,' said Drupada, lapsing into a mood of helplessness. 'But I don't know how you can escape that fate if he wins the test.'

'May I speak, Father?' asked Shikhandin, urged by a sense of duty, in spite of his hesitation.

'Yes, you may,' said Drupada encouragingly. He had acquired a new respect for his son.

'You have been the support of Dharma amongst kings. It would be *adharma* to break you solemn pledge. I agree. But it would be equally *adharma* to give our sister in marriage to Duryodhana who is living in *adharma*,' Shikhandin pointed out, summoning all his courage. He seemed to speak boldly, but his lips were twitching nervously and his hands were trembling.

Drupada looked at Shikhandin. 'Don't be so agitated, Shikhandin. Tell me precisely what you think.' And for the first time he spoke in an affectionate voice.

Thus encouraged by Drupada, the young man overcame his hesitation. 'Duryodhana, guided by his uncle Shakuni and supported by Karna and Aswatthama, is wickedness personified. There are no limits to which he will not go to secure his purpose.'

Drupada nodded agreement and Shikhandin proceeded: 'He organized the conspiracy to murder the Five Brothers. He got them banished. He had them burnt to death in Varanavata.'

'We have heard these reports. But are they true?' asked Drupada.

'They are true. I heard it from my teacher himself— how there was a plan to kill the Five Brothers, if they had not gone into voluntary banishment. And I heard from Yaksha Sthoonakarna how they met with their end. He was engaged by Duryodhana to build a mansion of lac and sulphur at Varanavata. Purochana was employed to set fire to it,' said Shikhandin.

Drupada exchanged glances with Dhrishtadyumna and Draupadi. No one spoke for a few moments.

'Who is this Yaksha?' asked Drupada.

'He is the person who gave me my manhood,' replied Shikhandin. 'He is waiting in the chariot outside. I will bring him in.'

Shikhandin went out and returned with a strange-looking, tall, lean individual with corded sinews and flowing hair and large red eyes, carrying a trident in his hand. With lofty unconcern he stood before Drupada and extended his hands in blessing.

Drupada looked at the extraordinary one and asked him 'Are you Yaksha Sthoonakarna?'

The Yaksha nodded without speaking a word.

Shikhandin intervened. 'Noble father, the Yaksha speaks only twenty words in a day. He has only five more words to speak before tomorrow's sunrise. You may put any questions you like. He will give you the appropriate reply.'

'You treated Shikhandin?' asked Drupada.

Sthoonakarna nodded assent.

'Did you construct the palace of lac and sulphur at Varanavata for the Five Brothers?'

Sthoonakarna again nodded assent.

'Who asked you to do it?'

'Duryodhana,' replied the Yaksha.

'Do you know who set fire to the palace?'

'Purochana,' replied the Yaksha.

'How do you know that he set fire to it?'

'Orders,' laconically replied the Yaksha.

'Whose orders?'

'Duryodhana's.'

'How do you know?'

'Heard,' replied Yaksha.

'You heard the orders being given, is that what you mean?'

Sthoonakarna put his fingers to his lips to indicate that he had already spoken his quota of words for the day and would not speak any more.

'Did you hear the orders yourself?'

Sthoonakarna nodded assent.

'Sthoonakarna, you can go now,' said Drupada.

Shikhandin took Sthoonakarna out of the room and asked one of the waiting attendants to take him back to the chariot. When he returned, Drupada said in a deliberate tone; 'It would be a heinous sin to let Duryodhana marry Krishnaa.'

Dhrishtadyumna nodded assent. Draupadi only smiled; her instinct had proved sound when she had decided not to marry Duryodhana.

'What should be done now? I am so confused tonight that I cannot make up my mind,' said Drupada helplessly.

'Father, will you permit me to speak?' asked Shikhandin.

'Speak, speak, by all means speak,' Drupada almost

shouted, irked by the too respectful manner in which Shikhandin was addressing him, 'You have something at the back of your mind.'

'If Duryodhana wins the archery test, Father, I want to intervene. It is my duty as a brother to save my sister from a sin,' said Shikhandin.

'What would you do?' asked Drupada.

'Before the assembly of kings, I will charge Duryodhana with having got his cousins burnt alive, and call upon the venerable *rishis* to pronounce whether an *aatataayi*[1] can take advantage of a pledge given in Dharma,' replied Shikhandin.

Dhrishtadyumna saw the implications of such a step and said; 'But that would lead to a war between the Kurus and ourselves.'

'It would be a war of righteousness. The kings would be with us. Vaasudeva would surely befriend us. It would be a war of Dharma,' said Shikhandin.

Dhrishtadyumna thought for a while and remarked, 'Father, this is a matter which has to be considered seriously.'

Drupada closed his eyes, frowned in concentration, and came to a quick decision. Opening his eyes he said. 'Dhrishtadyumna, I now see my way. I have made up my mind,' Then he paused. 'Shikhandin is right; he must denounce Duryodhana. I prefer leading a holy war to giving my daughter in marriage to an *aatataayi*.'

44

THE NIGHT BEFORE

It was midnight. A lone, majestic, three-quarter moon lit up the placidly flowing waters of the Ganga. The camps of the royal guests had settled down to rest after the hectic activities of the day.

In the camp of the Magadhan Emperor, trusted retainers, sturdy and grim-looking, stood guard outside the tent to which the Emperor Jarasandha had retired for the night. Immobile like stone statues, they leaned heavily on the handles of their upturned maces planted in the sand.

Footsteps were heard approaching, soft but unafraid. The guards shook themselves awake and moved towards the two men who, wrapped in scarves except for their faces, were approaching the camp.

'Stop there,' said the leader of the guards. 'Who are you and what do you want?'

By then, several other guards had gathered near their leader, ready to smash the head of any visitor who insisted on entering the camp.

One of the strangers detached himself from the other, took a step forward and said in a clear voice: 'I want to see the *Chakravarti.*'

'See the *Chakravarti!* At this time of the night!' exclaimed the leader. 'Have you gone mad?' The guard laughed, 'Go away,' he ordered.

The man who had spoken took off the scarf which covered his head and shoulders, disclosing a radiant diadem, a necklace of jewels, luminous ear-rings and a sword with a gold hilt—the insignia of very high rank.

The guards were taken aback at the strange visitor—a prince at least—coming at the dead of night, unattended and unheralded. They automatically folded their hands. Their leader respectfully said: 'We cannot let you pass, noble Prince. Our orders are strict.'

'Who is the Prince in charge of the watch? Will you take me to him? Or, better still, will you bring him here? The mission on which I have come does not brook delay,' said the visitor with a note of urgency in his voice.

'We cannot allow you to enter and we cannot bring Prince Vidanda here. He must be fast asleep.'

The visitor laughed in good humour. 'Then he must be awakened. The matter affects the life of the Emperor. I need to see him without any delay.'

'You can do so in the morning, lord,' replied the leader of the guards persuasively.

'I must see him now,' insisted the visitor as he fixed his compelling eyes on the leader. 'Don't hesitate to go and call Prince Vidanda; he will thank you for doing so. If you do not, I will blow my conch; it will wake up the whole camp, and the Emperor will not forgive you for being awakened so unceremoniously.'

The leader of the guards was confused. He took counsel with his companions and went to call Vidanda. The visitor waited facing the guards, with one arm on the shoulder of his companion who had now come up to him.

'What do you want?' Vidanda asked in a surly voice as he approached the visitors, his eyes full of sleep, his face showing his annoyance.

'Noble Prince, I want to see the Emperor immediately.'

Vidanda was very angry. 'At this time of the night! That is absurd! How can I wake up the Emperor?'

'I am afraid you will have to,' said the visitor quietly.

'He is sound asleep,' said Vidanda, and was turning away, when the visitor said in a voice of authority; 'You can wake him up all the same.' At this, Vidanda rubbed his eyes and looked at the visitor more closely.

'Who may you be, noble Prince?' he asked, with a new courtesy.

'I am the Yadava, Krishna Vaasudeva,' the visitor answered with a laugh. 'And this, if you want to know, is Uddhava, the son of my uncle Devabhaga.'

Krishna Vaasudeva! Vidanda opened his eyes wide. He could not believe them. He rubbed his eyes again. Could this be the famed Krishna Vaasudeva of whom

people had been talking all the time in the camp? But
there was no mistaking the dark colour and the
peacock feather which, as he had known from reports,
distinguished this Yadava hero.

'Will you wake up the Emperor and let me see him?'
asked Krishna quietly.

Vidanda knew what feelings of hostility they all,
and particularly the Emperor, bore towards Krishna.
'He will not see you lord,' he said apologetically.

'If the *Chakravarti* refuses to see me, will you
convey my message to him? If you canont do it yourself,
do it through *Yuvaraja* Sahadeva. Tell him: "Once at
Gomantaka, Vaasudeva saved your life. He wants to
save it again, if you will let him do it." And add this
also, if you have the courage: "Krishna Vaasudeva says
that if you do not see him now, nothing in the three
worlds can help you".'

Vidanda was dismayed when the meaning of the
message dawned on him. 'How dare I convey such
threats to the mighty *Chakravarti?*' he asked in protest.

'I am not uttering threats,' said Krishna mildly. 'I
have come here to save him,'

Vidanda reflected for a while. The matter was
serious, he thought, and he could not take the risk
of turning away so powerful a visitor.

'Will you please wait, noble Vaasudeva?' he asked.
'I will convey your message to the *Yuvaraja*. Do both
of you want to see the noble *Charkravarti?*'

'No, Uddhava will wait here,' said Krishna. 'Also

tell the *Yuvaraja* that I have no other arms except my sword, and even that I intend to leave here in the keeping of Uddhava. I have come on a mission of peace.'

'As the noble Vaasudeva pleases,' said Vidanda, still wondering at the curious message he had been asked to carry to his Emperor.

When Vidanda had gone, Uddhava turned to Krishna. 'You are very obstinate, Govinda. Why do you want to meet him alone?'

Krishna laughed. 'If he is bent on killing us, it is just as well that only one of us should be killed rather than both. And don't forget that, even if something happens to me, you have still to find the Five Brothers,' he said and affectionately patted the shoulders of Uddhava, who remonstrated no further, noticing the finality in his cousin's voice.

They waited for some considerable time before Prince Vidanda returned accompanied by Prince Sahadeva. 'Is it the noble Vaasudeva?' asked Sahadeva, but his voice betrayed his annoyance. 'Do you want to see the *Chakravarti* at this time of the night?'

'Yes, *Yuvaraja*,' said Krishna. 'I can understand your surprise and also your suspicion. I am not the Emperor's friend nor is he mine. And yet I have come to see him alone. I propose to go with you completely unarmed. I am even leaving my sword here with Uddhava. That should satisfy you that I have something important to tell him—even at considerable risk to myself.'

'Is it so very important?'

'It is. Do you think I would have come to your camp at midnight were it not very urgent?'

Sahadeva, realizing the validity of the argument, entered the tent and, gently waking up the sleeping Emperor, told him of the strange visitor.

'Lord, may I bring the noble Vaasudeva in?' asked Sahadeva.

'You may,' replied Jarasandha in a voice which clearly showed that the visitor was unwelcome.

Sahadeva led Krishna into the tent, where a dim light threw flickering shadows. The torch-bearers lighted the wicks floating in the oil lamps and withdrew.

Jarasandha was sitting on a huge bed covered with soft bear skins, his stalwart and heavy body unbent and unwrinkled in spite of age. His long hair and beard which he was gathering in his hands to tie up, gave a leonine appearance to his face, flushed as it was with annoyance.

No one spoke. Sahadeva brought a seat and placed it in front of the bed inviting Krishna by a gesture to take it.

Krishna sat down. Jarasandha acknowledged his presence by a grunt. For some time there was silence.

Courageous though he was and though he tried to maintain a bold, angry front, Jarasandha was perturbed. When he had heard of Krishna's presence at the *swayamvara* in Kampilya, he had had a premonition already; it boded no good for him. His plans had foundered every time the cowherd had intervened in his affairs in the past. So, when he found himself alone, and at dead of night, facing his bitterest enemy, he had a sense of impending calamity. In the flickering light, the visitor looked to him like an ominous apparition.

'Why are you here?' burst out Jarasandha ultimately, unable to restrain himself any longer.

'I will tell you why,' said Krishna in a matter-of-fact voice. 'You sought me in vain in Gomantaka; also in Mathura. Now you find me here in your camp, at dead of night, alone and unarmed.'

'You are my enemy,' growled Jarasandha, glaring at Krishna angrily.

'Yes, I know. Yet I am delivering myself into your hands,' said Krishna with a smile.

Jarasandha plucked at his beard and stared at Krishna silently for some moments. He was summoning all his strength of mind so as not to show his perturbation. 'Why have you done so?' he asked at last.

'Do you want me to give you the reason whilst the *Yuvaraja* and Prince Vidanda are present?' Krishna countered. 'Perhaps you would prefer our talks to be confined to ourselves. We are old enemies, you know.' And, with a mischievous smile at Sahadeva, he added: 'The younger men may best be kept out of our quarrels.'

For a moment Jarasandha hesitated. Then, with a gesture, he dismissed Sahadeva and Vidanda.

However, they did not want to leave the *Chakravarti*, formidable though he was, by himself, at the mercy of his young enemy, and stood outside the tent, ready to rush in at the slightest sign of danger.

'Why have you come?' questioned Jarasandha again impatiently.

'To save you from disaster', replied Krishna with a smile.

'I don't want your assistance now or ever. You are wasting your time,' blustered Jarasandha truculently.

'I am not wasting your time or mine. I have come to give you advice.'

'You! You give me advice!' Jarasandha snorted contemptuously.

'Yes,' answered Krishna quietly. 'My advice is: Give up the attempt to kidnap Draupadi.'

Jarasandha shook himself like a tiger getting ready to spring. His hands were clenched. 'What did you say? Kidnap Draupadi! You are impertinent. We have come here to win Draupadi in a *swayamvara*'.

'Then promise me that the Magadhans will not attempt to kidnap her.'

Jarasandha clutched at his bed in suppressed fury. 'How dare you? You demand a promise from me!' he shouted.

Krishna smiled indulgently. 'I am not quite a nobody. You wanted to kill me at Gomantaka, but it was I who saved you from the mace of my Big Brother. But for that, you would not have been alive today'.

Jarasandha bit his lips.

'You wanted to make the Princess of Vidarbha an instrument of your ambitious policies; I snatched her away from under your very nose'. Krishna coolly continued to enumerate the Emperor's failures. 'You wanted to destroy the Yadavas; they escaped your wrath to find prosperity and power. Don't you agree that, if I have come to warn you, it may be worth your while to listen to me?' he added in a persuasive voice.

Jarasandha gritted his teeth and sneered, 'You are a very conceited young man.'

'Yes', agreed Krishna uperturbed. 'But I think that I am rendering you a service even though I am no friend of yours'.

'I don't want to be your friend and do not want you as my friend either. No, never', said Jarasandha.

'I know that, of course. And I too will never accept you as my friend', replied Krishna.

'I will never forgive you for the way you killed your maternal uncle, my son-in-law', said Jarasandha.

'I have not come here to ask your forgiveness. I want to give you a chance to save yourself. Give up the idea of kidnapping Draupadi', replied Krishna.

'Who told you that we wanted to kidnap her?' Jarasandha's anger was rising at the effrontery of the visitor. 'And who are you to ask me to do or not to do anything? Don't threaten me, cowherd', he said menacingly. 'If you talk in this vein, I shall break your head'.

Krishna looked up defiantly and laughed. 'If you want to break my head, do it now', he said, 'But remember: if you do, it will be the sacred duty of the scores of kings assembled in Kampilya to take your life. The sacred canons governing the *swayamvara* enjoin that, if a visitor is killed, he who kills him forfeits his life.'

"The canons of the *swayamvara*!" exclaimed Jarasandha.

'Yes, the ancient canons upheld by Dharma. The *swayamavara* is a sacred ceremony.'

'I am sick of your Arya canons.'

"Then why do you attend an Arya *swayamvara*?" asked Krishna.

'Go away, go away', shouted Jarasandha impatiently, as he felt the force of what Krishna was saying. 'Don't meddle in my affairs'.

'I am going', Krishna made as if to rise from his seat.

'But I warn you again: If you try to kidnap Draupadi, wherever you are, your head shall fall.'

'I can cut off your head like this!' said Jarasandha and snapped his fingers.

'Try it if you dare,' challenged Krishna with a laugh.

'Don't try to challenge me, young man. The Magadhan warriors know their business,' Jarasandha boasted. But, bursting with wild, murderous rage though he was, he realized the truth of what Krishna was saying.

A shiver went through him. If he touched a hair of Krishna's head now, it would have a terrible impact upon the assembled kings. The Yadavas, the Panchalas, the Viratas, and even the Kurus, would combine to wipe out the Magadhans before sunset the next day. Whenever you stepped into an Arya ceremonial occasion you ceased to be your own master.

'You know that you cannot kill me tonight and you cannot kidnap Draupadi tomorrow', said Krishna and paused.

Jarasandha continued to glare at Krishna in silence, the wicked glint of an angry tiger in his eyes.

Krishna then quietly added: 'The only time that you could kidnap her would be when, surrounded by princesses, she ceremoniously goes from the *Yajna shala* to the *mandap*. At that time, I will be waiting for you on the main road. If you so much as try to divert the course of your chariot from the straight road to the *mandap*—to go to Magadha, for instance—my *Sudarshana* will sever your head from your body.'

Krishna continued to speak with the voice of Fate. 'The only other time you could make an attempt to kidnap Draupadi would be if no one wins the test or the winner carries away the bride and there is an uproar among the Princes. I will be there in the gallery of the kings then.'

'What is your object in telling me all this?'

demanded Jarasandha impatiently. He could see that this young man had anticipated all his possible moves.

'Don't forget that the Aryadharma prescribes that a man who abducts a woman has to pay the penalty of death', Krishna pointed out.

'You kidnaped Rukmini, didn't you?' Jarasandha counted.

'But I was not guilty of *streesangrahana*—the abduction of a woman. She came to me of her own choice,' replied Krishna. 'I want to warn you, mighty son of Brihadratha. It would be very dangerous for you or the princes of Magadha to join in the uproar'.

'I will not be threatened', shouted Jarasandha, almost choking with the self-restraint he had imposed upon himself so as not to lay hands on his visitor.

'I am uttering no threats', replied Krishna, quietly, 'I am only telling you what will happen if you try to kidnap Draupadi. I have only one other word of advice to give. Acharya Sandipani has prescribed a stiff—a very stiff—archery test. None of your princes can win it. Perhaps you might. At any rate, you may be tempted to try. But, would it look proper—consider carefully—if you at your age and in your position, enter the lists and win a young bride—you, with several sons and numerous grandsons? Think of it. And if you fail, you will be the laughing-stock of the assembly and of the crowds, and your prestige as an emperor will have gone. You may call yourself *Chakravarti* thereafter, if you like, but no king would care to keep your company.'

Jarasandha was an extremely shrewd person. He could visualize the exact situation in which he would land himself if he attempted to enter the test.

Krishna smiled. 'Perhaps you will see the wisdom of expressing your admiration for the test, bless the bride and withdraw. If you do not like my advice, enter the contest and risk the consequences. But don't say that I did not warn you.'

Jarasandha's head began to swim. He would have liked to give vent to the fury which he had suppressed so far and strangle this young man with his bare hands. But he saw that what Krishna was telling him was the plain truth. He could not do anything to hurt his visitor now, nor face the world if he failed to pass the test. He was sick of these canons of Arya conduct. Every time he tried to force his way into the Arya world, something or other prevented him from carrying out his wishes.

For a time there was silence between the two. Krishna got up from his seat, flung his scarf on his shoulder and said: 'Mighty son of Brihadratha, my mission is fulfilled. Do you want to know why I undertook it?'

Jarasandha did not reply. He was staring at his visitor without seeing him. His mind was obsessed with the realisation that again, when face to face with this man, he had failed.

'I have pledged myself to see that the *swayamvara* succeeds,' said Krishna. 'I shall not allow anyone to disrupt it. Think over what I have said.'

Without waiting for a reply, Krishna stepped out of the tent and left the camp, with a hundred Magadhan warriors waiting in vain for an order to smash the Yadava's head. The guards made way for him as, taking Uddhava's hand, he walked away.

Jarasandha looked at the opening of the tent through which Krishna had passed. He was baffled. He could not understand at all how, with so much power in his hands, he had not been able to crush this young man. Every time he was manoeuvered into a position in which neither his anger nor his power prevailed. Oh, how he would have liked to choke the life out of this Yadava upstart! But he could neither crush him, nor break through the rigid canons of Arya conduct.

The next moment the Emperor placed his hand over his eyes. His head began to swim. His limbs were rigid. His mouth sagged open and he breathed in quick, short gasps. His mind was clouded in darkness. In that darkness appeared, again, the naked ascetic with the garland of skulls—the Mighty Rudra, the God of Destruction. And he heard the words which he had heard before: 'You will never conquer Aryavarta till you offer the sacrifice of a hundred kings' heads.'

45

'YOUR PLEDGE SHALL BE FULFILLED'

*F*or some time, Krishna and Uddhava walked silently through the sleeping camps. The moon was sailing towards the western horizon. Scorpio rose in the heavens in radiant, majesty.

'Govinda, did you tame the Magadhan?' asked Uddhava hesitatingly. 'I was dying of impatience.'

'I don't think he will venture to kidnap Draupadi,' replied Krishna. 'But that leads us nowhere, Uddhava. There is no trace of our cousins yet.'

'None whatsoever. The Five Brothers do not seem to have arrived in Kampilya,' said Uddhava. 'Anyway, Siguri Naga has no news so far,'

'I am afraid they are not likely to be present tomorrow morning at the *swayamvara*. Then we will have failed, Uddhava,' said Krishna in a low voice.

'What will happen then?' asked Uddhava.

'In all likelihood, Duryodhana will win the contest; he is no mean archer. Satyaki may not, confident though he is,' Krishna answered. 'But Draupadi is determined not to marry Duryodhana even if he is the only winner—

and rightly. She might put an end to her life. Drupada also might break his pledge. That would mean an outburst of bitter fighting among the kings.' He paused and then spoke as if he was thinking aloud. 'If Duryodhana is the winner, the only way out would be for me to enter the contest and win it. But then....' He hesitated.

'Perhaps Duryodhana will not win, nor any one else,' Uddhava said hopefully.

'Then Krishnaa will be free to choose whomsoever she pleases.'

'That is quite likely. Shvetaketu told me that the test is very, very difficult,' said Uddhava.

'But don't forget that barring Karna and Arjuna, Duryodhana is the best archer among the assembled princes. I leave out Satyaki, you and myself,' said Krishna.

'I wish you had not taken a pledge not to enter the contest yourself, Govinda.'

'Uddhava, if I were to enter the lists, I would have failed in my mission,' said Krishna slowly, weighing every word. 'I have tried to build an empire of Dharma on the foundation of this *swayamvara*. If it ends in personal gain, the empire will be in the dust.'

'Let us not think of difficulties, Govinda. Let us go to Maniman's camp. Siguri Naga may have brought some news.'

'Yes, go and find out whether he has brought any news. I will wait for you,' said Krishna.

Satyaki, who was the only one in the camp who was, besides Uddhava, in the secret of his friend's visit to Jarasandha, was awaiting Krishna's return with an anxious heart. When Krishna reached their camp, he was standing at the opening of the tent which he occupied with Krishna and Uddhava, counting every moment with gloomy forebodings.

He had been afraid that Jarasandha would not miss the opportunity of wreaking vengeance on Krishna. He had, therefore, opposed the whole idea of Krishna meeting the *Chakravarti* alone, but had been firmly overruled.

Seeing Krishna returning safe, he could not restrain his relief and threw himself into his friend's arms.

'What was the outcome?' he asked in a whisper.

'I am sure he will not make an attempt to kidnap Draupadi,' replied Krishna tersely, as he handed over his diadem and sword to Satyaki, who returned them to their appropriate places.

The two of them sat down, each on his own bed. Krishna was lost in thought. The other respected his mood and was watchfully silent.

Then Krishna spoke. 'Satyaki, go to sleep. You will require all your strength in the morning. All depends upon your winning the test.'

'Oh, I am full of strength. And now that you have scored a triumph over that Magadhan, I am stronger than ever I was,' said Satyaki enthusiastically.

'Go to sleep, Satyaki. You need not wait for Uddhava,' Krishna urged. 'I shall wait for him.'

Satyaki laid himself down on his bed, thinking of his friend and that fine beauty in Dwaraka who had sworn to make him her husband. With a happy smile hovering on his lips, he closed his eyes in sleep.

When Krishna saw that Satyaki was sound asleep, he went out of the tent to await Uddhava's return.

Alone, in that vast silence, a doubt assailed him: Was he really born to establish Dharma?—Or was it all an accident that things had turned out as he had wished so far? In contriving this vast and complicated *swayamvara* he had risked all and, if he was unsuccessful, he would lose everything. And the Five Brothers—after all the trouble he had taken—would have equally lost all.

After some time, Uddhava returned and shook his head as he spoke in a whisper. 'Siguri has not been able to find the Five Brothers.'

Krishna looked at Uddhava. 'That makes things very difficult for us, Uddhava.'

Looking anxiously at Krishna, Uddhava put an affectionate hand on his shoulder and said: 'Krishna, you have always been good to me. Will you grant me a favour?'

'A favour, Uddhava! Have I ever refused you anything?'

'Then I want your permission to enter the test tomorrow if Satyaki fails,' said Uddhava.

'You! Would you care to marry Draupadi? You are softhearted and have no ambition to enter into powerful alliances. You would be unhappy with her. And you would break the hearts of the twins whom you love.'

'That is not the point, Krishna,' said Uddhava with the ring of earnest appeal in his voice. 'You have promised that she shall not marry Duryodhana. You will not enter the test yourself. Satyaki may not win. If he does not, let me enter the contest. I beseech you. Please don't say "no".'

Krishna put an arm affectionately around Uddhava's shoulders. 'Uddhava, how many times will you sacrifice yourself to maintain my pledge?'

'Krishna, you know that I live only to make your plighted words come true. Will you permit me to contest?' entreated Uddhava.

'Yes, if you want to. But I am not happy over it.' Then a doubt struck Krishna. 'What if both you and Satyaki fail and Duryodhana wins?'

'Even then I will see that Duryodhana does not win Draupadi,' said Uddhava in a firm voice, his face looking inspired even in the dimming moonlight.

'How?' Krishna turned to Uddhava, expecting a new solution.

'Don't say "no". Give me your blessing that is all,' replied Uddhava evasively.

'But what is your plan?' Krishna persisted.

'If Duryodhna wins and there is no chance of my winning, I know what to do,' said Uddhava, trying to sound casual.

'What will you do?' asked Krishna, his heart missing a beat as he sensed the grim earnestness behind Uddhava's words.

'I have seen the bow. It is heavy enough to crush me to death, if I so wish. If I am crushed,' said Uddhava, again trying to sound light-hearted, 'the *swayamvara* will have been defiled. It will have to be abandoned.'

'Uddhava, Uddhava!' Krishna's voice was choked with emotion. 'Why must you sacrifice yourself to redeem my pledge?'

'God's words must be fulfilled, Govinda. If you are a god, we will all live; if you are not, we are better dead— at least I would prefer to be,' replied Uddhava, his heart uplifted in surrender.

Krishna pressed Uddhava to his heart. His eyes were gleaming with tears.

46

DRAUPADI GOES TO THE
SWAYAMVARA MANDAP

$\mathcal{S}$ometime before the break of dawn, Draupadi woke up. It was the eleventh day of bright half of the month of Paush, the day of the *swayamvara*. For a long time the astrologers of Panchala had studied the position of the presiding planets and, after lavishly propitiating them, found that it was going to be the happiest day in her life.

Today, of all days, she thought, her fate and the fate of her family, and perhaps the fate of empires, was going to be decided, and she was to be the architect of this fate.

As she entered the waters of the Ganga for her early morning bathe in the company of her friends, a song was in her heart. It was the song of victory, lifting her towards a dazzling future. Even the sky and the earth echoed the song, she felt, for the wintry breeze, gentle and refreshing brought to her the gay notes of the boatmen's song as they sailed their crafts on the river.

As she dived into the chill waters of the Ganga, she

felt Krishna coming to her—as he had done in actual life the day before—and asking: 'Krishnaa, have you faith in me?' Yes, yes, she had complete faith in him, He had shown her the way to found an empire of Dharma! What a delicious feeling of happiness the thought created in her! 'I shall abide by your wishes,' she murmured. She could contain the exultation she felt, it overflowed.

After the morning bathe, she was given a ceremonial bath. Sanctified water mixed with milk and curds was poured over her by the officiating priests with appropriate Vedic chants. A fragrant paste of sandalwood, saffron and musk was rubbed over her body, as her friends sang auspicious songs.

This was the sixteenth day of the ceremonials. In spite of the strain of vigils, fasts and rituals, and the uncertainties of the situation as it changed from day to day, she felt as if she was in the high heavens. Men and things appeared to her merely to be forming a joyous pattern on some distant planet.

Only one man, Krishna, was real. He was by her side, buoying her up with faith which never wavered.

The final touches were given to her dress of gold cloth. She was decorated with rings, armlets and a girdle studded with gems. Flowers were woven into her hair. A coronet, blazing with diamonds and rubies, was placed on her head, a garland of sweet-smelling flowers on her neck.

Attended by priests and princesses, she went to the *Yajna shala.* In the shrine, the sacred fire had been burning in honour of her guardian deity, Agni, the Fire God, since the day Dhrishtadyumna and she were born.

She went round the sacred fire, her hands joined, her eyes downcast in humility, praying for the success of the great venture she was embarking on. Yes, it was a great venture. It might involve the rise and fall of kings. To that end she was prepared to welcome any trial, any suffering, any torture.

As she came down the steps of the *Yajna shala*, she found her favourite cow, Kshiraa, her dearest friend, waiting for her. She had fed her every day and milked her with her own hands. She smiled at the cow as she looked at her with mute affection.

'Yes, dear Kshiraa. I will never part with you,' she whispered to the cow. 'You are coming with me to my husband's house. Wherever my home is, there you shall live. You will be a part of me.' Kshiraa raised her head and received a loving hug.

Led by the priests and accompanied by fifty maidens singing auspicious songs, she proceeded along a path strewn with flowers on her way to the spacious arena, the *mandap*.

The procession, preceded by drummers, fife players and blowers of conch and horn, was joined by Dhrishtadyumna, Satyajit and Shikhandin. Acharya Shvetaketu, the principal disciple of Guru Sandipani and a teacher of the martial art, also joined them. To the surprise of many onlookers, a spirited horse, ready saddled, carrying arms, accompanied the procession. Shvetaketu had prepared himself for every contingency.

As she proceeded on her way to the *mandap*, Draupadi apprehensively looked around, but was relieved to find that no Magadhan chariot warrior was near the route. She smiled. Krishna had kept his promise. Nobody would kidnap her.

As she entered the huge arena, a murmur as of a mighty sea arose from the vast multitude which was waiting for the bride. Necks were craned; eyes were fastened on her. Till yesterday she had trembled at the prospect of facing this great assembly which had come to witness her *swayamvara*. Now it was a symbol of her triumph, no, the triumph of Dharma to which she was dedicated.

When she entered the arena, she saw her father sitting on his throne in a happy mood. The decision she had taken the day before had restored his determination. She prostrated herself before him; he gave her his blessing. Satyajit and Shikhandin, armed with bows and arrows, went and stood on either side of the throne.

In front of the throne was a large *vedi*, sacrificial pit, in which the God Agni had been placed. Around it were seated venerable Brahmans, headed by the old *rishis* Yaja and Upayaja. Her heart was full of gratitude for her guardian God, Agni. He was giving her a chance to affect the fortunes of Aryavarta.

In the middle, a little further down the *mandap*, was a pool of water in which, she could see, the target was fixed. She looked around and saw, as if in a dream, thrones arranged in a semi-circular gallery for the royal visitors.

She had never seen such magnificence before. Gold glittered everywhere. The kings were resplendent in their diadems, necklaces and girdles of gold coruscating with emeralds and rubies. Most of them wore scarfs of gold thread and had with them swords, maces or bows encrusted with gold—all reflecting the rays of the morning sun. Their eyes were fixed on her—some out of curiosity, others out of avidity, all in wonder.

She recognised some of the royal guests, who had been pointed out to her in the last few days. Shakuni's corpulence and perpetual unctuous smile were unmistakable. Duryodhana could easily be recognized; he sat next to his uncle, surrounded by his brothers— handsome, well-built, a magnificent golden diadem, studded with scintillating gems, on his head. Next to him sat Aswatthama, eyeing her with hawk-like intensity. There was no mistaking the charioteer's son, Karna; he sat next to Drona's son, handsome like a god, graceful in every limb. Oh, if only he had been born a Kshatriya!

She could identify some other kings too—Virata, Shalya of Madra, and Shishupala of Chedi.

She could easily tell the Emperor of Magadha. He sat surrounded by his court—massive of build, with bold eyes and a face full of self-conscious dignity. On his head was a huge crown of gold, a single ruby as large as an egg gleaming from it like the third fiery eye of Lord Shiva. His hair and beard, white as snow, were glossy with oil. A tiger-skin was folded across his broad chest. He was girded with a belt embossed with gems. Each of his arms was encircled with a massive bracelet of wrought gold. He bore no weapons. His heavy mace was held by a bearer who stood behind him.

Draupadi's eyes went in search of Govinda. There he sat in the enclosure occupied by the Yadavas. Next to him was a giant of a man; it must be Balarama. He had a miniature ploughshare in his hand. He was laughing—evidently at his own witty remarks.

Krishna was calm, detached and smiling, distinctive in his comparative simplicity. He wore a gemless diadem with a peacock feather and a single necklace, and glowed with charm and dignity, having none of the ostentatious magnificence which the other kings displayed. His eyes met hers. They had a message for her: 'Krishnaa, it is your duty to go through with the *swayamvara* keeping a stout heart.' Her eyes replied to the message: 'Yes, I will go through with it. I know you will never desert me, whatever happens.'

Then she turned to the semi-circular gallery to the right of her father's throne. On wooden planks were seated venerable *rishis* covered with deer skins and surrounded by their pupils; holy men, besmeared with ashes; Brahmans famed throughout Aryavarta for their learning and austerity.

At the far end, between the ends of the two semi-circular galleries, facing the *vedi*, was a huge crowd of men impatient to see the *swayamvara*.

Draupadi stepped towards the sacred fire and took

her appointed seat. *Mantras* were chanted. Oblations were offered. Sacred grains of rice were showered on her.

When the Fire God was propitiated, she was led by Dhrishtadyumna to their father, who again gave her his blessing. Then they walked up to the artificially-constructed pool of water. A long pole had been fixed in the centre, on the top of which a fish, fastened to a circular frame, was revolving rapidly, Guru Sandipani, old, lean and muscular, as the master of the contests, stood by its side.

Near the pool, on a mat of sacred grass, lay a bow, huge, tough and stout, adorned with flowers, with its gold-encrusted shaft glittering in the sun. A string of well-twisted catgut, firmly tied to its lower end, lay near it coiled like a long serpent. By its side was placed a quiver with five arrows.

After she had offered worship to the bow in the way Guru Sandipani prescribed, Drupadi went back to her brother who was standing near the *vedi*. The ceremonies were over. The sun had now risen. The crowd of kings looked like an assembly of gods.

Conchs and horns were blown. Drums beat a joyous rhythm. The bards sang songs of valour. Drupada, with a keen eye, looked at the kings as if trying to find out who would win his daughter.

The conchs, horns and drums were hushed. Dhrishtadyumna stepped up to the pool. 'Venerable Brahmans, holy ascetics, noble kings, valorous princes, the *swayamvara* will now be held,' he announced in a loud voice which rang throughout the *mandap*. 'My sister, Krishnaa, will wed the valiant bowman of pure birth and undefiled honour, who, with one of the five arrows, hits the eyes of whirling fish, after taking aim only at its reflection in the waters of the pool. This is the pledge of the noblest of Kings, Yajnasena Drupada, the mighty lord of Panchala.'

The announcement was greeted by a flourish of conchs and beating of drums. And by cries of *'sadhu, sadhu'* from the assembly.

The old *rishi* Yaja walked up to Draupadi with unsteady feet, bringing a golden cup full of *kumkum,* the auspicious powder. He dipped his fingers in the cup and applied it to her forehead, and placed a garland on her neck. She was now the bride. She felt more like a goddess whom the world had come to worship.

Draupadi's initiation as the bride was signalised again by the blare of conchs and beating of drums. When the final notes faded in the air, there were moments of complete silence—only interrupted by the loud breathing of many men in hope, despair, anxiety, curiosity. Who would pass the test, everyone asked himself.

She saw the kings looking at each other in mute enquiry as to who would make the first attempt. The smoke from the sacred fire blurred her vision. Through it, she tried to see the kings and was startled....

All the kings were standing defiantly, impatient to destroy each other, with arms upraised in wrath, a murderous light in their eyes. It was a terrifying scene.

A mighty river of blood was flowing in swirling waves from the heavens, enveloping them all, carrying them into the leaping flames of the sacrificial pit. In the centre of this eddying flood was Krishna, dominating all. His right hand was whirling his discus, *Sudarshana Chakra,* his eyes flashing, his lips set firm. Frightened, she would have liked to rush to him for protection, but he was standing as the presiding god of storms, remote and irresistible.

A shattering thought rose in her mind: Was she the cause of this blood-thirstiness? However, it did not matter. He was there by her side—like endless all-consuming time.

She rubbed her eyes again. The vision vanished. The *mandap* appeared as it was. The kings were seated where they had been. Krishna sat in their midst, looking at her with his heartening smile. The river of blood was nothing but the smoke spiralling from the sacred fire.

She looked at the kings' gallery carefully. Who would have the courage to make the first attempt? She had not long to wait.

Shishupala of Chedi stood up proudly and stepped down to the arena, good-looking, sturdy and of medium height. He was twirling his moustache. Immediately the bards announced his name and the name of his kingdom, recounted his ancestry, extolled his valour and virtues. She had heard all about him. He was the son of Damaghosha, the King of Chedi, and Queen Shrutashrava, sister of Krishna's father—a dauntless warrior, a pupil of Parashurama, the master of the martial art.

Just as he came down from the gallery, she could see that he shot a venomous glance at Krishna. It was a look of challenge, for Krishna had kidnapped his promised bride Rukmini at Kundinapura on the very day of her *swayamvara*.[1]

With supreme self-confidence, Shishupala walked up to her father Drupada, joined hands in salutation, strode towards the pool, looked at the revolving fish overhead, bent down and lifted the bow, though with some difficulty.

In his right hand, he held the free end of the string; with the left, he tried to bend the shaft of the bow to fasten it. With his lips set firmly, he brought the end of the shaft and the string together. But before he could tie the string, the shaft straightened with a rebellious jerk and escaped his grip. He tottered, and narrowly escaped falling on the ground.

Irrepressible laughter issued from the assembly. Shishupala turned to the assembly with a frown and walked back to his seat, without looking at the kings, most of whom enjoyed his discomfiture.

Draupadi could not help smiling to herself. The test was indeed stiff. One of the most redoubtable bowmen had failed to string the bow.

47

THE ALL TOO FAMILIAR LAUGHTER

After the interview which Jarasandha had had with Krishna the night before, he had lost all interest in the *swayamvara*. In bitter humiliation he had given up the idea of kidnapping Draupadi. Surprise was the essence of such a bold venture, but every move of his had been anticipated by the crafty cowherd.

Krishna was also right about his (Jarasandha's) entering the contest himself. At his age, if he won it, all the kings would treat him with scorn for coveting a young princess and would call him a senile fool. If he failed in the test, he would be the laughing-stock of the world.

As one king after another stepped forward to the pool, failed to lift the bow or to string it, and returned to his seat, the assembly, and in particular the Magadhan princes, looked at the Emperor with great expectation. He had come to win the Princess for his grandson and, now that Meghasandhi was out of the contest, something wonderful was expected of him.

He had to find a dignified way out of this impossible situation, he felt. He also noticed that Krishna, the architect of his misfortune, was waiting for an ignominious end to his matrimonial endeavour.

With a broad fatherly smile—he could assume such

smiles at will—he rose from his seat, pulled himself to his full height, and looked at the assembly. Thunderous applause went up from the assembly as he came down the steps of the gallery of the kings.

Slowly, with majestic tread, he walked towards the pool. He waited till the bards finished chanting his praise. Then he went up to king Drupada, joined hands in a formal salutation, made an effort to smile happily, stepped forward to the pool, glanced at the bow and slowly fixed his gaze on the revolving fish. Then he turned to Guru Sandipani, the master of the contest. 'Gurudeva, you have prescribed a wonderful test, fit for heroes,' he said and laughed.

Guru Sandipani extended his hands in blessing. 'May you live for a hundred years! Will the valorous *Chakravarti* enter the contest?'

Jarasandha, a seasoned master of moods and attitudes, any one of which he could adopt at his convenience, laughed again, this time heartily.

'I would certainly enter the contest,' he said in a clear voice, loud enough to be heard by the assembly. 'But how can I wed Draupadi? She is young enough to be my granddaughter. I must give a chance to younger men,' he added. The assembly, with appreciative laughter, heartily gave assent by shouting 'sadhu, sadhu.'

Jarasandha turned to Draupadi with the kindly air of a grandfather. 'Noble Princess may you win a bright young bowman as your husband! That is my blessing. I came here only to give it.' Then, after pausing a few moments for dramatic effect, he continued, 'I wish my grandson excelled in archery as he does in mace-combat. I would then have had the privilege of having you as my daughter-in-law. Having blessed you, my child, I will now leave for Girivraja.'

With a broad smile, he went back to the kings' gallery. He could see that there was wide appreciation of what he had done, for the cries of 'sadhu, sadhu,' reverberated for a long time.

When he approached his seat, he threw a challenging glance at Krishna, as if to indicate that he had come out unscathed from the difficulties created for him. Krishna smiled back in seeming detachment.

'Sahadeva,' shouted Jarasandha, 'it is very late as it is. We must start for Girivraja.' So saying he offered distant salutation to King Drupada and the assembled kings and left the arena to the blare of conchs accompanied by the Magadhan princes.

When Krishna had taken his seat in the gallery of kings, he had every reason to be gratified. With a friendly smile, he had responded to the respectful salutions of the kings, princes and learned Brahmans, as well as of the crowds. As he did so, shouts of 'Jaya Krishna Vaasudeva' had rent the air. Every one had felt that he was the central figure in the swayamvara and had, with a creator's touch, called this glittering world into being.

He now swept a glance over the assembly with an eagle eye. Yes, the swayamvara was a grand affair. Drupada presided over it like a Chakravarti. The occasion was even more impressive than a rajasooya sacrifice.[1] Only one obstacle was still to be overcome: Duryodhana. One hope remained unfulfilled; the Five Brothers had not arrived.

As he surveyed the crowd of kings, Brahmans and ordinary people, his eyes were arrested by what he saw in the Brahmans' enclosure opposite. Suddenly his heart bounded with joy. There they were! No mistaking it. In the midst of the Brahmans, the Five Brothers were seated, garbed as anchorites, in deerskins, their hair tied in matted locks, their bodies smeared with ashes. He had won.

He turned to his brother Balarama. 'Brother, the Five Brothers are alive.'

'How do you know?' asked Big Brother sceptically.

'Look at the Brahmans' enclosure. They are there. That giant can be no other than Bhima. Next to him is Yudhishthira. That handsome anchorite is Arjuna. The twins are seated behind them.'

The Big Brother rubbed his eyes, looked at the enclosure in which the Brahmans sat, recognised the Five Brothers in spite of their disguise, and smiled at his younger brother, slapping him happily on his back. 'You cunning fellow, it is all your doing, I know,' he whispered.

Quivering with impatience, Satyaki was awaiting Krishna's permission to enter the contest. He leaned over from his seat which was just behind Krishna's and asked: 'Lord, tell me when I should enter the lists.'

Krishna pressed his hand. 'Don't be impatient, Satyaki. I will tell you when the time comes,' he replied, and whispered in the ears of Uddhava who was also sitting behind him: 'No Yadava warrior must enter the contest till I give the word.'

'As Govinda pleases,' said Uddhava.

Duryodhana was filled with exultation. He was sure of winning Draupadi. He knew his own strength and skill. A little more time and he would hit the target. Sitting in the gallery, he had estimated the effort which would be required to string the bow and send a flying arrow right into the eye of the revolving fish. He could not fail.

Aswatthama had cleared up the misunderstanding with Drupada the night before last. The last hurdle had been crossed. The crowd also had received him well.

Pictures, stowed away in his memory, rose to the surface without relevance, and vanished.... He was anointed the *Yuvaraja* of the Kuru empire......The Five Brothers were burnt to death at Varanavata......Drona's efforts at dominating him had failed. Now the Princess of Panchala would be his wife. With Draupadi by his side, he would have resounding victories, outdoing his great ancestor *Chakravarti* Bharata.

Yet this feeling of supreme self-confidence was not complete. His whole reason insisted on telling him that he was going to win. Yet a foreboding, faint but insistent, continued to gnaw at the back of his mind: Would some stroke of ill-luck befall him? He brushed it aside. He was sure to win.

There was a lull after Jarasandha and his feudatories left the arena. Duryodhana, found that now all eyes were turned to him. The time had come. He slowly handed over his mace and sword to Duhshasana, his younger brother, rose from his seat, threw a friendly smile at the kings and stepped down from the gallery, his head held high. The bards sang his praise. He heard the achievements of his noble forbears with just pride. His handsome face was flushed with joy.

Like a king among men, he walked up to King Drupada and saluted him with joined hands. He was a little surprised to see a deep furrow on Drupada's brow and a determined look in his eyes.

He walked up to the pool, received the blessing of Guru Sandipani, stood for a moment and paid silent homage to the guardian deity of the Kurus. He shot a flying, admiring glance at Draupadi. He saw her lips trembling; possibly she was afraid of his not succeeding, he thought.

For a moment he looked at the bow, at the string and at the revolving fish and its reflection in the pool, and pulled himself erect. He looked at the assembly with an air of triumph. He would show the world what Duryodhana was capable of.

He lifted the shaft of the bow in his left hand, and let it slip till he held it by its upper end. Straining every muscle, he bent the shaft. His right hand began tying the string with practised ease.

A deep silence prevailed in the assembly. All eyes were fixed on him. A tingling glow of coming triumph was in his veins.

Suddenly a loud laugh cut the deep, expectant silence as if with a sword. His mind felt a shock. The laugh had a familiar ring, evoking memories as it echoed down the corridors of his mind. He had heard it all to often—insulting, challenging, humiliating—in his boyhood, adolescence and youth. It could issue only from one throat—his cousin Bhima's. Something seemed to snap at the back of his mind.

Bhima's laughter! But it could not be. He had been burnt to death under the cinders of the mansion at Varanavata. His funeral obsequies had been performed. His ashes had been scattered in the waters of the Ganga.

A shiver passed through Duryodhana's body. 'The Five Brothers are alive! They are here!' ran an under-current of his thought. With the Five Brothers alive, dire consequences would follow. For a split second, they flashed across his mind in dreamlike sequence.

With a supreme effort, he took his mind off these ghastly prospects and concentrated it on stringing the bow. What had seemed so easy a moment before, now looked well-nigh impossible. His hands trembled. His eyes lost their keenness. He was conscious of what was to follow: he was going to fail.

No, he could not fail—could not afford to fail. He must win the contest, whatever it cost. But the bow was no longer an obedient instrument. The string was rebellious.

He clenched his teeth and made a supreme effort to string the bow....

......The Five Brothers would be given a welcome in Hastinapura..... Old Bhishma would reinstate Yudhishthira as the *Yuvaraja*.......

He tried to shake off the thoughts which came tumbling in, one after the other. His nerves were on edge. His fingers had lost their cunning.

The end of the shaft escaped his grip. He tried to recapture it and failed. The shaft straightened with a terrific jerk.

The toe of his left foot, resting on the lower end of the shaft, lost its hold. He was thrown off his balance. He tottered.

He grimly steadied himself, maddened by the jeers of the assembly, which, like the roaring waves of the stormy sea, seemed to be pulling him down to his doom.

He bent down again, took the shaft in his right hand, shifted it back to his left and began to string the bow. The sound of jeers and laughter continued to swell. His fingers were now nerveless.

The shaft would not bend. The greater the effort the weaker he grew. The shaft escaped his hand once more and fell to the ground, bringing him down with it.

Loud laughter, issuing from a thousand throats, assailed his ears. He grew purple in the face. A clear, roaring voice came from the enclosure of the Brahmans: 'What can a blind man's son do?' He had heard the same taunt again and again since his boyhood. He stood up, blinded by rage, and began walking back to his seat. The words 'I have failed' rang in his ears.

For the first time in many years, Drupada smiled happily.

Krishna looked on, the smile on his face unchanged.

Draupadi, transported with joy, also had a smile on her face. But the smile froze as she looked at Duryodhana. His face, painfully distorted and pitiful, was turned to her. It was appalling, the face of a mad man full of murderous intent—a face which was to haunt her till the end of her life.

48

'VAASUDEVA, YOU HAVE KEPT YOUR PROMISE'

*W*hen the Five Brothers, in the guise of anchorites, started for the *swayamvara mandap* from the potter's house where they had been living in Kampilya, Arjuna, the third of the Brothers, felt the stirrings of a new life of glorious adventure.

Now, he felt, was the time to realize his dream, which he had nursed all the time, of high adventure and joyous experience; of performing exploits rivalling those of his ancestor *Chakravarti* Bharata; of winning a goddess for a bride like his forbear Samvarana, and fulfilling his life in poetry, dance and song.

Though he loved his mother and his brothers and shared their life and thoughts, he had a dream-world of his own in which he lived by himself. The months that they spent in Rakshasavarta had had a depressing effect on him. Whenever he saw Bhima making love to the fibre-topped Hidimbaa, he had felt, sensitive to beauty as he was, like dashing his head against a tree and ending his inglorious existence.

When they left Rakshasavarta, his drooping spirits had revived. They had plenty of adventures on the way to satisfy his longing for enterprise. For instance, he was very happy when he overcame an irate Gandharva, whose amorous sports were interrupted by his presence.

Bhima was very lucky. Adventures met him without his seeking them. At Ekachakra, for instance, he killed a Rakshasa who had extracted a daily tribute of a human being from the people of the town to satisfy his craving for human flesh.

As directed by the Master, they had then gone to the *ashram* of Dhaumya Rishi at Utkochaka Tirtha. Their stay there was a soothing interlude in their long journey through the forest with its thorny paths, crawling snakes, howling wolves, chattering monkeys and sparse meals of wild fruits.

But even the life of the hermitage, with its quiet air, sacred chants and lowing cattle could not lull Arjuna's restlessness. When would he live in palaces, he wondered, with damsels dancing and musicians playing? And when would he have a *Shastra shala*—an armoury—of his own, where he could weave bow-strings which would twang to joyous victories and sharpen arrows of miraculous destructiveness?

Arjuna was glad that Dhaumya agreed to be their preceptor and blessed them on their journey to Kampilya. He felt as if he was going to victory on a battle-field. All the kings of the past had gone on adventures of conquest, had had their own preceptors who had armed them with invulnerability by their blessings.

However, his satisfaction was not unmixed with annoyance. He could not foresee what was going to happen to them at Kampilya. How was Krishna going to usher them into the world of the living? Theirs was a strange lot, he thought—living and yet dead, to be resurrected only when someone gave the signal! Though he loved and admired his cousin Krishna, he could not help feeling that it was a humiliating way of existing.

At Kampilya they lived in a potter's foul-smelling, ramshackle hut. Oh, the misery of it—a congerie of huts surrounded by huge heaps, full of dirty children, braying donkeys, ceaselessly-turning wheels and the acrid smell of dung and urine!

He hated the idea of their attending the *swayamvara* disguised as Brahmans. If he had had his way, he would have intruded into the *swayamvara* on a painted elephant. But Yudhishthira, their Eldest, was quite firm. They were to remain disguised till Krishna gave the signal. That was what the Master had said and that was what they were to do.

Arjuna was annoyed at the way his brothers looked on the situation. Yudhishthira, always patient, never felt humiliated at the plight in which now and again they found themselves. He accepted every situation cheerfully. He considered every such occasion to be a fiery ordeal through which they must necessarily pass to attain to purity in their souls.

Bhima's spirit never wavered or flagged. He could always make a running commentary, hilarious, wry or cynical, on whatever happened, and was always irritatingly cheerful.

He also could see that Nakula was unhappy, but it

was not in his nature to complain. And Sahadeva remained wrapped in silence, oracular in his reply when a question was put to him.

Sometimes Arjuna felt irritated at being enmeshed by the bond of affection which tied him to his mother and brothers. But his urge to break it was invariably short-lived.

How could he break, he argued with himself, the bond of a mother's love—a mother who lived in each one of them and for them all? She was the embodiment of sweetness. Her severest rebuke only took the form of a look of pain. If she ever felt any resentment, it found expression only in tears of affection, which wiped out the very memory of the offence he had committed.

And how could he break with Yudhishthira—so wise and considerate, so solicitous of his well-being? Yudhishthira exercised a tyranny of the Spirit which drove Arjuna to fulfil his expectations. How could he possibly shake off that tyranny?

And he could never break with Bhima either. Bhima looked after each one of them every moment of the day and night, protected them from dangers and rescued them from falling a prey to despair by his ever-bubbling cheerfulness.

And the twins! Arjuna simply could not part with Nakula and Sahadeva. They served him, anticipated every wish of his and made themselves indispensable. Nakula looked upon him with such affection that it was clear that his heart would be broken if he, Arjuna, left him. And Sahadeva, the silent and the wise, was so foresighted that, without him, Arjuna would simply be lost in the labyrinth of life.

Each one of them lived in all, and all lived in each And above all, Arjuna was convinced, they needed him without his irrepressible spirit of enterprise, their life would be flat and stale. Severing the bond would be cutting the artery which carried the blood from the heart of each to them all.

Again and again he came to the same conclusion if he made any headway, it must be made for all. How was he going to do it? This question oppressed him all the time—a question which he did not share with his mother or brothers. He must find an answer to it himself, he decided.

On the way to Kampilya, whenever he was left alone he asked himself: what did he want—glory?—yes; pleasures?—yes; strength and vigour?—yes. What then should he do when he went to the *swayamvara*? Should he treat his cousin Duryodhana and his wily brothers with contempt? Should he contrive to humiliate them when there? Should he earn the plaudits of the kings and warriors of Aryavarta? Yes, he wanted all these things. Everybody had such ambitions. But he was not satisfied with them. He wanted something more which he had missed all his life. He wanted to be himself. Yes, he must be himself. That was the only solution.

Continually thinking over this insoluble problem, Arjuna foundered in indecision. He was angry with himself for having always to depend upon the Master, Vidura and Krishna to provide him with an opportunity to take his proper place in life.

He was full of such thoughts when, early in the morning, he and his brothers reached the *swayamvara* arena. They were now about to 'come to life'. Yes, but how and when? How were they to know how Krishna wanted them to enter life?

As he entered the arena and saw the kings and princes resplendent in their diadems and necklaces and shining arms, his heart was shot through with envy. He should have been among them, the handsomest among them, with bow and arrows, ready to win the Princess. Alas, that lot was denied him.

In the enclosure for Brahmans where they took their seats, an old, loquacious Brahman gave him the names of the kings seated in the royal gallery. He immediately recognised his cousins, the Kuru Princes. Oh, how he would have loved to fight them for having sought to murder him and his brothers!

However, his heart was filled with joy when he saw Balarama, Krishna and Uddhava, entering the arena with the Yadava *atirathis* and taking their seats, in the gallery. How would he, Krishna, bring them to life? Oh, it was so irksome to await the decision of others instead of making one oneself!

There was a fanfare of conchs and a burst of music and drums as the Princess entered the arena, accompanied by her brother Dhrishtadyumna and followed by a few princesses. From the description of her given by the Brahmans when they were on their way to Kampilya, he had expected to see a proud, princess bearing the marks of an ambitious, and hard temperament. Instead he found himself gazing at the dark eyes of the most vital woman that he had ever seen, with high colour in her cheeks. She had warm lips parted in great expectation, large, expressive eyes, long braids of dark hair woven with flowers sweeping down her back, strong white teeth between full red lips, and a finely modelled chin, which added strength to her face and matched its beauty—she was a young woman exulting in life. She bore herself with royal dignity, but without hauteur. The poet in him was stirred to life. Oh, if he could only win her!

Arjuna saw king after king going to the pool and returning discomfited. Many of them were unable even to lift the giant bow. He carefully observed the defective way in which they tried to handle it and wished he could show them the right way. He could have lifted it on the instant, but he had to wait—wait for someone to give the signal, which might not be given after all!

Seeing Duryodhana enter the contest, he felt bitter. Would his cousin carry away the bride whilst he himself, the best archer in Aryavarta, was sitting there unable to do anything? When Duryodhana was vainly struggling with the bow and the string, Brother Bhima could not repress himself. He laughed—a laugh which rang through the arena. Duryodhana failed—failed ignominiously, and became the laughing-stock of the whole audience. Arjuna felt happy. But his happiness was mixed with impatience. He looked at Krishna who sat unmoved like a god, serene and radiant.

When Duryodhana went back to his seat, there was an expectant hush over the assembly. Suddenly there was an outburst of many voices. Karna rose from his seat and stepped down from the gallery. He moved with matchless grace, saluted Drupada, walked up to the pool and swept the assembly with a defiant glance. Arjuna felt a pang, almost of despair. Karna had always been his rival.

Planting his left leg firmly in front, Karna bent down and picked up the bow in his hand with a smile in his eyes. In the breathless silence which followed, he strung the bow with a deft movement of his fingers. Then he lifted it with ease.

Draupadi, standing near Dhrishtadyumna, so far immobile like a statue, came to life, took a step forward and whispered something in his ears. Dhrishtadyumna, with a commanding gesture, stopped Karna from taking aim and came up to the pool.

'King of Anga, you cannot enter the contest,' said Dhrishtadyumna loudly, so that everyone could hear. 'You are a charioteer's son.'

Contemptuous, offensive laughter swept through the assembly. Karna smiled as he lowered the bow, and replied with dignity: 'I know I cannot win the Princess. It would be a *pratiloma* marriage'[1]—a heinous sin. I only wanted to show that the Kurus have friends who could win the test.' He laughed aloud. Unstringing the bow, he placed it carefully on the mat of sacred grass and walked away with dignity, his head held high.

The laughter died down as Aswatthama sprang from his seat. The son of Dronacharya, to whom the people had taken a dislike on his arrival in the city, ran down the steps of the gallery, blessed Drupada with rude impatience and made for the pool. He was angry, very angry. He bent down, lifted the bow, but found it difficult to bend it; gnashed his teeth and made another strenuous effort, straining every nerve; and failed. He threw down the shaft in an outburst of anger. 'It is not a bow; it is not a test,' he hissed. Indignantly he strode back to his seat. The assembly burst into laughter at his fury.

When quiet was restored, expectations ran high. Who would venture now that Shishupala, Virata, Duryodhana and Aswatthama had failed? All eyes were upon the Yadavas.

Arjuna saw Draupadi smiling in triumph and turning her face towards Krishna in mute enquiry. Her eyes, he felt, were waiting for the hero whom she was expecting, but who had not come.

A sudden urge seized him—an urge to seek fulfillment in action, He saw, as if in a flash, that he was stupid, blind, not to have made a decision himself. He must make it—the decision which could bring them all back to life; the decision which would usher him into power and glory; the decision from which there was no turning back.

He stood up. The Brahmans who sat near him, asked him to sit down; he was obstructing their view of the pool. He did not look at them, nor even at his brothers. He did not want to catch their eyes. Lightly he jumped down the steps. He stood and looked around, his handsome face flushed, his eyes flashing.

The assembly was gripped by surprise and annoyance. A young Brahman anchorite to enter the contest! Ridiculous! Grotesque! The kings, all except Balarama, Krishna and Uddhava, snorted or laughed in derision. The Brahmans were shocked. The youngster was making a fool of himself, turning the whole occasion to ridicule.

Yudhishthira himself was surprised. Never before had Arjuna taken a step without his permission. Bhima's large eyes glowed with wild joy; those of Nakula had pride in them; Sahadeva's were inscrutable.

With easy steps, Arjuna walked up to where Drupada sat, extended his right hand in blessing as was customary with Brahmans when saluting a Kshatriya, however highly placed he might be, and asked his permission to enter the contest.

Drupada looked at the anchorite's handsome face, his bright eyes full of assurance, his noble ash-besmeared, his shapely arms full of vigour, his sparse beard. Drupada almost saw in him the great Parashurama, the mighty warrior, as he must have been in his youth. He folded his hands. 'Best of Brahmans, you have my consent, now that you ask for it. But it is not needed. The contest is open to you.'

Balarama could not repress his excitement. Krishna pressed his hand: 'Control yourself, Brother.'

Duryodhana saw the young Brahman and recognised Arjuna. There could be no doubt about it. That insulting laughter, be had been sure, could have issued only from the throat of Bhima; his suspicion was now confirmed. The Five Brothers were alive and were here to win Draupadi. He immediately guessed who was at the bottom of this mischief and, turning his blood-shot eyes on Krishna, whispered to Shakuni; 'Uncle, they are here!'

The unfading smile on Shakuni's lips vanished. He spoke an unutterable word under his breath.

Duhshasana also recognised Arjuna, and, gnashing his teeth, turned to Duryodhana. 'Brother, they are alive. Is this a magic trick?'

'The whole *swayamvara* is a magic trick of the scheming cowherd's,' hissed Duryodhana.

Before the fascinated gaze of the assembly, the young Brahman blessed Draupadi and Dhrishtadyumna by raising his hand as he passed by them, and prostrated himself before Guru Sandipani, who blessed him with words; 'May you be victorious.'

With brisk steps, he walked to the pool, measured the distance to the target with one swift glance and looked at its reflection in the pool.

With a deft twist of his left hand—the young Brahman was left-handed—he caught the shaft of the bow in the middle, lifted it with a graceful movement, transferred it to his right hand, took the string and tied it with expert skill. Nothing mattered to him now. The weapon he loved most was in his hands, and his imagination could see the whirling target even better than his eyes could.

Every one caught his breath. Draupadi had seen the young Brahman and admired the dignity and confidence with which he had walked to the pool. Fascinated by the light shining in his magnetic eyes, she was waiting breathlessly for the outcome, which could not now be long in coming.

He stepped to the pool with a firm step, looked at the target's reflection in the pool, drew the taut catgut string back to his left ear, and, offering mute homage to Guru Dronacharya and to Krishna, shot the arrow.

The assembly gasped. The arrow sped, caught the whirling fish in the eye and cut it away from the revolving disc with neat precision. The fish fell into the pool below with a splash.

Guru Sandipani raised his hand and shouted, 'sadhu.' The whole assembly echoed with 'sadhu, sadhu.' The conchs blared. Drums reverberated. Fifes played. Tremendous excitement followed.

The Brahmans stepped down from their enclosure and rushed towards the winner.

As Arjuna was placing the bow on the sacred grass, Draupadi, her eyes glowing with excitement, came to him bashfully and placed the garland round his neck.

Some kings stood up in the royal gallery, their arms upraised. 'This is an insult,' shouted one. 'The Princess cannot be given to a Brahman. The swayamvara is only for the Kshatriyas,' shouted another.

Taking advantage of this confusion, Shakuni whispered in the ears of Duryodhana who, stunned, sat in his seat, not knowing what to do: 'This is the time to dispose of Arjuna. Let us make a rush.'

King Bhoorishravas, son of Somadatta, who was

sitting next to them, heard the whispered advice, stood up and placed his hands heavily on Duryodhana's shoulders. 'We shall not do anything of the kind. Don't you see that the Yadavas and the Chedis, the cousins of Arjuna, are there?' Not knowing what to do, Duryodhana sat glued to his seat.

Seeing some princes move towards Drupada, Bhima pushed forward, parting the crowd of enthusiastic Brahmans with irresistible strength. With a frightening roar, he uprooted a tree which stood nearby, and, placing it on his shoulders like a mace, stepped forward to arrest the onrush of the angry princes.

Everyone was taken aback. The giant, with flaming eyes, was ready to smash the skull of the first man that dared to come near Drupada, Draupadi or Arjuna.

Arjuna, picked up the bow, slung it on his shoulder and took an arrow from the quiver, preparing to let it fly.

'Arjuna, put back the arrow. Leave it to me.' So saying Bhima, with a broad smile, placed Daupadi's hands in Arjuna's and led them to Drupada.

As the bride and bridegroom prostrated themselves before the King, the crowd, in appreciation of the winner's miraculous deed, enthusiastically shouted, 'sadhu, sadhu.'

Balarama and Krishna, with the Yadava atirathis, made their way through the crowd, accompanied by Virata and other friendly kings.

Arjuna, as he turned round, saw Krishna's smiling eyes. He was holding Draupadi by the hand and he swiftly made her kneel as he himself fell at Krishna's feet, Krishna lifted them both from the ground and folded Arjuna in his embrace.

Then came the surprise of the day. Krishna, disengaging himself from Arjuna's arms, touched the feet of the giant who stood protectively near Arjuna and Draupadi. Bhima was the elder of the two.

The onlookers were amazed at this strange exchange of courtesies and were shocked to see the giant unceremoniously slapping the back of the great Vaasudeva, whom everybody had so far looked upon with such profound awe.

A strange Brahman this, thought Drupada, who fell at Kshatriya Krishna's feet! Still stranger was the conduct of Krishna in embracing the Brahman with the words: 'My blessing Kunti's son', and his falling at the feet of the giant. His eyes were opened wide in full understanding.

These were two of the Five Brothers, the sons of Kunti.

Hurriedly, with the vigour of a young man, Drupada jumped down from the pedestal on which the throne was placed and took Krishna in his arms. 'Vaasudeva, Vaasudeva, you have kept your promise.'

And joyous tears rolled down the cheeks of the gaunt King of Panchala.

∎

49

THE MASTER DECIDES

$\mathscr{T}$he town of Kampilya was in a highly festive mood. It was celebrating the *swayamvara* of Draupadi and her forthcoming marriage with Arjuna, the son of the Emperor Pandu of Hastinapura.

In the camp of the visitors, there were many broken hearts and disappointed ambitions. A few guests were sullen, while many were happy that the Five Brothers were all alive and that one of them had secured the Princess of Panchala. All were busy calculating what shifts in the balance of power in Aryavarta would follow from this alliance.

While the royal palace in Kampilya was decked out for the festivities, there was gloom among the few people who sat closeted in the throne room of King Drupada. It was a strange gathering. King Drupada sat leaning against the throne, with his head in his hands, and despair in his eyes. Dhrishtadyumna sat by his side to the left, frowning. Satyajit and Shikhandin sat behind him, watching anxiously. Next to them sat Draupadi, with a miserable look, with the white-haired Kunti gazing sympathetically at her, and two ladies of the royal family by her side.

To the right of King Drupada sat Krishna, his usual

collected self, smiling with understanding. Next to him sat the Five Brothers—Yudhishthira in placid dignity; Bhima, trying to look serious, though enjoying the gloom which pervaded the room; Arjuna, anxious and unhappy; Nakula, irritated; Sahadeva, detached, as befitted an oracle.

In front of the king sat the Master on a wooden plank covered by the skin of an antelope, with the old Munis, Yaja and Upayaja, to his right, and Dhaumya and Jaimini on the left. Guru Sandipani sat near the old Munis.

On Arjuna winning the contest, Krishna Dwaipayana Veda Vyasa, the Master, who was awaiting the result of the *swayamvaru* at a nearby Tirtha, was immediately invited to come to Kampilya. He had arrived that morning with Dhaumya and Jaimini, and was received at the pier by a crowd of kings, Brahmans and people, headed by King Drupada and Krishna Vaasudeva. The Master came walking from the riverside to the palace through crowds which had come to seek his blessing.

On his arrival at the palace, the Master was invited to join the family conclave on an urgent problem, too terrible to contemplate, which had marred the festive outlook for the royal family and which had been closely guarded from the public so far. The doors of the throne room were closed. Minister Udbodhana standing guard outside to see that no one eavesdropped.

'Noble King, you all seem to be very unhappy. What is the reason?' asked the Master, who could sense that a matter of life and death was oppressing the minds of all. His understanding smile invited frankness. Then, with a broad smile, he added: 'The *swayamvara* has been the greatest triumph of your life, noble Drupada. It is also a crowing achievement of noble Vaasudeva's', and he turned to smile at Krishna. 'Everyone in Kampilya is in a festive mood. The whole of Aryavarta, I am sure, will feel the thrill of joy. Do you need to be so miserable?'

Drupada removed his hands from his brow, looked at Krishna and, with bitter emphasis, said: 'I wish I had not held this *swayamvara*. It has been the greatest misfortune of my life.'

'But what is the matter?' asked the Master persuasively.

'Matter? These Brothers want my Krishnaa to marry all of them. Whoever had heard of wife having five husbands? It is gross *adharma*,' said Drupada, choking with indignation.

'But how did this difficulty arise?' asked the Master, trying to understand the situation.

'It was my doing, luckless as I am,' interrupted Kunti in a tearful voice. 'When Arjuna brought Draupadi to the potter's house where we were living, he said from outside: "Mother, I have brought alms—very valuable alms indeed.' Foolish woman that I am, I thought that it was the usual *bhiksha* which he had brought, and said from inside the house: "My son, divide whatever you have between all your brothers equally." Then, when I saw that it was a wife that he had brought, I was shocked. However, my sons have never allowed my word to remain unfulfilled. It has been a life-long pledge of theirs,' she added and wiped away a tear.

'Now, let me understand the whole position,' said the Master in a very soft and persuasive voice. 'Arjuna won Draupadi in the *swayamvara*, didn't he? She wanted to marry the best archer in Aryavarta. He has now come. Apart from Kunti's word, is there any other difficulty, Arjuna, my son?'

Arjuna looked up and replied in a sad voice: "Venerable Master, I won her as a bride, no doubt. But how can I marry when my elder brothers remain unmarried? It is against the eternal ordinance of *kuladharma*. I could never do it. So I requested the Eldest to accept her.'

'Arjuna, in a way you are right,' said the Master smiling broadly again. 'Why don't you marry Draupadi, Yudhishthira?' he asked, turning to the eldest of the Five Brothers.

'I did not win her at the *swayamvara*. Arjuna won her and she has chosen him as her husband. How can I filch her from my younger brother?' asked Yudhishthira.

'What about Bhima?' asked the Master and turned to Bhima with a smile.

'Even Bhima will not accept her,' said Arjuna.

'Yes, he is already married,' said the Master with loud, jovial laughter, which lightened the gloom in the air.

'He will not marry an Arya wife until the Eldest is married,' interjected Arjuna in an unhappy voice.

'He is right,' said the Master. 'A Rakshasi is a

different matter altogether, isn't she, Bhima?' asked the Master with a chuckle, turning to Bhima.

Bhima laughed aloud, a laugh which fell on the others' ears as inopportune. 'I had to marry the Rakshasi. Mother enjoined me to do it. It was an *apaddharma*—a way dictated by a calamity. If I had not married her, the Rakshasas would have eaten us all up. I assure you,' added Bhima with an irrepressible chuckle, 'I married the Rakshasi as a pious duty to save six lives.' Then he winked at the Master like a mischievous boy and added: 'Not that I was at all fascinated by Hidimbaa.'

The Master laughed outright. 'Don't tell me that, my son,' he said, and, pointing a warning finger, added: 'I have not forgotten the way you stole to her bed in the middle of the night.'

General laughter followed this sally. The Master had worked a miracle. The sense of oppression in the room was lifted.

'Now, tell me, Yudhishthira, what solution do you propose? You are a wise man,' said the Master.

'My Mother's word, though spoken unconsciously, is the only true solution. We all five should marry Draupadi,' said Yudhishthira.

'Great God!' interjected Drupada, with a loud sigh, 'For five men to share my daughter in common is horrible!'

'No, I will never allow my sister to marry five brothers,' said Dhrishtadyumna angrily.

Krishna, with one of his irresistible smiles, intervened. 'Venerable Master, it is a very serious matter.

It involves the prestige of the noble King and the future of Draupadi. The future of the Five Brothers is also in the balance. Calamity lies before us either way. If the solution which Yudhishthira had suggested is accepted, it will mean a stigma on the whole family of Bharata and a setback to the brothers' career. If, on the other hand, Draupadi rejects Yudhishthira's solution, it will be the greatest calamity that can overtake Aryavarta. All that the noble King has worked for and all that I have done during this present year will be in vain. In either way, dharma will be in danger.'

Draupadi, who was shedding tears all the time, broke into sobs. However, she could not help exclaiming: 'Five husbands! Oh, Great God!' She hid her face in her hands, sobbing violently.

'Yudhishthira, what have you to say?' asked the Master.

In his balanced and dignified way, Yudhishthira replied: 'Venerable Master, you know me well. I will not make a suggestion without deliberation. All my life I have tried to speak the truth and to live up to it. I have never allowed sin to enter my mind. And I think the only solution is the one which I have suggested. The Princess of Panchala should be married to all of us.'

'It is *adharma*,' burst out Dhrishtadyumna.

'It is not *adharma*,' quietly contradicted Yudhishthira. 'In the days gone by, Jatilaa, the daughter of Sage Gautama, the foremost among virtuous women, was married to seven brothers who were *rishis*. Also the ten Prachetasa brothers, all righteous and pure men, had one wife between them. So the ancient tradition says. If my suggestion finds favour with the noble King, we will not depart from it.'

'Would the ancient laws of the Aryas ever sanction as Dharma a marriage with five husbands?' asked Dhrishtadyumna, shocked at what Yudhishthira had said.

The Master smiled at Dhrishtadyumna in a disarming manner and turned to Yudhishthira. 'My son, you are very well informed about the ancient traditions of the Aryas. What you say is quite right. According to the ancient laws of the Aryas, brothers can, if circumstances so dictate, marry one wife between them. They do it even now. I have seen it among the Aryas in the hills.' And the Master again smiled broadly. 'Such marriages prove successful if the wife is wise and the husbands considerate.'

'How can a woman be married to more than one brother? How could she then be a *sati* as every Arya noble woman should—a chaste, devoted and dedicated wife who could bring the gods to her feet?' interjected Dhrishtadyumna.

Drupada, bewildered, looked at his son helplessly.

'You are right, Dhrishtadyumna,' said the Master. 'A dedicated wife, a *sati*, is the root from which spring strength and discipline which make life righteous,' continued the Master with an indulgent smile, holding up his right hand with the gesture of a teacher, bringing the tips of the thumb and the forefinger together.

'Then, O Venerable Master, why do you approve the *adharma* which Yudhishthira suggests?' asked Dhrishtadyumna.

'What is *adharma?* We must find it out, noble Prince,' said the Master. 'The divine sages have ordained that the family should revolve around a dedicated wife. If she falls, the family falls with her. Children grow up in unrighteousness. Chaos follows. Men and women begin to live worse than animals—a prey to all-devouring lust. Any disregard of the *kuladharma,* therefore, leads to destruction.'

'Does not the suggestion of Yudhishthira destroy the *kuladharma* altogether?' asked Dhrishtadyumna.

The Master paused for a moment, the others waiting for him to speak. He continued: 'Noble Prince lust, as I said, is an all-devouring fire. It reduces every noble urge to ashes. The animals are saved from it, for the gods have given them instincts to regulate it. Men and women, however, have no such instincts. They can only escape it through the alchemy of the marriage tie. You know what the ancient sages have taught. The seven steps, which the wife takes with her husband around the sacred fire, make man and wife one. They become the bone of each other's bone, the blood of each other's blood, the skin of each other's skin, living in and for the other'.

'But how can one woman married to five husbands perform that alchemy?' asked Drupada.

'Have a little patience, noble King,' said the Master 'Remember, men and women are not perfect. Their weaknesses have to be taken into account. They have to be protected against the temptation to succumb to promiscuous lust. So, the ancient sages have provided *apaddharma,* sanctifying unfamiliar ways of marriage in unforeseen calamities.'

Muni Yaja said: 'That is true, Best of Sages.'

'If the husband dies and the wife cannot cheerfully join him on the funeral pyre, she may feel the need of marrying again,' said the Master. The divine sages, therefore, have laid down that she can marry again and be a *sati,* a dedicated wife, again.'

After a little pause, the Master resumed: 'You know, noble King, that *Niyoga* is all too common in our midst. It is sanctioned by Dharma. By that ritual, a childless widow can seek the company of her deceased husband's brother or a learned Brahman, to beget children. It must not be a matter of lust, but a religious duty.'

'But surely not more than one husband at the same time!' exclaimed Dhrishtadyumna.

'Wait,' said the Master, raising a warning finger. 'In the same way, if a great calamity has to be avoided, a woman can marry more than one brother, say the divine sages, provided her devotion to each of them is equal and her dedication to all the brothers absolute and unreserved.'

'We have got a great calamity facing us, indeed,' said Drupada.

'Noble King, you are right,' said the Master. 'Vaasudeva has put it well. It is a calamity. The Five Brothers have just emerged into life. They have still to win their heritage. They have to face the implacable hostility of Duryodhana and the wiles of Shakuni, and perhaps the whole power of Hastinapura. Can we afford to give up the fruits of the *swayamvara* and try to secure another husband for Draupadi?'

'That is the difficulty, I know,' said Drupada. 'Oh, Master, I don't know what to do. Please guide us. You are the fountainhead of Dharma.'

'Noble King, you are wrong in asking me to find a way. Krishnaa Draupadi will find a way for herself. It is her choice,' said the Master, looking at Draupadi with his parental smile of indulgent affection.

'She will never choose five husbands, I can assure you,' said Dhrishtadyumna.

The Master laughed. 'You are so impatient, my son.'

'How can Draupadi solve the problem when all of us have failed to do it?' asked Dhrishtadyumna.

'Master, please don't put this difficult question to this unfortunate daughter of mine,' said Drupada. 'She has been sufficiently miserable these days. She has been crying all the time.'

'Noble King, you have forgotten that a daughter is a child only in her father's house. The moment she becomes a wife, she develops the power to deal with all problems. You do not know women, as my son Bhima does, for instance. Hidimbaa managed him so well,' said the Master, again introducing an element of lightness.

Bhima could not help smiling broadly, and said with wink: 'Master, how do you know all about women?'

'I know it by having dealt with wicked men like you,' said the Master, again with a hearty laughter. Then he turned to Draupadi. 'My child, don't cry. Don't become helpless. You are a brave young woman.' Then he turned to Drupada and commented: 'Noble Drupada, your daughter is the Goddess Shri.'

'Master, what can I say?' asked Draupadi.

'You alone have the right to decide, Draupadi,' said the Master. Three ways are open to you. I hope these venerable Munis will bear me out,' he turned to Yaja and Upayaja.

'Lord of ascetics, we hear,' said Upayaja.

Everybody waited in respectful silence.

'I will tell you the first way open to you, my child,' said the Master. 'Accept the *swayamvara*, regardless of the difficulties that have arisen. You have selected Arjuna as your husband. He has pledged himself to marry you. If you marry him, you will be happy, I have no doubt. He would be a good, loyal and devoted husband. With you by his side, he would certainly be able to carve out a career for himself. He could live here with your father, or he could go with noble Vaasudeva. Wherever he goes, he would be a good husband, a great warrior and a righteous man.'

The Master paused and then continued: 'But remember, he would have broken the vow that the Five Brothers have observed so far—always to fulfil their mother's wishes. Draupadi, you do not know Kunti.' The Master then turned to Kunti. 'She is the most wonderful mother ever born. She has lived only for her sons. By her love, she has knit the five into one. Departing from her wishes, Arjuna would have broken this oneness. And without it, the Brothers would never be able to meet the wickedness of Duryodhana, as they have done so far. Without it, they will never attain the status of *Chakravartis*—which I am sure they will attain some day, if they remain united.'

After a pause, the Master continued: 'Don't forget that, throughout life, Arjuna would carry wound in his soul that for you—his wife—he had had to be untrue to his mother and brothers. You might be happy with him alone, but your husband's heart would be torn by regrets. Remember, Draupadi, no man, in his heart of hearts, forgives a wife who separates him from his parents.'

Everyone heard the Master attentively. The old Munis, Yaja and Upayaja, nodded their heads in assent, muttering *'sadhu, sadhu'* whenever the Master paused. Draupadi heard the Master, her eyers brimming with tears, suppressing sobs which threatened to burst out every moment.

The Master continued: 'Let us examine the second way that you can take. You never bargained for this calamity. If you, the noble King and your brother feel strongly about it, let us reject Arjuna. It would be a brave decision and a right one. But your father would then have broken his pledge of giving his daughter to the winner of the contest at the *swayamvara;* he would have been put to shame before kings and men. The aim of his life—to triumph over Drona—would have been frustrated. Arjuna—why, all the Five Brothers—rejected by you, would be just cast away from life. They would no longer have the support of Panchala's noble King, your father. They would be easy victims of Duryodhana's enmity. And what would be your lot? You were a divinity at the *swayamvara,* coveted by kings: you would be left a rejected bride whom few would care to win.'

At this, Drupada frowned. Dhrishtadyumna's eyes burnt with smouldering anger. Draupadi was shaken by irrepressible sobs.

'Now, let us look at the third way,' said the Master. 'If you marry the Five Brothers, as Yudhishthira suggests, many people would scandalise you and call you unchaste—and there is no higher disgrace for a woman in the eyes of gods and men. You would be disowned by the princesses of your rank and scorned by your own maids. Wedded to the Five Brothers, you would be tortured day and night by the thoughts: "Do I fail to please one or other of them? Am I partial to one to the exclusion of the others? Am I sharing my favours equally? Do I make them jealous of each other? Do they all feel happy with me?"'

The Master, looking at Draupadi, added with a laugh: 'My child, you don't know how difficult it is to please one husband. Your problem would be to please five.'

'You are right, Master,' said Drupada, impressed by the way the Master explained it. 'My poor Krishnaa will always be unhappy.'

'But look at it this way, Draupadi,' said the Master. 'You will get Kunti as a mother for you—and no more loving mother was ever born. You will have as husbands, the Five Brothers—loving and considerate—united in will and deed. Their strength will have been cemented by your undivided devotion. They will then be strong enough to withstand the malice of Duryodhana and the wiles of Shakuni. They will either rule the

Kurus or establish an empire for themselves. And I assure you, my dear child, if they remain together, they can be the greatest *Chakravartis* known to men.'

The Master looked at Draupadi, paused and passed his hand over his flowing beard. The others waited intently for him to continue. Then he resumed: 'You will not have married only the Five Brothers; you will have married Dharma, whose instrument they will be. The aim for which your father has lived, will be fulfilled. The *swayamvara* will have been a unique triumph. The hope of Vaasudeva to establish an empire of Dharma will have been justified.'

Everyone heard the Master in breathless silence. Even Draupadi's tears were dried. Throughout, the Munis continued to nod their heads in assent.

'Think for a moment, my child,' continued the Master. 'Dharma often presents a conflict of ways. When it does, a righteous soul has to find the way which savours least of *adharma*. Yours is the choice, Draupadi, and never was a woman confronted with a more difficult choice, I know. I myself would not have liked to be in your place—not that I could be a fine young woman like you, however much I tried.' And the Master laughed loudly. Everyone laughed—even Dhrishtadyumna—at the possibility of the Sage being a young woman.

'You are a brave woman,' continued the Master. 'Make your choice, and wisely. Think over all that I have said. Perhaps you would like us to postpone our consultation till you are able to make up your mind. But, remember, the decision is yours; it will count with me, and I am sure, with the noble Drupada, the Five

Brothers and Vaasudeva, your adopted brother, who has staked his life on the success of your *swayamvara*.'

'I don't want any time,' said Draupadi, helplessly clutching at her throat. 'If these difficulties come to be known, it will mar the joy of all the people and our enemies will laugh at us.'

'What do you say, Dhrishtadyumna?' asked the Master. 'Should we make the decision now or postpone it?'

'No postponement, please, Master, I beg of you,' said Dhrishtadyumna, surrendering to the Master. 'We do not want evil rumours to spread. Whatever be the decision that we make, it must be made here and now, once and for all. I am sick of doubts.'

'I agree with Dhrishtadyumna,' said Drupada. 'We must decide here and now, and leave here of one mind. I have suffered enough in these days and I do not want to suffer longer. We must make our decision now.' 'It is not for you to decide, noble Drupada,' said the Master with a pleasant laugh. 'It is for Draupadi to make the decision.' he corrected.

'Yes, yes, I am sorry I said our decision,' said Drupada. 'Master, you rightly pointed out that the decision must be hers, for she will have to face the consequences,'

'My child, which way will you take?' asked the Master in a coaxing voice.

Draupadi looked down for a moment, looked up at the Master's friendly face, his eyes full of understanding. Then she looked at the Five Brothers. She could see that anxiety was writ large on the face of each one them.

Then she looked at Kunti, so good, so trusting, so affectionate, her eyes giving Draupadi a warm welcome, a little tremor of her eyelids indicating that she was afraid of Draupadi's making the wrong choice. She felt that life would be worthwhile with a mother like this, and that with the Five Brothers she would be the architect of Dharma in Aryavarta.

Then she looked at Krishna, who, by a glance, conveyed the message that, whatever her decision, he would stand by her. She had decided to go through with the *swayamvara* in faith as Govinda had said, and this was a part of it. She must not waver in her resolve.

She looked up, wiped a tear and said: 'Venerable Master, I have made my decision.'

'What is it, my child?' asked the Master.

'I will take the third way you have shown. I will marry all the Five Brothers according to the ancient rites,' said Draupadi and broke down under the strain of the very effort she had made. She prostrated herself before the Master.

'May you be blessed, my child,' said the Master, placing his huge, rough hand on Draupadi's lovely head. 'Didn't I tell you, noble Drupada, that she is Shri herself?'

'So be it,' said Kunti, her maternal instinct overflowing, and she clasped Draupadi in her arms.

'So be it,' said King Drupada with a sigh of relief. 'The knot which the gods have tied, no man can cut.'

Krishna smiled. Draupadi had won for him an empire of Dharma.

EPILOGUE

1. REACTIONS : DRONACHARYA

Dronacharya, the great military leader of the Kurus, woke up with a start. The sound of two or three chariots, coming to a grinding halt at the gates of the *Yuddha shala*, came to his ears. In the pallid light of the late moon, he could see the shadows of the chariots. He heard a familiar voice speaking to the watchman. It was the voice of Shikhandin, son of King Drupada, his disciple who was no longer a woman.

He was surprised. Shikhandin back in Hastinapura, so soon after the *swayamvara!* Something important must have happened at the *swayamvara* to bring him within a few days to Hastinapur in the dead of night.

Drona awoke his disciple Shankha, who, as usual, was sleeping at a small distance from him, and asked him to go and bring whoever had arrived. Shankha went, had the gates opened and, a few minutes later, brought a pale and exhausted Shikhandin into the presence of the Acharya.

With feeble steps, Shikhandin approached the Acharya as he sat on his bed, and prostrated himself before him, wiping the dust from his feet and applying it to his eyes.

'Shikhandin, what is the matter? Why have you come back so soon?' asked the Acharya; Shikhandin's eyes turned filmy. It appeared as if he would faint. Sthoonakarna, the Yaksha, who had followed him, helped him to sit down in front of the Acharya.

Shikhandin, his voice choking with breathlessness said: 'The Five Brothers are alive. They have married my sister.' Then, gasping for breath, he became unconscious.

Sthoonakarna laid him on a bed. Kripaadevi immediately went to his side, laid a pillow under his head and forced some water into his mouth. She also began to bathe his forehead and temples with water.

Dronacharya could not believe his ears. The Five Brothers alive and all of them married to Drupada's daughter! He turned to the Yaksha and asked him: 'Is it true?' The Yaksha nodded assent.

'How can that be? They are all dead.'

Sthoonakarna, who was under a vow to speak only twenty words a day, pointed at Shikhandin to show that the Acharya should ask him. By a gesture, he further conveyed that number of words that he could speak before sunrise had already been spoken and that he could speak only after sunrise the next day.

Dronacharya helped Kripaadevi to tend Shikhandin. After a littler while, Shikhandin opened his eyes, and seeing the Acharya sat up, feebly trying to stand, out of respect for his Guru.

'Don't try to stand, my boy. You are tired and should go to sleep. You may tell me everything in the morning,' said the Acharya.

'No, Acharyadeva,' Shikhandin spoke in a feeble voice after some effort. 'You must know it before anyone else does.' He drank the water given to him by Kripaadevi and steadied his mind with an effort.

'How did the Five Brothers come to life?'

'Uddhava, who has come with me, but gone to Vidura's house, knows all about the details. But this I know, that there was a miracle at the *swayamvara*. Arjuna, disguised as a Brahman, won the contest.'

'What happened to Duryodhana?'

'Duryodhana could not even string the bow. He came back, broken-hearted. Aswatthama could not lift it. Karna lifted it, but my sister refused to allow the charioteer's son to enter the contest. Other kings failed in the same way but Arjuna, at the very first attempt, hit the whirling fish and brought it down into the pool of water.'

'But when was he recognised as one of the Five Brothers?'

'Not in the beginning. Everybody thought that he was a Brahman. But when Draupadi, my sister, placed the garland on his neck in token of acceptance, some princes rushed towards King Drupada saying that he had insulted them by giving his daughter to a Brahman. Then his giant brother Bhima, with an uprooted tree in his hands, opposed them single-handed.'

'So, Bhima was there too?' asked Dronacharya.

'Yes, he was there,' replied Shikhandin. 'It appears that the other three brothers were parted from them in the rush of the crowd and returned to the potter's house where they were living.'

'But when was Arjuna recognised?'

'Only when Krishna Vaasudeva embraced him and prostrated himself before Bhima, his elder cousin.'

'Oh, I see. It is Krishna Vaasudeva again who is at the bottom of all this,' said Dronacharya. 'And who sent you here to inform me?'

A faint smile lit up Shikhandin's pale face. 'Krishna Vaasudeva. The Five Brothers also said that you, as the Guru, should be the first to receive the news that they are alive. My father was likewise eager that you should bless Draupadi.'

Dronacharya was puzzled. 'But you said just now that the Five Brothers were all married to Draupadi. How can that be?'

'Oh, it was a terrible thing in the beginning. It shocked everybody,' said Shikhandin.

'But how did it come to pass? How can an Arya princess have more than one husband? It is *adharma*,' said Dronacharya,

'Strange things have happened, Gurudeva. Arjuna, accompanied by my brother Dhrishtadyumna, took my sister to the potter's house where all the brothers, with their mother, were living. Before entering the house, Arjuna in a jocular tone, called out to his Mother Kunti, saying that he had brought home a valuable *bhiksha* (alms). From inside the house, the mother replied: "My dear son, share your *bhiksha* equally with your brothers." When she found that the *bhiksha* was my sister, she felt very miserable, for her sons had never broken their pledge to fulfil whatever wish she expressed.'

'But, that is no reason why the Five Brothers should marry Draupadi.' said the Acharya.

'It is all so puzzling, Gurudeva,' said Shikhandin. 'Arjuna would not marry my sister before his elder brothers were married. Yudhishthira declined, saying that Arjuna had won her by the strength of his arms and he would not marry her. Bhima would not marry her till the eldest brother was married. They were all in a difficult situation. Then Yudhishthira suggested that all the brothers should marry her.'

'Yudhishthira said that! Impossible!' exclaimed Drona. 'He is the most righteous man alive. How could he be so foolish? What did your father say?'

Father was shocked. He said the suggestion was against *Dharma*. The noble Vaasudeva said that it was a difficult matter; in either way it would be a calamity. Yudhishthira said that in ancient days Arya women were known to have married several brothers.'

'How did the matter ultimately end?' asked Drona.

'Next day, the Best of Sages, Veda Vyasa, came with Dhaumya Rishi, the preceptor of the Five Brothers. He was consulted. A long discussion followed,' said Shikhandin.

'What did the Master say?'

'He said that Mother Kuniti's wish, though expressed without giving it a thought, had a deeper significance,' said Shikhandin. 'If Draupadi married Arjuna alone, the brothers were likely to be estranged from each other. Things would be very difficult for them, for they would have to fight for their heritage with Duryodhana and his brothers, perhaps with the whole might of the Kuru Empire.'

'What did the Master say about the propriety of such a marriage?' asked the Acharya.

'He said that in the days gone by, under extraordinary circumstances, several brothers had married one wife. Among certain Arya tribes, he said, several brothers do the same. Some of the marriages he knew to have proved successful.'

'I never thought that the Master would have approved of such a marriage,' said the Acharya.

'The Master ultimately decided that the matter should be left to Draupadi and explained to her the ways she could possibly take. She could marry Arjuna and face the consequences of estrangement between him and his brothers. She could go back on the *swayamvara* and make everyone ridiculous. Or she could accept Yudhishthira's suggestion and face the possibility of being called unchaste. At first, my sister was unhappy. But then she accepted Yudhishthira's suggestion. The marriage was thereupon fixed for the next day. I left immediately. Duryodhana will be coming within three or four days. I was sent here to inform you in advance,' said Shikhandin.

Then Shikhandin told Dronacharya all that had happened to him since he had left for Kampilya with the Yaksha, Sthoonakara. He told him how his father got angry because he thought that his change of sex was a gift from his enemy; how Krishna saw his sister Draupadi and prevailed upon her to induce their father to accept him, Shikhandin; how Shakuni and Aswatthama gave a pledge to his father that even at the cost of his life, the latter would see that the Acharya would not leave Hastinapura; how they all decided to risk a war with the Kurus rather than let Duryodhana marry his sister.

As Shikhandin was telling the story, Dronacharya understood Duryodhana and Shakuni as he never had understood them before. He was lost in admiration of the miraculous resourcefulness of Krishna Vaasudeva. As he thought over the matter, he felt his life-long bitterness against Drupada ebbing away. He, however, disliked the giving of the pledge by his obstinate son— a son whom he loved above everything else; it created a difficult situation.

When dawn broke, he went to have his morning bathe in the river and to perform *sandhya* and offer worship to the God Surya (Sun) with sacred *mantras*. Suddenly he found a solution. Yes, that was the only thing to do: to divide the empire.

2. REACTIONS: DURYODHANA

A few days later, Duryodhana, with his brothers and friends, returned to Hastinapura. He felt beaten, crushed. The Five Brothers were alive and now were the sons-in-law of the powerful King of Panchala; his game was frustrated; his life's work was in ruins. He had been humiliated; made the laughing-stock of the whole of Aryavarta. Krishna Vaasudeva, the villain of the piece, had tricked him of his future destiny.

If the Five Brothers came to Hastinapura, he and his brothers would have no place there. The happenings at the *swayamvara* were in everybody's mouth. The people were jubilant over the Five Brothers being alive and married to the Princess of Panchala. They were dying to give them a rousing welcome. The only way out would be to have the Five Brothers disposed of before they arrived in the capital.

Next day, in the morning, Duryodhana, with Karna and Shakuni, went to see his father, the blind King. King Dhritarashtra had also come to know from Vidura all that had happened in Kampilya, and had feebly agreed that the best way was to give a royal welcome to the Five Brothers at Hastinapura.

Duryodhana shouted, stormed, crushed and gnashed his teeth. He chided his father for yielding to Vidura, his enemy. He wanted clever emissaries to be sent to Kampilya to create differences between the Five Brothers and Drupada, and set afoot a conspiracy to kill them.

Dhritarashtra had already promised Vidura that the Five Brothers would be made welcome in Hastinapura. However, as usual, he yielded to the vehement protests of his son, who was exasperated by anger and bitterness.

Karna, who was listening to the conversation between the father and the son, when called upon to advise, was against Duryodhana's plan. He called it impractical. With all the Five Brothers married to Draupadi, there was no possibility of their being disunited from each other. Drupada was not likely to disown his sons-in-law. Vaasudeva was still there to befriend them. The only way, according to Karna, was to assemble the Kuru forces in all their might, make a surprise attack on Kampilya and storm it, and inflict a

crushing defeat on Drupada, the Five Brothers, and
their allies. The Kuru forces, if properly mobilised, would
prove irresistible. Quite a few kings. who were
disappointed at the *swayamvara*, would join them.
Balarama and Krishna had to be fought, no doubt, but
they had only a negligible force at their disposal.

As they were discussing this plan, Vidura came in
to invite King Dhritarashtra and those who were with
him to join the Grandfather and Dronacharya in the
throne room, where they were discussing this very
problem.

Duryodhana then led his father to the throne room
where the old Grandfather was seated, discussing the
matter with Dronacharya, Kripacharya and some senior
ministers.

The old Grandfather, for once, was in a happy
frame of mind. With a faint smile on his lips, he turned
to Dhritarashtra as he was led to his throne.

'Dhritarashtra, it is a great day for us. All the five
sons of Pandu are alive. They have also married
Drupada's daughter. The stigma which was attached to
our house, that somehow we were responsible for the
death of the Five Brothers, has been removed. I hear
that the people are very jubilant over the unexpected
return of the Five Brothers. Tonight they are illuminating
the whole town, and from tomorrow ceremonial worship
is being celebrated in every temple to invoke the blessing
of the Gods on them.'

Dhritarashtra turned his blind eyes helplessly
towards the Grandfather. No one spoke. 'But what will
happen to my sons?' Dhritarashtra asked at last.

The old man's voice assumed its usual tone of authority. 'Dhritarashtra, how can we make a distinction between your sons and the sons of Pandu? To us both are equal.'

Dhritarashtra lapsed into silence.

Duryodhana tried to overcome the awe which the Grandfather always inspired in him, and hesitatingly exclaimed: 'But the Five Brothers were banished, Grandfather!'

'Yes they were banished, no doubt, to save trouble for Hastinapura. Now the Great God has not only kept them alive, but given them a high position among the kings of the earth,' said the Grandfather.

'If they come where shall we be?' asked Duryodhana, betraying his helplessness.

For a moment the Grandfather was silent as he looked steadfastly at Duryodhana. 'You will be where you are—in Hastinapura.'

'How can we share the empire with the Five Brothers? Either we are here or they are here,' Duryodhana blurted out impetuously.

'Don't say that, my son,' said Dhritarashtra, trying to intervene between the Grandfather's ire and his beloved son.

The Granfather's silence became oppressive, as he quietly went on passing his hand over his beard. Then he said quietly: 'Duryodhana, you should remember that the throne of Hastinapura is the throne of Dharma. Righteousness must prevail here and has been claim of the Kurus. Nothing ought to prevent us from giving the Five Brothers their proper placc.'

'Grandfather,' said Dhritarashtra meekly, 'we should see that there is no conflict between Duryodhana and his brothers on the one hand and the Five Brothers on the other. It would be suicidal.'

'If we intend to find a way, one is sure to be found.' said the Grandfather. His tone was kindly, as he placed a hand affectionately on the King's shoulder. 'I have been discussing it with Acharyadeva. The balance will always be held even between your sons and the sons of Pandu. We cannot deny them their rightful heritage,' added the Grandfather.

'What does the Acharyadeva say about it?' asked Dhritarashtra, who was torn between his fear of the Grandfather and his desire to keep his son happy.

'I agree with the venerable Grandfather, noble King,' said Dronacharya.

'But what will happen if Drupada's daughter comes to Hastinapura? Drupada is your bitterest enemy and there would be any amount of intrigues,' said Dhritarashtra. 'That is what you said when we discussed the matter of Duryodhana going to the *swayamvara.*'

'Noble King, many things have happened since', replied Dronacharya with dignity. 'Duryodhana has solved my difficulty. He got my son Aswatthama to give a pledge to Drupada that, if Draupadi married a Kuru prince and came here, he would see, even at the cost of his life, that I did not leave Hastinapura. Isn't that so, Duryodhana?' Duryodhana bit his lips and nodded assent.

'Duryodhana says it is true,' continued Drona. 'Aswatthama gave the pledge at Duryodhana's insistence, and I will not act in a way that would cost the life of my only son. The Grandfather has suggested a way to solve the difficulty. I entirely agree with it.'

Karna could not repress his feelings. He turned to King Dhritarashtra and said with a sneer: 'Noble King, even those who have flourished on your patronage are now turning traitor.'

Dronacharya gave Karna a contemptuous look and said: 'Son of Raadhaa,[1] if your advice is accepted, the Kurus will be destroyed.'

The Grandfather continued slowly to run his hand up and down over his beard.

Dhritarashtra turned to Vidura and asked: 'What have you to say, Vidura?'

'Lord, I can only add that it would be folly not to welcome the Five Brothers amidst us. The stigma of Purochana having burnt them alive has been happily removed. The kings assembled at the *swayamvara* have welcomed them. They are allied to the great King of Panchala, and have now Balarama, Krishna and Satyaki as their friends. How can you resist them? Whole of Hastinapura is dying to see them in our midst. The best way would be to forget the past and welcome them and give them the place that they are entitled to.'

The Grandfather stopped playing with his beard and said decisively: 'We are all agreed that the Five Brothers should be made welcome as the sons of Pandu.

We shall also find a solution which will not make Duryodhana unhappy.'

'Welcome the Five Brothers as the sons of Pandu!' muttered Duryodhana under his breath.

The Grandfather heard the words, and his eyes for a moment were lit in suppressed anger. Then, ignoring him, he turned to the King and said: 'Dhritarashtra, nothing more need be said. The Five Brothes are going to be given a royal welcome in Hastinapura. I am going to consult the Most Venerable Mother and, if she approves of my suggestion, Vidura will go with presents to Kampilya and bring back the Five Brothers. Vidura, give me your hand. Tell the Most Venerable Mother that I will see her after I have performed my *sandhya*.'

Without waiting for anyone to say a word, the old man got up, and with his hand on Vidura's shoulder, walked out of the room.

Duryodhana's blood was boiling. He was seeing red. But the old man was too powerful to be defied. He had not the courage to face his wrath nor to give up his ambition to rule over Hastinapura. As the old KIng was led out of the throne room, Duryodhana decided to play his last card.

The Most Venerable Mother sat in her usual seat in front of the sacred instruments and vessels of her worship, White-haired, quiet, with the traces of her beauty still unfaded, she was the very image of venerable age.

The maid-servant standing at the door hurriedly came, folded her hands and announced: 'Mother,

Duryodhana is waiting outside. He wants to see you immediately.'

The old Empress smiled indulgently. 'I am sure he is very unhappy. Let him come in.'

Duryodhana entered the room hastily, his face flushed red, his eyes clouded in distresss. He prostrated himself before the Mother, who blessed him by placing her hand on his head.

'How are you, my son? I understand that you returned from Kampilya ycsterday. How are you now?' asked the Mother in an affectionate tone.

'How am I.....?' burst out Duryodhana in a choking voice. 'How am I.....? Mother, Mother, I am the victim of evil planets. Everyone's hand is against me.' For a moment he was so overpowered that he sat down unbidden, placing his hand over his eyes.

'Don't lose heart, my boy,' said the Mother in a kindly tone. 'Failures and triumphs are both given to us by the Great God. We have to welcome them in humility as trials to be borne cheerfully.'

'Welcome humiliation?' burst Duryodhana, removing his hands from his eyes. 'I went to Kampilya to win Drupada's daughter. I failed disgracefully. I became the laughing-stock of Aryavarta. Bhima called me "a blind man's son." Arjuna, my enemy, won the bride. Suddenly the Five Brothers came alive—perhaps by some magic trick of that crafty Vaasudeva's.' His words tumbled forth one after the other. 'And now everyone is my enemy. Grandfather wants to send Vidura to welcome them. My own Guru, whom I have served the whole of my life, supports him. Father acquiesces in it. No one wants me,' he added as he broke down.

'Why do you say so, Duryodhana? You are as dear to me as any son of Pandu. I know your life has been one of frustration. But don't you think your *swabhava* (temperament) is responsible for that?' asked the Mother quietly.

Duryodhana folded his hands. 'Venerable Mother, I beg of you to come to my rescue. You are the guardian goddess of the Kurus' empire. If the Five Brothers are installed here, we cannot live here; we would have to leave Hastinapura. Don't let me and my brothers be destroyed.'

The Most Venerable Mother looked at him patiently with an indulgent smile on her lips. 'Duryodhana,' she said when the torrent of Duryodhana's words had been choked by his inability to speak any further, 'why do you take such a dark view of things, Duryodhana? They are your brothers, entitled to the throne of *Chakravarti* Bharata—even before you. They have suffered enough. Should they not be given an honourable place in their father's house?' she asked. The appealing way in which she put the question would have melted any heart but Duryodhana's. His face twisted into a grimace.

'They have no place in Hastinapura. Mother, of all people, you know the truth, They are not the sons of Pandu. They have no place in our family, nor in Hastinapura,' said Duryodhana, losing all control over himself.

A cloud of deep sorrow passed over the noble face of the old woman. For some moments she looked with infinite pity at Duryodhana, though his wicked words almost broke her heart.

'My son,' she replied in an almost tragic voice, 'when will you be able to control your temper and conquer your jealousy, envy and hatred?'

'I hate the Five Brothers,' said Duryodhana in desperation. 'I wish they were dead or I was dead.'

'All of you have to live in amity, Duryodhana,' she replied, her voice regaining its even but sad tone. 'Do you know what you have done, my son? You have opened up an old wound which I thought had been healed.' As she said these words, two tears rolled down her dark but still shapely cheeks.

Duryodhana looked in surprise at the agony which was evident on the Mother's face.

'Duryodhana, I thought that at your age you would understand,' she said, looking at him with compassion. 'You have said the cruellest thing that could be said of the Five Brothers—and of *me*. If you had said it to Bhishma, I do not know what he would have done. But I am a helpless woman,' she added in a subdued voice.

'But, Mother, Mother, you don't realise how everybody conspires against me,' said Duryodhana.

'That is again not true, my boy, said the Mother, 'You talk of the throne of Hastinapura as if it belonged to you. I have not told the story to any of you so far, and Bhishma and Dwaipayana are the only two other people who know it. Do you know how the kingdom had been built up and preserved during the last sixty years and more?'

Duryodhana looked up with curiosity. Even in the exasperated mood in which he was, he could see that the Mother was going to share with him a secret of the highest importance.

She looked up wistfully. A shadow passed over her eyes. Then she spoke in a sad tone. 'Listen to me, my son. When you are inclined to talk about the throne of Hastinapura, never forget how it came to be built up. It is an old, old story.' She closed her eyes as if recalling the picture of the days she was talking about.

Then, with half-opened eyes, she spoke reminiscently, in an unsteady voice: 'When my lord lay dying, he called me—a fisherman's daughter, whom he had elevated to the mightiest throne of Aryavarta. He said: "Devi, I want you to give me a promise. Since I inherited the empire of Dharma from my father, the Emperor Pratipa of glorious memory, I have tried to maintain its traditions. But now, it is in danger. Bhishma will not marry. He will not succeed to the throne. Your sons are very young. The burden of this empire will therefore fall on you".'

The Mother cleared her throat and began to talk as if she was describing an imaginary picture. 'My lord held my hand and continued: "Promise me, Devi to maintain the traditions of the Kurus. They have brought the rule of righteousness where none existed before. They have never let down the poor and the helpless. They have seen to it that men of learning and piety never suffered want; that the Brahmans well versed in the Vedas, the cows which give plenty, and virtuous women were protected; that ploughmen fearlessly enjoyed the fruits of their labour; that the strong were never permitted to oppress the weak; that armies curbed the violent and rescued the oppressed; that tributes were levied only to enrich those who gave them. This is what the empire of the Kurus has meant to me. Promise me that the traditions of the Kurus shall be maintained".'

As she spoke slowly, reminiscently, tears sprang to her eyes. She wiped them, cleared her throat again, looked at Duryodhana and said: 'I gave the promise to my lord. He died happily.'

The Mother again wiped the tears from her eyes, waited a while to control her emotions and continued: 'Do you know, Duryodhana, that, weak as I am, from that day, years and years ago, I have lived only with one aim: to see that the throne of the Kurus, on which my lord sat, should maintain righteousness and its tradition unimpaired?' She paused again.

Duryodhana, with wide eyes, listened to her well-modulated voice, which still retained the charm of her earlier days.

After a little while, the Mother continued: 'My son, you see Hastinapura as powerful as before. You want to rule it. But do you know what it has cost Bhishma and me to maintain it?' Her face grew reminiscent once more and she talked as if to herself. 'Bhishma would not accept the throne. I begged him to marry; he would not. My sons died without children. You claim to be the descendant of Bharata. My son, the direct line of the Emperor Bharata came to an end with them. You have as little right to claim the throne as the five sons of Pandu, or rather, they are as much entitled as you are.

Neither you nor they are the sons of the emperors of Hastinapura.'

Duryodhana opened his eyes in shocked surprise and listened to the subdued and tremulous voice of the Venerable Mother with its heart-rending pathos.

'However, I was determined to keep the promise which I had given to my lord,' continued the Mother. 'I therefore got my son Dwaipayana—the Master, as you call him—to perform *Niyoga* with the widows of my son Vichitraveerya. It was he who begot your father and King Pandu. I saw that the secret was buried in the hearts of a few. I did not want you all to be branded with illegitimacy. That would have led to internecine war and to the destruction of the Kuru empire.'

Duryodhana wanted to interrupt her, but the Most Venerable Mother held up her hand. She wiped her tears again. 'Your father, the elder, was born blind. He could not therefore succeed to the throne. As his son, you cannot do so either, according to our laws. Therefore, Pandu was installed on the throne, but he could not father any children. But I had to keep my pledge. By the advice of Dwaipayana, I permitted Kunti, with the sanction of Pandu, to beget sons by the ancient rites. Duryodhana, you are wild and impetuous. You cannot understand that, if the Five Brothers have no right to succeed to the Kuru empire, you have none either. You all have the right to the heritage because of me, a guilty woman.'

She cleared her voice, wiped her tears again and continued in a steady voice: 'Let me be frank. Old and weak though I am, I am going to maintain the noble traditions which my lord asked me to maintain.'

She raised her small pretty head with its venerable crown of fleecy hair in queenly dignity. 'Won't you, my son, even at your age, realize what the empire of the Kurus has meant to the whole of Aryavarta? What happiness it has brought to the people?' she asked.

Duryodhana could not look up. He felt like a drowning man. Even the last plank had slipped from his hands.

'My son,' continued the Mother, 'I beg of you, when you think of your rights and wrongs, to think of the poor old woman who has lived in the hope of passing on to you the heritage of *Chakravarti* Bharata.' Her voice had in it an appeal of moving pathos.

Overpowered by her own words, the Mother placed her hands over her eyes as tears rolled down her cheeks. Duryodhana was speechless. Neither of them spoke for some time. Then the mother wiped her tears again, paused till she regained her self-composure and spoke: 'Duryodhana, we do not want to be unjust to you or to sons of Pandu. But no one shall dare to dispute the paternity of any one of you. It is sanctioned by the most ancient laws of the Aryas.'

She continued: 'Think of the future of Dharma which the kings of Hastinapura are pledged to support. Bhishma and I have decided that you shall be the *Yuvaraja* of Hastinapura and Yudhishthira installed as King. The Five Brothers will be received in Hastinapura as the sons of *Chakravarti* Pandu. Do not let hatred dim your vision. The Great God may be pleased to restore peace and amity between all of you. Be generous. Let the Kuru empire flourish. Now go,' she added peremptorily.

NOTES

Chapter 5

1. Yudhishthira, the eldest, was respectfully referred to as the 'Eldest.'
2. Bhima was referred in the family as 'the middle', being the second of the three sons of Kunti; Nakula and Sahadeva as the twins.

Chapter 10

1. Duryodhana. A form of respectful address by wives when referring to their husbands.

Chapter 17

1. Referred to in detail in Parts I and II of *Krishnavatara*.

Chapter 21

1. Worship in which water is offered to the sun God.
2. Kunti's "Eldest" would be her husband's eldest brother, Dhritarashtra.

Chapter 23

1. *Krishi-go-vidyaa-Bhagavad Gita.*
2. Modern Lothal.

Chapter 29

1. In several villages in Jaunsar-Bawar (Dehra Dun District) where Bhima is worshipped as the

Great God, the practice still prevails of selecting the strongest among the tribesmen as the Bhima of the year. During that year, he enjoys the chieftainship.

Chapter 30

1. Now called Lothal in the Ahmedabad District, where excavation has revealed the remnants of an ancient port.

Chapater 31

1. *vide Krishnavatara,* Vol. I, *The Magic Flute.*
2. *vide Krishnavatara,* Vol. II, *The Wrath of an Emperor.*

Chapter 32

1. *Atirathi* was an expert chariot warrior who commanded a contingent of *maharathis* and *rathis,* expert chariot warriors of inferior ranks.
2. Time unit of 24 minutes.

Chapter 39

1. *vide Krsihnavatara,* Vol. I, *The Magic Flute.*
2. *vide Krishnavatara,* Vol. II, *The Wrath of an Emperor.*

Chapter 40

1. A prohibited form of marriage, prevalent among the Rakshasas, by which the bride was kidnapped by a bridegroom without her consent, is called the Rakshasa form in the Hindu Law texts. The Brahma marriage before the sacred fire was deemed to be the best. Among the warrior class, Gandharva marriage — a love marriage in which the bride ran away with her chosen bridegroom-was permitted.

Chapter 42

1. The ideal wife who followed the God of Death to his dread land and retrieved her husband from him.
2. Empress.

Chapter 43

1. People who are guilty of arson, poisoning, attacking another with a murderous weapon, dacoity, trespassing on land, or abducting a woman are classed as *aatataayis.* The Shastras enjoin that they should be killed at once. No sin is incurred in killing them.

Chapter 46

1. *Krishnavatara, Vol. II, The Wrath of an Emperor.*

Chapter 47

1. Sacrifice with elaborate rituals, generally performed by a king after winning victories.

Chapter 48

1. Pratiloma marriage, that is marriage between a higher caste bride and a lower cast bridegroom, was strictly prohibited by Hindu Law from times immemorial. The prohibition persisted till after Freedom, when it was removed by legislation.

Epilogue

1. Raadhaa was the name of Karna's adoptive mother-the charioteer's wife who found him abandoned and broght him up as her son.

█

APPENDICES

I. NAGAS AND RAKSHASAS

During the period I am dealing with, the Nagas, a large ethnic group, occupied most of the parts of North India where the Arya Kings ruled, and ultimately came to be fused with the Aryas in a common society, The Naga king, Aryaka, who figures in the *Mahabharata* and whom Bhima visited, ruled over a territory on the banks of the Ganga and Yamuna. He was the gradfather of Vasudeva and Kunti. Several Naga kings had matrimonial alliances with the Arya kings. Maniman, a Naga king, was present at the *swayamvara* of Draupadi. Uloopi is recorded to have wooed Arjuna and at last persuaded him to marry her. Possibly he had another Naga wife too, Airavati. Their social customs appear to have been different and the Nagakanyas enjoyed the reputation of being highly seductive.

The culture, civilization and arts of war of the Nagas, during this time, were markedly different from those of the Aryas. These people presumably belonged to the race which the archaeologists call 'Copperheads', who occupied parts of North India before the Aryas came.

The Rakshasas, to which ethnic group Hidimbaa, whom Bhima married, and others such as Jaraa, Koolakaa and Pulaamaa belonged, were another distinct race which lived in the inaccessible forests. They appear to have been ferocious cannibals. As the Epics and the Puranas show, the *rishis*, trying to spread their *ashrams* in the forests, were constantly harassed by the visitation of these Rakshasas, and more than one instance is referred to of an Arya king having to run to the rescue of *a rishi* to save his *asharam* from them. Often the Rakshasas were styled Asuras. Danavas or Daityas.

The Nagas and the Rakshasas also lived in Khandava Vana before it was burned down by the Five Brothers.

2. POLYANDRY AMONG THE PRESENT-DAY KHASA COMMUNITY OF JAUNSAR-BAWAR (DEHRA DUN DISTRICT)

In most of the areas of Jaunsar-Bawar apart from Mahasu, the favourite deities are the Pandava brothers, the heroes of the *Mahabharata.* Time seems to have stood still in these parts of the Himalayas after the Pandavas climbed to Heaven by Satopantha, a snow-peak near Mana, the last village on the IndoTibetan border.

Many important spots in these areas have associations with one or the other of the five sons of Pandu. Some of the Khasa villages have temples dedicated to the Pandavas, called *Pandavanki-chauri,* and the courtyards of most of the temples are called *Pandavon-ka-angan.*

Bhima is the most popular of the Pandava deities of this region, all of whom are very touchy and ready to take offence at the slightest lapse or misdeed.

The main feature of the social and religious festivals of these areas is the Pandava Dance, in which most of the people in the villages join. The persons who act as the five Pandavas are held in high esteem, and the Bajgis, the musicians, play a very important part on such occasions.

Bhima, as the hero of the festivals, has to perform prodigies of heroic dancing on such occasions. The man who impersonates him is selected with great care, and he has to prepare himself for the part of days beforehand. During the dance, his strength, endurance and agility are severely tested. It is believed that on such occasions, Bhima himself takes possession of the dancer, who, after the festival, enjoys the privilege of wearing a silver bracelet as a mark of distinction.

How the communities of Jaunsar-Bawar and the adjoining areas came to worship the Pandavas, is a very interesting question. No doubt, after his retirement, their father Pandu lived in the Himalayas with his wives, Kunti and Madri. The Pandavas were also born there, possibly near the place called Pandukeshwar, on the way to Badrinath. When Kunti enjoined that all the Five Borthers should take Draupadi as their common wife—a flagrantly unorthodox affair in Aryavarta—she may have been following the custom of the Himalaya regions where she had lived with her husband.

The most intriguing part of these areas are the few villages called Fateh-parvat, in the upper Rawain of Jaunpur, in the Tehri-Garhwai district. Their presiding deity is Duryodhana. He is the god and king of the people, and is offered tribute. Here his enemies, the Pandavas, are the demons.

In Fateh-parvat, Duryodhana is true to his reputation. If you visit any of its villages and fail to offer a buffalo, a goat, or even a rupee, to Duryodhana, he will see to it that you suffer some permanent injury. He even orders his people, through the *thani* of course, to steal a buffalo from the neighbouring villages or to kill someone.

Duryodhana in life was highly politically-minded and even as a god, his tastes have remained unchanged.

During the general elections of 1952 party organisers approached the headman of these villages for votes. The community was in distress. They had never heard such importunities before, and the did not know exactly what they should do. So the *pujari* invoked Duryodhana, who, through the *thani*, commanded that all the votes should be cast for a particular candidate.

It is difficult to explain why, of all the heroes of the *Mahabharata*, the wicked Duryodhana came to be worshipped. Did some of his adherents escape to the Himalayas after the battle of Kurukshetra and found this colony? Or, was there a war between the Pandava-worshipping Khasas and the Fateh-parvat Khasas, who, having won a victory, forswore allegiance to the gods of the others and accepted their enemy, Duryodhana, as their guardian deity?

The marriage customs of the Khasas and other members of these communities are most interesting. They observe Manu's *Law*. *Anuloma* marriage, i.e., a marriage between a higher-cast man and lower-caste woman, is valid; Pratiloma marraiage, i..e, a marraige between a higher-caste woman and lower-caste man is ordinarily not; at the same time, in many of these areas, *pratiloma* is permitted between the Brahmans and the Rajputs.

All the Khasa areas of U.P., Himachal Pradesh and East Punjab are polyandrous. In Jaunsar-Bawar, the bride generally goes through a marriage ceremony with the eldest of the brothers, but becomes the wife of them all. There is both polyandray and polygamy. The eldest brother, however is the master of the household. In his presence, the younger brothers do not even talk of the common wife. Whaterver domestic felicity they enjoy with her has to be found under the open skies.

In Bawar, on the other hand, every brother has a day allotted to him for consorting with his wife. The wife, however, has an alternative. She can get rid of her multiple masters by going away to her parents; then, after seeking divorce from the first set of husbands and with the consent of her parents, she is free to choose any other man she likes. The new bridegroom, however, has to pay a bride-price to the husbands.

Among the Khasas of Jubbal and Girupar in Sirmaur District, polyandry is restricted to only two brothers. If there is a third, he must marry another wife.

The impact of modern civilization is putting a great strain on the people of Jaunsar-Bawar. Recently, I hcard of an educated Khasa girl refusing to live with any of the brothers of the person she had married. This young woman insisted that, if in accordance with custom she was called upon to live with them, she would return to her father's house and live with any lover she liked.

I heard another report of a curious case. A boy from Jaunsar-Bawar came to a school in Dehra Dun. The whole class began to tease the poor boy by asking him: 'How many fathers have you got?' He innocently answered, 'Four', and his classmates made fun of him.

GLOSSARY

Adharma — Action contrary to Dharma.

Apadharma — Action not fully consonant with Dharma but done as Dharma in a cast of extreme emergency.

Arati — The ritual of waving lights before a deity or a very highly venerable person.

Aryadharma — Dharma governing Arya behaviour; ancient law and religion of the Arya.

Ashram — Hermitage of a Rishi; a sylvan school for imparting learning in scriptures, sacrificial lore and martial sciences.

Aswamedha — Horse Sacrifice performed by a king when he attains imperial status.

Bhiksha — Alms, mostly food, obtained by begging, on which the ideal Brahmin was supposed to subsist.

Brahmachari — A celibate student who spends years with his teacher to acquire learning.

Chaitra — A Hindu calendar month which falls in March/April.

Chakra — Wheel; discus.

Chakravartin — An emperor who commands the allegiance of vassal kings.

Champaka — A flower of sweet fragrance.

Chandrayana varta — A purificatory rite, involving fasting.

Darshan — Sight of divine or highly respected persons, which uplifts the soul.

Dhoti — Loose garment tied round the waist and covering the lower half of the body, with or without folds.

Dwipa — Island.

Gandharava — (noun) A celestial being noted for music; (adjevtive) applied to a form of marriage in which the religious ceremony was performed after marital relations commenced.

Gopal — Cow-herd.

Gopi — Cow-herdess.

Gopta — Defender; Protector; Keeper.

Gotra — Pedigree; the name of the *Rishi* from whom one is descended.

Homa — Rituals in which offerings are made to the sacred fire, generally of ghee.

Karttik — A Hindu calendar month (Octorber/ Nevember).

Kaumadaki — Name of Krishna's *gada* or mace.

Kuladharma — Dharma governing the behaviour of a family and its members.

Kumkum — Red turmeric powder applied to the forehead on auspicious occasions. Women whose husbands are alive are under a religious duty to have a *kumkum* mark on their forehead always.

Kunda — A flower of sweet fragrance.

Madira — Wine or other intoxicating drink.

Maharathi — A chariot-warrior of the rank subordinate to an Atirathi, often used as a synonym.

Mandap — A large area decorated by bunting and roofed by cloth or dry leaves of the plam tree, in which holy rites, ceremonies or other celerbration are held.

Marntra — Sacred chant or formula having the power to secure the blessings of God, specially Vedic verses which are accepted as divinely inspired.

Margashirsha — A Hindu calendar month (November/ December).

Mleccha — Term applied to an alien who does not accept the authority of the Hindu Shastras.

Muni — An ascetic of the highest order.

Nishadas — Forest-dewlling nomadic tribes.

Niyoga — A practice sanctioned by the Hindu *Shastras*, under which a childless widow can beget issues by her deceased husband's brother.

Panchajanya — The conch which Krishna obtanined by killing Panchajana, a demon.

Parishad — A meeting, generally of eminent people, to discuss serious matters of religion, statecraft, literature or art.

Paush — A Hindu calendar month (December/ January).

Piambar — Cloth, light yellow in colour, used as dhoti, generally made of silk.

Phalgun — A Hindu calendar month (February/ March).

Puja — Worship of God's images or holy persons with auspicious things like water, sandal-paste, flowers, etc.

Purohit — Family priest; preceptor who recites *mantras* and officiates at the performance of religious ceremonies, and teaches the *mantras* to the members.

Rajadharama — Code of kingly counduct.

Rajsabha — Council to assist the ruler, usually of ministers, preceptors and elders and other persons of rank.

Raas — A special kind of dance popular among cowherds and cowherdesses, associated with Krishna when he was in Vrindavan.

Rathi — Chariouteer.

Rishi — Man of learning and piety, living in austere poverty, who imparts the study and teachings of the *Vedas* and *Shastras* to his pupils, generally living with them in an ashram.

Sadhu — A holy man; also indicative of approval, equivalent of 'Well done.'

Sanjvani — A formula giving life.

Sati — Virtuous woman devoted to her husband; woman who follows her husband in death by entering his funeral pyre.

Satya — Truth which fulfils its purpose; Eternal Verities.

Shala — School; Shed; store-house; Hall.

Shanti — Peace; Benediction invoked at the end of rituals.

Shamiana — Pandal or tent decorated and furnished with ornamented seats for joyous gatherings.

Sharnga — Name of Sri Krishna's bow.

Shastra — Scientific, legalistic or canonical treatise.

Shimal — A flower with fragrant honey.

Sreni — Guild of traders.

Streesangrahana — Abduction.

Audarshana — Krishna's Chakra (discus).

Swabhava — Inborn nature; temperament.

Swayamavra — The ceremony of self-choosing husband; a gathering of princes in which a princess selects her husband.

Tapas — Rigourous self-discipline imposed by controlling the sense, pursued by the Munis.

Tapascharya — Observance of Tapas.

Tapasvin — Man enaged in Tapas.

Tirtha — Place of pilgrimage; river, tank, sea-shore and other water spots held holy because of their potentiality of wash away sin.

Triyambaka — Lord Siva's mighty bow with which He destroyed the otherwise indestructible Tripura demon.

Vedas — Scriptures of the Hindus, the oldest literary compositions that have come down in Sankrit. They were believed to be given by Gods to Rishis, and their injunctions are considered inviolable.

Vedi — A platform or a pit in which sacrifice is performed.

Vidya — High learning; sicence; art.

Yajna — A sacrificial ritual.

Yaksha — Being believed to have magical powers.

Yojana — Four miles; about 6 kilometres.

Yuddha shala — Military academy; place of training for warfare.

Yuvaraja — Crown Prince.

THE END